Jensen

"The pay convoy—gone, lord, gone!" the soldiers stammered. "Robbers with a demon—took everything, killed everybody—"

The pay convoy had been attacked by a demon, or at least the image of one. It had a horse's head, snake's fangs, dragon's body, buzzard's wings, hooves; fire shot from its eyes and nostrils. Bakarydes recognized the description from folklegend—the demon steed of the wizard Krusevo.

"We found one chest, just one," a soldier said. "Smashed to bits and pieces. Found men, too. Baggage boy, guide, others—they must have thought surrender would save them. It didn't." He shuddered.

"Their throats were cut. Like pigs."

THE
BOOK OF KANTELA
VOLUME ONE: THE THRONE OF SHERRAN TRILOGY

ROLAND J. GREEN AND FRIEDA A. MURRAY

THE BOOK OF KANTELA

VOLUME ONE: THE THRONE OF SHERRAN TRILOGY

A TOM DOHERTY ASSOCIATES BOOK

THE BOOK OF KANTELA

Copyright © 1985 by Roland J. Green and Frieda A. Murray
Cover art copyright © 1985 by Ilene Meyer
Maps copyright © 1985 by Dan Grant

Reprinted by arrangement with Bluejay Books, Inc.

First TOR printing: May 1986

A TOR Book

Published by Tom Doherty Associates
49 West 24 Street
New York, N.Y. 10010

ISBN: 0-812-53900-1
CAN. ED.: 0-812-53901-X

Library of Congress Catalog Card Number: 85-6236

Printed in the United States

0   9   8   7   6   5   4   3   2   1

To our mothers,
Bertha M. Green and Frieda R. Murray,
with love and gratitude

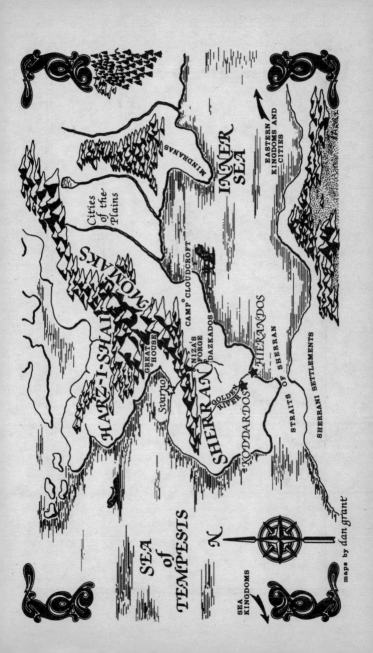

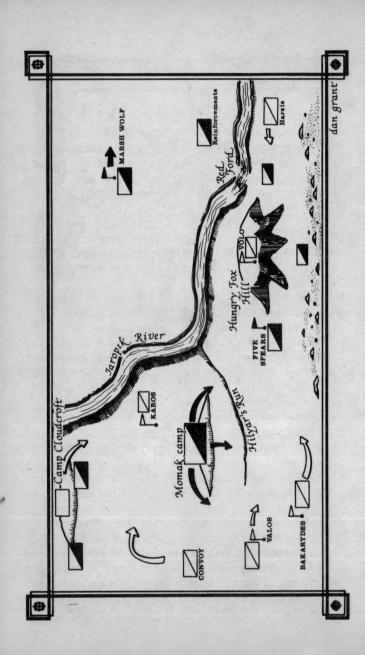

I

"HALT! WHO ARE YOU?"

Michal shan-Ouvram Kadran reined in his horse so abruptly that the gelding nearly reared. The Harzi simultaneously gentled it with his knees, laid hand to sword hilt, and studied the man who'd challenged him. Man? No, the long legs in their ragged trousers and the too-large hands gripping the spear showed Michal's challenger to be scarcely fourteen, if that.

Boy or man, he was standing squarely in the road before Michal and his mount. He might not use the spear if Michal tried to simply ride past him, but then again he might. Michal had not survived ten years as a fighting man by trusting overly much in "might."

Under the rider's steady gaze, the boy swallowed, licked his lips, and mustered the courage to repeat his question.

"A free man of Harz-i-Shai," Michal replied.

The next question was so long in coming that Michal was able to find the boy's comrades without shifting his own gaze. One thought he was hidden in the shadow of a stone wall that seemed to be part of a ruined cow byre. A second must have heard too many foolish tales; he was trying to hide in the lower branches of a bluethorn tree whose trunk had forked no more than three paces from the ground. He had no bow, either.

"What brings you to Niza's Forge?" the boy in the road finally said.

Michal rejected the answer, "My horse," in favor of a more polite, "Matters lawful in the eyes of both Harzi and Sherrani and all their gods." He would be interested in hearing someone argue that the service of the First Magistrate of Koddardos was *not* lawful.

Not here and now, though. It seemed wiser not to mention Lord Joviz without greater need. Tales of King Pijtos' sickness had met Michal when he landed in Svarno. On the road south he'd heard that Pijtos was dying, and the great lords flocking

1

to Koddardos like carrion birds scenting a feast. If this village of Niza's Forge was on the lands of such a lord . . .

Michal backed his horse a pace or two.

"Do you swear this?" asked the boy, taking a firmer grip on his spear.

"I swear by the Father and the Warrior that none of Niza's Forge, their kin, their beasts, or anything that is lawfully theirs will come to harm through me."

The boy swallowed again. "Do you swear it by the Mother and the Craftsman?"

"By these also, I swear it."

The boy looked as if he'd just been reprieved from a flogging, and slightly relaxed his grip on the spear. A Harzi, of course, was bound by no oaths save those sworn in the name of the Father or the Warrior, but the young Sherrani could learn that some other time. Right now he and his comrades were about to receive a short lesson in the skills of a sentry.

Michal snatched the horse bow from his back; the boy, seeing the action, froze. An arrow from Michal's saddle quiver followed. Nock, aim, draw, shoot—see the arrow *thunk* into the crotch of the branch supporting the second boy—see him fall out of the tree with a yell—a quick draw of the sword to guard position before the spear carrier's courage could push him to effective thrusting distance—move the horse a pace forward and aim a slash that took the spearhead clean off.

The boy looked at the head lying in the gravel of the road and clenched his hands on the shaft until the knuckles stood out white. Michal stifled laughter. There was nothing funny about such humiliation when it was yours and you could neither fight nor weep.

"The third of us would have run away and warned the village," the boy said, a little before he could control his voice.

Michal silently patted his bow.

"You might have missed," the boy replied.

"I probably would not have missed," said Michal. "Anyway, it's foolish to wager your life on a 'might.' Very foolish." He sheathed his sword, reslung his bow, and slid out of the saddle with empty hands, the sign of peaceful intentions all over Sherran. As the second boy came up, Michal went on.

"Had I been an enemy, I could have killed all three of you. As it is—let's see to your friend by the tree there. If he's hurt, I'll pay for his Healing and a blood-price. If he isn't, you three can groom my horse. In return, I'll teach you how to lie in wait so that no man but a warrior more skilled than I am will see you until you've learned what brings him to Niza's Forge, and also how to get rid him if you don't want him here. I promise this in the name of the Warrior."

The third boy was lying senseless beneath the tree, breathing normally and not bleeding. "Leave him alone for about a spell," ordered Michal. "And now tell me—why does your lord have the roads guarded?"

"Lord Volo didn't—" began the first boy, to be promptly and ungently kicked in the shin by the second. Michal rested two fingers lightly on the hilt of his sword.

"What did Lord Volo do or leave undone, that has you out here guarding your village? Besides, I haven't heard that the lords of Sherran commonly gave such work to—fledgling warriors." He'd almost said "children," which would have been a Father-forsaken bit of unwisdom! "Remember," he added. "I have sworn that I mean no harm. Do you repay me by hiding knowledge that might save my life, or help me save yours?"

Michal was nearly certain he heard the first boy mutter something about "Damned Harzis always wanting their price," but he thought it best ignored. Just then the boy from the tree groaned and sat up, shaking his head and limbs like a clumsily worked puppet.

"Lie still, fool," said Michal. He handed the waterskin from his saddle to the second boy. "Support him and help him to drink—slowly. If he wants to vomit, let him. Otherwise he should lie quietly for another two spells."

Thinking the injured boy would recover his spirits, if not his senses, faster if there was no Harzi looming over him, Michal withdrew to see to his horse, leaving the boys to tend to their comrade. The gelding was no trained and hardened Harzi war steed, but a long-striding Sherrani mount of the same stock as that used by the Great King's cavalry. He was faster than a Harzi mount for traveling the high roads of Sherran, but not as enduring.

Those high roads were well provided with inns and other conveniences for travelers, so it wasn't really necessary to use a horse you could be sure would see you to your journey's end. All the same, the hospitality of a village had saved more than one traveler from disaster. It was something most Sherranis took for granted, but Harzis could not always be sure of their welcome.

In spite of two centuries of coming and going and the fact that any Harzi who actually reaved children *or* adults would face outlawry from his clan and a painful death on either side of the border, the belief persisted that Harzis were stealers of children, especially girls, to sell into slavery in distant lands. Harzis did sell their own infants on occasion—when they were weak or deformed or a father could not afford to raise a daughter—but this was a painful decision, made at birth, never to be unmade even if a man ended up with no children at all. The custom had been twisted into a belief that you'd better lock up your daughters when a Harzi passed by. This belief sometimes made things unpleasant for Harzis traveling alone or in small groups, although Harzi skill in arms usually kept matters from becoming really dangerous.

Michal realized that his instinct to see soldiering done properly, even if only by Sherrani village boys, had led him to behave very much like the monstrous Harzi of popular fear, especially if the boy he'd frightened out of the tree was more seriously hurt than he seemed. Michal examined his mount's left forehoof and picked out a stone that was threatening to lodge in it. Other than that, the horse seemed fit to carry him well beyond Niza's Forge if necessary. He hoped the villagers would not turn the nether cheek or worse to him, especially since he might learn something worth knowing, but he'd hardly made an auspicious beginning.

Movement under the tree made Michal look up. The boy who'd fallen was standing—unsteadily but unaided. At least

Michal wouldn't have to ask Lord Joviz for blood-price and Healer's fees, whether or not he could bring the First Magistrate news of Lord Volo's doings.

Michal remounted as the three boys returned to the road, the first boy in the lead. "Lord Volo did not ask us to do this," the boy said. "He has gone to Koddardos with his men. They say King Pijtos is dying. Do you know of this?"

"I heard he was sick," said Michal. "That he is dying is news to me."

"Well, we heard that was what they told Lord Volo," said the second boy. "So he called up all his household fit to ride and went to Koddardos. Auntie Zelena went to Lord Volo's steward to ask him to at least leave the road-riders. He wouldn't do that. So she came back and said we would have to do something ourselves, or robbers would come too close to the village."

"Auntie Zelena sounds wise," said Michal. "I would like to speak with her."

The boys looked at each other. The first one said, "It is Sowing Eve. She will have much to do."

"So she will. Yet—" He hesitated, not sure how long it would take to carry out this promise if they accepted it. Would Joviz think what he might learn worth the time it would cost?

"If Auntie Zelena will speak to me, I will teach all the men of the village what I promised to teach you. Even the women, if they wish it," he added, although he didn't think he could teach much to Sherrani women. Most of them had never learned the simplest ways of steel.

"We can't promise anything in Auntie Zelena's name," said the third boy, speaking for the first time. "But I think we can promise to take you to her, and we will care for your horse whatever happens."

"Fair enough," said Michal. He pressed his knees into his mount's dust-coated flanks. "Lead the way."

The first boy returned to the road, while the other two led Michal along a winding path through fields plowed, dunged, and ready for sowing. In the corner of one a gang of men and women was erecting a shelter of poles and woven rush matting. The sign of the Mother was woven into the matting.

The mothers of Niza's Forge would keep vigil in the shelter tonight, while the maidens and the priestess sowed the first seeds of the year's planting. Michal tried to keep his distance from the structure. In some villages it was considered bad luck for an armed warrior, especially a Harzi, to pass by during the shelter's construction and use. If he gave such luck now, neither gold nor threats nor good service would open the lips of Auntie Zelena or anyone else in the village.

Beyond the shelter the path crossed a wooden bridge over a stream. Michal noted the possibility of making some of its planks removable to keep enemy horsemen from using the path. Beyond the stream rose two hills, the village filling the crest of the one to the right and part of the valley between.

The upper village was clearly the older part, as was usual here in the north of Sherran. An ancient wall of roughly dressed stone surrounded it with a good score of men at work on it. Some were rooting out brush at the base with mattocks, while others mortared a new course of stones in place atop it.

Michal considered the sight. He didn't know where Lord Volo stood among the men whose good will Magistrate Joviz would need if King Pijtos died. He'd have to find out before revealing all he'd said and done here to his new master. Lord Volo might not care to see his villagers so eager to defend themselves. A strange notion, but then, not ruling free men of Harz-i-Shai gave the lords of Sherran many strange notions. If Joviz told Volo everything Michal had seen at Niza's Forge, it might go hard with the villagers whom Michal had agreed to help.

It might even go hard with Michal if he taught them anything their lord didn't want them to know. No help for that, however. He'd made a promise in the name of the Warrior, and only a fool would break that. A man who did could never again trust weapons or comrades or war-luck.

The two boys now led Michal around the base of the hill and into the valley. The houses here were larger, newer, and mostly of wood, built since there'd ceased to be any fear of war in northwest Sherran. Michal hoped there was a plan to move all the people behind the walls of the old village if that happy time was now about to end. If not, he would see about providing one.

Michal dismounted in front of a house with a blue-painted door and a freshly thatched roof. He carefully stripped his mount of weapons and personal gear before allowing the horse to be led off. He was anticipating using a much-needed chamberpot within when the door opened and a sharp clear voice told him to enter.

Auntie Zelena must have been the village beauty when she was young, and she was far from ugly even now. She needed a stout stick or a strong arm in order to walk, so she sat by the hearth while one of her granddaughters brought Michal a cup of ale and some cakes.

"On Sowing Eve we all fast until morning. You don't have to honor our customs, of course, except for not having a woman."

Michal suspected this meant he was free to ignore their other customs as long as he didn't expect her to tell him anything. A woman was nearly the furthest thing from his mind right now, but he would have appreciated a hot meal. He reminded himself of a warrior's duty to seek victory even in small skirmishes and nodded.

"I will ask no more than this. Now, one has heard dire news from Koddardos, goodwife." He used the honorific appropriate to a small merchant's lady. "What is known of this news in Niza's Forge?"

Auntie Zelena told him hardly anything he hadn't heard from the boys. By the time she'd finished describing the steward's warts for the third time, Michal suspected that he'd become that classic figure of Sherrani comedy, a Harzi who'd been outwitted in a bargain. The boys would bear witness to what he'd promised in return for speaking to Auntie Zelena. He was now speaking to her, for all the good it was doing him, and he was bound to do what Lord Volo might call teaching his villagers to rebel!

He realized with a start that Auntie Zelena had finished her tale and was asking him if he wished to visit the bathhouse with the men. "If they know what you've promised to do, none of them will say a word. Most of them won't even give you a queer look. Anyway, we've nothing against Harzis here. Live and let live, for all you'd bargain for the water needed to save you from dying of thirst and you pinch a veysela until Veysel Sherran himself must feel the pain."

"Thank you, goodwife. But I think it would be better if no one knows what I'm here for until tomorrow."

"As you wish."

Michal's last remark was perfectly true, but also relieved him of explaining why, if he meant no harm and was outnumbered anyway, he refused to be parted from his weapons. It simply went against a Harzi fighting man's instincts to be away from his weapons among several-score able-bodied strangers. The Sherrani were not so bonded to their steel that they allowed for this in their bathhouses, as did the Harzis.

At least this village seemed to believe no worse of Harzis than that they were hard bargainers and close with money. The Land of the Clans was fair but hardly wealthy. Harzis learned to make a little go a long way.

There was nothing more he could do by sitting here except feel a bigger fool than ever. He laid his heavy gear in a dry corner and went out to see to his horse. The boys would keep their promise, but might need watching.

Very surely, he must learn where Lord Volo stood in whatever was happening in Koddardos, and not from any Sherrani either, if he could help it. Hakfor shan-Melech Hakatsar owed Michal more favors than he'd yet repaid for succeeding to Michal's old place as chief of Master Merchant Coron's caravan guards. It should be easy to find Hakfor if he still drank at the Blue Falcon, and no great merchant's chief guardsman would be without his sources of information.

As Michal walked toward the stables, he smelled smoke and heard voices. Where the path forked between the valley and the hillside, a bonfire now crackled. The village priestess stood by it, throwing pieces of bread from a tray into the flames, while a group of young girls in green tunics stood by, one holding the tray. A chant to the Mother rose antiphonally as the bread fell, growing louder as more villagers approached and joined in.

"Blessed is God the Mother,
  Who causes the fruits of the earth to sprout in due season."
"Honored is God the Mother,
  Who protects and prospers the seed in the ground."
"Gracious is God the Mother,
  Giver of sun and rain."
"Holy is God the Mother,
  May She keep us in Her unceasing care from seedtime to harvest, from harvest until seedtime."

Michal was out of hearing before the ceremony went any further. Harzis did not worship the Mother, but he hoped Somebody would answer those prayers and reward those offerings of the last harvest's bread.

As for his own offering—first he'd oversee the grooming of his horse, then he'd visit the village blacksmith to see if he had the skill to make spikes to be set atop the wall.

II

BY THE TIME THE FIRST MAGISTRATE'S LITTER REACHED THE southern bridge over the Amrakis Canal, it was nearly dark. The crowds in the streets between the canal and the palace were so thick that the lamplighters were battling their way from lamp to lamp, using the butts of their firelighters to clear a path.

The street cleaners had given up the struggle. Joviz saw three of them standing by the wreckage of their cart, a litter of planks, wheels, and shattered water jars. All were waving their brooms at the crowd, invoking all the lawful Faces of God and demons out of legend as well.

Joviz sighed and signaled to the troopmaster of his guards. The squarely built Harzi in turn signaled to the trumpeter, who blew a resounding blast. The troopmaster drew breath and shouted.

"Way! Make way there for His Excellency Joviz Orasur, First Magistrate of Koddardos! Make way for the First Magistrate and his business!" His voice rose to the bellow of a Harzi battle cry. "Make way there, you slowfooted witlings!"

The troopmaster's shouts and the judiciously flourished staves of his men slowly cleared a path, though there was little room in the street. The street cleaners' curses grew still louder as their pots and cart were trampled into still smaller pieces. Joviz pitied them and prayed that wood and crockery would be all that was broken tonight.

His duty was still to reach the palace, though, and this he would do even if all Koddardos had joined the vigil outside its walls.

In the narrow streets between the canal and the palace quarter, it sometimes did seem as if the whole city was afoot tonight. Joviz's troopmaster shouted himself hoarse, his men ran with sweat, and in places the magistrate's party still had to retrace their steps. In some streets the only way to clear a path would have been to turn half the people into apes so that they could climb the walls of the houses on either side.

Long before he reached the palace, Joviz was thanking God he'd taken his litter as usual, rather than following his secretary's advice to ride. The magistrate was one of the few in Sherran who could lawfully ride on the Island of Koddardos, but no law could make most horses keep their wits in such a mob. Joviz had to admit that only Harzi-trained mounts could be trusted to do that. Perhaps Michal, that new captain he'd hired away from Master Merchant Coron, could train at least a few of the horses in Joviz's stables.

Time to think about that later. Here was the palace, with the Swords of Sherran in their silvered breastplates mounting guard on the wall. Joviz's men fought their way to the tree-tall bronze-faced gates. The gates displayed all the lawful Faces of

God, but from the gate house on top of the wall there also hung a gigantic wrought-iron sigil of God the Divine Essence, "which has not the form of a face." It had hung there during all the fifteen years of Pijtos Sherran's reign.

As the troopmaster identified him and the gates swung open, Joviz smoothed his trousers and adjusted his robe so that it hung as well as any garment could on his lean body. A seemly appearance would not banish his fear but would hide it, and that was all his duty as one in the hierarchy of Rulers demanded.

Izrunarko the Teacher had likened the Ruler to the wise father of a family, who hides his fear in order to keep his children in good heart. Translated, this Teaching required the First Magistrate not to appear disheveled, nervous, or frightened. He composed his face and bearing to the necessary official sobriety.

The gates groaned shut behind the litter and the guide called the attendants to a halt. Joviz descended from the litter as a Captain of Swords approached.

"Your Excellency, the Captain-General of the Swords awaits you."

"I would rather see the High Steward of the Household or the Keeper of the Purse."

"They attend the King."

"Can they be summoned?"

"Not without much delay, I fear."

If a Captain of Swords said that the two most important officials of the royal household were attending the King and could be summoned only with difficulty, even the First Magistrate of Koddardos had to accept it. If there was anything else the captain could say on the matter, it would not be said in the presence of common soldiers and litterbearers.

Two of the Swords and two of Joviz's own guards took places before and behind him. With feet he hoped would not drag he began to mount the long marble stairs to the palace doors.

Within the palace all was seemly, or at least nothing was so unseemly that Joviz saw cause for more worry than he already

11

felt. Few servants were in sight, but it was night and there were no guests in the palace now. Those few he saw seemed to be about their duties. The Attendants' Chamber was not only empty but unguarded; otherwise the outer palace showed no sign that anything was wrong.

The Captain-General met Joviz in a small chamber off the corridor to the Hall of Audiences. Like the rest of Pijtos's principal officials, he seemed to have been modeled after the King. He was even taller than Joviz, gray, austere in manner and still more so in dress, slightly stooped, and had the unworldly air of a contemplative priest about him.

In fact, only Pijtos himself and two of his officials had ever been consecrated. It had been Pijtos's pleasure to surround himself with men who had the manners, if not the standing, of priests. The Captain-General had once been a captain in the same regiment as Joviz, and his manners had not always been so austere. The night they'd rescued five girls the Momaks had been carrying away, for example . . .

The blank stare in the Captain-General's eyes turned Joviz's thoughts from past frolics to present dangers. "I have come to learn the condition of Pijtos Sherran, which it is my right to know," said Joviz.

"I do not deny your right."

"I thank you. How is he?"

The Captain-General seemed reluctant to reply. Joviz continued. "Do you yourself not know how the King fares? It is your duty to know! You must have inquired."

"Yes. Yes, I have. I asked the Healers, at least those I thought would answer. Not all of them are willing to speak freely, you know."

"I also know that snow melts in the spring. Did you have any luck in finding one who would speak? If so, what did he say?"

The Captain-General frowned. "None would say more than that they had not given up all hope."

That was not a good sign; Healers used that phrase when they did not wish to talk about a patient's condition. It could mean that the condition was embarrassing, felt to be none of the inquirer's business, baffling to the Healer, or about to kill the patient. Joviz had never liked the habit, and by employing it now when the patient was the King himself, the Healers were venturing out of Healing and into Ruling. Knowledge of the King's condition was not supposed to be kept from certain of the lesser Rulers, and perhaps it was time for one of those to so remind the Healers.

"I need to know more than that," said Joviz. "I think I had better speak to them myself."

"The chief Healers still attend the King," replied the Captain-General. "Several of the lesser ones have gone back to the First Temple to fetch—certain instruments."

That could mean much or little. It could mean that there was no need to move the sick man to a temple of God the Healer, where the apparatus for the most potent Healing magic was kept. It might also mean that Pijtos could not survive even such a short journey or that no more could be done in a temple than could be done in the palace.

Joviz felt a surge of anger. The Captain-General had no business behaving like a stubborn, wary fish to Joviz's angler. He knew perfectly well what was at stake in the matter of Pijtos's life or death. Lacking other bait, Joviz was about to appeal to their old comradeship when he heard feet and voices in the corridor.

Peering out, he saw a Healers' procession advancing toward him. First came a bald, gray-bearded man whom Joviz recognized as one of the four highest Masters of the First Temple of God the Healer. Two apprentices followed, carrying a litter between them.

On the litter stood two carved poles. Between the poles ran a silvered axle of fine steel, and around the axle turned a wheel of gilded bronze filigree so fine it reminded Joviz of lace.

Behind the litter walked another high-ranking Healer Joviz didn't recognize, flanked by two apprentices festooned with leather pouches and silk-wrapped glass vials. Two of the First Temple's guards, armed with light staves, brought up the rear.

Joviz watched the procession pass, then turned back to the Captain-General, who could not meet his eyes.

"Pijtos has a congestion of blood in his brain, does he not?"

"Yes. But—how did you guess?"

"I know how the Wheel of Gaida Lerikur is used," said Joviz. "When there is a congestion too deep within the body to be reached by a surgeon, the Healers use the wheel on it. When the wheel is turned, Gaida Lerikur's spell transforms the rotary motion into pressure which a second Healer focuses on the congestion, 'grinding' it away. The pressure may be changed with the speed of the wheel, which is easier to alter than the strength of a spell."

"So I also have heard. How did you know the congestion was in his brain?"

"Had it been anywhere else, we might have seen signs of its presence before this, but Pijtos was to all appearances hale and fit. Also, had it been anywhere else, yet so serious that he has not named an heir, he would almost certainly be dead by now. A man may live some time with a congestion of blood that has destroyed his brain and muted him without doing him other harm. I am sure you know this as well as I do."

"So he may," said the Captain-General absently. "How do you judge that he has named no heir?"

"You would have told me if he had. Not perhaps the name, for that must go first to Queen Kantela and the heir himself, but certainly that the name was known. You know your duty and mine under the laws too well to do otherwise. The law says nothing about what you are to do when the King has not spoken and may never speak again."

Joviz now understood the bleak situation of the Captain-General and the other royal officials. The laws of Sherran and the traditions of the Swords clearly spelled out their duties to both the King and his heir. But in this case there was only Pijtos. The Captain-General had not wished to bring shame to the King's deathbed by revealing that he'd failed in one of his most necessary duties: the naming of an heir.

Still less would he encourage panic by spreading the news. But now the Captain-General would have to keep up the spirits of men who had no sworn master and deal with attempts to influence the Swords at every level from the newest-joined

14

Swordsman on up to the Captain-General himself. No wonder he was keeping his mouth shut!

Joviz grasped the Captain-General's wrist and smiled. "Thank you for your help. When the time of mourning is done, I shall be inviting some of my old comrades to my house. There are not so many of us left as there were, and we should drink to old times before we become still fewer."

"I will come, Joviz."

Retracing his steps as far as the Attendants' Chamber, Joviz found the chamber not only occupied but guarded. Two Swords in full armor flanked the door, blades drawn and shields propped against the wall within easy reach. They did not challenge Joviz when he strode to the door and peered into the chamber.

The dozen or so armed men lounging on the benches under Zurik Nevestur's fresco of the arrival of the first Silver Fleet could be nothing but a great lord's household guards. Joviz noted the fine leather riding coats and breeches, goldwork on boot tops and coat skirts, silver-mounted scabbards, and general air of foppish confidence.

Their captain stood with his head just below the painted bow of Overlord Berov Barjachur's flagship. The silvered helmet under his arm, the plate-sized cloak pin, and the gilded hilt of his peace-bonded sword all displayed his master's badge.

"So Lord Ikos has come to Koddardos out of his concern for King Pijtos's health?" said Joviz.

One corner of the captain's thin-lipped mouth twitched. "Is that your concern, First Magistrate? Your powers do not extend to the palace itself, as we both know."

"True," replied Joviz. "Yet how are you and your lord to reach the palace without passing through Koddardos, where my powers do run? Or has Lord Ikos worked unlawful magic, to let him pass from outside Koddardos to the palace without passing through the city?"

Neither the captain's mouth nor any other part of his face moved this time. Joviz was almost regretting the revealing sharpness of his words when he looked again at the guardsmen. Two were exchanging uneasy looks, a third had turned away from the magistrate, while a fourth actually seemed to be changing color.

Joviz withdrew before his own face revealed what he'd learned. After all, it was not any part of his duty to teach discretion to the hired swords of one of the most notoriously turbulent great lords of Sherran.

In the corridor outside the Attendants' Chamber, Joviz's troopmaster was waiting and announced that his litter was ready.

By the time the litter passed out of the palace gates, it was raining. Not heavily, but along with the absence of news and the knowledge of a day's work to be done tomorrow, it was enough to be sending the crowd homeward. Joviz felt a moment's reluctant gratitude for the discretion of the palace officials. If the crowd had known they were keeping a deathwatch, nothing it would have been wise to do could have dispersed them, nor any weather short of a storm from the Inner Sea.

Joviz realized how late it was as his litter passed over the Amrakis Canal. From below rose the shouts of the bargemen collecting the nightsoil and garbage of Koddardos for hauling to the gardens and farms downriver. So did the stench from their barges.

For a moment Joviz actually wished that he had a scented sponge to hold to his nose against the reek. For another moment he contemplated what that told him about the passing of years, as well as watches. He was appointed First Magistrate of Koddardos ten years ago. Then, he'd have no more contemplated such a fancy lordling's trick than he would have contemplated visiting a common house of women.

The bridge, the canal, and the stench all fell behind. The litter bearers settled down to the fast trot they favored when the streets lay clear ahead. Its familiar steadiness calmed Joviz, letting him turn his mind to the inevitable question: What is to be done?

For the space of several streets there seemed to be no answer at all. Then Joviz realized that even he had been recoiling from the thought of Pijtos dead without a declared heir.

16

Very well. Usurp the Healers' duty, declare Pijtos dead, assume no named heir, and then ask the question again. Now answers came more easily.

First, he would speak to the supervisors of Markets, Streets, and Water. Ask what they would need, see what they could be given, and pray to God that the two were not separated by much. Also see that the baths in the temples of the Mother did not lack fuel or water.

As long as Joviz had breath in his body, Koddardos would stay fed and clean, whether it held no King or thirty.

Second, he would find out how many men Lord Ikos had brought to Koddardos and also who else among the lords of Sherran might be on his way to the city. Ikos was not the first; Lord Volo had come two days before with enough men to fight a small war.

However, Lord Volo also had a reputation for the caution of a merchant with only two spare gold pieces to invest. He'd left most of his men outside Koddardos and brought into Joviz's reach only enough to double the guards on his town house. It seemed likely that he would watch and wait, ready to apply his strength only after others had shown him where to do so most profitably.

Joviz had to admit that he would have done the same, with Ikos Muzkur dar no Ballos taking the field. God might restrain Ikos's impulses. Nothing mere men could do or leave undone, short of murdering him, promised to do so.

Third, he would visit the temples of the Mother and the Healer. Not tonight—that would be something extraordinary, and for the First Magistrate to do something extraordinary would sow rumors. He'd go tomorrow, as soon as he'd seen the supervisors. At the First Temple of the Mother he could also speak to the Reverend Lady Lilka about the bathhouses and pray to God before the Faces of the Mother and the Healer. Joviz did not like to make his devotions in public, but at times like this the First Magistrate not only must make all the proper observances but must be seen to make them.

Honor God and also prudence before the Face of the Giver of Knowledge, by sending a large anonymous contribution to that temple. If Lord Ikos was indeed dabbling in unlawful magic, it was not a matter for sharp jests to his hired soldiers but for writs of investigation from the College of Priests. Ikos's rank and temper made it unlikely that he'd stop for anyone less, unless he was caught openly practicing blatantly illegal sorcery.

The primary duty of the college in the four hundred years since the War of God the Destroyer had been to ensure that sorcery never ran wild in Sherran again. In recent years the college had largely become an appendage of the temples of the Giver of Knowledge, which provided most of its support, but the duty still remained. Students serving the Giver of Knowledge experimented with magic with great care for their own safety and still greater care for the safety of others. Neither the temple nor the college tolerated those who did otherwise, and frowned on those who did not work directly under the supervision of one or the other.

Joviz discovered that his meditations had brought him home. As the litter bearers turned in through the gate of his house, he stretched his legs and thought with longing and relief of his bed. He also thought of one more duty for tomorrow: send a message to Queen Kantela requesting an audience. She might have no wisdom to make his work easier in the days ahead, but surely she could be kept from making it harder.

III

LORD IKOS STIFFENED. HIS THICK-HEELED RED BOOTS brought his dark eyes to a level with the Queen's. Kantela forced herself to meet his gaze. She refused to admit even to herself that there could be any substance to the rumors that the notoriously ill-tempered lord before her was also a secret sorcerer.

"I have no Gifts from God—" Ikos began, with what was obviously meant to be a reassuring smile.

"They would not be from God, unless God has turned to you a face unknown to the true followers of Izrunarko," Kantela replied. Her fingers twitched, but she restrained them from making either a fist or a sign of aversion.

"That is not a matter we shall resolve tonight, if it is to be resolved at all," said Ikos piously. "I refer only to what may be given me by the coming death of King Pijtos."

"Have you knowledge that I lack?" said Kantela. "Or have you done what will surely interest both the magistrates and the masters, dabbling in prophecies of the King's death? That is both treason and unlawful magic."

The anger crackling in Kantela's voice halted Ikos. The dark eyes grew veiled. The smile grew broader if no more convincing.

"Forgive me, Your Grace. My words were ill chosen, but truly, I spoke out of concern for you, for King Pijtos, and for the Throne of Sherran. Surely you would not wish me to lack such concern?"

"I would not." Kantela had heard it said that this man, now professing friendship and concern, was as deadly as a nest of spellbound serpents to his enemies, who learned that he called them that only after his fangs were deep in their flesh.

At the moment Kantela would have agreed with this description of Ikos. She sighed. It was more than a few spells into the northwatch, she had been awake since before dawn, and her fifth talk with Master Healer Zali Bitrinur was fast approaching. She did not want to make an enemy of Ikos merely by dismissing him when he might have something to say worth hearing, but neither did she think she owed him much of her fast-shrinking time and strength.

"Your concern does you honor, and I am grateful for it. I will be still more grateful if you are brief."

"I shall do my best." A look of sober grief replaced the smile. "Death is coming to all of us, and to some sooner than to others. It is seldom that so many Healers come to a man whose death is not near. Is that not so?"

"Yes."

"So King Pijtos will be with God soon, and with a heavy burden on his spirit. He has named no heir to the throne,

19

leaving it and perhaps the survival of the kingdom at stake. Leaving you alone as well. Would it not be a noble work to remove this burden from the King and protect both yourself and Sherran?"

Kantela hoped that her face showed nothing and that the pause while she controlled her voice did the same. "If my lord Pijtos does in fact bear this burden," she said, "how do you propose that we do the noble work of lifting it?"

This time Ikos's smile seemed genuine. "Ah, you understand that it must indeed be done by us both together. How, is simple. You will swear by all the Faces of God that Pijtos did indeed name me heir when he summoned me to the palace four years ago, but in your hearing and yours alone. He did not wish this known because he feared that my enemies would flock around the throne and peck at him until he changed his mind.

"Now that my enemies can do Pijtos no harm, it is proper that his wishes be known. It seems to me that this is a small lie for you to tell, to win so great a prize."

"A prize?"

"To sit on the throne beside me, with as much power as it will be proper for you to have. More than you have ever had from Pijtos, once you have borne me a son, and that will not be long. I am no priest disguised as a king, like Pijtos."

"I have not heard that said of you," said Kantela warily.

Ikos laughed out loud. "You sound doubtful, Your Grace. Well, I will not ask you to buy the stallion without testing his paces. There is ample time and you will find me apt enough for—"

The idea of taking Ikos to her bed while Pijtos lay dying in his, presented itself to Kantela with appalling clarity. It choked her, shook her from coronet to ankles, made her mute and deaf and blind all at once.

It did not keep her from pushing at Ikos's shoulder with one shaking hand.

Ikos promptly lifted the hand to his lips and threw his other arm around her waist, pulling her against him. Rage and astonishment hadn't numbed Kantela's nose. When she smelled the wine on Ikos's breath and the oil in his beard, she reacted.

Her right knee shot up, driving squarely and hard into the part of his body whose qualities he had just proposed to demonstrate. Luck was with her. Rage, pain, and lack of breath kept Ikos completely speechless until Kantela could strike the gong for her chambers' guard of the Swords of Sherran. By the time Ikos had his breath back, he could also hear the fast-approaching footsteps of more witnesses than he could afford to buy, as well as more men than he could hope to fight.

"God will forgive Pijtos for more sins than he was capable of committing, for not naming *you* as his heir," snarled Kantela. "I swear to be silent on this—episode, but never speak of this matter to me again or I will forget the dignity due to both of us and publicly spit in your face."

She straightened as the Swords entered. "Lord Ikos appears to have been taken ill," she said. "If there is an apprentice or other lesser Healer free to cast a purgative spell on him, he might be the better for it."

Ikos salvaged what remained of his dignity by walking out on his own feet, keeping in step with the guards, and almost holding himself straight although his bow was too shallow and shook noticeably. Kantela watched him go, thinking a brief, unseemly prayer that he might find himself in the hands of the most inept Healer in the palace.

When Ikos and the Swords were out of sight, Kantela let herself sag into a chair. She felt an overwhelming need to cleanse herself of Ikos's touch, while the semiformal robe she had put on to receive him threatened to smother her. She struck the gong again for the chief of her lady-attendants.

"Summon the bath maids to draw me a bath. I will want a fresh robe afterward, but a summer one. Not one of these Momak burial shrouds, by all the Faces of God!"

"Yes, Your Grace," said Zensko Lilkura. "The Master Healer will surely wish to see you before—"

"Tell him to wait or else come in and talk to me while I'm bathing!" Kantela shouted. "If he's any kind of a Healer he must have seen enough naked women to last him ten lifetimes. If he hasn't, maybe it's time he started so he won't end up another dried-out useless husk of a priest!"

Lady Zensko flinched. Kantela realized she must have mouthed silently the words she'd managed not to say aloud: Like Pijtos.

Kantela made an inarticulate sound, leaped up, and ran for her bedchamber.

In the bath, her hair spreading fanwise around her, Kantela's first desire was to sleep. The idea of slipping under the water and drowning kept her awake and also made her laugh.

Yet what might happen if she did drown—or die some other way—would be nothing to laugh at. With both the King and the Queen dead, there would be no one to give orders on any matter, great or small, concerning the future of Sherran.

Or rather, there would be too many *trying* to give orders. Two of the greatest lords of Sherran were already in Koddardos, and the other three probably on the way. A score of lesser lords was already in the city and twice as many on the roads, all ready to sell their friendship or influence or armed men to the great ones. A few would surely be thinking of climbing to greatness themselves over the bodies of anyone who stood in their paths.

Together, they could rend Sherran like a pack of wolves.

The Queen of Sherran would have to be the she-bear standing between her cubs in their den and the wolf pack.

Kantela sat up and hugged her arms across her breasts. She suddenly realized that being able to do something of her own free will—indeed, having to do something of her own free will because there was no one to direct her—was more exciting than frightening, and not at all unpleasant.

She stepped out of the bath and reclined on the couch beside it while the maids did their work with pumice, oil, perfume, and scissors, letting them fuss over small matters she normally endured rather than enjoyed. She might have little time for a proper toilet in the days to come. Also, at the moment the bath maids were giving her time to think, something she needed more than well-trimmed toenails.

The idea of being her own mistress grew more agreeable each time Kantela thought about it. It would not have had to be very agreeable to seem more pleasant than the life she'd lived during her fifteen years as queen. Pijtos had never treated her ill or caused her to be more than impatient with him, but her presence was one more reminder that he was no longer the priest of the Divine Essence that he had been and that God had clearly made him to be.

God had made Pijtos a priest. But God had not withheld the plague that slew Pijtos's eldest brother before he'd begotten any heirs, nor the shipwreck that claimed Pijtos's other brother and both his children. Thus it came about that the palace officials knocked on the door of a temple of the Divine Essence, to inform a man very much at peace in the robes of a priest that he must now wear, however uneasily, the robes of the King of Sherran.

For fifteen years Kantela had been Pijtos's hostess at court functions great and small, dealt with the details of running the palace, held her peace through the concerts and philosophical discussions which so delighted him, and sometimes shared his bed, although that so infrequently and ceremoniously that she wondered what it was like to lie with a man instead of a priest. (No one thought she'd heard the bawdy jokes on that subject which ran about the palace like rats in the cellar. That was one small blessing.)

Fifteen years of this had left her with a great desire to do something and—she recoiled as she would have from a snake or a precipice—very little idea of what that "something" should be. What could she do, and whom could she trust to give advice?

The palace officials would be a broken reed, and not necessarily from ill-will. The ones she knew best, the household officers, knew only a little more of the affairs of Sherran than she did, if as much. As for the King's Servants, let alone the great lords—

"Your Grace, the Reverend Master Zali Bitrinur awaits

without. So does a messenger from the Captain-General of the Swords." It was Zensko Lilkura outside the door.

"In a moment."

Kantela pulled her trousers on, let the maids drag a shift over her head, heedless of the shambles it made of her hair, and pulled on a robe long enough to hide her bare feet. Healers set little store by anyone's dignity save their own and were discreet into the bargain; young officers on palace duty were another matter.

Reverend Master Zali bowed to Kantela, then smoothed his beard before he spoke. "Your Grace, all that can be done has been done for the King. The congestion of blood in his brain has not diminished."

Trust a Healer to spend ten words pronouncing a death sentence when two would do well enough!

"Then there is no hope for Pijtos."

As if she'd asked a question, the Healer shook his head. "By all our Gifts of Healing, Your Grace, we see none. His mind is already dead. His body may live watches, days, surely no more than weeks. There will be nothing within him of what lets us tell men from animals."

A very tactful way of saying that Pijtos would never speak again, and therefore could not be expected to name an heir.

No heir of Pijtos's body, and now there would be no heir of his choice. God be thanked that Healer ethics permitted the details of a deathbed to go only to the next of kin, and not always to them. The longer it took Sherran to fully absorb the news . . .

Meanwhile—

"The Throne thanks you for all your services, Reverend Master."

The ease with which Kantela slipped into the ruler's usage surprised both the Healer and the Queen. He blinked. "Your Grace, do you wish us to cease—the measures to prolong the King's life?"

With her eyes on the floor Kantela said, "Would you advise it?"

"Life will depart sooner or later. The sooner, the less pain for Pijtos. If someone I—had duties toward—was as Pijtos is now—I would say to let him pass."

"Then let it be done."

The Healer bowed himself out. Kantela forced herself to lift her head to greet the messenger, fearing what might be scrawled on her face. *God be merciful, does everybody know that Pijtos and I were only bound by duty?*

And why do I care?

No answer to either question. She took a deep breath and faced the messenger. He had the stocky build of the northwest, where Sherrani and Harzi had been mixing their blood in one way or another for two centuries.

"Your Grace, the Captain-General of the Swords bids me tell you that the Lord Arkan Batur dar no Chintek has reached the bounds of Koddardos."

"Has he sent to request audience?"

"No, Your Grace. Truly, I do not think he will come tonight. He brought half his household with him. It is almost the second northwatch, and I think he will be seeing that everyone is properly settled."

Kantela smiled at the officer's quick wit in seeing that she did not wish to be disturbed further. He blushed.

"Thank you, Captain—?"

"Ersko Shumur, Your Grace."

"You have served the Throne well tonight. It shall be remembered."

"Thank you, Your Grace." The officer was blushing again as he backed out, nearly tripping first over his sword, then over his own feet, then over the door jamb.

Kantela wondered what had made him blush, the Queen's favor or the woman's smile. She'd better assume it was the first and make sure she remained in a position to pay any favors she promised. Now—

The third great lord had arrived, surely enough, and she'd doubtless hear of Korul and Bihor before long. She felt a vindictive satisfaction at the thought that all of them would be disappointed in their hopes of being named heir to Sherran—at least by Pijtos Sherran himself.

The closing of the easiest way to the throne still left the field open to armies, daggers, poison, gold, silver, and spells. More subtle ways, too, such as advising a Queen who badly needed counsel . . .

Kantela rose, nearly knocking down the tiring-maid, who had come forward to strap sandals on her feet as soon as Captain Ersko left and whose presence she'd never noticed, and called her chief attendant.

"Lady Zensko!"

"Your Grace?"

"I shall be in the Queen's Garden. It is quite safe, but you may send a few of the Swords there if it will ease your mind."

"As you wish, Your Grace."

The maid had strapped on only one sandal. Kantela endured a lopsided gait as far as the door to the garden, then kicked off the odd sandal and walked barefoot out onto the dew-sodden grass.

It was a mild night for this early in the spring, but the heavy dew on the grass soaked the hem of Kantela's robe. At last she stopped pacing up and down and sat on a marble bench in the farthest corner of the garden. No longer moving, her feet grew cold until she tucked them under her robe and sat cross-legged on the dew-slick bench.

Twenty years ago she'd sat in the same position on a wooden bench in her father's garden, watching her brothers and sisters playing, too old to join them, too young for marriage. Five of them then, and two more five years later. If she hadn't been one of eight children, would she now be the almost-widow of Pijtos Sherran? It had been no secret that his councillors were looking for a mare from good breeding stock. Had they also known even then that they were dealing with a most reluctant stallion? Kantela didn't know and didn't really care. Most of the councillors of those days had long preceded their master in death, and God alone could judge their wisdom now.

Of her seven younger siblings five still lived, none of them the worse for their sister's being queen, although none of them had ever lived at court or among great affairs. For the first time in years she wondered if she could have arranged matters otherwise. Probably, but that was also as past remedying as was the judgment of the councillors who'd plucked Kantela Phaedura dar no Tinos from her father's estate and dropped her into the King's bed. Her kin would know even less than she what to do about the present state of affairs, and neither she nor the kingdom could afford ignorance.

Where could she turn if not to kin? Certainly the five great lords would take it ill if they were completely ignored. She would have to risk Ikos's wrath; his advice would be worse than none at all.

The newly arrived Lord Arkan would hardly be better. He was the wealthiest of the great lords of Sherran, with little thought for anything except increasing his lands, caravans, and fleets. He had enemies not only among his fellow nobles, but among the great merchants as well. Could she afford to make his enemies hers?

Korul Zenur dar no Olav would not do at all. He was the poorest of the great lords; his income barely met his expenses, and he was frequently in debt. He'd also burned two wives without getting an heir to his House from either, though he did not lack offspring from less formal liaisons.

Bihor Mindur dar no Pomos was young, handsome, and by most reports also rash, vengeful, and quick-tempered to the point of easy violence. Such a man would gladly use the Queen's ear as a weapon against his enemies if she gave it. Volo Deningkur dar no Tivest had made a career of being cautious to the point where he would hardly tell his breeches the color of his tunic, let alone give anyone advice without playing some deep game—

Kantela realized that over the years she must have absorbed more of matters of state than she'd ever been aware of knowing. Certainly she'd never been given a list of the great lords' idiosyncrasies to study.

She recalled the priestess of the Giver of Knowledge who'd visited her parents when Kantela was sixteen, newly removed from the supervision of the scholar-apprentice who was the family tutor. The priestess had told Kantela's parents that their daughter might well benefit from a year or two of study in the First Temple itself. Her parents, fearful of losing their eldest daughter to the temple, then having to wait six years until the next was of an age to figure in matrimonial alliances, had put the priestess off with vague answers. Kantela wondered briefly if what she'd missed would have helped her now.

She could still be tutored, of course. She also recognized, with twinges of disgust, that she was past submitting to a tutor or to anyone who either offered or threatened to lead her anywhere, even to a safe haven away from the disorders that might be about to engulf Sherran. A moment later she realized the folly of *that* thought as well. Where would such a haven be? Northwest in Harz-i-Shai? In the tents of the Momaks? In the Cities of the Plains? Truly there could be none, and anyone who offered her such was either a fool or a liar.

"Queen of Sherran," she told herself, "here you are and here you will stay because there isn't any place else for you to go."

She'd still need advisors, but at least she didn't have to rely on Pijtos's. If any of those disliked the fact of new councillors she would tell them that as long as she did not ignore the Teaching of Izrunarko or break the laws of the land, whose counsel she accepted was none of their concern. She would not accept any grumbling "—and you will do well to cease before *I* cease to even listen politely."

Kantela realized that she'd spoken out loud, as if the men were standing before her, frowning, tugging at their beards, and exchanging looks they thought she didn't see. A shadow moved at the end of the garden, bringing her completely back to the present. She rose to challenge it.

"Who is there?"

Zensko Lilkura's voice replied. "It is I, Your Grace. Word has come from the Healers. The spells to banish pain have been lifted from the King."

Now her husband had sunk even below level of an animal who could at least feel pain. There was no state lower than this, save death itself.

"I thank you."

"I have brought your sandals, Your Grace."

"I thank you."

"Your Grace, it would be more seemly—"

"For you not to tell me my duties and leave me in peace." Was Pijtos going to reach out from barely this side of the pyre to keep her caged still?

Forgive me, Pijtos. You did nothing, you could have done nothing, to earn such a reproach. If I have troubled your last earthly sleep with unworthy abuse, I am ashamed.

"Your Grace . . ."

"Leave the sandals on the path and wait by the guards. I will join you in a moment."

Kantela bowed her head and sat down again as Lady Zensko's footsteps receded toward the garden door.

What was she to do now? To whom could she turn for counsel? The questions would not go away and Kantela knew they would not do so tonight or for many nights to come.

"Your Grace—"

Kantela's hands tightened into claws. She wished there was something close at hand to throw. "Zensko Lilkura. If you think your place is by His Grace, go to him. If not, come out here to me and we will pray for him together."

"Your Grace, some would not consider it seemly—"

"You can surely bear witness that nothing seemly goes unsaid." She fought to keep both anger and pleading out of her voice. All she knew was that if she went back into the palace, let alone all the way to Pijtos's deathbed, she would feel like a trapped animal. That would be a far more unseemly farewell to her husband than anything she proposed to do out here.

"As you wish, Your Grace." Footsteps approached along the path. Kantela smiled.

"God can hear us as well here as anywhere else, I think." She was kneeling by the time Lady Zensko reached her.

"Blessed be God, the One, the Holy, the Almighty," Kantela began.

"O God, Who only art great, have mercy upon us," Lady

Zensko replied. Steadily they alternated in the phrases of the Litany for the Dying:

"O God, Who only art Holy,
    Have mercy upon us."
"O God, Who has graciously revealed Thy Faces to men,
    Have mercy upon us."
"O God, Mother of all living,
    Be with us from our life's beginning unto its ending."
"O God, Father of all people,
    Guide us and protect us each day of our lives."
"O God, Healer of the world's ills,
    Come to us in trouble, sorrow, and sickness."
"O God, Source of all Knowledge,
    Mercifully grant to us of this Thy great gift."

Kantela started as other voices began the next phrase before she did and looked around to see who'd joined them. Then she remembered that the north windows of the palace temple gave on the garden. People must be gathering there now to say their own prayers for the departing spirit of Pijtos Sherran.

"O God, Creator of the Universe,
    Grant that our works may find favor in thy sight."
"O God, strong in battle,
    Be Thou our Sword and our Shield in the day we must
        fight."

Now she could hear not only new voices, but shuffling feet.

"O Holy Essence,
    Come into our hearts and draw us closer to Thee."
"O God, Who has ordered our living and our dying,
    Look with mercy upon Thy servant Pijtos."

A pale wavering light now shone from the windows. They

must have lit the soulfire. The garden ceased to be blackness and became a dim pattern of light and shadow.

"Grant him easy passage from this world,
    And show mercy to him when he sees Thy True Face."
"Grant peace to us who shall mourn,
    And give us strength to carry on."

Almost done, now. Kantela was relieved to find herself growing calm and accepting. When the prayer was finished, she would not find it hard to go and say farewell to Pijtos. It would not be as long a journey as the one he was about to make.

IV

THE PRIEST OF THE WARRIOR LIFTED THE POT OF GLOWING charcoal and handed it to the Reverend Master Charko.

"I bless thee, O fire," Charko intoned, making the sign of blessing, then raising the pot. A brief puff of wind blew its smoke past Kantela. She fought down the would-be sneeze.

"The last fire, the fire that frees," Charko continued.

The chanted responses rose from all the priests and priestesses on the wooden stairs, from the priestess of God the Craftsman on the first step up to the Reverend Lady Lilka standing just below Kantela. The Queen hoped that the sound of seven voices together would hide her silence, for her mouth was too dry to let her speak. Her own prayer was that this would end before the pot reached her. She could not disgrace herself and give an evil omen for all in the Palace Square to hear by not properly pronouncing the Kin's Blessing just before she lit Pijtos's pyre.

The Reverend Master Charko passed the pot up one step. "I bless thee, O fire," said the priest of the Divine Essence, his voice thin and reedy. The smoke blew past Kantela more thickly, but she no longer feared a sneeze.

"The last fire, the fire that frees," and this time some of the crowd pressing close to the guards around the pyre joined in. The priest of the Divine Essence winced as he passed the pot up to the Reverend Lady Lilka. The people's voices at this time were not part of the ritual. Instead of a sneeze Kantela suppressed a smile, which would have been still less a part of the ritual.

"I bless and consecrate thee, O fire," said the Reverend Lady Lilka, making the sign of consecration, and "The last fire, the fire that frees," came with even more spectators joining in. Kantela didn't care. She'd somehow found her voice, and all would be well if she could just make her hands obey her.

Lady Lilka held up the pot, and Kantela reached for it. She felt her fingers tremble and twine helplessly in the air, looked down, and saw Lady Lilka's strong brown hands tighten on the pot as she pretended to pass it on to the Queen.

For a moment they stood with all the appearance of Kantela's taking the pot and all the burden really on Lilka. Kantela licked her lips, took a deep breath, and let it out again.

Once more her hands felt like part of her body. She took the pot, looking at the First Priestess of the Mother with more gratitude than she could ever put into words. Lilka's thin lips twitched into a faint smile.

"The sacred fire," said Kantela, raising the pot and surprising herself with the strength of her voice.

"The sacred fire, the fire that frees." She almost shouted the words, but other voices from the stairs and from all around drowned her out.

Kantela held the pot a moment longer, until the crowd quieted and all eyes were on her, then spoke the Kin's Blessing.

"O God, set now Thy servant Pijtos free from all impurity and grant him the sight of Thy True Face. Farewell, Pijtos."

Then she dipped the head of the long torch standing beside her into the pot and threw the torch onto the resin-soaked wood of the pyre.

The flames gushed up with a hiss and a rumble. The silk-wrapped bundle that was everything remaining of Pijtos

Sherran was on a level with the top of the movable stairs, but flames were rising around it almost before Kantela could turn around.

On the walls of the palace more flames appeared, as the Swords of Sherran lit their torches. From before the gates drums thudded and boomed in a rhythm going back to the remotest days of the worship of God.

To the beat of the drums the assembled priests and priestesses of all the temples of God took up the Chant for the Dead:

"O God, Thou has been our safety from generation to
    generation.
Before anything was, Thou wert and art and ever shall be.
A thousand generations of men in thy sight are but a
    moment, but the blink of an eye.
Thou has given us three generations to our life, and though
    we may have some few years more, yet they are but toil
    and sorrow, and soon gone.
Teach us, O God, to apply our days to wisdom; yea, even in
    those times in which we are afflicted, in which we see
    evil.
For Thou are our trust, our strength, and our refuge, even in
    that day in which we go to the generation of them that
    bore us."

By the time Pijtos's corpse had vanished in the flames the crowd was joining the prayers. They drowned out the sound of the drums, but the men on the ropes attached to the movable stairs didn't need the help of the drums to do their work. Ten of the Swords on one rope, ten picked servants of the palace on the other, they heaved away and the stairs began to roll back from the pyre.

Kantela turned to look at the flames, eyes half-closed against the glare and one hand raised to shield her gray silk mourning cap from falling embers. Pijtos was on his way to a True Sight of God, or so she had been taught. Certainly he was gone forever from Sherran and from her.

A corner of the pyre fell in, dropping half-burned wood onto red-hot coals. Flames growled like wild beasts and a wave of heat washed out from the pyre. Kantela shielded her face with both hands, but through her fingers saw the guards around the pyre holding their places.

Michal felt the surging heat at his back before he heard the sound of the flames. The crowd was no more than twenty paces from his squadron's line, and it was making too much noise for him to hear anything else or for anyone to hear him for that matter. He still raised his voice.

"Steady, men. Steady on this line."

It would not do for men of Harz-i-Shai sworn to the service of the First Magistrate of Koddardos to flinch at a little heat, still less to do so before what must be half Koddardos.

The heat grew until Michal was glad of the arming cap under his helmet and mail coif. Without them, his neck would have blistered. What held good for his men about not flinching held ten times over for him. He was not only their captain, he was a Harzi who had endured being tricked by a Sherrani grandmother!

At least there was little smoke from the pyre. Michal could sweep the whole two hundred paces held by his men without moving more than his head. He studied them again, saw nothing amiss, and raised his eyes to the crowd beyond.

Counting the people before him would have been meaningless. Every area the size of a kitchen garden held as many people as a good-sized village and the Palace Square was larger than fifty kitchen gardens. Michal could pick out the guards around the lords and merchants by their weapons and badges and also by the way they clustered together, but even they were beyond easy counting.

Michal frowned at the number of armed men. His frown deepened as his eyes took in the badges of all the great lords and so many lesser ones that he didn't know them all.

Perhaps one man in four bore arms. As for the others—bath attendants elbowed goldsmiths for a better view. The reek of tanners cleared small spaces around them, even though they were bathed and clothed in plain summer robes instead of their working trousers. A lady carpenter stood next to a wine merchant. He saw gray mourning robes, workday clothes, plain robes in colors other than gray, robes and mourning hoods on every sort of servant of Sherran's God. Michal felt his head begin to spin and hoped it was only the heat of the pyre.

In another spell he noticed that the heat was no longer clawing at his skin. It no longer kept back the crowd either; people were beginning to press forward toward the pyre. Michal's men raised their twelve-span staves before he could raise his voice. To his left the Swords of Sherran and to his right the Magistrate's Watchmen were doing the same. The forward press slowed, until only a few pushed by those behind them kept on coming. Michal saw one woman lose her balance trying to avoid the staves, but neighbors caught her before she fell.

Wait, though. Cries of pain and outrage were rising from the far side of the pyre. Michal risked a quick look behind him. What he saw elicited a quick "Eyes forward!" from him to his own men. Then he turned completely around and shifted his position for a better view.

The far side of the pyre was guarded by regular troops from the Thunder Hill garrison outside Koddardos. It was both their right and their duty to provide some of the guards on an occasion like this, but even those who weren't recruits weren't as well trained in working with crowds as the Swords and the city forces. The regulars were guarding the side nearest the palace, the side least likely to breed trouble, but also the side that had held the movable staircase for the priests and the Queen.

The staircase had now been moved back, and the priests and Queen Kantela were retiring toward the palace gates, but one couldn't tell the Queen to hurry, and there was a gap left by the notables. The crowd was flowing toward the gap as naturally as rain finding the one hole in a roof. The army men not only had their staves up, but were pushing the people back with more vigor than judgment. In a minute someone would stumble and be trampled. Worse yet, some of the soldiers were beginning to jab and even strike with the ends of their staves.

Michal yelled, "Halt! Staves up!" in his best imitation of a Sherrani troopmaster. It was good enough to freeze the soldiers. No longer provoked, most of the crowd slowed its forward movement. A Commander of Swords who'd been approaching the line from the gates at a brisk trot looked around in surprise, then saw the source of the trouble.

Now the matter was out of Michal's hands. He turned back to his own men, listening to the shouts from the Swords and Watchmen behind him as they urged the people into retreat.

"Back! Back, there!"

"This is supposed to be the King's funeral, not yours!"

"Can't you wait for your own pyre?"

Michal couldn't hear what the commander was saying to the garrison troops and rather regretted it. He regretted still more that he couldn't claim honor or reward for what he'd just done. Even if he could prove his deed, there was not so much good will between the First Magistrate's Harzis and the regular Army of Sherran that the latter would care to be reminded of a mistake by an honor given publicly to one of the former.

The uproar on the other side of the pyre faded. Michal was allowing himself a little smile of inward pride, when a small boy bolted into the open from the crowd on the near side of the pyre.

The boy had almost reached the line of guards before he saw the looming figures with their staves. He stopped, looked around frantically, and started crying. The nearest guard laughed and handed his staff to his neighbor, then stepped forward.

"What's your name, lad?" he asked.

Frightened wails and sobs.

"Come, come. Is this any way for a big boy like you to behave? Besides, I don't eat boys. I've a grandson at home, much your age."

Now Michal remembered the man's name—Yiftat shan-Melkor—and noticed his graying beard. Michal leaned down.

"It's true, he doesn't eat boys. I've known him for quite a while. Now, what's your name?"

The boy took one look at Michal, with the plume nodding above his burnished helmet adding to his height, his elbow-length saffron-hued gloves, and the rest of his captain's panoply. Too late, Michal realized that he must look remarkably like the demon-Harzi who was supposed to carry off bad Sherrani children. The boy squalled desperately and threw himself into Yiftat's arms.

Michal felt his face glowing like the coals of Pijtos's pyre and glared at the older man, who grinned and turned back to soothing the boy. He'd just succeeded when someone in the crowd shouted "Sapsko!" A comely, buxom woman appeared, elbowing her way through the crowd and looking rather like a young sow coming to the rescue of one of her litter.

"Thank you, thank you, and the Mother's Face smile on you," she said as she picked the boy up under one arm. "Thank you more than I can say," she went on, raising her voice to be heard over the boy's protests. "A pity you've been put to the trouble, but if there's a drink or a bite you ever want, ask for Niko Tovskura at the Full Trough. You'll not go short of either, for the next moon at least, either of you.

"Sapsko's lively as a flea, of course—they all are at that age—and he's got no mother to do for him, and his father's run off to ride with some lordling God couldn't teach let alone Izrunarko, so that's why he's my charge and no easy one he is, but you've made it easier and for this I thank you—"

Niko Tovskura thanked them several times before they were able to herd her back into the crowd and send her on her way. By then the last of the unburned wood on the pyre had vanished in the flames, and where Pijtos was only the Father knew. Queen Kantela had disappeared into the palace, and most of the notables had left the square. The rites were nearly done, although it would take the rest of the afternoon to clear the square without, the Father willing, anyone getting trampled or any more small boys straying. Michal's squadron would be off duty by nightfall with their funeral bonuses to spend and their choices of Koddardos's taverns to spend them in.

Michal decided to accept Niko Tovskura's invitation. Free food and drink for him meant that much more to spend on drink to loosen other men's tongues. It was never a bad idea to make oneself welcome in a place where people were apt to be less than discreet.

"Close the shutters and summon Lanach Tashinur," said Joviz.

"Yes, my lord," said the understeward. A moment later the bronze-strapped oak shutters squealed closed across the south window of Joviz's office. The damp breeze died; the chill it had brought stayed behind.

"And bring up a brazier and a bucket of charcoal." It was going to be a long night, following on the heels of an already too-long day.

"Yes, my lord." The understeward went out. Joviz sat down, draped his cloak over the back of his chair, and turned to the papers on his desk.

The first was a report from Kosovo about two robbers who'd stolen purses from a bathhouse. They'd been caught by a captain and four men in the service of Lord Volo, who'd left the baths and chased the robbers through the streets naked save for shoes and swords. The picture that emerged even through the humorless language of the magistrate there caused Joviz to smile thinly.

Still, the magistrate might well have reason for his lack of humor. Robbers were seldom bold enough to steal from bathhouses in broad daylight. Nor were the men of a northern lord like Volo often found bathing a quarter-watch's ride from Koddardos. Joviz would commend the men for their zeal; he would have commended them more if they'd been at home where they belonged, not here close by Koddardos leaving villages like Niza's Forge to be defended by grandmothers and boys, even grandmothers shrewd enough to trick a Harzi into teaching the boys.

Several more reports told of similar incidents, except that in one case it was a lord's men breaking up a tavern; they claimed they'd been overcharged. Very probably they had been, but a

38

wave of tavern brawls in Koddardos was the last thing Joviz needed now.

A knock on the door—his secretary's, not the understeward's. Joviz swallowed. Giving pain to a faithful servant was occasionally a duty but never a pleasure.

"Come in."

Lanach Tashinur entered silently. He was hardly ever noisy. His deceptively youthful appearance made him quite easy to ignore, a quality that had proven useful in the past and would doubtless continue to do so. In one hand he held a stylus and two wax tablets; under the other arm he carried a bundle of scrolls.

"I took the liberty of bringing the household accounts for your inspection, my lord."

"The regular or the special?"

"Both."

"Good."

The "special household" was the polite name adopted for those who served Joviz purely as spies and informers. He hoped he would not need to add to their strength in the moons to come, expected that he would, and knew that he had to be sure of the money to hire them regardless. He'd need silver for so many things, and that was part of the problem. In an emergency the First Magistrate could request extra funds from the Throne. These generally came out of the Privy Purse, or if the need was great enough, out of the Treasury by a special edict. But such funds could only be obtained by personal petition to the Throne—and who was keeping an eye on the royal silver these days? One more thing to ask when he had audience with Queen Kantela . . .

Joviz pulled himself back to the present. Before he could discuss finances with Lanach, he had to do something unpleasant.

"Lanach, your name day is the first of next moon, isn't it?"

"Yes, my lord. My niece and her husband have invited me to celebrate it with them in Hierandos. I have not yet accepted, since I thought your need for my services might make it prudent for me not to leave Koddardos."

It's a pity that Lanach can't really read people's thoughts. It would save me so much trouble.

"I had hoped to release you from the Spell of Discretion you have borne these many years in time for your name day. However, as things stand now—well, I just can't do it. It grieves me to disappoint you in this matter. If I were completely my own master I would do otherwise, but I'm not."

Lanach smiled. "God and the Ruler's duty are masters of us both, my lord. Indeed, I would have refused my release if you had offered it."

"Refused it?"

"My lord, I do not know who would be lifting the spell. If it were Reverend Master Charko or one of the other high masters in the temple of the Giver of Knowledge, I would have little fear, although even they might not be sufficiently discreet among their fellow priests. If a scholar-apprentice did the work, however, could we be sure that such a one's tongue could not be bought in spite of his oaths? If the great lords are willing to pour out silver to raise armies, they will not be slow to buy secrets as well, and yours most of all."

"They will not."

"If the Spell of Discretion were lifted, I would have the choice between either going in fear of being abducted to be tortured and killed after giving up whatever secrets I could not hold back, or else having my memories worked upon by a spell far more dangerous than the Spell of Discretion, so that I would have no secrets left to betray. Either would be a sorry end of my service to you. Shall I be disappointed that you have spared me both?"

Lanach's voice held a faint note of reproach, which Joviz might have resented if he hadn't been so tired. But if he hadn't been so tired, he would have seen the logic of the secretary's case beforehand and not wasted time on a matter that need never have been raised. Joviz swore a large oath that even if the earth itself opened to swallow Koddardos he would not again stint himself on sleep.

"Very well," said Joviz and beckoned for the accounts.

Joviz was foresworn immediately because he and Lanach were up well into the northwatch going over the accounts. There was enough ready silver to hire a fair number of new spies, if that were all he needed, but with the state of affairs in Koddardos bound to exhaust the city's regular funds and the almost certain difficulty of obtaining the usual emergency supplements, the situation was not so favorable.

"The money will be still less ample, my lord, if we wish to lay in a stock of salt and pickled provisions," Lanach added. "The prices for such are higher than usual, even for spring."

Meaning that everyone else was laying in supplies too, in case banditry or even civil war halted trade. Some might even be preparing to stand siege in their own homes, as Lanach was plainly suggesting that Joviz be ready to do.

The magistrate did not ask if Lanach knew something that his master did not. Lanach would not have held anything back, even if the Spell of Discretion had allowed him to do so. The secretary was no fool, however, and if that was how he saw the present situation. . . .

"By all means, let's not be short of food," said Joviz at last. "Spend up to two orbs at your discretion. If anyone asks why you're buying, say that we expect to have to provide hospitality to the lords before fresh food starts coming to the city. Don't sound too eager about the hospitality, though. Some of the lords must have sold their wives' breechguards to hire men. They will be as shameless as the beggars of Hierandos in flocking to our table if we let them."

"Precisely, my lord."

"That means still more money for the extra men we'll need to maintain order in Koddardos. Men like Captain Michal will do extra work for only a small addition to their regular wages, but I don't dare hire too many Harzis. That would look as though I were planning something myself, or else that I feared riot and insurrection in Koddardos at any moment.

"I'm going to ask the Queen about the emergency funds from the Treasury as soon as I have audience. After that I'll ask you to arrange meetings with the Keeper of the Purse and the First Lord of the Treasury, unless Kantela will do that for me—and when is my audience with her, anyway?"

"The day after tomorrow, my lord, at the second eastwatch. And my lord, it were best if you wore your mourning dress and dispensed with your official panoply."

"Why?"

"The Queen has proclaimed the strictest mourning, my lord. She will see no one, she says, unless the need is urgent. Your mourning dress will convey an impression of urgency and at the same time respect for her wishes. Your formal robes would not."

Joviz doubted that Kantela was so grief-stricken and said as much.

Lanach continued. "This is what I learned, my lord, when I went to the palace to deliver your request for an audience. The man who told me is likely to be reliable; he is a commander under Uzichko Kalinur dar no Rodu, Overlord of the Fleet."

The Magistrate of Hierandos and Overlord of Sherran's Fleet hadn't attended the funeral, and as far as Joviz knew hadn't even left his city. "Is Lord Uzichko coming to Koddardos?"

"No. The man who spoke to me was sent here to represent Lord Uzichko at the funeral and to bear his apologies to the Queen. The Fleet makes its spring sailing soon, so duty holds the Overlord in Hierandos."

"Duty?"

"Perhaps more than that, but certainly nothing less. No man has ever held the Overlordship of the Fleet as a more sacred trust than Lord Uzichko."

That was certainly true. "Anything more?"

"Lord Uzichko's sister is married to an uncle of Lord Volo's wife. One of his sons is married to a cousin of Lord Bihor. If he were to come to Koddardos, either those to whom he had ties of kinship or their enemies might doubt his lack of partiality."

Also true enough, but for once it was a pity that Lord Uzichko was so relentlessly honest. If he were in Koddardos now he could give advice that Kantela would sorely need, and he would not intrigue for the throne on his own behalf or anybody else's. Which reminded him—

"I wonder if the Queen is trying to avoid any particular petition by proclaiming strict mourning? Oh well," he yawned, "this way she avoids them all"—another yawn—"impartially." He stretched. "Have some more charcoal and a pot of hot tea sent up, then go to bed."

"I took the liberty of ordering the tea some time ago, my lord. It will be sent to your bedchamber. Let me see you to it, and—"

"Lanach, you're my secretary, not my nurse!"

"I will perform what duties seem necessary, my lord. Does not the Teacher say—"

"Oh, a plague take you and the Teacher both!" Joviz tried to draw himself up sternly and completely ruined the effect with another yawn. He sighed and stood.

"All right, Lanach. I will go to bed. And so will you. Tomorrow will be another long day for both of us."

"Yes, my lord. Good night."

Lanach left, and Joviz started to follow, then stopped. They had worked so late that his evening devotions were closer to being his morning ones, but they still had to be made. He drew the curtain from the oratory in its niche and knelt.

The icon on the shelf was of a kind seldom found outside shrines of the Divine Essence. Instead of a representation of a particular Face of God, the frame held only a cloudy gray crystal about five fingers in diameter. The same sort of crystal was used in scrying glasses, but Joviz had no talent for scrying. However, it was said in the temples of the Divine Essence that one might catch a glimpse of the True Face of God in such a crystal if one were pious enough in one's actions and devout enough in one's prayers.

Joviz had no opinion on that proposition, but he did agree with the teaching of the Divine Essence's priests, who held that too much gazing upon manmade images of the Faces of God led one to lose sight of even the idea of the True Face. When praying in front of a finished icon, Joviz often found himself meditating on the artist who'd made the image and what the image said about that person's concept of God. He preferred to meditate and pray before something less distracting.

"Blessed be God, the One, the Holy, the Almighty.

Unto Thee, O God, will I lift up my voice; yea, unto Thee will I cry.

For Thou has ever been our help in times of adversity.

Our ancestors called upon Thee and Thou didst hear them; they cried, and Thou didst deliver them.

Let not my prayer go unheeded, but deliver me from danger.

And let me never forget thee, O God, though I stand surrounded by foes, or feast with friends."

The Prayer in Time of Danger and the meditations afterward calmed Joviz. He went to bed in good heart, to find that he'd been granted the gift of untroubled, if brief, sleep.

V

IN THE SEVEN DAYS AFTER THE FUNERAL, KANTELA ESTABlished a royal widow's routine. Morning prayers with Zensko Lilkura, breakfast alone, bath with only one attendant, then meetings with those who could persuade her that their business was urgent.

Usually there were enough such meetings, mostly with officials of the palace, to last until noon. That was more than she would have liked, but the household had always been her charge. She could not have neglected it, even had she been in the deepest grief for a husband who had been the light of her world. Not without throwing the palace into chaos, at any rate—and a fine portent that would be for the rest of the kingdom!

At noon she entered the Queen's Garden to eat lunch and consider in solitude what was to be done next. Some of this considering was done sitting on the marble bench, but most of it while striding rapidly up and down fifty paces of the garden's length, the only exercise her mourning allowed her.

She was aware that many people thought the Queen was secluding herself because she was or might prove to be with child. Kantela knew she wasn't, but since for safety's sake announcements were rarely made before the end of the second moon, the mere possibility gave her the better part of another two moons in which to maintain authority. As long as no one obtained proof that she wasn't breeding, that is—or decided to take action in case she was . . .

After a half-watch of meditation in the garden, Kantela returned to her chambers and read, mostly chronicles of Sherran's history. She wasn't sure she'd find anything of immediate use, but at least dead scribes had no ambitions to advance. When word of her choice of reading matter leaked out, as it doubtless would, it would also indicate that the Queen wasn't planning to quietly leave the palace when her period of mourning was done. That in turn would lend strength to the rumors that she might be pregnant, and was searching out precedents for a regency.

In the evening another bath, evening prayers, a late and very light supper, and another quarter-watch or so of reading. This time it was the day's reports of the Swords, the Magistrate's Watchmen, and Harzis. Reading them was the best way she had of finding out what went on in the city. The Captain-General had been surprised when she asked for them to be sent to her, but he'd obeyed without protest.

Finally she retired. On those nights when her mind turned back to the eternal question, whom to trust? she sometimes lay awake, tossing, turning, even weeping in frustration. Most nights she slept, and thanked God for that small blessing.

On the morning of the eighth day no one came to Kantela's chambers for audience on palace problems. By mid-morning she'd begun to hope that she really might be free for the rest of the day. Her joy at this prospect was tempered by the thought that the palace officials might have finally decided to use this time of uncertain royal authority to enrich themselves by unlawful means, but one day proved nothing much one way or the other. A quarter-watch earlier than usual, she let herself into the Queen's Garden.

It was a day of summerlike heat. The air in the garden was almost too close for pleasure, heavy with the scent of flowers and the humming of gratified bees. It was also cloudless, like every day since Pijtos's funeral. Such a stretch of fine weather at this time of year was rare, but neither unknown nor, after the heavy rains earlier, unwelcome. Folk would be talking less of omens and portents and more of rich harvests.

The grass was growing along with everything else; it was up to Kantela's ankles. After a moment's hesitation and a mental note to have the gardeners trim it, she pulled off her shoes and padded barefoot over to a blossom-laden bronze hawkbill. Plucking a blossom, she tied it into her hair, then bent over the pond in the middle of the garden to study the results.

She decided that the blossom would neither make nor mar. Otherwise the pond told her nothing she hadn't already learned from her mirror: that she looked a good five years less than her actual age and still less like either a grieving widow or a queen.

She pulled the blossom free, dropped it into the pond, and sat down on the marble bench, toes twined in the grass. She was going to miss the peace of this garden when she finally left the palace. Knowing this made her more determined than ever to stay. Yet how? The full strength of her desire to remain didn't provide the answer.

Three of the great lords—four, if one chose to count the Overlord of the Fleet—were married and had children. The moment one of them took the Throne, Kantela would be destined to return to her family's estates, doubtless well-gifted but almost certainly pledged not to marry again without the new King's consent.

Marry one of the unmarried lords and remain as his queen? One of those was Lord Ikos, and at the mere thought of him her stomach knotted. The other was Lord Korul, who had the least resources of all the great lords and a pack of acknowledged children to provide for.

A lesser lord as king? Perhaps. She did not know all or even many of them, but there had to be some reasonable ones unmarried. On the other hand, a King of Sherran without some strength of his own in land, silver, and men would either have to raid the kingdom to gain it or strike bargains with allies, and what price would those allies ask? Kantela would have no assurance of her own freedom then, and she'd risk enslaving her husband. She could not inflict that fate on anyone worth marrying.

Another thought had been knocking tentatively at the gates of her mind for some days. Now she let it in and looked it in the face. Suppose she called a man to her bed—a virile and discreet man—and passed off the result as the fruit of Pijtos's loins? She could be regent for a son for the best part of twenty years.

She would also be completely at the mercy of the man, her next moon-time, and any of her household who knew about it. That was a lot of mercy to expect God to provide in defense of a lie. It would be even more foolish to expect God to guarantee her a son, and a daughter would only postpone the question of the succession, not settle it.

No law or Teaching forbade reigning queens in Sherran. But there had never been one before, not in all the centuries since Veysel Sherran first wore the five-pointed crown. Fear of the unknown would do more to bind men to inaction or drive them to folly than could any law or Teaching.

The idea of passing off some other man's progeny as Pijtos's was one to be considered, if she were to truthfully say she'd considered every possibility. But then it would be put firmly away.

No, not quite. It was leaving something of itself behind— the idea that she could now ask a man to her bed if she wanted him there. Would he come? She did not think her reflection was that of a woman from whom most men would turn away in revulsion.

Not *if* she wanted a man, either. *When*. She couldn't have ignored a faint warmth in her nipples and loins if she'd wanted to, which she did not.

After a spell or two she discovered that the warmth was becoming less of a pleasure and more of a worry. Right now she couldn't rule Sherran or even Koddardos. Was she losing command of her own body?

She'd heard of *parodis*, women enslaved by lust, and even seen a few of the miserable creatures. She prayed to God to spare her such a fate. Not even the Healers knew what caused this malady, but its victims were objects of dread and disgust.

She tried to ignore the ill-timed warmth, and was relieved to feel it pass away in about three spells. Quite another appetite couldn't be satisfied by ignoring it, however; Kantela realized that it was well past her normal lunchtime. She was going back to the gate to ring for it when Zensko Lilkura hurried into the garden and bowed hastily.

"Your Grace, the Reverend Lady Lilka is without and wishes audience."

Kantela stopped. "Lady Lilka?"

"Yes. I have told her—"

"Never mind what you told her. She may come out here." Kantela remembered her bare feet and added, "When I summon her." She lifted her robe and ran back to where she'd left her shoes, while Zensko Lilkura retreated almost too hastily for proper etiquette.

"I will now receive the Lady Lilka," Kantela called out as she slipped on the second shoe. Now she had as much dignity as she could hope to have. Whether or not that was enough for facing the First Priestess of the Mother, even when one presumably had her good will, was another matter.

"My duty to the Queen's Grace."

Lilka's words were deferential, but the stride that carried her across the grass to Kantela was not, nor was anything else about her. Seventy years of life, most of them devoted to service and personal austerity, had grayed her hair and stretched her brown skin tightly over fine bone and sinewy muscle, but her carriage was straight and her eye keen. A sword and dagger would not have been out of place on her belt, instead of the distaff and purse with the Mother's sigil she actually wore.

"First of all, my thanks, Reverend Lady, for your aid on the day of Pijtos's funeral. I was and remain grateful for it."

The way one gray eyebrow quirked upward made Kantela wonder if she shouldn't have stuck to the traditional "Honor to God and you, Reverend Lady."

"May I have leave, Your Grace?" said the priestess, indicating the bench.

"Of course." Too late, Kantela realized that she was now standing to face whatever the seated older woman said. She felt as if she was fourteen again, facing her governess after going frog catching at night clad only in shift and trousers.

"I am indeed grateful, you know," said Kantela, grasping desperately at any words that would come. "The Throne of Sherran is facing enough perils right now without whispers of evil omens."

"They would not be whispers but shouts from the rooftops. Although not all of the shouts would come from unpurchased throats, to be sure. Also—my daughter, you and Sherran have been deprived of support and guidance. God and human wits demand that I help you both. Does not the Teacher say—?"

Lilka went off into a long, fluently-rendered quotation from Izrunarko, about the obligation to aid those who had the burden of Ruling. Long before she'd finished Kantela had to force herself not to fidget. She felt more than ever like a girl, suspected that she was being tested, and knew that interrupting the Reverend Lady Lilka was not a right given to mere queens.

When Lilka finished, Kantela again grasped at the first words she knew would come out smoothly. "True, Reverend Lady. Pijtos was our king and guide, and now he is gone. But—" Queens did have the right to take the initiative "—I do not think it was to discuss the deeds of Pijtos Sherran that you came today."

Lilka gave a brief, approving smile. "It was not. It is a matter which concerns the honor of the Throne and your duty."

Kantela recognized the phrases and was quite sure that any reply except an expression of devout attention would launch another quotation from Izrunarko. She could do without that.

Lilka took Kantela's silence properly. "The temples of the Mother have not received their contribution of broken meats from the palace these seven days."

"Seven days?"

"Not from the palace itself. Some of your people have sent from their own tables, but from the palace kitchens, not a morsel."

"That—that is outrageous!" The broken meats sent to the temples of the Mother were given to the poor and the sick. How many had gone hungry because of this?

"Those swine in the kitchen! Gorging themselves while—!" Indignation reduced her to spluttering. It was followed by a stab of fear. Why had she not known about this? In all of those overlong interviews with the palace officers not one of them had so much as hinted . . . What else had she missed?

"I have not heard that they were eating the food themselves," Lilka said. She clearly had heard something else. Just as clearly, Kantela would have to figure it out for herself. Once more the ghost of her old governess took the place of Lady Lilka, waiting for her to say what the proper penalty for her immodest and foolish behavior should be.

Once more Kantela resisted a temptation to kick the older woman in the shins.

"If they have not been eating it themselves, it has either been going home or . . ." She hesitated. "Or they have been selling it to the men of those lords who are not providing for them. Many of the lords have come to Koddardos without any thought of what they will do here!" Her voice crackled again. "They are taking for themselves what belongs to God! I will have order in the palace if I have to whip every servant in it, including the Captain-General of the Swords himself!"

The anger in Kantela's voice didn't drive out the fear inside her. If her own servants were turning against her, if the palace was becoming a trap rather than a refuge . . . ? She looked wildly around the garden, wanting to lie down and curl up.

"My daughter," said Lilka, "it is my thought, and to some degree my knowledge, that the palace servants have not done this for any reason that makes them your enemies. Like you, they have lost their protector. Unlike you, they have the right to expect a new one."

"Meaning me?"

"The palace needs more attention than you have given it, clearly. I believe most of your people are honest but afraid of what the future may bring. So they are driven to robbing God, that they may provide for their kin. A great fault—but are you sure that yours is not greater, since few of them would have done this without a belief, correct or not, that you lacked a proper concern for palace affairs?"

Kantela thought back over recent days. Yes, she had given orders for the continued provisioning of the palace, and she had overseen the payment of the servants' wages. That was necessary or the lower servants might be cheated. But she had only assumed, not verified, that the charitable offerings were going out as usual. Furthermore, her proclamation of strict mourning, combined with her reluctance to give audience, could have given rise to the belief that Queen Kantela wouldn't notice what was going on in the servants' quarters.

Pride and the passage of years kept Kantela from ending now as she had done with her governess—crying on the older woman's shoulder. Instead she sat down on the bench beside Lilka and sighed. "Certainly I will tighten my rein on the palace servants. And—I do not ask for God's secrets, but perhaps you can help me in judging which are frightened and which are merely greedy?"

"Of course, my daughter. What I know and can lawfully tell, you shall know."

"Good. If I can put the palace in order, at least I may not have to guard my back."

"Will you content yourself with that?"

Kantela closed her eyes. She did not want to see Lilka's face twist at her confession of what in the priestess's eyes would be ignorance compounded by idleness. "I would not if I knew what to do next. It is not that I believe I can sit and wait for God to dispose of events, nor even that I doubt my own wits. What I doubt is my knowledge, and I fear those who will use this lack to give me only advice that will serve them."

"You can trust me, my daughter."

Kantela opened her eyes at the warmth in Lilka's voice.

Then she blinked twice, to keep her eyes dry. "Thank you. But I do not want to follow in Pijtos's footsteps, exalting one Face of God above the others. Were I to make you my chief counselor, many would say that the temple of the Mother now rules in Sherran. There was such talk about the Divine Essence during Pijtos's reign, and no one questioned his right to rule."

"You are right to fear that—to a certain point."

"What is that point?"

"When fear of consequences prevents you from taking any action at all. Now, you are right in not offering a palace post to me, which I could not accept, nor could any other First Priest of Koddardos. You were also wise to think upon the King's Servants and the lords, Kantela, for they will be your enemies if you pass them by entirely."

"At least one already is, Reverend Lady." She described Ikos's behavior the night of Pijtos's death, then went on to summarize the virtues and vices of the other great lords and the various courses of action she'd considered. She was halfway through explaining why she would not pass off some other man's child as Pijtos's when Lilka started to chuckle.

Kantela glared. "You find my thoughts amusing? Do you perhaps think I am better fitted to be a street entertainer than a queen?"

"No, no, my daughter. What amuses me is that you doubted your own wisdom. I am sure it has been anything but amusing to you, so forgive me."

"I haven't felt very much like laughing this past moon, Reverend Lady."

"Then it is very important to find someone you can laugh with."

Kantela was only kept from laughing now by realizing that if she started she might not stop. She'd done the thing she most feared: revealed all her thoughts. Yet Lilka called it no shame and even praised her "wisdom."

"Reverend Lady, are you turning pander now?"

"No. Although I believe it would be well for both you and Sherran that you marry again, at a time when you may choose freely."

52

"That time may never come."

"It certainly will never come as long as you sit here and doubt, rather than stand up and act. You doubted your own wisdom and the honesty of those who have the knowledge you lack. Your wisdom as it stands is greater than that of any lord who abandons his lands and comes to Koddardos to intrigue. As for advice—why have you slighted one of the best sources in all Sherran and one close at hand as well, First Magistrate Joviz Orasur?"

"Lord Joviz? Oh, I know his reputation as a most worthy First Magistrate, Reverend Lady. But all of my dealings with him have been purely ceremonial. He never came to the palace while Pijtos was alive save on official business, and when he came for audience after the funeral, he conducted himself according to the most rigid etiquette I have seen these fifteen years."

She did not add her impression that if she had confided in him, Joviz would have treated her like a troublesome daughter interrupting him at a busy moment. It seemed that she had been wrong. "You recommend that I trust him, Reverend Lady?"

"Joviz is one of three men in Sherran you can trust, both to give advice and to be circumspect in their dealings with you."

"You say three men? Who are the others? The Overlord of the Fleet is one, I suppose, but what would bring him to Koddardos?"

"Nothing short of a command from Izrunarko's spirit, I admit," said Lilka. "Even if you sent him a direct order, he would send a polite excuse, as he did for the funeral. And the other man is almost as bad. The Captain-General of the North would not leave the frontier during the spring raiding season to attend his own wedding."

"So it seems that I must deal with Lord Joviz." Kantela felt enough at ease to dare one more question. "Have you and he been taking counsel together on what to do about Queen Kantela?"

Lilka had the decency to blush. Kantela mock-glared. "So, if I do not deal with you openly, you will continue to plot

53

behind my back. All for the good of Sherran, of course," she added hastily.

"Izrunarko teaches us that it is better to use one's breech-guard as a bandage than to see another bleed to death for fear of appearing unseemly oneself."

"Well, I will do much to prevent Sherran's bleeding to death. Not bed Lord Ikos, of course—"

"Ikos has the manners of a wild boar, the morals of a serpent, and the appearance of the runt of the litter," said Lilka. "He is a good soldier, and not without some following because of that, but he has so many enemies that if you bedded him, half Sherran would be saying that the Queen is no better than the lowest kind of drab who will open her legs to any man for a copper bit because she is too lazy or stupid to follow an honest trade."

"Indeed," said Kantela. "Short of such follies—well, you and Lord Joviz can trust me that much, at least. Now, would it be too much to ask that you cease giving me advice until we have eaten lunch? I am so hungry that the only thing I can hear clearly is my stomach rumbling."

VI

IT WAS SUMMER-HOT IN THE PLAINS, OR SO THE MESSENGERS and escorts for the supply convoys said. Here in the hills it was still no more than spring by day, and at night one could even believe in winter. Bakarydes Linzur dar no Benye looked behind him to the dark path his horse was leaving across crisp, frost-whitened grass.

Light reflected from a polished silver mirror flashed from a tree fifty paces ahead, the one piece of virgin timber left on the edge of a stand of second growth. Bakarydes rode on until he could make out the scout's horse tied inside the grove. Good at hiding his mount, that man. Of course all the men with Bakarydes were picked, and he trusted his own judgment. One did not become Captain-General of the North through constantly doubting oneself. But only God was infallible.

Bakarydes reined in his horse and allowed the score of riders behind him to come up. He sat loose-reined and relaxed to set a good example for the men, but there was no hiding excitement from a horse. Well, in proportion to his years Lightning was as much a veteran as Bakarydes himself. He was one of those northern-bred mounts of whom it was said that they could smell a Momak half a watch's gallop away.

The scout peered out of the branches, thrust his signaling mirror into his belt, and waved both hands at Bakarydes. The other ambush force was in position, covering the Momaks' other line of retreat. The troop acting as beaters for the game was on its way into position, but not there yet.

Bakarydes swore under his breath, then had to gentle Lightning. If he could talk instead of neigh, Lightning might be a better leader for the beater troop than its newly joined captain.

Perhaps that wasn't just. Bakarydes hadn't forgotten that he was once such a captain; that was why he'd sent the boy into that position. The captain might be a son of Tapan Vodarkur dar no Chorap, but Lord Tapan expected his sons to fight when he sent them into the army, not just to look pretty on parade. Also, the beater troop came from Captain Kalaj's own squadron, and their troopmaster was a veteran with eyes in the back of his head.

Still, Kalaj Lesnur was acting as beater for the most dangerous of all game, the wild horsemen of the plains. There was no way he could really know how dangerous, either, not without some substantial fraction of Bakarydes's twenty years' experience on the frontier.

The mirror winked again, three times in rapid succession. The Momaks were in sight, the beaters still were not. Bakarydes was past swearing now. He hoped it was the scout's eyesight going back on him, not Captain Kalaj forgetting his orders.

The *thubthubthub* of a Momak signal drum told Bakarydes that the Momaks were not only in sight but close. Unless their horses had wings, it would now be his troop that rode into them. Quite unnecessarily, Bakarydes tested the easy draw of his sword and the balance of his throwing darts. Lozo Bojarkur would rather bed a Momak stallion than leave his Captain-General's weapons unfit for their work.

Thubthubthub again, closer—until the drumming ended in a chorus of neighs and war cries, both Momak and Sherrani. Wherever the beater troop had been, it now seemed to be among the Momaks.

Bakarydes didn't wait for the scout to signal what his own ears told him plainly. He pressed his knees to Lightning's flanks. Clods flew as the stallion climbed the hill.

The scout dropped from the tree, landing so hard that he rose limping. One of Bakarydes's men swerved aside and flung himself out of the saddle to help the scout remount. That was the frontier way: a helping hand to the next man from the day he joined to the day you either drank to his retirement or laid him on the pyre.

"Archers to the left, lancers follow me!" shouted Bakarydes as he reached the crest of the hill. Then he looked back. By the Face of the Warrior, he must have his first-battle-of-the-year frets worse than usual, to think the men behind him would forget their orders! They'd already been dividing before he drew in the breath to shout.

Lance butts stayed in their buckets as Bakarydes led his right wing downhill. On the left, crossbows rose, bolts snicked home—then the bows fell and curses rose. The beater troop and the Momaks rode into sight, so thoroughly entangled that no archer could hope for a safe shot.

One fool let fly anyway. Bakarydes didn't bother trying to see who it was. The left-wing leader would know and arrange to deal with the man, probably behind the barracks some dark night, where neither Captain-General nor squadron commander need take notice of it.

From below came Sherrani horns: the Momaks were too busy fighting to drum, if not to shout. The din from below was welcome. It would deafen the Momaks to the approach of Bakarydes's men.

Downhill they rode now, reining back the horses to a canter although they'd caught the excitement and were ready to gallop if given the slightest chance. The ditch appeared ahead, the one that Bakarydes was relying on to pin down a flank of the Momaks. The plains riders' tough, sure-footed little ponies could not jump like the longer-legged Sherrani cavalry mounts.

"Sherran!"

Bakarydes shouted it as a war cry. Lightning tucked up his legs and soared over the ditch, landing so smoothly that Bakarydes hardly noticed the impact. Nine out of the ten men behind the Captain-General followed, if not as neatly. The tenth separated from his mount in midair; both landed hard.

The man should be safe if he wasn't too badly hurt to crawl into the ditch itself. With the fight at such close quarters, it would be sheer bad luck if a Momak archer saw him and had time to shoot before having to forget about his bow and defend himself hand-to-hand. The thirty men of the beater troop were already doing a pretty good job in the matter. Bakarydes's twenty would make a bad situation for the Momaks still worse.

He urged Lightning to the right around a patch of scrub certain to offer unsure footing, giving himself time to draw with one hand his sword and with the other a throwing dart. Then Lightning hardly needed urging to wheel and plunge straight at the Momaks.

A half-score of Momaks in the rear of the band wheeled their mounts out into the open. Their leader was pointing uphill toward Bakarydes's archers. He and his men had their flank toward the Captain-General, and Bakarydes put a dart into the leader's horse before the Momak could notice his mistake, let alone correct it. The other Momaks wheeled again to face Bakarydes.

One seemed to rise from the ground almost under Lightning's hooves. Bakarydes took in the familiar details of the Momak rider at a glance—sleeveless sheepskin jacket, leather breeches, heavy compound bow, and quiver slung with an elaborately tooled leather strap that might be the most valuable thing he owned other than the bow and the horse. Dark intent eyes above a reddish-brown mustache reaching almost around to his ears, below a scale-mail cap that was his only armor except for a plate guard on his right arm.

That right arm was raising a short throwing spear now, and Bakarydes slashed down at it. He misjudged the distance—his eye was always out in the first battle of the spring, curse it!—and the spear point drove against his mail. Then the Momak's pony reared to nip at Lightning's neck with his long yellow teeth.

Lightning reacted to the insult as his master would have reacted to the offer of a boy as bedmate. He reared too, spoiling Bakarydes's second slash even more thoroughly than his first. His iron-shod hooves crashed against the pony's neck. The pony reeled sideways, so out of control that not even a Momak could stay on his back without dropping the spear and clutching the shaggy gray mane. With both hands occupied, the Momak didn't even bother to look up as Bakarydes's sword came down for the third time, biting through sheepskin, shoulder blade, and upper ribs.

In any hand-to-hand battle it was hard to tell what was happening to anyone but yourself. In a cavalry action it was impossible. The best-trained, best-managed mount still had a mind of his own and would do unpredictable things at times and places of his own choosing. If Bakarydes hadn't had Lightning under him, he might have listened to those who doubted the wisdom of the Captain-General's engaging the enemy hand-to-hand. The example of such leadership was inspiring. A dead Captain-General was not.

Bakarydes killed at least one more Momak without remembering the details. He seldom remembered more than his first fight of any battle. The charging archers hit the Momaks who'd turned to face them. Bakarydes was thrust past the nearest Momaks into their main body of troops like a cork from a bottle. He would have been dangerously isolated if the main Momak force hadn't already been disintegrating under the sheer ferocity of the beater troop's attack.

Bakarydes had an interesting time for what he later learned was about a spell, slashing at Momaks who seemed as numerous and elusive as biting midges over a pond. Then he found himself sitting on a somewhat blown Lightning, holding a bloody sword and watching the Momaks scatter with more haste and fewer backward-shot arrows than usual.

Almost automatically, Bakarydes counted the fleeing survivors, arrived at a figure he didn't believe, and managed a second count before they were out of sight. The figure came out the same both times. At least fifty Momaks were on the way home, perhaps daunted but certainly alive.

More carefully, Bakarydes began to count the bodies on the ground. When he reached thirty without looking beyond spear throw, he began to wonder if he'd taken a blow on the head without noticing it. The best part of a hundred Momaks was a damnably large band to be found this far over the frontier at this season. He couldn't recall one as large this early in more than ten years.

He thought again about his intended reproaches to Kalaj Lesnur. If the beater troop had obeyed its orders to follow the Momaks without engaging them until Bakarydes had done so, Bakarydes would have ridden into action against odds of three or four to one. Reinforcements would have been close at hand, but "close at hand" often wasn't close enough when you were fighting Momaks. The Face of the Warrior did not smile on soldiers who ignored that fact.

Captain Kalaj rode up, his helmet pushed back and his face shiny with sweat. He raised his open palm in salute to Bakarydes, then began, "My lord Captain-General—"

Bakarydes returned the salute and grinned. "No apologies necessary, Captain. You did well." Later, in private, he'd find out if the boy had really weighed the alternatives or just been eager for a fight. Right now, why question God-sent good luck? Half of war was luck anyway, and the older Bakarydes grew the less he hoped anyone but God could change that.

"Thank you, my lord." The boy didn't even look away in embarrassment. Something might be made of him, if he went on as he'd begun. "I was going to say that a clan chief is among the Momak wounded needing the Mercy. Do you wish to give it?"

The custom of the highest-ranking Sherrani giving the highest-ranking Momak the Mercy stroke must be nearly as old as the war between Momaks and Sherrani. Certainly men who'd commanded squadrons when Bakarydes's father was a baby said it had been old when they first rode against the Momaks.

"I won't stand on rank today," Bakarydes said. "The victory is more yours than mine, so let the stroke be yours, too."

Kalaj proved that he was still as much boy as man by turning scarlet and nearly coughing himself into a fit. Muttering a strangled, "Yes, my lord," he wheeled his horse and rode over to the clan chief.

Bakarydes watched how he kept his distance, in case the chief was still lively enough to launch a final attack, and how cleanly his lance thrust down into the Momak's chest. He even muttered the old dedication of the man to the Warrior, a prayer that went back to before Izrunarko and perhaps even to before Sherran, without being reminded and getting most of the words right. That was more than Bakarydes could recall doing with his first Mercy stroke. The boy definitely had promise.

However, he also had a good deal to learn, such as stationing sentries and keeping half his men mounted while the others searched the Momak bodies and gathered in the Sherrani both alive and dead. Bakarydes went about this quietly and had the work done by the time the other ambush force appeared to the west.

When they saw the bodies they started cheering wildly and shouting "Bakarydes!" like a war cry. Bakarydes rode to meet them, but only half his mind was on a proper reply to the greeting.

A hundred Momaks, led by a clan chief, this far inside Sherran this early in the year. Clearly, the Momaks had heard of the illness and perhaps of the death of Pijtos and might be wagering on what would come of it. This little victory might daunt them for half a moon, not to mention encouraging his own men in the face of slow pay and scanty supplies. It would not keep other clan chiefs from sooner or later thinking as this one had, or keep the frontier cavalry in good heart if their pay was late one more time.

If the delays had been caused solely by winter weather, the men would be in better spirits now that spring had opened the roads. In fact, the local freeholders did a fair job of keeping the roads clear even in winter; doing so was in their interest as much as in the army's. But the pay convoy had now been late three times running. Almost as annoying, the last supply convoy, while bringing almost everything Bakarydes and his Chief of Supplies Captain Belas Batur (only an ordinary cavalryman, but a genius at conjuring lance points and baking pans out of what seemed to be thin air) had ordered, also brought several querulous letters from the Purveyor's Office, questioning the need for this and the use of that and the quantity of something else.

To be sure, the next pay convoy was said to be on the way— but better to send a squadron southward to be sure. If anyone in Koddardos questioned the use of frontier troops outside the north, Bakarydes would say he wanted to be sure small scouting bands of Momaks weren't lurking on the Sherrani side of the frontier—which made sense, come to think of it. Make that two or three squadrons going south.

Also he decided to send a messenger to Koddardos, one with enough rank to ask for more fodder money and to command the escort of the convoy bringing it north. This spring there could be no waiting to bring the horses up to battle fitness, and the effort to avoid such a wait would take more cut fodder than he could afford with what his treasury held now.

VII

"WELCOME, YOUR EXCELLENCY."

"My duty to the Queen's Grace." Joviz gave the full ceremonial bow, although this was not required for the kind of private audience he was receiving.

Kantela motioned Joviz to a chair. He sat, trying to judge the mood of the woman seated across the ivory-inlaid table without staring at her too obviously. She certainly seemed more at ease than she had at their previous meeting.

"In the matter of the palace servants selling the broken

meats of the Mother . . ." Kantela began formally, then trailed off. Joviz waited. "In this matter, it has seemed proper to the Throne to withhold punishment for all but three of the people involved. One has been sent back to her native village."

Joviz suspected that would be the one said to be from Kantela's own family estate. It was both unlikely and unnecessary that he ever know for sure.

"As for the other two, the Throne has sworn a warrant giving them up to the First Magistrate's justice, for their crimes seem to have come from Godless greed and not from simple fear." She lifted a sealed scroll onto the table and pushed it toward Joviz.

She'd spoken so rapidly that Joviz didn't realize what she'd said until he picked up the scroll and saw the Great Seal of Sherran on it. Then he had to be still for a moment to keep his fingers from trembling with joy and triumph.

To release royal servants to the magistrate's justice was the act of a reigning monarch. Kantela was going to exercise the Throne's powers and expect to be obeyed. He certainly wasn't going to quarrel with her, and the fact that she'd begun by doing something both shrewd and just made it less likely that anyone else would either.

She hadn't bothered to take counsel or make a formal assumption of the Throne's power. She was simply doing it. Well, that might be the best way.

Kantela was the only person in the kingdom entitled to wear a five-pointed crown; in the absence of another wearer, to disobey her orders was treason. In the capital, at least, a number of people were accustomed to obeying her. With a little good luck and a great deal of mercy from God, that habit would spread to the entire kingdom.

Joviz glanced at Kantela's right hand. Yes, the royal signet ring was on her third finger. He was sure that she intended it to be removed only from the hand of her corpse.

As he broke the seal on the scroll and started to unroll the parchment, Kantela giggled. "You don't need to pretend you aren't happy to see me doing something you've been praying for for half this past moon. In fact, if you try I'll call it an offense against the dignity of the Throne."

"Your Grace—"

"No, you may not ask if I conceived this myself, as much as you obviously want to." She did not giggle again, but her grin was that of a little girl—a good-hearted but definitely unruly little girl.

"However, since you need to know, I will tell you that the Reverend Lady Lilka spoke of this matter to me." She paused. "Your Excellency, the last time we met, we managed so precise a demonstration of official etiquette that two pedants would have looked rowdy by comparison, and all the good it did either of us or Sherran would fit on the point of a needle." Another pause.

"It is unseemly for a queen to beg, but if it were not, I would beg you to speak, and speak plainly, to me whenever you think something needs saying." The little-girl look was almost gone now and replaced by earnestness and a touch of hope.

Joviz smiled. Queen Kantela taking command would probably be no less maddening than Queen Kantela frightened into numbness by her lack of experience. She would surely make enemies. Yet the prospect of all this made Joviz happier than he had been since learning that Pijtos Sherran was doomed.

"I shall have to find some way of thanking Lady Lilka that will not have her curses descending on both our heads," Joviz said. "In the meantime, I beg Your Grace to consider that Lady Lilka's experience in running the largest and busiest temple in Koddardos has given her a greater knowledge of the laws and customs of Sherran than anyone else save those masters in the temples of the Giver of Knowledge who have made them their special study."

"Such as the Reverend Master Charko?"

"Has he been offering his counsel—?"

"Your Excellency, this is not a temple schoolroom and I am not your pupil. Please do not bandy question for question when I wish an answer."

Harshly put, but not unjustified, Joviz thought. He bowed his head. "No, Your Grace. Reverend Master Charko's knowledge is of magic, but it is very great. He is also an authority on the history of Sherran since the War of God the Destroyer. This knowledge has given him much influence in the College of Priests. If you need advice in these matters, his is worth having."

Kantela nodded slowly, stared at Joviz for a moment, then gave a trilling laugh. "Your Excellency, you clearly want to know if I need advice in such matters. Why don't you ask?"

"Your Grace, I—"

"If you go on restraining yourself with such dreadful persistence, Your Excellency, the next time I give you audience there will be something in the wine to make you talk freely."

Joviz had been reaching for the wine jug on the silver platter in the center of the table. Now his hand stopped in mid-air. Kantela had the decency to stifle her laughter.

Joviz reflected that he had prayed for Kantela to be at ease with him and speak freely. His prayer had been answered. Now he could say once again that both common sense and the Teacher Izrunarko said the same thing: that God sent men the knowledge of how to pray, but seldom the knowledge of what to pray for. Kantela at this moment reminded him of his daughter's youngest girl, a child alternately appealing and dreadful, one you wanted at times to kiss and ply with sweet cakes, at other times to turn over your knee and spank into order.

"Forgive me, Lord Joviz. This is not a matter for jesting." Kantela filled Joviz's wine cup and handed it to him. She seemed reluctant to let go of it, and for a moment their eyes met across the cup.

In that moment Joviz would have sworn that the Queen no longer had anything resembling the air of a little girl. Instead she had the look of a woman studying a man with an eye to his fitness as a bedmate.

Joviz had found a celibate life prudent in his office, and at sixty he also found it no dreadful hardship. He hadn't been celibate before his marriage, and that marriage had been an agreeable one of twenty years' duration. He was quite capable of recognizing the look he was now receiving from Kantela.

He was also quite capable of dealing with such a look in a situation where it was impossible to respond to it. He smiled gently, more like a father than a lover, and took the cup from Kantela a moment before she would have let it go. Then he looked away entirely while he took two or three sips. By the time he looked back to the Queen, the appraising look was gone.

Joviz's opinion of Kantela rose. If she ever found the right man at the right time in the right place, it seemed unlikely that she would have to fear refusal. He also told himself firmly that this good opinion of Kantela did not arise from her flattering his virility. Still, he thought, best move away from this quaking, boggy ground as fast as possible and stand on the firm footing of serious business.

"As to your needing advice from Master Charko, I can say that I have so far heard of no serious problems resulting from unlawful or imprudent magic. So your duty does not require consulting him or anyone else on that subject right now. As to your curiosity, I cannot speak for you."

"What you wish to avoid saying for fear of offending me is that I am no scholar. That is certainly the truth. Whatever abilities of that sort God may have given me, I fear that seeing Pijtos's friends here at court drove them out. I do not mean to be disrespectful to Pijtos's memory, but in this matter only God could have bridged the gap between us."

"We can only make use of the gifts God gave us," said Joviz. "We can pray for the ones we need, but since we are not given foreknowledge of what those will be, we can only pray that with God's help the ones we have will suffice." That was another point where Izrunarko and common sense taught the same thing.

Kantela rose and led Joviz over to a draped alcove. Pulling back the draperies revealed a large parchment map of Sherran in a wooden frame elaborately carved with shellfish and octopi.

"That frame—this is one of the Overlord of the Fleet's own maps, isn't it?"

"Yes. He is said to have the best mapmakers in Sherran in his service, and I knew I would need a good map. All the maps in the palace are from the reign of Pijtos's father. Pijtos never had them replaced. The Captain-General of the Swords had none to spare, or so he said. I asked Lord Uzichko to have one made for me, and instead he sent me one from his own palace."

Looking more closely at the frame, Joviz judged that Lord Uzichko had sent a map not just from his palace but from his own chambers. The man was as clean as the seas his ships sailed of any ambition for the throne, and had now shown that he was willing to aid the Queen. If he agreed that she was the legitimate ruler of Sherran, still more aid might be forthcoming. And was Captain-General Ludo trying to hinder the Queen, or just holding on to his equipment in case he had trouble replacing it, or . . . ?

Joviz made a mental note to send a private message to Lord Uzichko as soon as he reached home. Then he turned back to the map, realizing that Kantela had been talking all the while about the lords' armed bands that were infesting Koddardos.

"I do not fear for the peace of Koddardos so much," Kantela said. "The lords seem to have their men fairly well in hand. Or at least you have said nothing to make me believe otherwise. If there was danger to the city, you would have said so even when you thought me unwilling to listen."

Joviz could think of no seemly reply to that, so contented himself with answering her open question. "No. As to common brawls, thefts, and the like, we have less of a problem than I feared. I think even the greatest lords fear the united wrath of the merchants."

"Do the merchants have a leader, or at least one man who can speak and listen to me for them?"

"They would be as greedy as allies as any of the lords, who would be slow to forgive you for setting the merchants above them."

66

"Magistrate, do not think so far ahead of me. I was only asking if I can listen to one merchant and learn something, or if I must listen to fifty."

"The merchants of Koddardos may be about to make your task easier," said Joviz. "They have asked me for permission to form a Council for Public Order. The chief among the petitioners is Coron Sirotur dar Trati, and no doubt he will be chief of the council if it is formed. He is generally trusted, and I myself know him to be a good judge of men."

"Yes, and this trustworthy good judge would still give me no advice that did not make him richer and more powerful, whatever it did for me!" Kantela raised her eyes to the frescoed ceiling. "God, take bronze or clay or wood if flesh will not do, and make me an honest man. Just one. I need a hundred, but I will not ask for too much. Send me one honest man, and I will be on my knees thanking you every morning and every night!" For a moment Joviz thought she was going to burst into tears of rage and frustration.

The moment passed. Kantela sighed and turned to the map. With her back to Joviz she said, "Tell Master Coron that I wish to speak with him. And tell him that I will hold him personally responsible if I find out that he has told me anything less than the whole truth."

"As you command, Your Grace."

Kantela continued to look at the map, then suddenly turned. "So riots and robberies in Koddardos are not to be feared— yet. But for the rest of the kingdom—do *you* know what will send this pack of idle intriguers back to their lands?"

Joviz would have given the remaining years of his life to be able to say yes and suggest it. Instead he shook his head. "Letting it be known that you now Rule may help. Lord Batur, for example, would probably like nothing better than to accept you—or someone—and return to minding his caravans. But until they all accept you, they will stay here to keep an eye on one another."

"As I thought. What of our other dangers—Momaks and bandits?"

"More bandits than Momaks this early in the year. A bandit

does not have to travel as far to find an unwary merchant as a Momak does to cross our frontier. But unchecked banditry will still disrupt trade and tax-collecting, and even cause hunger if food cannot be transported safely. Also, enough bandits on the northern roads could end up aiding the Momaks."

"How is that?"

Kantela now seemed a girl again, but one eager for instruction. In spite of himself, Joviz found he was using a schoolroom tone as he explained about the widely scattered settlements along the frontier.

"They produce enough food for their own needs, but seldom have much to spare for the army. Regular supply convoys are essential to keep the frontier garrisons fit to fight."

"So we could not solve the problem of the lords' men by making a great war against the Momaks, one that would take them all north?"

"You know the state of the Treasury better than I, Your Grace," said Joviz diplomatically. "I think it would beggar the kingdom to feed such a mass of men that far north, especially now in the spring. Even if we could feed them, they would still not be at their posts of duty on their own lands. And if by some chance the Momaks won—"

"God forbid!"

"God has not seen fit to forbid Momak victories in the past, Your Grace."

Kantela paced up and down the chamber, sometimes sitting down but always jumping up again, the fingers of one hand twined in a fold of her robe.

"What of the city guards and Watchmen?"

Joviz rejoiced at hearing the question, but not at the answer he had to give. "It shames my fellow magistrates, but they have relied on the local lords to catch bandits for so long that few of the city forces would be much use at this work. Not all have enough fit men or the right sort of weapons, and most lack horses. Without horses—"

"There can be no chasing bandits, I know. Well, I do not know the Treasury as well as I might. But I will be very surprised if it cannot bear the cost of enough horses to make the city forces fit for such work. Please send to all your fellow magistrates to learn how many they will need." She grinned. "Unless you have reason to trust them, assume that they are asking for twice as many as they need. If they are honest, only half again as many."

Looking at Joviz, Kantela laughed out loud. "Do not look so surprised, Lord Joviz. I have learned something from dealing with palace servants these fifteen years. Are magistrates all that different?"

"No, Your Grace." Joviz was trying hard to keep both delight and relief off his face. If Kantela were no worse than untaught, and would continue wise in her choice of those who taught her . . .

She would still need a husband to beget an heir, though, and soon, before she passed her childbearing years. Joviz swore that if God sent Kantela her honest man to serve her in that matter, he would be down on his knees beside her, joining his prayers of thanks to hers.

VIII

As BAKARYDES AND HIS ESCORT RODE DOWN INTO THE valley, fog thickened the darkness. By the time they reached level ground, they had to slow to a trot.

At last Bakarydes heard the lead horse slow to a walk and his hooves sound on a harder surface, the hard-packed gravel of the Royal Road. Unless they'd lost their way, another quarter-watch would bring a bath, hot food, and a night's sleep in a real bed.

Bakarydes found his eagerness for those pleasures a trifle disquieting. He liked to believe that he was still up to a lancer's work, but it seemed that God had not made him so that he could be at thirty-eight what he had been at eighteen.

Perhaps, but then how to account for men such as Lozo Bojarkur, his Bannerbearer? If Lozo was less than fifty, he must have killed his first Momak while still in swaddling clothes. Yet he could ride any man on the frontier into the ground, then prepare Bakarydes's dinner, tuck him in bed, go off to drink all night, and wake him in the morning. It was said that Lozo had been suckled by a brood mare; perhaps the tales that claimed that practice held magic for a fighting man were true. Perhaps—

"Hold up there," came Lozo's voice ahead. "Somebody's coming." The riders drew rein, and in the sudden near-silence Bakarydes heard it too: three or four horses approaching at an irregular trot, as if their riders were inattentive or the mounts exhausted.

"Hold!" came the Bannerbearer's voice again, this time addressed to the unknown riders. "Stand and identify yourselves."

The riders reined in. From the noise, one of them fell out of his saddle. The others huddled together but didn't answer. Bakarydes ordered a torch lit, and by its light saw the markings of the Twelfth on the men's armor and harness. He spurred Lightning up the road embankment and in among the men. Closer inspection showed all four horses lathered and looking half-dead, and their riders swaying and wide-eyed with fatigue—and something else, Bakarydes realized, looking more closely.

"Do you recognize me? I am your Captain-General," he said, holding the torch so that it lit his face. "Tell me what happened," he commanded. "You first," he added, pointing at the nearest man.

"The pay convoy—gone, lord, gone!" the soldier stammered. "Robbers with a demon—they used it to scare the horses, then came in and took everything, killing everybody—" The other men started babbling agreement, until Lozo Bojarkur bellowed for silence. He got it, too—the men seemed more afraid of him than of the Captain-General.

Making the men talk one at a time brought the story out faster. The pay convoy had been attacked by a demon, or at least faced by the image of one. It had a head like a horse's, fangs like a snake's, the body of a dragon, wings like a buzzard's, feet like an elk's, and it shot fire from eyes and nostrils.

Bakarydes recognized the demon steed of the wizard Krusevo from the tale of Krusevo and Ratevka. For him, that settled the question of image or reality.

Lacking Bakarydes's knowledge, the horses of the pay convoy hadn't been so levelheaded. Both cavalry mounts and pack animals went completely out of control and scattered across country in all directions. The four men facing Bakarydes had eventually controlled their mounts, but by then they'd been carried so far that it was nearly dark before they had gotten back to the road to see what had happened to their comrades and the pay chests.

"Found one chest, just one. Smashed to bits and empty," said the man who'd fallen off his horse. "Found men too. Baggage boy, guide, one of ours. Our man—he'd died of wounds. Others must have thought surrender would save them. Did 'em no good—their throats was cut. Like pigs," he added with a shudder.

The other men added small details but no new facts. Bakarydes heard them out anyway, then asked, "Does the camp know?"

One of Lozo's distinctive warning coughs told Bakarydes too late that he'd said something monumentally silly. It was hardly likely that men coming from the south on half-dead horses would have been able to warn Camp Tin Lake still some miles to the north. By the Great Stallion's prick, he must be tired!

"This news stinks like a Momak cookfire," he said. "Give these men something to drink. First Lancers Zago Kopanur and Ludo Zelenur, ride on ahead to camp as fast as you can. Take the news to Commander Chukan Vodarkur and no one else. Have him send out a squadron to search for other survivors. We're in no condition to do it ourselves."

The look of relief on the faces of the men around him was barely concealed. Even the most hardened veteran couldn't have had an easy mind about taking a single troop against an unknown danger that had already slain three times that number.

The two messengers rode off with set faces. Bakarydes dismounted to spare Lightning while the men of the Twelfth drank wine. Lozo Bojarkur posted sentries, then also dismounted and walked over so close to Bakarydes that no one could hope to overhear them.

"My lord, I think we ought to go to the back gate of the camp, coming in tonight. The men won't be happy with this news."

"The magic or the lost silver?"

"Both."

"If Chukan Vodarkur doesn't babble—"

Lozo's reply was an eloquent look. They both knew that there were precious few secrets in a frontier camp, and none where pay, wine, or women were concerned.

"The men aren't going to riot tonight, by the Face of the Warrior!"

"It isn't a riot that worries me. Just the hotheads who'll go looking for somebody to blame. Like you."

Bakarydes grinned. "Your concern for my dignity does you honor. But I'll lose more of it sneaking into my own camp as if I were one of the robbers. The sober men won't make trouble and if we don't stand here arguing all night no one will have time to get drunk."

"Yes, my lord." Lozo sounded respectful rather than convinced.

Two of the men of the Twelfth reached camp riding double, their own mounts dead by the road. Otherwise the journey to camp passed uneventfully.

Contrary to Lozo's fears, they did outrace the news of the stolen pay chests. One other man had stumbled into an outpost, but thanks to a head injury he'd been past making sense. The Healer guessed much of what had happened from his ravings, but held his tongue and put the man in a private cubicle, saying that he needed quiet.

"At least he showed some sense," said Lozo, as if a Healer showing discretion was the exception rather than the rule.

72

Bakarydes forced a smile at his Bannerbearer's chronic pessimism. He himself was not only tired, but by now too tired to be hungry. He wanted only a bath and bed.

By the time Bakarydes left the bathhouse, the news was out. Peering through the shutters of his bedchamber window, he saw nearly a hundred men milling around in front of his quarters. Some looked angry, some frightened, most just uncertain. None were drunk, as far as he could judge.

He also saw Lozo Bojarkur standing at the foot of the steps, one hand on the hilt of his sword. "—don't care what you do, as long as you do it quiet. You can stand on your heads or bugger each other until the demon steed of Krusevo carries you off, for all I care! You keep the Captain-General awake, though, and there won't be enough of you left for the demon steed!"

Lozo was making more noise than any five of the men could have done all shouting out loud, but it was a familiar, comforting noise to Bakarydes, almost soothing. The Banner-bearer had appointed himself the mother hen and Bakarydes the one chick twenty years before, and only death would change him.

Bakarydes lay down on the bed, wrapped himself in the blankets, and was asleep so quickly he barely remembered his head touching the pillow.

Five more men of the Twelfth and a wounded baggage boy came in during the night. By the time Bakarydes was awake and eating breakfast, they'd been questioned by Commander Chukan and Lozo and seen by the Healer. Their answers to the questions added little. The Healer was another matter.

"I have used the Spell of Clean Hands on all the survivors, save the man with the head injury," the Healer said. "He may have bleeding within his brain. It would be too dangerous for him."

"I would doubtless agree, if I knew what the Spell of Clean Hands did," said Bakarydes, picking up another sausage.

"Your pardon, my lord," said the Healer. "It is the simplest test to show whether a man is or has recently been under the influence of magic."

"And?"

"I found no traces of magic in any of the men."

"Which means?"

"Some spells of illusion draw on what is in a man's mind, his fears, hopes, and memories, then give it visible form. Such spells leave traces of a kind which the Spell of Clean Hands can usually discover."

"Since all the men saw the same thing, it doesn't seem very likely that sort of spell was used. However, you did well to make the test. Whoever cast the spell might not have been content with only one, and we could have bespelled men here now under who-knows-what foul influence. Anyway, since this wasn't a spell that left traces, what was it?"

"A very powerful illusion spell, altogether apart from the men and horses it was intended to frighten. Such spells are forbidden, my lord, as you might expect, and certainly they are not commonly known."

"Thank you, Reverend Balar. I commend your work in this matter." Bakarydes's gesture held such evident dismissal that even a loquacious Healer could see it clearly enough to obey.

Reverend Balar really had done well, Bakarydes realized. However, his confirmation of a powerful, forbidden spell used to ambush a military convoy made up Bakarydes's mind.

Spring raiding or no spring raiding, he was going to Koddardos himself. The pay chests alone might be replaced on his written order, but just replacing them would not be enough. When the new money came north it would have to come with an escort strong enough to fight off any band of robbers, and with a couple of skilled priests to guard against more illusion spells or any other kind of magic. The Purveyor's Office would not produce such an escort for just any captain with a message, and the same applied to the College of Priests in the matter of guarding against magic.

Even the stolen pay chests might need a man who could by right demand access to the Chief Purveyor or the Throne itself, while the illusion spell would need to be laid before the College of Priests. Bakarydes knew little more than the average frontier officer about the inner workings of the college or how to approach it directly. As Captain-General, however, he had access to people high enough to answer his questions, and possibly even the right to ask them to keep their mouths shut after they did so.

"Lozo!"

"My lord?" The Bannerbearer might not have been listening at the door, but Bakarydes would not have wagered on it a cup of any wine worth drinking.

"Pick the six best riders from the Banner troop. We are riding relay to Koddardos."

"My lord," came out respectfully, but Lozo's face remained a stiff mask.

Bakarydes suppressed a sigh. "Very well, the twelve best riders."

"My lord." Lozo sounded happier, but he still made no move to go.

"Oh yes. Send a messenger to Commander Chukan with my compliments. He is to pick a full squadron to ride south with us as far as Three Ravens' Ford. They can search the countryside for other convoy survivors and traces of robbers on their return." Two squadrons sweeping to the south of the camp would also turn up any lurking Momaks.

"My lord!" Lozo's reply told Bakarydes that he'd laid to rest all the Bannerbearer's fears for his safety.

The Bannerbearer went out, and Bakarydes finished the last sausage before calling his servants to pack his saddlebags and his secretary to draft a letter to Chief of Horse Berov Godinur, leaving him temporarily in command in the north. He considered having the servants pack his one suit of court dress, then realized that it had been so many years since he last wore it that he could no longer be sure it would fit, and it was unlikely to survive the journey in a state fit to be worn at all. Not to mention that packing it would be as good as announcing his destination before he was safely past the old tin mine on the south shore of the lake.

He considered at somewhat greater length having Kalaj Lesnur join him, but finally decided against that also. The boy deserved some reward for good work in his first battle, but going to Koddardos this time might not be the best one. Bakarydes knew he would have to make enemies at court if there was no other way to do his duty. He would gladly make them for himself, but not for the boy.

Even if goodwill prevailed from first to last in all matters of duty, there were still the intriguers who'd flocked to Koddardos after Pijtos's death. They had no sense of duty, but a keen nose for anyone who might have secrets worth learning. The boy might not have to fear magic, abduction, or violence, but wine and women were another matter. A man who could resist those at eighteen was hardly a man at all.

IX

THE DOOR TO THE REVEREND MASTER CHARKO'S CHAMBERS stood ajar when Lord Ikos reached the top of the stairs. After a moment's hesitation, Ikos slipped through the gap and pushed the door closed behind him. The unmistakable *click* of a lock eased his mind about intruders, but not about having his retreat cut off.

The room before him was low ceilinged but otherwise large and well proportioned. A bronze oil lamp at one end of a tile-surfaced table lit up two padded chairs, benches, a rank of four identical carved chests along one wall, a tapestry on another, a pair of crossed boar spears on a third wall, a shadowed alcove—

Something moved in the alcove and Ikos started. "Reverend Master Charko?"

"Be welcome in the name of God," said a strong voice from within the shadows.

Reverend Master Charko Tashinur's body hardly matched his full voice. He was as tall as one of the boar spears and only a little wider. With a long nose jutting over a gray mustache and beard and prominent ears sticking out from under thick gray hair, he reminded Ikos of an old greyhound of his. Wolfsbane had led the hunting pack by cunning and skill long after he could no longer do so by sheer strength. The lack of strength did for him in the end, but even then it took a she-bear's claws.

"Honor to God and you, Reverend Master," said Ikos. He would limit himself to polite formalities until Charko stated exactly what his purpose was in inviting Ikos up here.

"Please be seated," said Charko. He rested a hand on one corner of the table and somewhere just outside the room a bell went *dingdingding* rapidly. Ikos looked around, hoping his roaming eyes would not be noticed. He found another alcove; it contained a door, painted to match the plaster of the walls, and nearly invisible in the shadows.

"I have not broken our understanding that we were to be alone," said Charko. "No one else is within my chambers save my secretary. He is bound by the Spell of Discretion. Even if he were not, your disguise as a priest of the Craftsman is so perfect that I doubt his ability to penetrate it."

Ikos felt called on to reply, if only to prove that Charko's reading his thoughts back to him wasn't unsettling. "That is well," he said. "But what of the other priests? Did you bind both their eyes and their Gifts before you summoned me?"

"I did not summon you, Lord Ikos. I only told you that if you did not choose to meet me within the temple precincts at this hour, it would appear that you honored God too little to be worthy of what counsel I, God's servant, might be allowed to give you.

"As for the other priests—we do not, within or without these consecrated walls, abuse God's gift of knowledge in order to satisfy idle curiosity."

And I can believe that or not as I choose, thought Ikos. *Of course, if I choose not to believe it, then I have to believe that my visit here is no longer a secret. If that is so, all my further actions will be suspect. I'm doomed any time Charko wants to take offense, and the best I can hope for is to drag him down with me.*

Something of this must have shown in Ikos's eyes. Charko actually took a step backward. Ikos wanted to shout his war cry. By God, when a scholar-priest faced a warrior-noble all his knowledge could not keep the courage in him! Best be gracious, however.

"Forgive me, Reverend Master. I did not wish to insult your brothers and sisters in the service of the Giver of Knowledge. I spoke from ignorance of the ways of the temples, not out of malice."

"At least not out of malice toward me," Charko said with a thin smile. Neither the words nor the smile encouraged Ikos in his hopes of a victory. Before the nobleman could try again to regain ground, Charko's secretary entered.

He carried a tray with a jug, cups, and a plate of cakes. He also bore a strong look of Charko on his youthful face. Blood-kin, certainly, possibly even an acknowledged son. If either, his being in Charko's service was bending the laws of the College of Priests. Ikos was not as ignorant of such matters as he was choosing to seem.

The air in the chamber already seemed oppressive, and yet there was undeniably something in it that Ikos could almost taste and that he wanted—badly. He started to shake his head, then stopped. He didn't want to lose more ground at this point by appearing to succumb to the mere atmosphere of the chamber. He returned his eyes to his host's face. It was tempting to unsettle Charko by pointing out the probable kinship of his secretary, but Charko might just be using his secretary's presence to test Ikos's discretion. Even if he wasn't, the comment would give Charko knowledge of Ikos's own powers of observation, which the priest might otherwise underestimate. Ikos was no fool, but he didn't care who thought he was as long as that mistake was to his profit.

Ikos poured both cups full and lifted his own. "To peace in the land and a strong Throne of Sherran!" Charko repeated the toast, although Ikos noticed that he only sipped. Then the priest set his cup down and with another thin smile said, "What action do you propose to take to achieve this worthy end?"

Ikos matched smile for smile. "Before taking action, it is well to gather knowledge. May I ask what knowledge you have, Reverend Master, that led to your . . . invitation?"

"It will be best for Sherran if the question of the next Ruler is settled quickly. You are a man of action, Lord Ikos, not one to wait upon events as are many of your fellow lords. God often favors the bold, and certainly Sherran needs no timid ruler now. So . . . how might I or this temple aid you?"

Ikos swallowed more wine and looked down at his clothes, smoke-stained and heat-cracked leather from head to foot. "The story I have told is that I am a smith as well as a priest, seeking a way to find easily worked lodes of iron. I am not really sure that I would not choose that as the greatest gift anyone could give me."

"Indeed, God did not make Sherran rich in iron."

"As the smiths and armorers know too well. Now, if one were able to supply them with iron more cheaply than the Harzis, would they not be grateful? And if that gratitude took the form of supplying weapons and armor in payment for the iron . . . ?"

"That would indeed be fortunate, for the one who earns their gratitude. Also, he would be following the Teacher, who said that a Ruler can never put all men in fear. He must always earn the love or gratitude of his people.

"But the temple cannot give you what it does not have. Would not gold or silver do as well, if you wish to buy the hands of smiths and armorers?"

"It would buy their hands, but what about their tongues? Men will ask the source of gold, but not of iron."

"If you had either gold or iron to buy the hands of smiths and armorers, what would you have them make? There is no great want of arms and armor in Sherran."

Ikos's grin this time was wry. "Quite the contrary, and too many of them in hands bound neither by law, wisdom, nor reverence for God. Now that the better part of the lords of Sherran have abandoned their duty to keep the peace on their lands, bandits threaten to devour everything outside Koddardos to the bare bones."

This was an exaggeration of present conditions, but an all-too-likely prophecy of things to come soon. Bandits were like jackals, sharks, and Momaks—quick to scent prey.

It seemed to Ikos that Charko hesitated a trifle longer than usual before replying. Again, Ikos sensed that something in the air that he could almost taste. "No good can come of that," said Charko, finally. "So began the War of God the Destroyer."

"Indeed, I do not think we need to fear matters going that far," said Ikos quickly. "Some lords remain at their posts. Your own house, for example."

"That is good news," said Charko, with unmistakable and unfeigned relief. Ikos was glad it was also the truth, as far as he knew, although he doubted that the House of Rishi was staying home out of virtue. With the most powerful master in the College of Priests willing to serve his kin, in spite of his vows to put his service to God and the people of Sherran before all other ties, they probably saw no need to come to Koddardos and intrigue on the spot.

"If I could come by arms and armor cheaply enough, I would raise my own army," Ikos said. "Then I would lead it wherever other lords' neglect had let the bandits loose upon those they were sworn to protect."

"A man who did this might earn the gratitude of many," replied Charko. "Even Queen Kantela—"

Ikos choked on his wine. "That—!" He took a deep breath. "I doubt if she has it in her to feel grateful to anyone and surely not to me. There are between us . . . many insults to me and my house. These are not my secrets to reveal, so I must beg you not to—"

Charko made a gesture that was halfway between a dismissal and an aversion. "I do not need to know the story of your dealings with Queen Kantela. As long as you do not plunge the kingdom into chaos by leaving the throne empty, I do not even care to know."

Charko had emptied his first cup of wine in the time it took Ikos to empty four. Now he poured out the last of the jug and rang for his secretary to refill it. With his long fingers laced about the stem of the cup, he stared at Ikos until the nobleman had to work hard not to fidget.

At last he spoke. "The first lord who curbed bandits outside his own lands would earn the gratitude of many. But if the work had already been begun by others, a lord who tried it might seem ambitious and arouse fear rather than gratitude. Certainly he would have spent no small share of his substance to little purpose."

"Who else is likely to do the work?" said Ikos with a shrug. "If you can name me the man, I will embrace him as a brother." *I will also know rather more than I did before, including how much* you *know of events outside this cursed warren of a temple!*

"Those lords who have remained in Koddardos might return home if Queen Kantela were to declare herself the lawful ruler—"

"Lawful ruler, my left ball!" Ikos took a deep breath, hoping Charko's mention of Kantela's name hadn't been cracking the whip to see how high the dog would jump. "With all due respect, Reverend Master, Kantela's arse will stay on the throne only as long as it will be more trouble to pry it off than to let it sit there. Once she's made a big enough mistake—"

"God may give her the wisdom to avoid such a mistake."

The note of warning was unmistakable. Ikos sighed again. "I do not deny the power of God. But Kantela will need much help. Am—are we to sit around on *our* arses waiting for God to show Kantela what to do?" Ikos did not sigh a third time, but admitted to himself one truth. In any contest of who could learn more about the other's weaknesses, he simply wasn't Charko's equal. At least not here. Outside the temple, perhaps—

"The Teaching of Izrunarko does not ask that of us. We are, however, asked to use all our knowledge so that when we must act we may do so wisely."

Which is why I am letting you treat me like a schoolboy, was what Ikos did not say. He shrugged. "Indeed. Yet many of the lords will sit in Koddardos at least through the spring and summer, waiting to see what Kantela will do and whether she is with child. Do you know—can you learn if she is?"

"There are ways of learning, but they require access to the Queen's person. By the time you could . . . obtain . . . the aid of one of her women, you would know anyway. And the bandits would not be idle while you did so.

"And suppose the Queen were to act, sending the Army of the North and the garrisons of the great towns against the bandits? They will obey her, I think."

Was this another test? The conversation had veered into Ikos's territory now. While it didn't seem likely that one as full of knowledge as Charko claimed to be would be ill-informed on the state of the army, still . . . had Charko made his first mistake?

"If the Momaks don't keep the greater part of the army busy in the north from now until the snow falls, I will walk barefoot from Svarno to Hierandos and back!" said Ikos. He had little fear that he would ever be called on to fulfill this vow. If he was, he would do so gladly, for it would mean that the curse of the Momaks was lifted forever from Sherran.

"As for the garrisons, the Overlord of the Fleet might be willing to aid the Queen, but he can hardly spare her many men if he is to keep order in Hierandos and guard the mines of Mindranas as well. The Koddardos garrison is up to its breechguards right now in new recruits. It will have enough to do getting them into shape and running errands for the House of War to keep it from being used to chase any bandits more than half a day's ride from the city. In Svarno and Dazkados, those men fit for work in the field who will not be called north against the Momaks are mostly Harzis."

"So I have heard. Despite the prejudice against them, Harzis should be able to make short work of bandits. Could not the Queen hire the guards of a number of merchants, add some of the Overlord's Harzis, and form them into an army?"

Ikos grinned to himself. *So, this priest does not know everything.*

"If it were that simple, I'd be on the road with an army of Harzis already. Except in Koddardos, most of the farmers and many of the townsfolk south of Dazkados still believe that Harzis are monsters who kidnap girl children to sell into slavery abroad. Outside the north they can't serve in more than squadron strength. Also, in the north they bar the road to any raids by their countrymen. No Harzi raider can approach the walls of Svarno or Dazkados without fear of slaying fellow clansmen or even blood-kin, sworn to fight for Sherran by oaths not lightly broken."

"Sherran hasn't had to fear Harzi raids since the time of Ruchan Sherran," said Charko. "Do you really think we have that to fear, as well as everything else?"

"Keeping Harzi garrisons in the north helps preserve the peace," replied Ikos. "Also, the Harzis have found it more profitable to work here than to raid. If the land goes up in flaming chaos, this could change.

"If you take the Harzis away from the north and set them to chasing bandits in the south, not only will central and southern Sherran complain about the presence of both bandits and Harzis, but the border will be open. Do not think King Daivon will not see it, either. Might he not be tempted? He is a cautious man, but what he starts, he finishes. He might not bring the clans south just to seize territory, but if we give him the blood of Harzis slain by Sherrani to avenge—well, if Kantela brings that about, her own kin will be among the first to throw her from the balcony of the palace!"

"That appears to be the fate you most earnestly wish for her, is it not?"

Ikos sputtered for a moment, then cleared his throat and wits with more wine. "I will not mourn if it comes about. But I would not pay the price of Daivon's leading an army on Koddardos! Remember, the clansmen think one Harzi is worth three Sherrani in battle. All the Faces of God will be turned away from us if we tempt them to prove it!"

Ikos finished emptying his cup without taking it from his lips, then slammed it down on the table. He forced both anger and wine from his voice and said, "So the sooner I—or some other man equally fit—gathers strength of his own, the better. Sherran has enemies both within and without, and not the strength to face them all."

Charko put his own empty cup down on the tray, picked up a

cake, plucked a crumb-sized piece from one end, and chewed it with elaborate care. At last he nodded.

"You are fit for this task, Lord Ikos, and with God's favor you may accomplish it."

"I will pray for God's favor. Yet gold, since there is no iron, also has value."

"Will you accept silver—ingots, not coined?"

"Not if they've been stolen from the mines of Mindranas. I'm not that big a fool, thank you, Reverend Master. I may be a traitor before this ends, but I'll not begin as one!"

"They will not be from the mines of Mindranas. I swear—"

Ikos rose. "Master Charko, you can swear by all the Faces of God and by Izrunarko's pubic bone as well, but this needs more than oaths. What proof do you have?"

"I will not reveal God-given knowledge merely because you need to learn courtesy! I am a master in the service of the Giver of Knowledge, not a conjuring street entertainer."

Ikos nearly put his hand on his dagger, but stopped himself in time. Despite the anger in Charko's voice, he would not have gone this far if he didn't value Ikos as an ally, but he had not gone too far to turn back.

"I understand that much magic is neither easy nor safe. Yet why else conceal the origins of the silver, if it is not from the mines?"

Charko managed to smile again. "Do you not know that the coins used for the pay of the army are marked, so that men who steal them or defraud soldiers may be detected?"

"Have you robbed an army pay convoy?"

"I will say no more than this. Before long word will reach Koddardos of a pay convoy routed by the appearance of the demon steed of the wizard Krusevo, then looted by bandits. When that word comes, consider when it happened and how I could have known of it tonight. Then consider whether if I am telling the truth about this, I might also be telling the truth about the silver."

"Where is this convoy being robbed?"

"Somewhere between Three Ravens' Ford and the Green

Heron Bridge. I know where the demon steed appeared, but I do not know where the bandits caught up with the fleeing men."

Ikos frowned. Three Ravens' Ford was so far to the north that if the robbery had taken place within the last four days, there was *no* way Charko could have known of it without magic of a sort not commonly used. And knowing exactly what had caused the convoy to flee, if that were true . . . Ikos suppressed a shiver.

"I will say neither yes nor no to you until that word comes. If it then says that you have told the truth you and I may find another occasion to speak."

As Charko let him out, Ikos prayed quite sincerely that the occasion would not be in the temple of the Giver of Knowledge. More meetings in that atmosphere would addle his brainpan long before it could be crowned.

X

MICHAL WAS INSPECTING A WORN STRAP ON A LANCE BUCKET when he heard the trumpet signal—two long blasts, then two short—for a mounted party approaching the High Bridge. He straightened up, jerked a nod of approval at the stable hands, then gathered up Yiftat shan-Melkor with a glance and headed for the door.

As they stepped into the dawn light, Michal wondered if Yiftat was as weary of inspecting the First Magistrate's stables as he was. It wasn't wasted effort; Michal didn't need to have memorized Izrunarko or anyone else on Ruling to know that people had to be watched more carefully than usual when a land had no king. Being caught in the civil war in Shakora City, away east on the plains, would have taught him that, even if his Harzi's common sense hadn't. Besides, his own mount was stabled here, and no Harzi boy passed his sixth year without being taught (sometimes with a whip) that, "He who neglects one horse, will neglect all."

So far, nobody in the stables seemed to be neglecting the horses. The harness and weapons were almost as well cared for; the smithy was in the practiced hands of Bariv shan-Yiftat, who could have shod a horse in the middle of an earthquake. Only the feed stores, which skimped the best feed, wanted looking to.

It also seemed more than likely that the chief farrier was selling some of the manure privately to the gardeners of lords and merchants with large town houses or estates close to the city. The stables lay in a triangle formed by the north channel of the Golden River, the Amrakis Canal, and the High Bridge Road, so anything as common around a stable as manure could leave by several different routes without anyone noticing.

Few had noticed. Fewer still seemed likely to talk to a newly appointed Harzi captain against one of the veterans of the First Magistrate's service and (so it was said) an old comrade of his army days. Michal greatly doubted that Joviz was the sort of man to shield even an old comrade who'd betrayed his trust, but over such a small matter and without firm evidence . . .

Michal wanted an opportunity to demonstrate his zeal and increase Joviz's trust in him, but reporting this would only do the first. Otherwise it would just make a weary man's burdens heavier, and none was grateful for that. On the whole, the affair of the stolen manure smelled like something best left alone for now.

Michal put both the thought and the smell of manure behind him as he climbed the stairs to the guard post on the roof of the stables. Here he could look outward to the High Bridge or inward to the courtyard, and see without being seen or at least without being distinguishable from the score of other armed Harzis on guard duty.

A dozen men on obviously tired horses were riding off the Koddardos end of the High Bridge, and the soldiers at the gate houses made the open palm of respect as the raiders passed. That gesture made Michal take a second look.

The men rode like soldiers, and as they trotted toward the

stables Michal saw a mail cap under one man's hood and a frontiersman's mustache on the broad-shouldered man in the lead. Their horses, though, looked like borrowed mounts from the royal relay stables. An important messenger from the north, so important he deserved an army escort? Perhaps, and it was odds on that he brought word that the Momaks were out in force, early in the year as it was.

Michal had been thinking of how pleasant it would be if he were standing on the hillside range above his home village, a bow in his hands and the clean chill of the upland wind in his face. Now he could see himself equally well leading a squadron of Joviz's Harzis against the Momaks. It would have to be his Harzis who rode north if any of Joviz's men were sent; not even for the sake of politeness would Michal call the Magistrate's Watchmen fit for the field.

Suggest that to Joviz? No; wait until it was certain that the trouble really was Momaks. Otherwise it would look as if Michal had too much zeal for fighting and not enough for the more ordinary side of his work.

But oh Father, how he wanted to be away from the profitless intrigues of Koddardos where a fighting man could flicker out like a neglected candle in a breeze simply because someone with gold enough to hire daggers didn't like his looks! He didn't want it badly enough to be careless of how he left, but quite enough to give getting away a certain amount of thought.

The riders were turning toward the stables now, either to leave their horses or receive permission to ride on into the city, probably to the House of War or even to the palace. They were bunching up as they did, and Michal had a good view of the man bringing up the rear.

"By the Warrior!"

"Yes, captain?" said Yiftat.

"I'm going down to have a word or two with those men. Wait a bit, then follow me down but pretend you're not with me."

"Ah."

Yiftat clearly understood as much as he needed to— including that there was a chance of profit for both of them—

and would have obeyed even if he hadn't. Michal couldn't afford to have favorites in his squadron this early in his command, but he and Yiftat had grown closer than duty would have allowed through taking advantage of Niko Tovskura's hospitality at the Full Trough. Yiftat respected Michal's judgment and quick wit without envying either; Michal knew that Yiftat was utterly reliable and his opinion always worth having, even when that opinion was that his captain was showing the wits of a tuppiebird.

If there'd been any real danger, Michal would have kept Yiftat closer to his back. However, Captain-General Bakarydes would not ride to Koddardos with an escort of men prone to brawl with Harzis, or anyone else for that matter. Bakarydes was well known to wink at a great many minor vices but to be utterly ruthless with anything that left a man unfit for duty.

Which was all very well, but why was Bakarydes here at all? Reluctantly, Michal set aside his notion of a Momak invasion. That was the last message Bakarydes would have brought in person.

Michal quickened his step. Whatever had brought the Captain-General of the North to Koddardos might not promise a battle, but it could promise something more profitable and less tedious than inspecting lance buckets and ejecting drunks from bathhouses, while never leaving your back or your words unguarded.

Lozo Bojarkur pushed his empty porridge bowl halfway across the table and stood up. He heard benches scrape as the rest of the escort took this as the signal to do the same.

"Sit down and finish your breakfasts!" he growled without turning around. They were as tired as he was of waiting for the Captain-General to return with the orders that would let them ride to the House of War and their real business here in Koddardos. He'd seen the cubbyhole where the glorified clerks who handed out those papers worked, though. If they all followed Bakarydes upstairs, the chamber would be packed, the clerks annoyed, and the papers delayed. One Banner-bearer, on the other hand . . .

A shrine of the Warrior stood in an alcove at the foot of the stairs. Lozo pulled the curtain aside, bowed his head, and rested his fist on the hilt of his sword.

God, if I prayed for what I really wanted, it would be for the Captain-General never to have to come here at all. Izrunarko says we can't pray to be spared our duty, though. So I'm praying that nobody else gets in the way of Bakarydes doing his duty and riding north again fast.

He turned, shifting his grip on the sword, as he heard someone pulling the curtain the rest of the way open. A man in his mid or late twenties stood there, a Harzi by the look of him. That square build and thick blond hair didn't come with any other blood. Right now he smelled of stables, but his trousers and overtunic were of fine leather, his dagger hilt had silver inlays, and the First Magistrate's badge was pinned to his tunic.

"May the Face of the Warrior look favorably on you," Lozo said.

"And on you," replied the Harzi. He held out his clenched right fist and let Lozo punch it lightly. That was conceding Lozo superior rank from the start, but did that mean the Harzi knew who Lozo was?

Damned Harzis. You never know what game they might be playing.

"Would you be Bannerbearer to Bakarydes Linzur dar no Benye, Captain-General of the North?"

"Supposing I was, what would that be to you?"

"I'm not here to interfere with his or your duty to Koddardos. In fact, I may be able to do another soldier some good."

Lozo's first instinct was to forget all his experience of dealing with Harzis and either question this one's truthfulness or ask his price. The first might make him draw steel; the second would certainly silence him, but since this man obviously knew something, Lozo didn't want that either.

Let him talk some more.

"We don't forget people who do us good. Or the other kind either."

"Of course not. But you should be able to forget your saddle sores in better quarters than the barracks on Thunder Hill. Better and closer to wherever the Captain-General's duty takes him, which I suspect is the House of War."

"Among other places, yes." Lozo was about to ask how the Harzi knew so much when he recognized the black cord of captain's rank on the Harzi's shoulder, almost invisible against the darker leather. Oho! This was someone who might have the ear of the First Magistrate himself. Maybe the Harzi wasn't the only one who'd end up learning something if they went on talking.

"I'm Lozo Bojarkur, and I am the Captain-General's Bannerbearer. Who are you?"

"Michal shan-Ouvram, Captain of Harzis in the service of the First Magistrate. Also a regular customer at an inn called the Full Trough."

Harzis thought they had to tell more of the truth to a fellow soldier than to anybody else. Not the whole truth, but enough so that if Michal said he was a regular customer at the Full Trough he probably had actually drunk there.

"Is there something I ought to know about the Full Trough besides its existing at all?"

"Quite a lot. The wine is good, the food not so good but better than barracks messes—"

"Faint praise, that is."

"I'm not going to raise false hopes, Bannerbearer. You wouldn't thank me for it."

That at least was the whole truth. "Go on. This begins to be interesting."

"As I said, good wine and fair food. Beds with good rush mattresses and not too many fleas."

"Company for the beds?"

"It's an inn, not a women's house. Not that there's much fuss made if a girl comes freely and willingly. It's not a temple of the Divine Essence, either."

"Where is it?"

"On the Street of Victory—and by the way, do you know what victory the street's named after? Nobody around here seems to know, so I thought a soldier like you—"

"Whose statue is close to it?"

"You have your choice of about a dozen, from Veysel Sherran himself down to Queen Kantela's grandfather Kalaj Kopanur. They're no help.

"Anyway, it's on the Street of Victory with its back to the Amrakis Canal. You can't see it from the street because there's a vintner's in front of it. The inn gives on a little courtyard with a fountain."

Lozo conjured up the best mental map he could of Koddardos. He had a good memory for open countryside but not for cities, and anyway he hadn't been to Koddardos in five years. Not much had changed in the Island City, of course—it had been built solid from one end to the other a century ago.

On the west bank of the Amrakis Canal meant no more than two miles from the House of War, probably less. No bridge to cross, either. And on the canal, where the cleaners' barges could carry away the manure, just might mean . . .

Lozo hoped he didn't sound eager when he said, "Does this place have a stable?"

"Two dozen stalls, half of them empty. Fill them for, oh, ten days and it shouldn't cost more than your stabling allowance."

It would probably cost less than that, if you weren't getting your cut, you Harzi son of a lame ass. Still, if the man was willing to name a price . . .

"How much?"

"Half a veysela a day for bed and board for each man. Half a veysela and a brass for the horses."

Lozo had to force a stern expression on to his face. For what the Full Trough seemed to offer, he and the lancers of the Banner Troop could have afforded a good deal more. As it was, they'd be well enough off and without having to ask the Captain-General for money. He'd give it, of course, but Lozo knew too well just how thin Bakarydes's private purse was and how long it would take the Treasury to pay him back.

If Thunder Hill had been in the Island City or the House of War had been on the South Shore, Lozo would have sent Michal shan-Brass Weigher packing with a clear conscience. Same thing if there'd been accommodations for Bakarydes's escort in either the House itself or the palace barracks. As it was, Bakarydes would be staying at the House of War while his lancers enjoyed the hospitality of Thunder Hill at night, then rode to join him for his day's work.

From the barracks on Thunder Hill to the House of War the only way was either by ferry (with their outrageous charges for horses!) or across the floating Market Bridge. Lozo remembered that bridge as jammed at all hours of daylight with everything from small boys carrying baskets of eggs to cartloads of wine and roofing tiles. Then there'd be the Grand Market itself *and* one of the bridges over the Amrakis Canal to cross through the usual crowd of porters, litters, and God knew what else.

Though the Captain-General would have been happy to dismiss his escort and save them all that riding, Lozo refused to allow it. There were his dignity and, in the current state of affairs, his safety to consider. Besides, Lozo didn't want to have anything to do with the rats who'd think Bakarydes didn't trust his men and would start crawling out of their cellars to find out why. He'd rather be staked out on a Momak torture mound than to have to listen to those jackal-begotten sons of midden pits without the right to answer with his sword. Listening to a Harzi with a scheme in mind was a real pleasure by comparison.

"I think that's a brass too much, but I'll go look the place over before I scream. Who's the innkeeper?"

"Her name's Niko Tovskura. She'll listen to you for the price of a cup of good wine, so you're not risking much. Look for the vintner's sign, Malko Orasur's Cup of Peace." Michal grinned. "Malko says his wine's so smooth it makes everybody love everybody else."

"Maybe we'll buy a barrel and try it out on some of those girls," said Lozo. He wouldn't say it was exactly a pleasure to be outbargained by a Harzi, but there were worse fates, and not being able to stay close to Bakarydes's back would have been one of them.

Besides, it was too soon to know who'd gotten the better of the bargain.

XI

THE MARE BEGAN TO PRANCE THE MOMENT SHE LEFT THE cobblestones and felt the grass of Queen Kopana's Garden underfoot. Bakarydes reined her in long enough to make sure the horse path was as empty as usual at this time, then let her out. It was a good two miles to the end of the Island City, and while the relay-stable mare wasn't Lightning she had spirit enough to resent a regimen of confinement in the stables of the House of War.

Clods flew as the mare worked up to a canter. Bakarydes held her at that. She was too hard-mouthed to be safely let gallop in the garden, and it would have been difficult for his two bodyguards to keep up.

The three riders swept down the horse path as far as the shrine on Elktree Point, then trotted back to their starting point. By the third time they passed the shrine, the sun was above the horizon, striking pale fire from the gilding of the shrine's dome. By the fourth time they returned, Koddardos was waking to another day.

Bakarydes dismounted and watched shutters swinging open, chimneys starting to trail smoke in the light breeze, and the boats of the center span of Market Bridge being winched into place. The moment the Watchmen at either end of the center span raised their staves and stepped aside, the quiet of the morning vanished for good. Men shouted, cattle lowed, horses whinnied, and asses brayed as half a townful of the market bound poured onto the bridge.

The mare whiffled and nuzzled Bakarydes's shoulder. "Quick learner, aren't you?" he said, reaching in his pouch for the half of a wisdomfruit. The mare took it from his hand, tossed her head, and munched away while Bakarydes unslung the leather jug of watered wine and the sack of army bread that he ate in this morning rite.

He'd been taking a ride every morning that weather or duty

permitted since he'd been given his first pony thirty years ago, and taking wisdomfruit, bread, and watered wine since he first tied on the sash of an officer. He wondered what he would do if he ever found a horse perverse enough not to like wisdomfruit and realized uneasily that he would not much care for it. It was no jest to call this a "rite." Fortunately, God had yet to make a horse who could resist wisdomfruit.

One of the bodyguards shouted a challenge; Bakarydes heard Lozo Bojarkur replying. A moment later the Banner-bearer rode into sight, flawlessly turned out as usual even to the waxed mustache, but at the head of only five lancers instead of ten.

"Morning guard reporting for duty, my lord," said Lozo, saluting.

Bakarydes trotted past the men once; he found nothing amiss and hadn't expected to. The men of the Banner Troop feared God, Lozo, their Captain-General, and the Momaks—in that order. He trotted past a second time, signaling as he went for Lozo to follow him out of earshot.

In the shade of a blackwood tree, Bakarydes raised his eyebrows. "Morning guard?"

Lozo didn't blink. "Four guards and a messenger in case we need to send for the evening guard."

"I see. Or at least I think I do. There hasn't been any trouble at the Full Trough, has there?"

"No." From Lozo's tone Bakarydes knew there really hadn't been, as opposed to there having been some about which he would be better off not officially knowing. "Mistress Niko's too glad to have us instead of some lordling's hired swords. Those Harzis in Joviz's service won't let anyone—er, dirty up their well."

Bakarydes nodded. The silence lasted until Lozo realized that more of an answer was necessary. "Seemed to me, we ought to save the men's strength, seeing as how we've been here five days without—with no sign we won't be here a while longer. Unless you think we should ask for some of the Swords?" Lozo's tone made it clear that he'd rather clean out

94

privies with his bare hands than accept the help of the Swords of Sherran to guard his Captain-General.

Bakarydes stifled a sigh. There was no good answer to that except the truth—that it did seem as if they were going to be here longer, much *too* long. A day spent trying to see the Purveyor, a day spent in futile argument with him and failing to see the First Lord of the Treasury, and three days spent asking people what they might be able to supply in the way of money, men, and magical knowledge if they were allowed to do so—that was how five days had gone.

So, very nearly, had Bakarydes's patience. He doubted that ten thousand Momaks had swarmed over the frontier the moment he crossed Three Ravens' Ford; the grazing wouldn't support such a horde this early in the year. He was quite sure that every day he wasted in Koddardos and every barrier he faced to paying his men would weaken the army when the Momaks did come.

So would losing his temper with any of the glorified scribes who wore officers' sashes and fearlessly bestrode chairs and stools in the Purveyor's Office. At least it would if he learned nothing in return . . .

"Lozo."

"My lord?"

"When I become Great King of the Flyaway Islands, I shall appoint you my ambassador to the world. Your diplomatic skills are quite wasted as a mere Bannerbearer in the Army of the North. If you ever exercise them on me again, however, I shall give you a squadron of your own."

While Lozo struggled between fear of being parted from Bakarydes and joy at the possibility of a fighting command, Bakarydes continued. "Send your messenger back to the Full Trough. Have the evening watch turn out ready for duty at the south gate of the House of War at—" he looked at the sun "—the second eastwatch. We are going back to the Purveyor's Office and either get some answers or learn why we aren't getting them."

Lozo couldn't help grinning as he saluted. "My lord!"

* * *

The second eastwatch was being struck on the large bronze gong in the watchtower above the south gate of the House of War when Bakarydes rode up at the head of his escort. He reined in to allow the flankers to come up and the guards to salute. The gate was as wide as any in Koddardos; it easily took three horses abreast.

A captain stood in the middle of the courtyard, obviously waiting for Bakarydes, just as obviously having run to his place at the last moment. Bakarydes stayed in his saddle, ostentatiously looking off at the watchtower, until the officer had caught his breath, then acknowledged the captain's salute and greeting with a curt nod.

At that point Bakarydes caught sight of two soldiers escorting a young woman in work trousers and mortar-specked smock from the fountain in the center of the courtyard. She was carrying two full buckets toward the shrine of the Warrior, where a tiler and another apprentice were at work on the sloping roof.

Bakarydes was torn between indignation at the sight of soldiers neglecting their duty to "help" a woman who obviously needed none and a desire to go on watching the apprentice. Certainly she was admirably constructed, with long strong legs in trousers that couldn't avoid clinging where they'd gotten wet. The other apprentice was also a woman, he realized, and as far as he could tell her best points were somewhat higher than her legs. . . .

It struck him that he must have carried his fastidious avoidance of camp trulls to an unreasonable extreme, if he could moon over a couple of tiler's apprentices this way and while yet on duty. At least he was now in Koddardos where a man could find a woman fit to please any taste and, moreover, one who was interesting before and after as well as during.

A cough from Lozo brought him back to the present. He dismounted and strode after the captain without looking back to see that his escort was following; Lozo would see to that. They stopped at the portico of the Purveyor's wing. His escort took positions by the serpent-carved columns on either side and saluted as he entered.

Inside, all was the same as it had been five days ago: the cool shadows, smelling of dust and parchment and oil, the dark wooden paneling, the tiles underfoot worn by thousands of feet over the generations, including the boots of Bakarydes's nineteen predecessors as Captain-General of the North. No wonder the men here seemed to have much in common with moles, hating light or disturbance. A pity, but their burrows were going to be disturbed whether they liked it or not.

The office of the Purveyor himself was in what had once been part of the ancient fortress. The stairs up to it were winding, dimly lit, and even more worn than the tiles on the ground floor. Stopping by one of the barred windows, Bakarydes found himself looking down an alley to the North Channel.

A boat was putting out from one of the piers, a large flat-bottomed affair crowded with armed men—Bakarydes could see helmets and weapons glinting—and flying a banner he couldn't make out. Not the royal banner, he was sure of that. One more lord whose men were in Koddardos to lend strength to his intrigues while bandits preyed on the soldiers who were already busy fending off Momaks, and on others much less able to defend themselves.

The Purveyor's antechamber had the same watchdog as before, a paunchy, nearly bald commander wearing a green tunic instead of a blue one but with winestains in nearly the same places. He rose as Bakarydes entered.

"Honor and greetings, my lord Captain-General. How may we serve you today?"

"I wish to speak to the Purveyor again on the same matter as before."

"Did no one inform you? The Purveyor has gone to Hierandos. He expected no further request from you until the First Lord of the Treasury had agreed to meet with you. Has this been done?"

"It has not." *Let the man wriggle out of that one.*

To do him justice, the commander frowned in either genuine or convincing confusion. "Surely there has been some mistake. The First Lord knows his duty too well to refuse such a request."

"I have no doubt of that. What I doubt is whether my request was sent. Somebody's knowledge of his duty is—not what is needed at a time like this." Bakarydes would have cheerfully used a harsher phrase, but he was not yet prepared to relieve his frustration at the expense of dispelling what little hope of cooperation might remain.

"I will certainly look into the matter, my lord. But even hanging a scribe and two clerks will not bring the Purveyor back from Hierandos before the day after tomorrow." He smiled then pulled his face straight at Bakarydes's glare.

"Have I the right to know what detains the Purveyor in Hierandos that is more important than the pay of the soldiers who stand between Sherran and the Momaks?"

"Of course. You spoke last time of the poor quality of the remounts for your cavalry. The Purveyor is thinking of buying horses in the cities of the Inner Sea and wished to speak to the Overlord of the Fleet about transporting them."

Again Bakarydes had the sense of either being told much of the truth or at least watching first-class acting.

"So. The Purveyor is not here. Even if he were here, he could do nothing without the approval of the First Lord of the Treasury, who may or may not have received my request. It will take still more time to discover which. Suppose I were to visit the First Lord myself?"

"My lord, the laws of Sherran clearly state—"

"Oh, a plague carry off the laws of Sherran and you too!" Bakarydes snapped. "Do you think I don't know one end of a horse or one office of the kingdom from another? I also know that whoever placed the Purveyor's Office under the Treasury instead of the Great Captain should be impaled!"

The moment the words were out of his mouth, Bakarydes knew he'd said too much and far too loudly. He heard feet scrape in the hall outside the door and something that might have been the chink of metal against metal. He saw the commander's face suddenly become a mask—a plump mask, but not so plump that it hid two watchful eyes.

Bakarydes wanted to spit in those eyes. Once again he strangled the impulse before it could harm his men. *Now let's see,* he thought. *I can twiddle my thumbs until the First Lord and the Purveyor decide to act. Over my dead body on a Momak torture mound! Which is where it could end, if I can't kick these* umgrutzhags *into action pretty soon. But if I go over their heads to the Throne, accusing the Purveyor's Office of neglect of duty, even if Kantela gives me what I need, will these motherless sham-soldiers see that I get it? Not that I've much to lose, since they won't even pass on my request for audience with the First Lord. I'll give them one more chance to cooperate. . . .*

"It should be known to you that as a Captain-General I may appeal directly to the Throne."

"It is. Do you intend to make that appeal?"

"I do. Nothing you can say or do, short of killing me, will prevent me. However, I can word my appeal so that the Throne need never know just how you've hindered me these past five days. You can all appear men who've done your best but could not do it quickly enough. Do I need to describe the alternative?"

The commander's shoulders sagged a trifle. "You do not."

"Good. You need not fear that alternative if you answer a few questions. No, not about the matter that brought me here, unless you wish to. Mostly why I'm being treated like a suspected criminal!"

The commmander's look of relief made Bakarydes breathe a little easier. His threat had been a gamble of the sort he disliked to take unless he had no choice, and it was bad tactics to have no choice in the first place. Sometimes, though, you had to fight the battle at a time and place of the enemy's choosing—which seemed to be the case here.

"Or perhaps—perhaps I can answer that question myself. Would it have been better if I'd given—shall we say—a more *detailed* explanation of why I needed new pay chests, two squadrons to escort the convoy, and a couple of priests of the Giver of Knowledge to ride with it?"

The commander looked as if he'd been reprieved from having his sash burned. "The Captain-General's reputation for great wisdom has been fairly earned."

"Save the flattery for people who care about it. Am I right?"

"To a great extent, yes. I swear by all the Faces of God and the name of my mother that for no other reason did we stand in the path of your duty. You asked for a great deal of silver, my lord. Enough for a gift to all your men, to bind them more closely to you. With another half a regiment and priests with knowledge not commonly found among the Healers serving your army, who could say what might come of it?"

"I say that absolutely nothing would have come of it, but of course I can't expect you to believe me." He found, rather to his surprise, that he wasn't particularly angry now, not even in the face of the mortal insult of being suspected of plotting against the Throne.

"I believe you, my lord. At least I do now." The commander swallowed. "I believe—I believe you, because you did not tell any of the other men you saw during the past three days what you would not tell us."

Bakarydes didn't waste time resenting being spied on. "Are you sure it's wise to tell me that you're doing something that isn't according to law or custom or even within the powers of your office?"

"I will ask your discretion about our spying in return for our cooperation in drawing up the appeal to the Throne. Believe me, my lord, it is not something we would do if we thought we had any choice in the matter."

Bakarydes laughed. "If we all sit around doing stupid things because we think we have no choice, the Momaks will overrun Sherran and then we really will have none—those of us who are still alive. That's not Izrunarko, that's Bakarydes Linzur dar no Benye speaking out of his boot soles and twenty years in the army."

"That is true, my lord. It is also something in which you can be of great assistance, if you can see fit to stay here for . . ." His voice trailed off at Bakarydes's slowly shaken head.

100

"Not until the north is on a safe footing and the Momaks are back around their fires. My duty lies there. After that, if you've helped me with the appeal to the Throne, I'll scrape parchment or carry a hod to rebuild the walls of Koddardos if that's what's needed." He punched the commander's outstretched fist hard. "Now let's see about that appeal."

The commander sounded a small gong hanging in a polished wooden frame at one end of his desk. The man who appeared in response didn't look like much of a fighter, but he did wear a helmet and sword and came so quickly that it was obvious he'd been waiting just outside the door.

"Summon a scribe under Discretion and dismiss the guard at the door."

"Yes, commander."

From the noise in the hall, Bakarydes guessed the guard outside must have been six or eight men. He sat down, more than ever relieved that he'd avoided a quarrel with the commander. Now that he could look around and see clearly, Bakarydes realized that such a quarrel would have done a considerable injustice. It wasn't only riding a chair and drinking wine that made the commander's shoulders sag and his eyes red. The man was on the ragged edge of sheer exhaustion, yet he'd managed for the most part to control his temper in the face of a fair amount of provocation, and also stand up to a man very much his superior who was known to despise clerks.

Bakarydes was even more relieved that he hadn't yielded to a very real temptation to tell everything to Master Charko at the College of Priests. The man had looked down at Bakarydes and shrugged when Bakarydes hesitated over mentioning the demon steed of Krusevo.

"My lord Captain-General," he'd said, "unless you speak more frankly, I can do little or nothing for you even if the Treasury and the Purveyor's Office bid me to do it. I cannot send priests north without knowing if they are to fight earthquakes or greenfly swarms. Knowledge is not made all to one pattern to be used in one way like swords or lances.

101

"Would you send men against an opponent whose strength you did not know if you could help it? I thought not. Well, neither can I put at risk those who have studied under me and who may be needed against greater troubles than stolen pay chests."

That might not have been a dismissal, but Bakarydes had chosen to take it as such. His desire to trust Charko or even go on talking with him had been swept away by the man's overflowing self-confidence. Bakarydes didn't expect from a Master of the Giver of Knowledge the deference he normally received from more modestly Gifted men and women whose spells healed men and animals or purified water, but neither did he expect to be treated like a Momak brought before a royal judge.

Perhaps he'd better learn what he should expect from high-ranking Koddardos priests. It looked as if Charko wouldn't be the last one he'd have to deal with, and the army's modestly Gifted sorcerers were as unlike them as a camp woman was like a high noble's concubine—and there he was, thinking about women again. . . .

The guard returned with the scribe, who made such an elaborate business of unpacking his gear that both Bakarydes and the commander were exchanging Shall-you-hurry-him-or-shall-I? looks by the time he'd finished. At last he sat down and looked up at Bakarydes with the expression of a dog waiting for what he knows will be poor food.

Bakarydes started pacing up and down, then clasped his hands behind his back and cleared his throat. "To Her Grace Kantela, Queen of Sherran—"

"Begging your pardon, my lord," said the scribe, "but that's not her proper title. 'Queen' all by itself means she's Queen Regnant, and there's no such thing."

"At least there hasn't been," said Bakarydes. "Maybe . . . But what else can I call her?"

The scribe looked blank. "Queen Dowager? No, she's the widow of the old king but not the mother of the new one. Queen Regent? No, a regency is always on behalf of somebody else—"

"And there isn't anybody else," Bakarydes finished. "So let's call her 'Queen' and leave it at that. Certainly the letter won't go astray. There's nobody else around with any claim to any form of that title."

"But, my lord—"

"It's either 'Her Grace Kantela, Queen of Sherran,' or I write the damned appeal myself, and may the Great Stallion piss in your inkwell! I'd rather send Kantela an illegible letter than an insulting one!"

The scribe looked at his commander in mute appeal, found the appeal rejected, and bowed his head over the wax tablet. Bakarydes was accustomed to dictation, so it did not take long for the scribe to rough copy a single sheet that gave a discreet version of the past half-moon's events, assured Kantela of Bakarydes's great respect for the law but equal need to satisfy his loyal men, and petitioned for her judgment in this matter, a judgment he knew he could trust.

Bakarydes devoutly hoped that last was not going to be a mere polite formality. If Kantela had no judgment worthy of the name Sherran could end up prey to worse than Momaks. However, his own difficulties notwithstanding, she obviously hadn't let the government dissolve completely. He recalled Lozo's mentioning a rumor (no doubt picked up from the Full Trough's pet Harzis) that Kantela was relying heavily on First Magistrate Joviz's advice. She could do much worse. Although Joviz might well be good only for common sense and matters particular to Koddardos or the law; he hadn't been a soldier since before Bakarydes put on his sash.

Bakarydes read through the rough copy, nodded, and handed it back to the scribe, who retired to an alcove holding a small table with a candle at one end and a padded stool. He lit the candle, drew a brass phial from his belt pouch, and somewhat pompously sprinkled a line of reddish powder across the mouth of the alcove. Two passes with his hands and three formulas, and the alcove vanished behind a gently swirling reddish fog.

The commander struck his gong again and sat down. "It's a pity that the Spell of Veiling can't be extended far enough to be used on the battlefield."

"If it needs powder, it wouldn't be much good even if it could be extended," said Bakarydes. "A stiff breeze could blow the dust away, or the Momaks could send riders through it to scatter the dust."

"I've seen other ways of Veiling, but would the Momaks really charge without knowing what's in front of them?"

Bakarydes merely nodded. It was no good replying with the question, "Have you ever faced the charge of a hundred Momak death riders and listened to their death song growing louder with every stride of their horses?" The answer was so obvious that the question itself would be insulting. Bakarydes had lost the wish to insult the commander, for all that he still doubted that any pen pusher or desk rider had ever lanced an enemy or even baked a batch of ration bread.

He was saved from having to reply at all by the arrival of two guards and a woman with a wheeled tray laden with cheeses, cakes, fruit, and jugs of wine and water. To Bakarydes's mild relief the woman, though fresh-faced and light-footed, had obviously seen the last of her youth about the time he made his Boy's Vows.

The cakes were fresh from the oven, and their appetizing smell made Bakarydes realize he was hungrier than he really should be. Was fighting clerks going to prove harder work than fighting Momaks?

"I have ordered lunch sent out to your men as well," said the commander. "Now, my lord, may I ask in return for what we have done for you one small favor? Could you tell your men—or have your Bannerbearer tell them—not to station themselves as though they expected to have to rescue you from our clutches and fight their way out of the House of War!"

He threw open the shutters. By leaning out the window Bakarydes could see the whole courtyard, including the portico of the Purveyor's Office. He began to laugh softly. The commander might not be very warlike, but he knew men ready for a fight when he saw them.

The Banner troopers couldn't have been more on the alert without drawing their swords and cocking their bows. Only one man had his attention on the tiler's two apprentices as they climbed up and down the ladders in their snug trousers, and as Bakarydes watched, Lozo noticed this. The Captain-General listened for a moment to Lozo describing eloquently how useless the man would be to any woman if he ever let his eyes wander like that with Momaks around, then cupped his hands and shouted.

"Lozo! Take the men off guard! The matter's been settled as well as we can expect today. They're sending lunch out to the men."

"Yes, my lord."

By the time the men had gathered around Lozo, the old woman had led out four guards with more trays. The tiler set down his trowel and mortar bucket and watched dubiously as his two apprentices scrambled down the ladder to serve the wine. Bakarydes grinned at the tiler's uneasiness. The man obviously suspected the soldiers' intentions but didn't know Lozo's discipline; those young women were as safe as they wanted to be.

He turned back to the room to find his plate and cup filled. He sat down and bit into a cake. He couldn't tell if he'd won a victory by appealing to the Throne, but at least he was no longer fighting the Purveyor's Office on their own ground. And he could pray that Queen Kantela hadn't been frightened into seeing plotters and usurpers under every bed.

XII

KANTELA SWEPT THE CHAMBER WITH HER EYES TO SEE IF anything was out of place or unseemly, but found nothing. The curtains were freshly ironed and hung in elegant folds, the new-washed marble of the floor gleamed, as did the brass frame of the newly hung map of Koddardos. All the wood in the room, including the frame of the map of Sherran, exhaled the scent of fresh oil.

Kantela wondered why she had ordered the chamber made

as fresh and sweet as a maiden on her marriage day but found no satisfactory answer. *Well*, she thought, *when a Captain-General appeals to the Throne he ordinarily receives a full audience of state. While I'm in mourning this is the best I can do, and it does keep up appearances.*

She sat down in the high-backed chair facing the door and resisted the temptation to fiddle with the amber and silver brooch that was her one concession to court attire. The table in front of her was piled with wax tablets and styluses, paper, pens, and ink. Doing one's own writing was as good as having it done by a scribe under Discretion, and she had been brought up to write a good fair hand. Since it was said of Bakarydes that he could shoe his own mount and fletch his own arrows if need be, he would hardly disdain a queen doing scribe's work.

She struck the gong and the door to the chamber swung open—both halves for a Captain-General. She heard the Swordsman outside clear his throat.

"Bakarydes Linzur dar no Benye, Captain-General of the North, seeks audience with the Queen's Grace."

"The Captain-General may enter."

Somehow she had expected the man who strode through the door to wear a mustache, like nine out of ten frontier cavalrymen, but he was clean shaven. Looking at the full upper lip of the wide mouth, she had to admit that this did his face no harm.

As for the rest of Bakarydes, it was clad in an obviously new gray mourning tunic of fine linen with the gold cord of a Captain-General looped around the right shoulder and cinched in by the gold-fringed deep scarlet sash of an officer, and snug gray wool trousers tucked into soft brown boots. Bakarydes's legs were slightly bowed from all his years in the saddle, but even so were quite fit to stand the exposure of trousers tighter than most men could have worn. His parade sword rode in a black leather scabbard, and over everything else he wore the Captain-General's cloak of dark red lined with gold, which flowed admirably down from broad shoulders to pool around him as he made his bow.

"My duty to the Queen's Grace."

106

"The Throne honors those who have served it well," she replied as he rose.

"Your Grace is most gracious." Bakarydes frowned as he realized his poor choice of words, and Kantela bit her lip to keep from smiling. In spite of his natural dignity and grace of movement, Bakarydes was living up to his reputation of being less than the perfect courtier—and the plague take anyone who cast that slur on him, unless they'd done half as much for Sherran as he had!

"Be seated, my lord Captain-General, if you please."

Bakarydes managed to seat himself without catching either his sword or his cloak on the chair. As he folded his hands one over the other on the table in front of him, Kantela noticed that he wore no marriage ring, only a gold signet. She told herself firmly that the rush of pleasure she felt upon noticing this was due only to the fact that if he had no heirs whose advancement he might hope to procure, his dealings with the Throne would be that much more disinterested.

"Now," Kantela continued, "you mentioned a matter which requires swift action by the Throne. If I do see fit to act, I can do so more swiftly if we dispense with further ceremony and come to the matter at once."

"Your Grace is wise."

"Borrowed wisdom," said Kantela before she could stop herself, remembering too late Lady Lilka's advice not to answer half a question when she couldn't answer the other half.

"That's the best kind," said Bakarydes. His smile not only curved the mouth, it lit up the deep-set eyes. "An officer who tries to invent new tactics for every battle doesn't last very long."

"The same can be said of Rulers," said Kantela, trying not to stare too hard at Bakarydes. That was a remarkably graceful reply for a man reputed to be no courtier. What other unsuspected virtues might the man have?

"I have here a letter from the First Lord of the Treasury that says you refused to give adequate reasons for needing new pay chests for the Army of the North. Is this—complaint—true?"

Bakarydes's mouth opened like a gaffed fish, then closed enough to let out a couple of words in what Kantela assumed was the Momak tongue and best left in it.

"Well, my lord?"

Bakarydes took a deep breath. "Forgive me, Your Grace, if I seemed to imply that the First Lord is treacherous. He thought—thinks—that there is reason to suspect my loyalty. He would not have known of my appeal to the Throne when he wrote that letter, and even if he had, no doubt he thought it was his duty to warn you about me."

"I appreciate the compliment to Ikarotikos Zaralikur, my lord. However, I can't say that you've answered my question."

The moment the words were out of her mouth, she realized that though they might be true, they also had the effect of making the Captain-General uneasy. He seemed at a loss to how to go on, opening and closing his mouth once or twice without actually speaking. While that certainly argued no prepared tale, Kantela was far from easy herself at this speechlessness. She remembered that he had mentioned in his appeal, "the discretion which I have chosen to exercise, but which the First Lord and Purveyor seem to consider excessive, I submit to Your Grace's judgment." Her tone had implied censure; perhaps he thought she had already made up her mind, or that she placed full trust in First Lord Ikarotikos.

"I ask your pardon, my lord Captain-General, if I seemed to give judgment at this point. Your appeal was quite frank about your quarrel with the First Lord, although discreet as to its cause. I do not think either of you has acted from motives which I can censure." She caught a final remark "—and I am glad to know that you do not seek to come between me and my servants—" before it left her mouth.

"May God amend us if we have, Your Grace," said Bakarydes. "But let me stop exercising discretion, and maybe you will see why I thought I had the right to it."

Kantela listened as Bakarydes told the story of the magically aided robbery of the pay convoy, his decision to ride south, the signs of unpatrolled roads and active bandits he'd seen on the way and what had happened (or not happened) since his arrival in Koddardos. As he spoke, she found that to put him at ease it seemed to be enough to let Bakarydes speak as Captain-General of the North rather than as courtier or royal petitioner. He was not a soldier who could see nothing beyond the end of his sword, but he saw most clearly the work he'd been doing since he was hardly more than a boy. Not even "hardly more"; she remembered that he'd taken his first Momak at fourteen, the last time the frontier was seriously shaken. . . .

She realized that she was paying as much attention to Bakarydes's face as to his words. Definitely it was the better for being clean shaven; a mustache would have broken the smooth flow of the lines down either side of his high-bridged nose as well as concealing part of his mouth, and of course a mustache tickled when a man was kissing a woman—

She couldn't stop that line of thinking quite before she felt herself blushing, God be thanked, she was able to stop it before she felt the warmth in loins and nipples that would have been beyond all enduring here and now! It still had caused her to pay less than proper attention.

"Excuse me, Lord Bakarydes. I was trying to remember the penalty for desecrating a shrine and murdering priests, so that we can do proper justice to those bandits in Cloud Valley."

Bakarydes frowned. "Your Grace, I would want to be sure the priests were dead before I punished anyone for killing them. We found no blood, no bodies, and no signs of a fight in the shrine or anywhere close to it. Plenty of signs that the bandits had sat down to count their loot and feast on some stolen cattle but nothing else."

"Did the priests—join the bandits?" Kantela tried not to sound as appalled as she felt.

Bakarydes shook his head. "From what we heard in the nearest village, they were two old men and a servant girl. I suspect their courage failed them and they ran off when they saw the bandits coming. The bandits weren't interested in chasing three people over rough country with night coming on."

"They still forsook their duty as priests by abandoning the shrine to desecration."

"They did, Your Grace, but it's not so hard to panic in the face of a stronger enemy that I'd condemn them for it." He made a wry face. "They weren't soldiers, and *I* soiled myself thoroughly in my first real battle. For the sake of both our dignities, I ask your permission to spare the details."

Kantela laughed. "You have it." She hesitated. "Was that when you took a Momak at fourteen?"

Bakarydes laughed. "When I was fourteen, I was too young and too stupid to be scared. That's why I took my Momak instead of ending up on his head pole. No, when I soiled myself it was my first battle as an officer, and if it hadn't been for Lozo Bojarkur's giving me the chance to change my trousers . . .

"But I promised to spare you the details. We told the villagers that the priests might have been carried off, and in any case the bandits were too strong for either us or them to pursue now. I escorted their messenger to the nearest armed estate, but it belonged to Bihor Mindur dar no Pomos, and his men are few enough when they're at their posts, so I don't know what will come of it."

Kantela mentally condemned Lord Bihor to have his private parts rearranged with red-hot pincers, while Bakarydes finished his tale up to the moment of his arrival at the palace this morning. There was nothing extraordinarily complicated about it, and nothing especially sinister except the magical assistance for the bandits.

If renegade sorcerers were taking up banditry, there was danger for all Sherran, but at least it was not a danger arising from the intrigues or follies of people close to her. The First Lord and the Purveyor didn't seem to have been guilty of any crime worse than doing the wrong thing for the right reasons, and considering how easy she'd found it to suspect everyone and everything, she did not feel particularly cleanhanded herself.

At the same time, she could not see that this matter was one to be settled by simply writing out a royal edict for the new pay chests and everything else Bakarydes had requested. If the

Momaks were really likely to make more trouble than usual this year, the army and the fleet had to be brought up to wartime efficiency. No, not the fleet; Lord Uzichko had a sea eagle's vision for the smallest mistake and wouldn't have much to do with fighting Momaks anyway except by sending some of his Harzis ashore. But the army clearly needed to be taken in hand, and the best man in Sherran for telling her how to do that was sitting across the table.

"Lord Bakarydes, you said that your escort and Bannerbearer were lodging at an inn frequented by Harzis. Are you sure they haven't said anything they shouldn't?"

"It would have to be dragged out of them by spells, and so far there's been no sign of that. As for loose tongues when they're drunk—Lozo Bojarkur's orders are almost as good as a Spell of Discretion."

There was no mistaking the warmth in his voice as he spoke of the Bannerbearer. *God send me someone I can trust like that.*

"And the Harzis?"

"They're all the First Magistrate's men. I won't absolutely swear that none of them are picking up odd bits of knowledge and posting them off to King Daivon. You know Harzis. But I don't think any of them are likely to tell Daivon anything it would hurt Sherran for him to know. In fact, if we told him ourselves—but forgive me, Your Grace. I presume to give you advice without your permission and on matters where you are better informed than I."

Kantela wanted to throw an inkwell or pull Bakarydes's hair or do something to bring him back from formality to at least the beginnings of companionship. "I very much doubt that I know so much about the relations of Sherran with foreign kings that you can tell me nothing worth hearing. I seem to remember that you've met King Daivon of Harz-i-Shai, and that's more than I've done."

"True, Your Grace." He smiled tentatively, and Kantela swallowed a look of relief.

Then she looked at the watchglass on the table and threw up her hand in feigned horror. "Forgive me, Lord Bakarydes. We have had so much to discuss that now I cannot do justice to your case without taking up the time of the next three audiences. I would like you to return to the palace tomorrow night at half past the second southwatch to dine with me and finish our discussion that has begun so well."

This time there was nothing tentative about the smile. "That will be a privilege and a pleasure, Your Grace. I hope I'll be worth my rations."

Kantela laughed, and unbidden but hardly unwelcome came into her mind Lady Lilka's words, "It is very important to find someone you can laugh with."

For a moment Kantela considered sending a message to Lord Joviz inviting him to dinner as well. He would be a source of good counsel as usual, and she could learn much about the army simply by hearing the other two talk.

He would also be a third person at a time and in a place where there should be only two, one man and one woman.

When she'd accepted that, she also found herself accepting how she intended the dinner to end. No—*hoped* it would end. One could not compel a man except by unlawful means, even if one were so lost to good sense and common decency as to wish to do so. If she tried any of those means on Bakarydes, the Ruler of Sherran would be no better than a *parodi*.

She felt no inner warmth, but this time it was not such a relief. Her body hadn't betrayed her when she chose to remain celibate. Would it do so now when she chose to abandon celibacy in the hope that it would help bring to her side as well as to her bed a man of honor and wisdom?

That was in the hands of God, if it wasn't impious to ask God's blessing in this matter at all! Still, no law or Teaching absolutely forbade what she wished to do, and as for custom, honor, or loyalty to Pijtos—she alone would judge those.

Discretion would be needed, of course. Otherwise she'd be risking the peace and good order of the land, present and future, just to satisfy unseemly desires. However, in the person of Bakarydes, loyal and disinterested counsel had come to Koddardos. If she could keep it here without committing

112

any crimes, her problem of finding someone she could trust, without crossing the gap of age that lay between her and Lady Lilka or Lord Joviz, would be solved.

She rose and noted that Bakarydes seemed uncertain whether to kiss her hand as his Queen or salute her as his commanding officer. She held out her hand; he bent over it only as far as manners required, but it seemed to her that he held it to his lips for a trifle longer than that, although not longer than manners allowed.

She still felt no warmth except in her hand as she watched him back out of the chamber, but an unbidden thought had definitely entered her mind.

Tomorrow night, God willing, she might find out what it was like to lie with a man instead of a priest.

XIII

THE DOOR CLOSED BEHIND THE SERVANTS CARRYING OUT THE last of the dinner dishes. The lighted lamps on the mantelpiece and on the sill of the shuttered window exhaled the faint scent of the dried graceflowers crumbled into the oil. Kantela pushed the wine jug toward Bakarydes, almost but not quite daring to reach out far enough to touch his hand as it lay with long brown fingers lightly curled around the stem of his goblet.

"You have been more than worth your rations, Bakarydes," she said as he poured himself more wine. "I only hope you've found them to your taste."

"It wouldn't be extravagant to say that I haven't eaten so well in years," he said. He drank, then laughed—rather more loudly than he had at the beginning of the meal, Kantela noticed. "It wouldn't be a sufficient compliment to your cooks, either. No one stays in the army for the fine meals in the messes, not even the Captain-General's."

"I've known some senior officers who lived well," said Kantela. "Your predecessor was one."

"He could afford it," said Bakarydes so shortly that Kantela feared she'd given offense. She looked at her own goblet and then at the jug. Had she drunk more than she'd realized, out of an uneasy mind? Perhaps, and if so the light dinner of broiled fish, bread, soup, and fruit in tart sauce would not do much to fight it. But indigestion or a rumbling stomach would have been worse, and after all, God had made women so that they did not need to fear as much as men the consequences of too much wine for bedsport.

"I beg your pardon, Your Grace," said Bakarydes. Apparently he'd taken her looking away as a sign that *he* had given offense. "The House of Benye can be traced back to before Veysel Sherran, but we haven't had much silver to clink together for more than a century. My great-grandfather was the last head of the house to keep any sort of state, and he did it when he shouldn't have. My kin had to starve their tenants and tighten their own belts to send me into the army with more silver than a Mother's Child going for a baggage boy."

"I beg *your* pardon. I did not know this." *But thank God, I know it now. Is that why he has the reputation of trying to do the work of five men—to justify all his family did and sacrificed for him?*

"And now, let us leave off begging each other's pardon or we shall do nothing else the rest of this evening." She thought of adding, "And it was not for that I invited you here," but decided that any such remark would be better left unspoken. Bakarydes could hardly be so drunk that he wouldn't take warning and perhaps take flight; he had certainly eaten enough to have kept his wits about him in spite of the wine.

"By all means, Your Grace." He rose and held out his hand to help her up. It wasn't the first time he'd touched her this evening—that had been when he was helping her to sit down at the table—but it was the first time he'd touched her as if she weren't made of the thinnest silk. Kantela hoped it was more than the wine, but she was too happy with the firm touch to worry about the *whys*.

As close together as if they'd been arm in arm, they walked

to the sturdy worktable of silver-inlaid pear wood set up in the alcove to the left of the door. Two cushioned chairs stood side by side behind the table.

The servants had arranged the chamber this way three times before, when Kantela invited Joviz for lunch to be followed immediately by a conference. Except that Bakarydes was here for dinner instead of for lunch, no one could notice anything different about this time. Even the graceflower in the lamps had been one of Pijtos's few indulgences. What could be more proper than that his widow chose to entertain in the same style?

Tonight, Pijtos's dislike of formal entertaining was finally proving useful to his widow. At his private entertainments, almost the only kind he'd given during the last five years of his reign, his custom had been to dismiss the servants to their own quarters as soon as dinner was over. When it was time for the guests to leave, he would escort them himself either to the Swords' antechamber or down Bavno's Staircase to one of the side gates. (Bavno Sherran had reigned a century ago, and he'd liked to disguise himself and go on northwatch frolics in the city.) The servants who'd waited at dinner, now in their own quarters two floors below, would assume that she'd follow Pijtos's custom. Even Zensko Lilkura had been dismissed for the west- and northwatches.

Bakarydes sat down at once. Kantela walked over to the shutters as if to inspect them. She knew her high-collared robe wasn't quite opaque when she was silhouetted against the glow from the lamps, and that what Bakarydes should be seeing was a well-formed woman who might be wearing undertunic and trousers, or might not be. She'd chosen both garments for their snug fit, then pulled the lacing of the undertunic so tight that her nipples showed through it.

She heard nothing, but when she turned around she had the satisfaction of seeing Bakarydes look quickly away and take an even quicker gulp of wine. He started choking, and Kantela hurried to his side, wiping his mouth with one hand and pounding him on the back with the other.

She went on wiping and pounding even after his coughing

faded into wheezes. She wanted to rest the hand at his mouth against that tanned cheek, feel its warmth, and stroke it. She wanted to slip the hand at his back under both his tunics and feel more intimately the play of the long taut muscles under his shoulder blades—

The thought of disloyalty to Pijtos came again, then went away almost at once—and she sensed that it would not return. What she'd done tonight had finally brought home to her that she had a life to live without Pijtos, though not necessarily with this man made so differently from Pijtos. Her father had been a notable hunter, who'd taught his children never to count the bag until the last bird was in hand.

Kantela realized that while she'd been contemplating her own desires, Bakarydes had lifted his own left hand and clasped it gently over her right hand at his mouth, so that it was held against his cheek. She let it stay there, but didn't quite dare leave her left hand in place at his back.

Bakarydes wriggled his shoulders as she lifted the hand. "Thank you, Your Grace. There wasn't anything wrong with your wine. I fear I was just being greedy." He unclasped his own hand, but Kantela was quite sure it wasn't just her imagination that his fingers trailed lightly along hers, even if the warmth that seemed to pass from one hand to the other might be.

"The Throne's servants left you no time to sample the pleasures of Koddardos since your arrival," she said, "so it is the Throne's duty to help you solve that problem as well." After feeling his back under her hand and his fingers trailing along hers, she couldn't have avoided double-tongued remarks if she had wanted to, and she did not. She also didn't want to throw them at him until she'd insulted his intelligence and caused him to doubt hers, so she stepped back and sat down.

Her chair was closer to its companion than it had been when she'd met with Joviz; that and the unlocked door to the bed-chamber were tonight's only departures from custom. Neither would be visible to even the sharpest-eyed soldier if he didn't know those customs. As for the servants, she'd moved the chairs and unlocked the door herself during a brief moment alone.

Only a miracle would give her servants whose discretion she could trust completely, since she could hardly enspell every servant in the palace and she'd have neither discretion nor good service if she simply replaced the present staff. The penalty for a royal servant who gossiped about palace affairs, let alone took bribes to reveal them, was dismissal in disgrace at the very least, but Kantela knew that she was not yet so firmly seated on the Throne that she could be sure her servants would count that threat more potent than some lord's silver. As often as she'd found Pijtos's reclusiveness a burden when he was alive, she now found it a real blessing.

Kantela turned to Bakarydes. "It seems that we have talked about everything God made except King Daivon of Harz-i-Shai, when your meeting with him was the reason I invited you to dine!" She refilled both their goblets, and this time she didn't have to imagine his hand clasping hers warmly as he took his.

"I wouldn't go so far as to call it a meeting," he said. "It was twelve years ago, when I was a commander. There were too many commanders for the regiments and other posts needing them, so I was like a fifth leg on a sheep. Then they heard that Daivon was going to visit Svarno incognito, just another Harzi clan lord visiting friends among the garrison of Svarno.

"Of course, it's easier for Daivon to play at not being king, since by our standards he really isn't one. His title is *Givron na Givron*, which means 'chief over chiefs,' and he does the things a king does only because Clan Kadran is the biggest and most powerful of the nine Great Clans. So when he's not sitting in judgment or leading in war, he really is just another clan lord or chief or whatever."

"I've never understood why we trust the city closest to the Harzis to a Harzi garrison. One would think that's the last place we would want them."

From the look Bakarydes gave her, Kantela was afraid she'd made a fool of herself, playing the witless woman asking silly questions to flatter a man. Please God she hadn't; Bakarydes didn't seem the kind of man to take a woman like that, any

117

more than he'd tolerate a lame horse or a drunken lancer in battle.

Then Bakarydes grinned. "Have you ever been to Svarno? I'm sorry, Kantela—ah, Your Grace. That was a silly question."

"Not altogether, Bakarydes. One doesn't see much on a royal progress. Everybody is giving you their best and hiding everything else." Not to mention that Pijtos hadn't made a progress in the last eight years of his reign and barely left the palace during the last four. The seclusion of a priest of the Divine Essence had always been more congenial to his austere spirit than the public appearances of a king.

"I wonder if Svarno has a best. Oh well, if it does, they wouldn't have given it to a mere commander." He rose. "I can show you better on the map." He reached down without invitation or hesitation; although he only took her hands to lift her, he held them so long she was afraid she'd have to pull them free if they wanted to do any more business this evening.

At last he turned and led the way to the map. He did not sway or stumble. Instead he walked with elaborate, almost desperate precision. When she found herself walking two steps behind him, matching her pace to his with the same precision, she knew that she'd definitely taken more wine than would have been good for her under any other circumstances.

She was even more certain of this when she came up to him and had to fight down the impulse to wrap her arms around him from behind, to feel the muscles of that straight back hard against her breasts and the muscles of his chest and shoulders under her hands. Would they be as fine and hard? Would the fire burn her or warm her, if she put her hands to it?

Bakarydes turned, and one arm seemed to float up to drape itself across her shoulders. With his free hand, he pointed to Svarno, Sherran's gateway to Harz-i-Shai, northernmost city, and principal port on the Outer Ocean.

"Half the people in the city are Harzis themselves, and most of the horse breeders and farmers along the shore have Harzi kin, unofficially at least." He frowned. "In many ways, Svarno *is* a Harzi city, because a good many clansmen from

118

Harz-i-Shai itself like to come to Svarno to trade. Svarno's also the port from which they sell most of their unwanted infants.'' Another frown. ''That's why we need men who can understand Harzi customs in a way nobody else can, for keeping the peace there.

''No man serves in the garrison of Svarno unless he's sworn the Oath of Iron and Fire to the Throne of Sherran, so he'll do anything needed against pirates, bandits, or disturbers of the peace. Even if the Harzis did mutiny, take a good look at the mountains.''

Bakarydes ran his finger along the ragged bow of peaks in northern Sherran. Kantela nodded, remembering how the mountains looked worn and soft until one was in them, riding along a road with a cliff two hundred paces high on one side and a gorge four hundred paces deep on the other.

''They'd not only have to mutiny, they'd have to do it so fast that no messengers made it over the passes to warn Daz-kados.'' He pointed at the city just south of the mountains. ''Otherwise the garrison would be out, picketing all the passes. There are places in every one where a hundred men can stand off two thousand if they have enough arrows. When they run out of arrows they can still fight a while longer by rolling rocks downhill.

''Of course, our trusting the Harzis didn't mean the Great Captain wanted Daivon wandering around like a rogue stallion. So he put together a handful of senior officers who were free at the time and sent us north to ride herd on Daivon.

''We met him when he landed on a gravel beach to the west of the city. I half expected him to ride a horse off the ship, but he came ashore on his legs . . .''

She'd known that Bakarydes had a soldier's gift for remembering what he'd seen. Now she learned that he had almost a storyteller's gift for putting those memories into words that others wouldn't forget either. She could see the big blond man in a mail shirt with a design in gold and red wires twined into it, the red-sailed ship that had brought him, the harsh blue northern sky overhead and the dark gray waters of the Outer Ocean endlessly rolling onto the beach. She could hear the seabirds riding past on the wind, smell the salt and the fresh horse dung, even feel the chill; without being told, she could be sure that the visit had been in the autumn, just before the storms ended sailing from Svarno for all but the south-bound or the foolhardy.

She shivered and felt Bakarydes's arm tighten across her shoulders. Unbidden, the thought came that she hadn't been this close to a man since the night of Pijtos's death—if one wanted to dignify one of God's less memorable creations by calling Lord Ikos a man. Not quite unbidden, another thought came, one that made her laugh.

"Yes, Your Grace?"

"I was just thinking of the last time I stood this close to a man. It wasn't nearly as agreeable, believe me."

She described the incident with Ikos, leaving out any details that might identify him. She'd given her word not to make the incident public, and even if she hadn't, what good would come of provoking Bakarydes? He might want to challenge Ikos to single combat for her sake or for reasons of his own, but he'd run hard up against the ironclad rule that forbade army and fleet officers to give or receive such challenges. Officers were supposed to put their duty to Sherran before all private quarrels; one who did not had to hang up his sash.

Bakarydes had finished using his right hand as a pointer and was now standing as if he wanted to take Kantela in his arms and wipe ugly memories from her mind. She could smell the wine on his breath, but that similarity to Ikos just heightened the contrast with her current situation. Far from wanting to strike, Kantela felt so comfortable that she had to force herself to finish her story.

Without moving away, she added, "Nothing like this had happened before, but now I am a queen—a woman—alone. It could happen again. What should I do if it does?"

"Well, I can't give you real lessons in hand-to-hand fighting tonight. Not dressed like this and with only a marble floor to fall on."

"I didn't mean I wanted to be trained against assassins. That's going to be in the hands of God and the Swords, at least for a while. What I need is ways of discouraging unwanted men."

"Ah." He stepped back and walked slowly in a circle around her. She wasn't absolutely sure that what he was giving her was the look of a man who is mentally undressing a woman, but she wouldn't have wagered that it was anything else.

"You're tall enough and strong enough to have a good chance against most men," he finally said. "Or at least you're strong enough if you're fit." She might have been a brood mare he was appraising.

"Not as fit as I might be or as I will be again," said Kantela. "I used to love riding, but as Pijtos—as the years passed, my duties kept me more and more in the palace."

"Good enough," said Bakarydes shortly. If she hadn't seen the look in his eyes as he studied her, she might have believed he was now too sober and serious to even be aware she was a woman. "Now, if you want to put your hand on my shoulder . . ." and suddenly his voice wasn't quite steady.

Kantela stretched out her right arm and planted the heel of her hand against Bakarydes's shoulder, which felt as solid as she'd expected. Of course the whole matter would be completely different this time, and not only because of the way she intended it to end; Bakarydes was a good head taller than Ikos, and—

Bakarydes's arm went around Kantela's waist.

The fingers of her right hand curled down to clutch at the linen of his tunic. Her left arm rose and went around him; again she felt the back muscles, then the springy silkiness of the hair at the nape of his neck as she ran her fingers up to it. Now he had both arms around her and his eyes suddenly seemed to have grown to three times human size. For a moment she thought of an owl. For another moment she wondered if he would kiss her, or would he lose his courage at the last moment and force her to kiss him, and would she be able to carry herself over that last barrier—?

His lips brushed lightly across hers, brushed not so lightly across her cheek, then returned not lightly at all to her lips.

121

She opened her mouth to let out a sigh filled with relief, triumph, and other things she didn't have it in her to name.

Now he had one hand around her waist, his lips against her neck. She felt her own grip tightening in response, and his free hand groping into the narrow space between them for the buttons of her robe's collar. They came undone and his lips hurried down to explore the newly exposed skin. The hand also crept downward, and she sighed again as she felt fingers tugging at the lacing of her robe.

She moved backward and then to the side, drawing him around in a half circle until they were facing the door to her bedchamber. She was careful not to break away from his touch, and it wasn't entirely because she was afraid that even now at the last moment she might frighten Bakarydes away. She felt the warmth in her loins and nipples again, not as strongly as before, but this time she knew she wouldn't have to fight it for any longer than it took them to reach the bedchamber.

That was time enough for Kantela's robe to become completely unlaced, so she could easily draw it over her head. As she lifted it, Bakarydes laughed and slipped his hands up under it, unlacing her undertunic so fast and so completely that his hands were on her bare skin by the time the robe was on the floor. She giggled as his hands reached the ticklish spots at the base of her ribs, sighed as they slid upward under her breasts, and for the first time moaned out loud at a man's thumb and forefinger caressing her nipples.

The moan came unbidden. Kantela was just clearheaded enough to know that it no longer made any difference, because Bakarydes was far past being able to tell calculation from passion.

She wasn't clearheaded much longer. She didn't remember how she came to be standing in front of Bakarydes bare to the waist, a state in which Pijtos had never seen her; they had joined in the darkness decorously clad in sleeping robes. She didn't remember at what point Bakarydes stepped back and began taking off his own clothes with hands that she did remember were shaking like those of a palsied cripple but somehow able to do their work with great speed.

122

She did remember that a moment came when she was lying on the bed, naked except for her breechguard, and a Bakarydes not even wearing that much was kneeling beside the bed. She also remembered feeling a chilling memory: Pijtos kneeling beside her bed, praying that the union would be fruitful and fit in the sight of God, a prayer which to Kantela had always seemed to last half the night.

Then Bakarydes had one hand over her left breast while the other undid her breechguard. She sighed happily, arching her back to press the breast more firmly into a hand that wasn't gripping as tightly as she really wanted, and knew that at last she'd discovered one important difference between a man and a priest.

When a man knelt by a bed where a woman waited, he did not kneel to pray.

XIV

BAKARYDES KNEW DAWN WELL, HAVING BEEN UP THAT EARLY or before most mornings of his life. He even knew how far dawn was advanced without opening his eyes, if his bed lay somewhere that let him feel the sun on his skin.

This bed did so, and he judged that the sun was well up, higher than it usually was when he rose except when he'd been attending a party or inspecting pickets in the field late at night. He stretched out his arms and legs. From what they met he judged that the bed was large and lavishly furnished, and that he was not alone in it.

A moment later one hand reached his companion. He ran his fingers down the companion's body, discovering the other to be female, of an age suitable for bedding, and naked. He opened his eyes, turned his head slightly, and found himself staring at Queen Kantela, her dark hair tumbled over the pillow and her full mouth slack in a deep slumber.

Memories crashed in on Bakarydes. He rolled toward the edge of the bed and gathered himself for a convulsive leap to the floor. Fortunately the bedclothes had tangled around his legs, and his leap turned into an ignominious sprawl, chest and arms on the rug and legs still in the bed. An ax seemed to sink into his head; from the taste in his mouth the wine had been good, but he'd drunk far too much of it for his head to stand being thumped about. He pulled himself back into bed, untangled his legs, and looked back at Kantela. That much movement his head could endure.

In the course of his antics Bakarydes had stripped the bedclothes off Kantela. Under them she was as his fingers had hinted: bare as a newborn babe. Sleeping soundly as one, too, for which Bakarydes gave thanks to God. Whatever might have passed or might yet pass between him and the Queen, no good could come of her remembering him leaping from her bed as if she'd been a poisonous serpent.

A moment later, Bakarydes became aware that Kantela's eyelids were fluttering, and that her revealed beauty was having an undeniable effect on him. Bakarydes tried to remember the last time he'd had dealings with a woman who would not regard that as worth an extra fee, and failed. He had avoided amorous intrigues among noblewomen, which frequently involved more intrigue than amorousness, and experience had taught him that far too many merchants' women who were willing to sleep with him expected to be paid in army contracts for their husbands or fathers or themselves.

Quickly Bakarydes drew the bedclothes above his waist. Reluctantly he drew them up to Kantela's shoulders. He could not keep his hands from lingering briefly on her shoulders, and under their caress Kantela's eyes opened. She turned her head, saw her bedmate, and smiled.

"Forgive me, Bakarydes. You must think me a very poor hostess, concerned only with her own pleasure and not letting her guests choose their entertainment."

Bakarydes knew that if he started laughing he might not be able to stop. He took a deep breath and shook his head cautiously. "If I seem too bold, Your G—"

"Please. I think we can be Bakarydes and Kantela, at least here and for now."

124

"If I seem too bold, K-Kantela, you must forgive me. But the—entertainment—you offered was—was—would have been my choice too if I had dared to speak my mind."

"You should always speak your mind, Bakarydes. You did so very well, once the wine was in you and even better afterward. Yet—" and she blushed "—we cannot spend all the time you have promised to stay in Koddardos in bed, as much as it might please both of us. You shall have to be as bold in giving advice as you were in . . ." She was blushing harder now, and turned her face into the pillow.

Bakarydes absently stroked her hair. "All the time you have promised to stay in Koddardos" seemed a meaningless phrase. Or had he promised to stay in Koddardos and advise the Queen?

That thought made him sit upright, with a sensation like that of riding a horse into an unseen mountain stream. He ignored his throbbing head and dry mouth and looked down at Kantela.

She survived nudity, daylight, and as much sobriety as he had achieved better than any woman he could remember bedding, but that didn't prove she was telling the truth. Possibly she thought he'd drunk so much that he would remember nothing and she could tell him anything and be believed. Since he could remember a great many of the pleasant details of last night and much of what they'd talked about before, he couldn't have been that drunk, and if she thought so she was very foolish, to say the least.

It was much easier, and certainly more comforting to a Captain-General with a morning-after head, to believe that the Queen of Sherran was neither foolish nor wanton and that he really had agreed to stay in Koddardos and advise her. She would hardly have needed to arrange for last night in order to ask or even command his counsel or his presence; under any circumstances his duty to the Throne would have required him to obey her. Unless and until the Momaks crossed the frontier in force, that is, and then Kantela would probably be the first to admit that his duty lay in returning north to lead his men. Somehow he could not imagine her being that ignorant of a soldier's duty.

125

Meanwhile, his most immediate duty to her was not to compromise her reputation more than she was prepared to allow. "Kantela, I can't imagine having to leave Koddardos soon enough not to give you a great deal of advice. The Treasury and the Purveyor's Office will want a good deal of setting to rights, for one thing. But I think we'd better discuss it some other time and place. The servants—"

"Won't even come upstairs until I send for them, and you can leave without any of them seeing you. There's a secret stairway in the wall with a hidden door in the paneling behind that tapestry." Kantela slid out of bed and crossed the room. The slanting golden dawnlight on her skin made her so glorious that every thought went out of Bakarydes's mind but that of drawing her back to the bed and starting where they'd left off the night before.

He managed to restrain himself while she lifted the tapestry, whose simple design of interlocking circles made the ornately carved wall paneling look even more so, and opened the door just enough to show its location. He'd have to get out on hands and knees, but somehow he doubted that most of the people who'd used the door in the past had cared greatly.

"Bavno Sherran was a cunning rogue," said Kantela. "Everyone knows about his staircase, but when he really wanted to come and go unnoticed, or when he wanted someone else to do so, this is what he used. It hasn't been used since at least the time of Pijtos's grandfather, so it's been almost forgotten. Even the Captain-General of the Swords doesn't know.

"So you see, I'm not the first Ruler of Sherran whose bedmates aren't according to custom, even if not unlawful." She picked up a bedrobe from a bench and draped it over her shoulders. It was pale yellow silk and adorned without concealing.

She returned to the bed and sat down beside Bakarydes, slipping an arm around his waist. "Not the first Ruler, but I think one of the most fortunate." She laughed. "Certainly one with good taste. Do you know that you're beautiful?" Bakarydes felt what he thought was a moment's hesitation, then the bedclothes flew back and she was studying him from eyebrows to ankles.

"That scar there, on the inside of your left thigh. Wasn't that a dangerous place to be wounded?" Her fingers prodded.

"It certainly was. A finger to the left and I'd have bled to death in the saddle. Three fingers to the right and I might have lived but I would have been—well, unfit for what we were about last night and—ahhh . . ."

Kantela's fingers had moved the appropriate distance to the right. This time Bakarydes could feel the hesitation even through the delight. So he waited until the hesitation was gone before he slipped the robe from Kantela's shoulders and gently pressed her down onto the bed, moving his lips across her cheek and down her throat. . . .

The sun was no longer shining directly through the window by the time Bakarydes sat up again. One thing he knew now for certain; all the rumors he'd heard about the late King Pijtos not knowing what to do with the woman—with the God-sent treasure!—in his bed were true. Nothing else could have left Kantela as she was, not a maiden but indeed worse off than one, for she'd been allowed to taste without being allowed to dine.

"Kantela, is there any water we can have without summoning the servants? Our last bout cured my head, but not my thirst."

"Of course, there's a pitcher on my side of the bed." Kantela poured a cupful and handed it across. Bakarydes drank thirstily, grateful both for the water and for not having remembered that there was bound to be water somewhere in the bedchamber. If he could forget something like that, he could have forgotten half a dozen promises to a beautiful woman, not just one. Although he might do well to watch his drinking; if it was beginning to affect his memory, perhaps he was losing his hard head, and when that head might soon be stuffed with the Throne's secrets . . .

"Thank you. Now, I really think I should—"

"I really think you should sit down and stop worrying more about my reputation than I do." She took a firm grip that he neither could nor wished to ignore, and his impulse to get out of bed and search for his clothes died. "I can also have a breakfast sent up through a shaft in the wall without anyone knowing if the Queen has a visitor or not." She smiled. "Unless you ask for bullsroot. I can't even stand the smell of it, let alone the taste, so the cooks would know I wasn't ordering it."

"Actually I was thinking of asking for wisdomfruit and bread." He hesitated, wanting to tell her of his morning rite but afraid to shatter something that was already good and might become precious to him. If Kantela laughed—

Instead she listened in silence, hands folded on her knees, until he'd finished. Then she said softly, "Some morning— may I come riding with you? My first horse was an old mare who always insisted on wisdomfruit as a snack."

"Kantela, I—"

"Didn't know I could ride? My father raised cavalry mounts. Riding was my favorite exercise, when I—had the time."

Bakarydes nodded, swallowing a futile anger that even in private this woman felt she had to be careful of the reputation of her bloodless clod of a husband! No doubt there was a Ruler's duty in it, but no justice that he could see.

He looked back to Kantela. Her hands were still folded on her knees, but her lips were trembling slightly. She looked about sixteen, asking her father for a favor. Did she know just how much she was asking?

She couldn't, not unless she could read his mind, but that didn't matter. Bakarydes knew that his morning ride would never be quite the same after this without Kantela beside him.

"You have my word of honor, Kantela, that whenever we are together and it is safe, it will be *our* morning ride."

Kantela's lips stopped trembling and curved into a distinctly impish smile. Bakarydes noted this with a less than easy mind. He had the feeling that Kantela would put a very loose meaning to the word "safe" any morning she really felt like riding with him.

Meanwhile, Kantela had been scribbling on a small wax

128

tablet. She tied the cover over it, lifted the lid of the bedside table, and dropped it into a small slot in the bottom. Bakarydes waited for the sound of its hitting bottom, heard nothing, and raised his eyebrows.

"Another aid to discreet bedsport?"

"Actually, Pijtos had it put in, so that I could order meals or papers or anything else I might need without making enough noise to interrupt his meditations." She grinned. "It goes down a shaft to a box outside the duty steward's office. I oversaw its building, but I confess I never thought of using it for this. I was innocent in those days." She rubbed her stomach. "Now I'm just hungry. I don't know about you, but that was the hardest night's work I ever did."

Bakarydes tried to keep his face straight, but it twisted into a smile in spite of himself. Kantela kissed him and the smile turned into a grin; she embraced him and they both started laughing; she pulled him down on top of her and he rolled to one side so that he could bury his face in the pillows and stop howling, but somehow he found his face buried between her breasts instead. . . .

XV

MASTER CHARKO LIFTED THE AMULET ON ITS SILVER CHAIN over his head and laid it on the table in front of him. The Double Veiling was in place; it not only drew a murky curtain across the alcove but would keep anyone who might be listening with ears or Gifts from overhearing his conversation with Lord Ikos. A sharp-eared eavesdropper might perceive sounds but would detect no sense.

Of course, there might be somewhere a technique for penetrating even the Double Veiling; he'd thought of working on one himself, and what he could think of, others could also. He doubted if anyone else had half the knowledge necessary to make that thought a reality, but perhaps it would be wise to learn if anyone was even trying?

Yes. If matters between him and Lord Ikos proceeded as Charko intended, they would soon have more interest than anyone in Sherran save Queen Kantela in Spells of Veiling that remained inviolate.

Charko turned to Ikos, who had seated himself while the Veiling strengthened. Charko noted with amusement that Ikos had seated himself in the smallest of the four chairs in the alcove.

"Honor and greetings, Lord Ikos. I am glad that we have been able to meet so soon."

"Indeed. I'm not accustomed to the kind of summons you sent. I accepted it because I know you'd be even less willing to come to me. Also because I wanted to see if you put the same importance on what hasn't happened that I do."

"By that do you mean the Captain-General of the North remaining in Koddardos or something else?"

"The first. Also, I don't know if you've heard the rumors—"

"I hear all rumors. Whether I give them any weight or not—"

"Is a matter for your judgment. Spare me the lecture. Do you judge it important that Bakarydes is said to be the Queen's lover?"

In spite of Ikos's sharp tongue, Charko felt an inward satisfaction. He knew both matters the nobleman had mentioned, and to him they seemed to create a situation that required a countermove. With or without Bakarydes, Kantela was moving ahead, slowly and not always surely, but no one in Sherran was really opposing her.

The money and horses she'd sent to the city magistrates had already led to progress against bandits in some places, and won the Queen some goodwill. If this went on, she could end up Ruler by default.

She had not struck at the nobles yet; all of them were capable of defending themselves, but as anyone who played Siege knew, even an effective defense could tie you down and bleed you to death slowly. Charko was prepared to take whatever action was necessary to put Ikos on the throne, but as even Ikos (whose impetuous facade was mostly just that) knew, before taking action it was always well to gather knowledge.

"I judge it important that Bakarydes is still in Koddardos, and I also judge it important to know why. That he is the Queen's lover is only rumor as far as I know. Do you have firm knowledge?"

Ikos shrugged. "If you mean have I actually seen them in bed together, no. I have only learned from certain persons in the palace that Bakarydes has moved from the House of War to the palace and that he spends more time in the Queen's chambers than the amount of business they have done would seem to justify. Also, he frequently dines with her and they work late into the evening."

"I am not sure we are the best judges of how much time Kantela needs. Remember, she is new to Ruling and may still be feeling her way cautiously, taking one step back and another sideways for every two she takes—"

"If Kantela were like that, she'd *have* to seduce Bakarydes to keep him in Koddardos even this long. Bakarydes's sense of duty makes wrought iron look like paper, and he's never suffered fools gladly, no matter how well intentioned. Kantela has to have either wits, wiles, or a warm—" an obscenity that made Charko flinch and Ikos grin at the flinching "—to keep him on hand."

"And will the—warmth—be enough by itself?"

"Knowing Bakarydes, probably not. So let's assume that they've found something in common besides an urge and private parts that fit like lock and key. In fact, they must have, or Bakarydes would have gone north with the new pay chests days ago." Ikos rose and began to pace the alcove. "I wish to God I could think that double-slotted *parodi's* daughter hasn't an idea of her own, but I begin to wonder." He looked around the alcove. "Is there anything to eat or at least some wine here?"

Charko shook his head. "The Double Veiling has other effects than concealment. One of those is to hinder the systems of the body that affect eating and drinking. While we are here, we would be wise to do neither, save for water. You may have that if you wish."

Ikos grimaced. "I came to you for information, not a course of austerities. Drinking water will hardly put me on the throne—!"

"I recommend that you embark upon the Fifth Level of Discipline, however."

"Why? My Healer says that I should live to be seventy at least."

"I do not speak of your health, but of your Gift."

"What?"

Charko smiled inwardly. His own observations and a few tales of Ikos's youth had led him to put *livala* in the lamp oil on the occasion of the noble's previous visit. Those tales had been of a young man who might have proven notably Gifted if he hadn't been so impatient to take up his position as head of the House of Ballos. Ikos's reaction to the *livala*, to which only the Gifted were sensitive, had been most gratifying. The nobleman's Gift was yet another reason why Charko was determined to put him on the throne. The bond between pupil and teacher in the development of a Gift was rarely broken, and Charko would be Ikos's teacher, both before and after he was king.

"You are past the best age for bringing out whatever Gift you may have, but it is not impossible that you could find a very considerable one if you studied properly. The first step in preparation for such studies would be exercises in austerity for the disciplining of the body—"

"I thought that manure came from the priests of the Divine Essence, not the Giver of Knowledge."

"You are a soldier, Lord Ikos. Do soldiers train on soft beds and rich food?"

Ikos grimaced again. "Even if I have a Gift, studies would take time and austerities would take strength, both of which I will need for leading my men. After our victory—well, I'll be willing to listen, at least. A Gift might be no bad thing on the throne, after all. Certainly better than Kantela's active—!"

The obscenity came again. Ikos's obsession with Kantela made it certain that he would support any move against her, but would that be a true advance in Charko's attempt to capture the throne? The two of them had the advantage that the other

132

side's king was known, which was rare this early in a game. But the king was quite effectively defended by her general, or in this case Captain-General. Or should he be considered her champion? She had other defenders too, including Lord Joviz.

One thing at least was certain. She had no sorcerer worthy of the name on her side. The sorcerer was a difficult piece to use in Siege, but perhaps not when his name was Charko Tashinur dar no Rishi. . . .

To take the king one had to remove his defenders. "Let us return to the man who seems to be occupying—that part of the Queen you were referring to. Consider that while he is in Koddardos, he cannot attend to his responsibilities in the north. Which do you think will be best: that he stay here, that he return north, or that he be—eliminated entirely?"

Ikos gave him a startled look. "We don't want him eliminated. Not now, at any rate! Bakarydes's name is a terror to the Momak chiefs, all by itself. If there was even a rumor that he was dead, we'd have three or four hundred-head chiefs swarming over the frontier, thanking the spirits for destroying the thousand-head chief of Sherran. Berov Godinur couldn't stop them, either. He does well enough under Bakarydes's direction, but he's not fit to deal with the unexpected."

Ikos resumed pacing, the four steps up and four down that were all the alcove permitted even his short legs. "Bakarydes wouldn't be here at all if he couldn't reconcile it with his duty. So, what is he doing. Mucking out the channels between the House of War and the Treasury? That would have to be done sooner or later; Pijtos let too many idle pen pushers accumulate among the King's Servants. Strengthening the Army of the North? It's possible for it to be too weak to stand against the Momaks, especially now."

"At least without aid. The man who brought that aid would earn the gratitude of all Sherran, especially if the Captain-General seemed to be dallying here in Koddardos instead of being at his post."

Ikos looked at Charko with both respect and wariness. "That would be a damned delicate matter, Charko. Momaks aren't pieces to be moved on a Siege board. They move fast, and once they get inside your defenses it's every band for

133

itself. That's why we can always defeat them in the end, but the cost—Charko, may God turn the True Face forever away from me if I sell or even lend half Sherran to the Momaks to rule over the rest!"

"Of course, Lord Ikos, and I am urging no such thing. Let us return to Bakarydes. Since the Queen seems to have been persuaded to make the army one of her chief concerns, is there anyone else whose counsel she might take, who could diminish Bakarydes's influence?"

"Not yours, at any rate," said Ikos with a grin. "You're no soldier. As for me, she'd probably empty a chamber pot over me if I came within range. Still, it's an idea. If enough of an outcry could be raised questioning Bakarydes's presence here and demanding that he return north or resign his post, we'd be somewhat further ahead without risking men or silver." He looked at Charko, his eyes now bright with anticipation. "Is there anything else, Reverend Master?"

Both the words and the tone told Charko that Ikos had reached the end of his patience with the interview. Charko merely inclined his head, sat down in the largest of the chairs, leaned back, and began breathing slowly and regularly until he felt calm enough to put on the amulet and begin undoing the Double Veiling.

Bakarydes picked up the chicken leg as etiquette prescribed, between the thumb and forefinger of his right hand, and nibbled the last scraps of spicy meat off the bone. As he finished, the light coming through the window took on a yellowish tinge. He heard the chink of armor and the thump of boots as the Swords escorted the torchlighters out of the courtyard.

Kantela rang for the servants, who lit the lamps in the chamber and brought in honey-soaked nut cakes and a jug of chilled pale wine. When they were alone again, she poured full goblets for both of them and raised hers.

"To the downfall of the Throne's enemies!" They clasped hands as they drank.

"And to the new First Lord of the Treasury, may God send him soon," Kantela went on.

Bakarydes held his cup short of his lips. "Were you planning on giving God some help in the matter?"

"Yes."

"Might I ask how?"

"Did it seem as if I wasn't going to tell you?"

Bakarydes frowned. The woman might like to be flattered; the Queen definitely wanted the truth. To give the woman precedence over the Queen would quickly set them at war with each other, and that would do neither Kantela nor Sherran any good.

Nor him, Bakarydes suspected. He wished he could be sure, but eight days after his first night with Kantela, most of what he had learned about her was how much more there was to learn.

"It did seem as if you might be asking for my approval of a decision you had already reached."

"And what would you have done then?"

"That's a meaningless question unless I know whether you've announced the decision yet. If you have, I can do nothing except loyally support you and do my best to carry out your wishes. However, in some cases I might be able to do my best work at my post in the north rather than here in Koddardos by your side."

"Are those 'some cases' the ones on which you disagree with me or merely those on which I don't consult you?"

Bakarydes stifled a sigh. Kantela's constant struggle to learn how much she could trust him and against letting her body decide for her was an unsettling business to watch. Until she made up her mind on the matter, he couldn't help her with her other decisions without making things worse! At least he knew his own mind; he no longer pretended that feeling Kantela awakening to God's gift of love wasn't influencing his decisions.

"There isn't a simple answer to that question."

"Then give me a complex one without regard for my lack of knowledge of Ruling."

One thing Bakarydes did know was that Kantela's ignorance of Ruling still hurt her, as well as being dangerous to her. Without regard for the justice of it, he mentally damned Pijtos for inflicting that wound on her. It would be slower healing than her ignorance of love and much harder for him to aid.

"I don't have the right to withdraw my advice and counsel for either cause. It's only a question of how much good I could do if it seemed that you didn't trust me."

"Who would know?"

"No one, at first. If it happened often enough that you ignored my advice or didn't seek it, however, word would slip out sooner or later. Then it would be known that the Queen didn't trust her Captain-General, and if I were still in Koddardos you know what they'd say then. Before matters went that far, I'd have to ride north to save you, far more than myself."

Kantela looked down into her wine cup as she said, "Bakarydes, there isn't anything worse than having no advice. If you ever had that experience, it must have been so long ago that you've completely forgotten. I've had to live with it since I knew Pijtos was doomed, and I don't see that I'll ever be able to leave the memory behind. Just as well, too. If all of Pijtos's advisers hadn't been cut from the same cloth that he was, much might have changed, though perhaps not all for the better. . . ." She squeezed her eyes shut briefly, then said, "I should not shame Pijtos's memory, I know. But he left so much undone that I—that we—must do now that sometimes I find it hard to be charitable."

Bakarydes decided it was his turn to look down into his wine cup. What he really wanted to do was leap across the table, take her in his arms, and assure her that she could dance on Pijtos's monument for all he cared.

If only they could arrange to ride together some morning! Bakarydes knew they couldn't have done it yet without open scandal. He also knew that his obsession with his morning rite was about as rational as a Momak's committing suicide because his stallion split a forehoof, but there was no denying that anything from a military trial to a beautiful woman was easier for him to face after a morning canter. Maybe the ride would be the way he'd been seeking, to show Kantela that she could trust him with more than her body, that Ruler or not, she didn't need to stand like a Harzi warrior in ordeal, suffering alone on a glacier.

For now, he only took her hands and held them until she raised her head.

"Forgive—no, I'll stop apologizing, Bakarydes. Pijtos was too good a priest of the Divine Essence to have much left over for being a husband or a King of Sherran, and I'll leave settling that to God. We have to settle matters in Sherran, and the first of those is either teaching Ikarotikos that he does not Rule the Treasury or else finding a new First Lord for it."

"Who were you thinking of putting in Ikarotikos's place?"

"The Fourth Lord, Lajos Zenskur. Either him, or bringing in someone from entirely outside the Treasury." She looked at him and frowned. "You look as if you're having second thoughts about replacing the First Lord."

"I hadn't been thinking about replacing him one way or another. Now that you've put forward your choices, I'd advise against it."

Again Kantela looked down into her wine cup, this time as if she expected to find in it the explanation for her ears betraying her.

"Very well. Why?"

"The Fourth Lord would have to be advanced over two other men, both of whom probably think they have a better right to the post than he does. Someone from outside the Treasury would be even worse. If he was a junior man, he'd be resented both as an outsider and as a junior. If he was senior enough in his own office, he might be too set in his ways to learn Treasury work."

"The Treasury has a very comprehensive book of rules and regulations. In fact, that's part of the trouble. They have something written down to cover every case, even those where a man ought to be able to use his brains if God gave him any!"

"That wasn't what I was thinking about. I meant the unwritten customs, who's friends with whom, which servants can be trusted to do you favors and keep their mouths shut, and so on. It would be like bringing in the head gardener of your brother's estate to be steward of the palace."

137

Kantela laughed. "He'd never come. He's as firmly rooted on the estate as any of the trees he's planted. But I begin to understand. Either advancing the Fourth Lord or bringing in someone from outside would not do what needs to be done as far as making the Treasury move faster. In fact, it might move slower."

"Yes. Either the new man wouldn't know the work or all the people whose help he needed would resent him and wouldn't pull in harness with him. Those people might even resent you, and a clerk or a scribe with a grievance is the best friend one of your enemies' spies could pray to have."

Kantela frowned. "Do you mean they'd steal from the Treasury? Or something else?"

"They'd probably steal from the Treasury, but I'd be more worried about information. Knowing what you're spending money on will help your enemies know what you're doing or planning to do."

"I see." She grinned. "I remember now trying to hide the hire of musicians Pijtos didn't like in the palace accounts. I seldom succeeded. He'd kept the accounts for his temple of the Divine Essence and a column of figures held few secrets for him."

Bakarydes nodded. "I found an officer of mine doing the same to hide the real cost of some barracks repairs he was supervising. The builder had bribed him. When that was discovered, he killed himself to avoid having his sash burned—to avoid being dismissed in disgrace," he added as Kantela looked a question at him.

Kantela silently gripped his hand. "So—what do you suggest?"

"How many people in the Treasury are old or sick enough so that they can be honorably retired with generous pensions?"

"I'd have to ask—discreetly, of course—but I should think quite a few. I know the Third Lord was bedridden for a whole moon last winter and had to spend the early part of the spring on his estates."

"Let's pray that he takes this as a message to lay down his office. If he doesn't, that's where you can give God a little

138

help. Retire him, promote the Fourth Lord into his place, then bring in a new Fourth Lord from the Purveyor's Office.

"The real problem is the fight between the Treasury and the House of War over the Purveyor's Office. The First Lord apparently thinks it's his duty to God and the Throne to make the House of War account for every horseshoe nail we purchase. We used to be able to appeal to the Great Captain when things got too out of hand, but Pijtos didn't appoint anyone when Vitko Jankur retired. Ikarotikos must have hired fifty clerks with no other duties than to carve the lists from the Purveyor's Office to a size and shape that pleases him. Of course, I'm a soldier, so I can't claim to be impartial, but if the army and the fleet had control of at least their routine peacetime expenses—"

He broke off at an urgent knocking on the door. Kantela raised her voice. "Yes."

"It is Zensko Lilkura, Your Grace. A message from the city. There is a riot near the market wharves. Some of the lords' men are said to be fighting."

Bakarydes used a Momak obscenity and strode to the door. Flinging it open revealed not only Lady Zensko but four of the Swords and his own Banner Troop messenger.

"Which lords?" he asked the messenger.

"Lord Bihor and Lord Volo have been named, my lord."

Kantela used a somewhat more dignified but no more complimentary epithet for Lord Bihor. "I'm not surprised at his men being involved. They must be hungry as winter wolves on what he pays them. Lord Volo surprises me, though."

"It surprises me also, Your Grace," said Bakarydes. "I'd best ride down and see what's going on. If the great lords are part of it . . ." Before such a potentially indiscreet audience he dared say no more, but Kantela's eyes told him she understood how tonight's troubles might affect the army.

"Talzo Devochur, ride to Lozo Bojarkur and have my escort meet me at the palace gates. You," pointing at one of the Swords, "I request that you go to the Captain-General of the Swords and say that I recommend the palace be placed in a state for defense. With Your Grace's permission?" he added, looking back at Kantela.

She swallowed. "As the Captain-General advises." She swallowed again. "But you're not going down into a riot with no armor or helmet." She pointed at the nearest of the Swords. "You. Lend the Captain-General your helmet and breast-plate."

Bakarydes looked back at Kantela and smiled. "Ka—Your Grace, I'd rattle around in that man's armor like a pea in a walnut shell. Besides, I won't leave a man unarmored when we don't know what may happen."

"All the more reason for protecting yourself. The Swords will at least have some warning if the riot comes closer. You'll be in the middle of it. Or have you forgotten Garzan Sherran, who died of being thrown by his horse when she shied at a flung torch?"

In fact, Bakarydes had completely forgotten the fate of King Garzan in his eagerness to get to grips with some enemy more tangible than incompetent scribes and their obstructive superiors. Now that he'd been reminded, he had to admit that he might be of more use tonight if he didn't have the itchy feeling that comes of a bare back and an unprotected head in a close-quarters fight. That this was a riot instead of a battle only made it worse; he couldn't simply clear a circle around himself by killing everyone within reach, not without turning the riot into a rebellion.

By the time Bakarydes had put on the least ill-fitting armor, the Swords had discreetly withdrawn and Lady Zensko was standing where Bakarydes hoped she was just out of hearing, although her wide eyes left him somewhat skeptical.

"I think we can trust the Swords and my messenger, but what about your lady-attendant?"

"If Lady Zensko raises so much as an eyebrow, she'll be keeping house for her uncle. He's a priest in the temple of God the Warrior that serves the garrison of the Mindranas mines."

"God be merciful." Bakarydes thought of the blazing sun of the silver-rich peninsula, the ever-present stink of the slave pens, and an aging man's whims to cater to. Personally, he

140

would have preferred the fifty lashes for insolence to an officer.

"God help me if I ever make you angry with me," said Bakarydes. Without quite realizing it, he let Kantela grip his hands.

"Then just be careful tonight and come back," she said. Her grip tightened. "If you don't come back, I'll never forgive you."

Bakarydes wanted to laugh at that, but he was afraid Kantela would think he was laughing at her. Instead he untangled his hands, stroked her cheek gently, then turned and almost ran down the hall toward the outer palace.

XVI

THE MARKET WHARVES LAY NEARLY AT THE OPPOSITE END OF Koddardos from the Full Trough, but to Michal the uproar sounded as if the inn were already on fire. Shutters slammed, bolts and locks clanked into place, feet pounded on stairs, and men and women shouted protests, questions, or oaths.

One of Michal's men appeared at the head of the stairs, still buckling his sword belt. Behind him came a smiling girl, wrapped in a blanket and holding out one hand to him— whether to hold him back from danger or collect her money, Michal didn't know. Nor did he have time to inquire, not when he was trying to put on his helmet, muster his men, reassure Niko Tovskura, and give Yiftat shan-Melkor his orders, all at the same time.

It didn't help that Lozo Bojarkur and most of Bakarydes's guards had also been settling down to an evening's drinking when word of the riot came. Once everybody was mounted and on the move all would be well; the Harzis and army men together would be much too tough a nut for rioters to even think of cracking. Right now, though, it meant another dozen men to bump into, chase out of the privies, and argue with over the sausage and bread Niko was providing as field rations in case they had to stay out longer than overnight.

"I don't think there's enough danger that you'll lose honor by not going into it at my back, Yiftat," said Michal. "I also don't think you're too old to take care of yourself," he added for what seemed like the tenth time. "We do need someone to guard our baggage, and you're the only one they'll trust here besides me." He lowered his voice. "Also, if the Warrior does decide my luck has run out, you, better than anyone else, can take the reports of our men and add them to my letters."

Most of those letters were to Michal's kin and could have been sent off by any man. One was to Daivon *Givron na Givron*, and that Michal would not have entrusted to any man except Yiftat, but that was not a reason for leaving Yiftat behind that could be discussed now.

"As you command, my chief," said Yiftat with a grin.

"Oh, Yiftat!" It was the man at the head of the stairs. "If I don't come back, Devoche Shumura here has first claim on my pay after my kin, to the amount of three brasses and a fourth if she needs it."

"*After* your kin?" came the voice of Niko's doorkeeper. "Is this how a Harzi pays his debts?"

"All right, take it from my funeral expenses."

At that moment Lozo Bojarkur burst out of the hall that led to the stables, followed by Niko Tovskura. The Bannerbearer was calling on the Great Stallion to piss on Niko's stable hands; she was defending them and looked ready to brain Lozo with the soup ladle she was carrying over one shoulder.

"What's wrong, Lozo?"

"Those lackwits in the stables—"

"Never mind what he thinks they are, Michal," said Niko. "Two of the Banner Troop's horses have come up lame, or so he says."

"Or so I say!" shouted Lozo. "Look here, you—"

"Be quiet!" Michal had used his battlefield voice; it got results. In the brief silence he stepped between Lozo and Niko.

"Forgive me, but we haven't time to reckon up who did what to whose horses. Thanks be to the Warrior, we've all our horses fit to ride, and we're leaving one man behind. Lozo, if you have a man who can handle a Harzi-trained mount—"

The Bannerbearer grunted indignantly. "The Banner Troop can ride antelopes or he-goats if they have to. Say no more, I'll send Zago Kopanur over at once."

"Well and good. Whoever you leave behind can guard Yiftat's back as well as your own baggage." Not that Yiftat's back needed much guarding, as anyone who thought otherwise would learn in his last moments of life, but it was always better to look as if you were trading favors rather than giving charity. Lozo would resent it less, and Bakarydes himself would be less worried about his most trusted men being too much in debt to outsiders, let alone Harzis.

Lozo hurried off and Michal turned to Niko. She now held the ladle in both hands and seemed about ready to bend it double.

"We'd like to leave you more than one man apiece, if we could spare them. If your people can shout warnings and deal with fire setters, two should be enough."

"Oh, I think we can do that. But two men . . . ?"

"Anyone who sheds Yiftat's blood will be at feud with all his clansmen in Sherran and all the First Magistrate's Harzis as well. We swear to be as clansmen to each other. That isn't something I'd like talked about, by the way, although it isn't exactly a secret." She nodded.

"As for the Banner Troops—they smell to me like men who'll fight each other's battles and take a good vengeance. Lozo certainly will, unless Bakarydes orders him not to.

"So anyone who comes at the Full Trough through Yiftat and the trooper is going to have more enemies than any sensible man wants. If he's not sensible, of course, you may have blood on your floors before morning, but something always rests with the gods."

Niko nodded. A lock of her black hair had fallen down over one eye, and for the first time Michal noticed that those eyes were very large and a deep slate-gray, almost like Harzi eyes. Did she have Harzi blood? Certainly she was standing her ground to defend her people as a Harzi woman would have done.

"Captain! Your mount's ready!" came a shout from down the hallway.

"Coming!" Michal tied the last thong of his helmet into its ring on his mail shirt and twisted his head back and forth to see that it moved freely. He saw that except for Yiftat he was the last Harzi left in the dining room.

"Take care of yourself," said Niko. She spoke as if he were kin or guest-friend, not just a paying customer. Michal couldn't think of any words to reply and he had to resist the temptation to squeeze her shoulders or kiss her, so he only turned and hurried down the hall toward the stables.

In spite of the noise all around him, Bakarydes heard the sound of his mare's hooves change and looked down. He'd ridden off the cobblestones of Silk Square onto the wooden planking of a wharf. He reined in and saw his guard of Swords moving up on either side of him before they did the same.

Bakarydes couldn't help wondering how far the Swords would go to keep him safe as a jeweled tiara wrapped in silk inside a strongbox in a locked cellar. He also wondered how many of them, in doing so, would meet the deaths they no doubt feared less than the wrath of their Captain-General and their Queen if anything happened to him. At the moment he would have given two fingers off either hand to have Lozo and the Banner Troopers at his back instead of this cordon of good soldiers forced to behave like bad ones!

Since neither two fingers nor anything else save the mercy of God would procure him Lozo, Bakarydes dismounted and walked to the edge of the wharf. To the west a river longship was tied up, riding so high in the water that her stern castle blocked his view. A pile of casks on the wharf told of cargo either just unloaded or about to be loaded, and the glint of helmets and spear points over the ship's railings told of a crew armed and on guard. Some people at least were taking thought to their own protection; Bakarydes would not worry about being surprised from that direction.

To the east the wharf stretched empty for fifty paces to end in a tangle of warehouses deserted for the night, and aged houses whose inhabitants had either fled or bolted their doors. Nothing was burning, but a few doors standing ajar, one with a body lying halfway out of it, showed that trouble had already passed this way.

To the two fingers for Lozo, Bakarydes added one more for First Magistrate Joviz. He'd sent a messenger to Joviz before leaving the palace, and two more for the magistrate and one for Lozo as he rode toward the market quarter. After that the Captain of Swords began to think respectfully but very loudly that if he had to send off any more messengers he couldn't guarantee the Captain-General's safety and they would have to turn back.

At the time Bakarydes would rather have been impaled than turn back, which would have meant waiting out the riot, or at least Lozo's arrival, in the palace. Now he was beginning to wonder. He'd seen the First Magistrate's men out and about, but none of his messengers had returned, nor had Lozo caught up with him. God willing, nothing worse than stone throwing or crowds of people trying to escape rather than cause trouble were blocking the streets, but he was still out here on the wharves with no more than a score of men and plenty of roofs that could hide archers within easy bowshot—

As if his thoughts had been a spell, a shadow moved on the roof of the house with the body lying at its door. The starlight and a faint glow hinting of distant torches gave it a distorted but human shape. In a doorway at the edge of the light cast by torch-bearing Swords, another shadow moved. Bakarydes heard the *snik* of a crossbow, then a gurgling scream, then only shouts and curses as he suddenly found himself solidly walled in by his escort.

"Stop protecting me so well I can't see what's going on!" he roared.

"My lord?" came a faint but familiar voice from the darkness.

"Lozo! Where are you?"

"With Lord Volo's men, coming past the Drunken Dancer."

"Lord Volo—?" Bakarydes realized the futility of a

145

shouting match and dug in his spurs. The Swords moved to block him; he snatched at one Swordsman's reins and nearly drew his sword on a second. Before the Captain-General could actually come to blows with his escort, Lozo and his men filed out of a narrow street to the left of the house where the archer had waited. Lozo led half the troopers on foot with his sword drawn; the other half were mounted and leading their comrades' horses. As they came into the open the crossbowman slipped out of his hiding place and joined them, then a solid mass of armed horsemen loomed up behind the Banner Troop.

Bakarydes saw that the Swords were too surprised to be worrying about him. He spurred his horse through the nearest gap in their ranks, and the Banner Troop's cheers made her prance. "My thanks for your good and loyal service in guarding me," he shouted over his shoulder as he brought the mare under control.

Two of the horsemen behind Lozo were dismounting to examine the fallen man, while others lit torches. In their glow Bakarydes saw a second band of horsemen coming up behind the first with Lord Joviz at their head. Bakarydes let out a gusty sigh of relief. His luck had turned; now he had other choices besides hiding in the palace or wandering about without plan or purpose.

A moment later he saw the first band of horsemen making the open palm of respect to the leader of the second and realized he'd made a mistake. He also realized that it was an easy one to make, as Volo Deningkur dar no Tivest rode out into the open.

Lord Volo might have been Joviz's ten-years' younger brother, or indeed kin to almost any wellborn Sherrani. No doubt he found the fact that he could be dropped into a crowd of fifty and vanish useful in his intrigues. Right now Bakarydes only hoped that neither he nor Joviz had any mortal enemies on the prowl tonight.

"Honor and greetings, Volo Deningkur," said Bakarydes. "I understand that your men have become involved in tonight's troubles."

Volo nodded. "You've heard the truth. Lord Bihor's men

certainly started the fighting, but I'll admit that mine may not have been innocent in everything that's happened since. Right now, I think we want to join forces and try to sort out my men from Lord Bihor's. That will end the most serious fighting. Lord Joviz's men and the merchants' guards can deal with any thieves and fire setters who don't crawl back to their holes in time."

Sensible words, Bakarydes knew, but not free of at least one problem: who would command the combined band? In the north Bakarydes's rank would be unquestioned; on his own lands Lord Volo would lead. What about here in Koddardos where neither had a right to command more than his own men? And what if Lord Volo himself was not entirely innocent of tonight's troubles?

Bakarydes decided to gamble. Volo might have guilty knowledge at least, but he had been in Koddardos more often, longer, and more recently. To command the united band needed knowledge of the city Bakarydes didn't have, and one of the privileges of being outside his lawful area of authority was that he didn't need to pretend infallibility.

"Lord Volo, the Banner Troop and the Swords of my escort will ride with your men."

The Captain of Swords opened his mouth and raised one hand, no doubt to order a messenger off to his Captain-General asking for permission to obey Lord Volo. Theoretically he was within his rights, but Bakarydes couldn't afford to either wait for the messenger to return or leave the Swords behind.

"Forget asking for permission, Captain. Your orders were to protect me, and you certainly can't do that if you don't ride with me and Lord Volo. You're allowed to obey any man of rank if it's the best means of carrying out a previous order."

As Bakarydes turned his horse, the Swords were falling into line. He was at least slightly avenged for half a watch of drynursing, and he saw Lozo fighting not to smile as he mounted.

XVII

"HOAA! THAT MAN HASN'T HAD HIS SWORD PEACE-
bonded!" shouted Michal.

The man turned and shouted back, cupping his hands to be
heard above the mounting roar of the flames in the next street.
"I'm one of Lord Arkan's men. We didn't start this!"

"I see your badge, but right now I don't care if you serve the
Great King of the Sun and the Moon! Either peace-bond that
blade or give it up!"

"Who's going to make me?"

Michal didn't dignify the question with an answer, merely
waved four of his men forward. They grounded their staves
and advanced on Lord Arkan's swordsman with their hands on
their own weapons' hilts. The swordsman took a long look at
the odds, shrugged, and let Michal's men do their work.

The man was either a very good actor or genuinely innocent
of anything except being in the wrong quarter of Koddardos on
the wrong night. He strode off with a look of injured dignity
that would have made Michal ready to apologize if he and his
squadron hadn't already picked up a dozen bodies.

Besides, Lord Joviz's orders were strict: persons leaving the
riot area with a house, guild, or temple badge should have
their weapons peace-bonded. Anyone leaving the area without
such a badge should be disarmed entirely. By his authority as
First Magistrate, Joviz had decreed the arrest of anyone not in
his service (permanently or temporarily) who appeared in
public on the Island with a weapon not peace-bonded. This
presumably would let law-abiding citizens defend their homes
and shops, while discouraging troublemakers of all sorts from
roaming the streets.

Michal hoped Joviz had given some thought to the practical
details behind this theory, such as having enough men in the
streets outside the riot area to keep common cutpurses from
preying on unarmed or peace-bonded men on their way home.

Here on the western edge of the riot area, Michal and his fellow Harzis didn't even have enough leather thongs for peace-bonding or enough tallies to provide receipts for confiscated weapons. They'd been able to cut leather strips from the belts and clothing of the dead and a couple of abandoned saddles; the tallies were another matter. One man had already died, refusing to give up his dagger because he didn't trust Harzis to return it. Michal hoped he would be the only one.

Right now he had a more immediate problem in the form of a burning four-story building just down the street. The building stood between a brick warehouse with a tile roof and a shrine faced and roofed with slabs of granite; neither was in immediate danger. The danger was to the building's more distant neighbors on either side of the street and in the warren of sagging wooden tenements that began just beyond the far side of the street. If the fire spread into those, Michal didn't want to think about how far it might go or what it might destroy before it burned out.

Most of the windows on the two upper floors of the building were already belching flames and smoke. Michal had sent one of his men up onto each of the half-dozen nearest roofs, leading able-bodied volunteers from the quarter with buckets to wet down the roofs. What he needed, what he'd sent for, and what hadn't arrived yet was a Gifted priest from the temple of God the Craftsman to raise just enough of a breeze to carry the embers away from the tenements and toward the warehouse. Beyond the warehouse lay the river with nothing on it that burning embers could reach before they burned out but a few ships whose crews could damn well look to their own rigging tonight!

Michal was cursing slow-footed priests, slow-footed messengers, and lords who took their men away from their duty and then let them riot, when half a dozen of his men came up carrying heavy coils of rope.

"Where did you get that, Nikot?"

"From the warehouse."

"Was anyone around to . . . ?"

Nikot shook his head and Michal waved them forward. As long as nobody had been on hand to be given a tally for the confiscated rope, the matter could be dealt with later. Right now it might save a few lives and a lot of sweat if the buckets for soaking the roofs could be hauled up on ropes instead of having to be carried up stairs.

Michal couldn't see anyone moving on the smoke-hazed street that led into the riot area. He suspected that everyone who hadn't already left was dead, injured, hiding, or staying for reasons that wouldn't bear the close examination they would receive when Michal or someone else in Joviz's service rounded them up! Meanwhile, he decided to go over and do what he could to cheer up the doleful crowd of tenants who'd fled the burning building. Some of them were clutching bundles or had spare clothing draped over their shoulders, and one small girl was carrying a cat in a basket, but most of them stood to lose everything they had except their lives.

Michal had just joined the refugees when the roof of the burning building caved in. A single groan rose from all the refugees, followed by sobs. Flames and embers shot up from the building like a volcano erupting. Michal didn't waste his breath cursing; he held it as a wave of hot air swept over him. When it had passed he saw three men hurrying down the street toward him, two supporting a woman who stumbled and lurched as if she was drunk or hurt.

Two of Nikot's men led the men and woman past the burning building and Michal himself led them to the refugees. He didn't bother searching or disarming them; the three men, black as barge cleaners, slumped exhausted where they sat down, while the woman was coughing as if her lungs were half burned out. Michal sent off a man to get her some water and turned back to watch the street and the fire and wonder what had happened to the priest. Should he send another messenger, or would he need every pair of hands here to keep the fire from spreading without using magic—?

Screams from the refugees spun Michal around. Two of the men were waving knives and snatching bundles and clothing

150

from cowering people. The third man had his hand up under the woman's skirt. She was no longer coughing and had a knife in her own hand. As the man pulled out both a knife and a short lead-weighted club, the refugees scattered like sheep fleeing a wolf pack and Michal's men came running up.

In the confusion one of the thieves got clean away. Nikot threw his staff like a spear and caught the woman in the stomach. The breath *whuffed* out of her and she went over backward to be jumped on by half a score of refugees and two of Nikot's men. She promptly started screaming for mercy, something Michal hoped nobody would be in a hurry to give her.

In the confusion Michal found himself squarely in the path of the last two thieves. One of them was a full head taller and moved like a fighting man; Michal decided to take him first. The other man tossed his chief the lead-weighted club as Michal drew his sword, and the man swung before Michal had time to guard. The sword went flying out of Michal's tingling fingers and the man rushed in.

Michal sidestepped the rush while launching a kick at the man's groin. His boot only caught the man's knee a glancing blow, but that was enough to stop him and swing him around. Michal's fist caught him twice in the stomach, and on the third punch he folded and went down. Michal would have cheerfully killed the man a dozen times for his treachery and for preying on refugees but knew that he had to be captured alive in order to name his partners.

The man's fall must have been at least partly a trick; the moment Michal was within reach he rolled and kicked at the same time, sweeping Michal's feet out from under him. Michal landed on top, but he was too busy keeping the man's hands from his throat to thank the Father and the Warrior for what might still turn out to be too small a favor to save his life.

Michal was just getting ready to drive his knee into the man's groin when he saw the man's eyes widen. At the same time he heard a voice shout, "Down, Michal!"

Michal rolled off the man as the last thief struck overhand with his knife and a Harzi launched his staff at the thief. Both blows went home, although only the Harzi's struck its intended target. The thief's knife went into his leader's chest, and a moment later he was rolling beside the man, clawing at a throat crushed by the staff and wheezing his life away.

Michal stood up and brushed the street filth off his leather trousers with elaborate care. He would have been much happier if at least one of those gallows cheaters had remained alive and somewhat happier if he'd been able to kill them himself. Having been deceived as he had touched his honor rather nearly.

"Just like the man," said the staff wielder, pointing at Michal. "First I took over a thankless job to set him free for the First Magistrate's service. Now I save his life. And what does he do? Preens himself like a stallion before his favorite mare."

"Hakfor shan-Melech!"

"So my mother avers and my father believes. Oh, by the way, Master Coron's guards are in Joviz's service now, and I brought them around to relieve you here on the magistrate's orders."

"Wait. Did Joviz bring the orders to Coron himself or send a messenger?"

"A messenger, of course. I'm sure Joviz would—" Hakfor broke off. "You're not doubting *my* word, I hope?"

At this point Michal was prepared to doubt a great many things but not the word of the friend who'd succeeded him as chief of Coron's caravan guards. However—

"Not yours. But I'm not sure about the messenger. Someone could be pretending to be one of Joviz's messengers to suck you and your men into the trouble without having the law on your side and make Harzis a target—"

"I know, I know. I thought of that all myself, and so did Joviz." Hakfor reached into his belt pouch and pulled out a silver medallion with Joviz's sigil on it. "Hang it around your neck and put your right hand on it."

As Michal suspected, the medallion was bonded to Joviz's hand and seal and imprinted by the Spell of True Voices with a message from him. When his hand touched the cool silver, he seemed to hear in his mind as clearly as he could have in his ears Joviz's voice saying: "By my order, the Harzis and Sherranis sworn to Master Merchant Coron Sirotur dar Trati are entered into my service under the command of Hakfor shan-Melech Hakatsar. They may perform all work of the First Magistrate's office for which they are judged fit."

That left open the not-so-small question of who judged the fitness of Hakfor's men—which was perhaps why Joviz had ordered them into his service under the eyes of their old captain. Harzi and Sherrani alike, Michal knew most of them and had himself led all but this spring's newest recruits in the field.

Joviz, Michal decided, was a very long-sighted man—no bad thing in any Ruler and especially not tonight.

"Did Joviz say what I was to do after your men relieved mine?"

"No."

That meant either that Joviz had forgotten, sent another messenger who'd managed to lose himself, or else trusted Michal's judgment. The last notion was so flattering that Michal's pride fought and lost a brief but savage battle with his common sense.

"I'll take you around to my posts and show you the ground," he said finally. "If I haven't received any more orders by then I'll assume I'm free to act as I think best. And by the way, have you seen a priest of the Craftsman who was supposed to come here and help us keep the fire from spreading?"

Hakfor laughed. "He came with me. While you were doing your wrestling practice with that thief, the priest went up on the nearest roof and went to work, him and his apprentice."

Michal's eyes followed Hakfor's pointing finger. On the roof of the building stood a broad-shouldered figure in a short-sleeved leather tunic and leather breeches with a massive collar of what looked like copper nuggets around his neck who held a silver-mounted horn in both hands. Behind him stood an apprentice, whirling a fuming pot on a brass chain around his head, first to the left, then to the right. Every time the apprentice reversed the pot's direction, the priest blew a blast on the horn, loud enough to drown out the fire.

Michal noticed that the bucket party on the roof had backed off to the far edge, either from fear of the spells or from fear of being brained by the swinging pot. He also noted that the spell was working or at least making *something* happen to the flames. They now rose almost straight, and as Michal watched they began to lengthen and waver. Michal was reminded of a snake charmer captivating a nest of Kamini fireworms.

"Why can't he raise buckets of water and drop them on the roofs or even on the fire?" asked Michal.

Hakfor shrugged. "I asked the same thing. I may have understood one word in four of the man's answer. It seems that you're working *with* nature if you change the course of something without changing its tendency, like making a flame rise to the east instead of the west. It's still rising. If you try to raise something that has a natural tendency to fall, like a bucket of water, you're working against nature, and either he can't or he won't or he shouldn't do that.

"Oh well, it could be worse. If he'd been a priest of the Giver of Knowledge, I'd have only understood one word in ten."

Michal grunted agreement and led Hakfor off on his tour of the position. By the time the two captains returned, the priest's spell was definitely working. The flames were streaming toward the river, and nearly all the embers with them.

"Now if the priest's breath just holds out . . ." said Michal. "Better send some men into the warehouse and see if there's anything there that will burn. The building itself is safe, but it could get hot as a bake oven inside if a lot of burning bits fall on the roof. Any messages or orders from Joviz, Nikot?"

"No, Captain."

"Then I think we'd better move in."

"The Father and the Warrior guard you, Michal."

"And you, Hakfor."

They gripped shoulders, then Michal led his men off. The Warrior's curse lay without question on disobedient soldiers,

154

but neither did He look with favor on a soldier who simply sat about and waited for orders. When no orders were forthcoming but the battle wasn't over, a worthy follower of the Warrior was supposed to get up off his arse and do *something*.

The clatter and jingle of approaching horsemen made Bakarydes look around the little square to see if it was fit for defense in case the newcomers were hostile. A quick look reassured him.

Between Lord Volo's men, the Banner Troop, and the Swords of Sherran, the number of armed mounted men in the square was enough to beat off any likely attack by sheer weight of numbers. In addition, Volo's captains knew their business; they'd been swift to post archers on commanding roofs. Bakarydes was glad to see this. He knew very little of this unwholesome business of fighting in narrow streets with walls all around, and he suspected the Captain of Swords of knowing little more.

If it hadn't been for the glow of burning buildings that silhouetted the archers when they moved, Bakarydes would have been well content. As it was, too much of the good work done tonight in arresting or slaying troublemakers and protecting the law-abiding could be undone by the spreading flames.

The hoofbeats and harness jingle grew louder; someone shouted a challenge. A commanding shout replied, then the guard called, "Pass, Your Excellency."

Lord Joviz rode into the square, and Bakarydes now saw him and Volo side by side for the first time. They might indeed have been close kin, although Volo was broader across the shoulders and also thicker through the belly. He hadn't run to fat, still less to dissipation, but it was well known that intrigue wasn't his only pleasure in life.

"Well met, Lord Joviz," called Volo.

"That's yet to be proved," Joviz replied.

In the silence following this remark, Bakarydes noticed that the mouth of one alley into the square was apparently out of any archer's sight and unguarded on the ground as well. A silent hand signal sent four Banner troopers to picket the alley, enough to hold it against anything from the demon steed of

Krusevo to the three drunken scholars of the song. What was more, they obeyed quickly and without argument, which was more than he could have trusted the Swords to do. Bakarydes was not anxious to have either Volo or Joviz guess what the Swords' real orders were.

"If we are ill met," said Volo at last, "then tell me how so that I may seek a remedy."

"We can best seek the remedy together," replied Joviz. "We must enter the area where the fire setters have been at work and remove any who would impede the work of putting out the fires."

"Indeed, the Captain-General and I were about to begin that very enterprise."

Bakarydes decided to keep his mouth shut and let Volo go on braiding rope for himself. After all, he did not *have* to be hanged afterward.

"Without thinking of protecting your rear? A bold stroke." Bakarydes decided that Joviz would need no help in setting a noose for Lord Volo, once enough rope was available. He also appreciated the magistrate's tact in not criticizing too harshly a plan that was supposed to be partly of the Captain-General's devising. Bakarydes knew that he was a horse in a bog in Koddardos tonight, but he would be happier if the rest of the world didn't learn it.

"Not as bold as all that. We hoped to be able to wait for the soldiers from Thunder Hill. Then the Captain-General could have led them in blockading the area of the fires while I led my men in to subdue it."

"You knew that the soldiers were on the way?"

"No, but we were sure that neither you nor the garrison's officers are fools. This has also been a bad night for messengers going astray."

Joviz smiled briefly, acknowledging Volo's hit. "The garrison will be called out if necessary. But I do not think half-trained recruits and pensioned veterans are the best men for firewatching and riot duty. I intend to hold the line around the fires with the Watchmen and Harzis of my service. Then you may indeed lead your men into the area of the fires and bring it back under the authority of the Throne. My captains can hold the margin without further assistance, so my guards and I will ride with you."

Volo's face showed no sign of irritation at this plain hint that Joviz did not trust him. Instead he shrugged. "That is the same plan under another name, and I do not quarrel with it. However, may I ask for the rearming of some of my men who were sent away peace-bonded?" He held up a hand as if Joviz had begun a protest. "No, I do not doubt your Harzis and Watchmen. It is merely that the more strength we can bring with us, the better."

"Certainly. Only I think it best that we take no more men than we can lead ourselves." Joviz smiled. "Unless you have changed since you were in the army and now let your captains go on ahead of you . . . ?"

Volo actually laughed, and Bakarydes wanted to. It was as obvious as the Great Stallion's member that Joviz didn't trust Volo out of his sight or Volo's captains out of their lord's. But by playing on Volo's pride in his old army reputation—that of a man who always led from in front whether he should or not—Joviz had quenched that particular ember before it could start any more fires.

Not to mention that going into the area of the fires with insufficient strength was sure to be dangerous. Letting some of Volo's captains go unpunished for whatever they might have done or left undone to cause tonight's troubles might not be.

Joviz gave an order and four of his guards rode off in different directions. The rest maneuvered their horses until they were two or even three deep around Joviz and he was barely visible.

This time Bakarydes did laugh. It was some consolation to discover that it did not need a queen's good intentions for a chief to have men so intent on their duty of protecting him that he might find it hard to do his duty of leading.

XVIII

FIVE STREETS TO THE EAST AND FOUR STREETS TO THE NORTH was a distance that under other circumstances Michal could have walked in the time it took to let a horse breathe after a hard gallop. Tonight it seemed as long as a journey from Koddardos to Hierandos along the River High Road. Every building had to be searched from roof to cellar; the law-abiding protected; the helpless, sick, or hurt aided; the suspicious rounded up and escorted to where they could do no harm; and the outright criminals dealt with as briskly as possible.

So far there'd been only one of the last: a man caught rifling a shop with the corpse of the shopkeeper bleeding at his feet. No one would say a word about his prompt dispatch, which was just as well. Michal knew he was stretching his authority to the limit by taking his men into the riot area to clear it. If he left a trail of even the most flagrantly guilty corpses behind him, he might turn out to have gone too far. Fortunately, except for that fool in the shop (and the Father grant that he had died before he'd bred any equally foolish sons!), no one seemed disposed to provoke the wrath of fivescore armed Harzis.

Michal was keeping his men together not only because they were more formidable that way, but also to keep the less experienced ones from getting lost and to have extra hands ready for any work that needed doing. He'd already been able to clear an alley of an overturned cart with a single order that sent the dozen nearest men running to lift it bodily and haul it out into the street.

As they turned the corner into what a marker stone said was the Street of the Hammer, Michal knew he'd most likely brought his men as far as they would come tonight. The roofs on the near side of the street were lined with men and women dousing falling embers with buckets of water or beating them out with wet blankets. On the other side of the street rose an old square of buildings, faces to the streets and backs to a common courtyard or garden. Half the buildings facing Michal were burning, two had already collapsed, and as Michal watched, flames shot out of a window in yet another house. Through gaps in the smoke pouring up from the buildings facing the street, Michal saw that buildings on at least two more sides of the square were also burning.

Here on the Street of the Hammer, the square of old and mostly wooden buildings faced stone and brick ones that were almost as good as a firebreak. If the people on the roofs kept at their work, everything beyond the firebreak was likely to be safe enough. Everything in the square itself was as good as doomed. Nor could Michal see, in the smoke and the glare, how far back the wooden buildings stretched.

Michal called a halt and sent parties off down the street to either side of the burning square; other Harzis scurried up the stairs to the various roofs to see if the people needed any help. This stripped Michal of nearly half his men and the most experienced ones, so he gathered the rest where he could keep them under his eye. With luck the fire fighters on the roofs wouldn't need much help, and the men he'd sent up there would be back down soon.

He'd pulled off his helmet and was pulling off his mail shirt when he heard someone calling.

"Captain! Captain Michal!"

It was Ulev shan-Bilat, the leader of the men he'd sent down the south side of the square, black faced as a smith and leading a man with pale eyes staring out of an even blacker face. The man's mouth kept opening and shutting but no words that Michal could recognize came out.

"His wife's caught under a collapsed stairway, I think. At least there's one in the building he was pointing to."

"Is the building on fire?"

Ulev nodded. Michal shrugged. "Then she's probably already dead. I can't risk our men on a slim chance—"

The man whimpered, then shouted, "No! No! Stones between her and fire—" He babbled on until Michal couldn't decide whether he was addled in his wits by the disaster or simply didn't speak Sherrani well.

At last Michal thought he had a picture of what had happened: a stone staircase that by incredible good luck had collapsed so that the man's wife was trapped but not crushed and for the moment protected from the worst of the heat. If that was so, it just might be possible to dig her out before anything more came down on top of her or the heat became too deadly. And the alternative was leaving her to be slowly roasted alive.

Michal nodded. "We'll do what we can." He ignored the man's gape-jawed grin and started giving orders. "Zemer, run back to where we left the priest and bring him up. We may need him to keep off the heat. Yafshi, run and shout to the people on the roof that we need a Healer and extra hands with buckets. Ulev, were all your men safe?"

Ulev nodded. "I had two trying to find the woman and two more fetching water while the others stood guard."

"Good. I'll come with you, then we can send the two sentries out to guide the priest when he comes."

The man tried to embrace Michal, who gently pulled his arms away. "Thank me after there's something to thank me for." Michal had never felt for a woman what this man obviously felt for his wife, but he'd lost a sister to fever and two blood brothers to Momaks. He wasn't utterly blind or deaf to what the man must be enduring.

He finished pulling off his mail shirt and laid it on the pavement beside his helmet. Armor now only promised to make a hot job still hotter.

"Come on."

The heat made him feel as if he were on an anvil with the blacksmith hammering away at him. On the far side of the street, the wooden shutters over all the windows were already black with soot; Michal hoped they weren't starting to char. The cobblestones of the street caught the heat and threw it back like the griddle in the Full Trough's kitchen, and Michal wondered when he was going to start turning brown and curling up at the edges like one of Niko's flatcakes. He wished he'd remembered to soak his face and clothing before starting down the street and hoped his forgetting it didn't prove he wasn't in command of himself. The flames would not gossip as his men would, but they would have far less mercy.

At least the dry wood of the old buildings here was burning without much smoke, and what there was mostly rose straight up to shut out the sky without coming anywhere near the street level. So Michal saw his men long before he could make himself heard over the roar of the fire. His companion's wild scream and dash forward told him that the Harzis had found the trapped woman.

She lay in an ancient building pieced together of bricks, stone, and timber, which explained how part of it had fallen while the rest still stood. The top floor was a mass of flames, but where the woman lay it was still no more than hot. It would be hotter very soon, probably before they could move the woman. A massive stone section of the stairway had come down on her left leg, pinning her firmly in place but leaning on the wall so that it hadn't fallen all the way to crush her. Seeing the blood on the woman's trousers, Michal realized that she would probably lose her leg. Indeed, it might be wiser to cut it off straight away and not even try to move the stairs, which must weigh the better part of a greatstone and offered places to grip for only a fraction of the men needed to lift it.

Still, there were such things as levers—and the man was holding his wife's head against his chest in a way that clearly said they'd have to kill him before they either abandoned her or hurt her any more. Michal sent two Harzis off to escort the priest, relieved one of the sentries himself, and sent the other and the two water bearers off to find something that might serve for a lever. Then he began to pace up and down, hoping that something or someone would turn up to save him from the need to die at his post merely to avoid looking like a man who could not produce magical rescues to order.

The three lever hunters returned with a variety of sticks of furniture, none of which looked heavy enough to move a baby's cradle, let alone that mass of stone. Michal was about to tell them as much when he saw the priest scurrying toward him, his head wrapped in wet cloths against the heat. Behind the priest came half a dozen Sherrani and four Harzis similarly dressed, most of them carrying buckets of water or wet blankets. As the priest came closer, Michal saw that he carried a large sack over his shoulder, plain leather without the sigil of the Craftsman on it. Several wooden handles stuck out of the sack.

Michal looked a question. "Barring a miracle, this is work for a stonemason," replied the priest. Michal looked another question. "I was a stonemason before I discovered my Gift and entered the temple of the Craftsman," the man added. "Not a bad mason, either, if I do say so myself. Maybe even good enough to do what needs to be done here." He unslung the sack and set it down with a clinking thud, then started hauling out mallets, hammers, chisels, and wedges of various sizes.

At this point Michal, waiting for the priest to select his unpriestly tools, definitely felt like a teat on a stallion. He also knew he would as soon have interrupted the High Priest of the Father in the middle of a sacrifice as this priest in the middle of his work.

At last the priest came up with a hammer and a selection of chisels that seemed to suit him. He dropped the rest of his tools on the cobblestones, except for a couple of wedges that he stuck in his belt. Then he advanced on the stone slab, and if he'd been the Father Himself coming to pass a judgment people couldn't have cleared a path for him much more quickly. Of those who could move, only Michal and the woman's husband were close when the first hammer blow gouged stone chips out of the stairs.

Five blows and the priest pulled out a wedge and stuck it into the crack. Four more blows and a slab of stone the size of a newborn kid fell with a crash. The section of stairs shifted slightly, and Michal saw blood start from the woman's dust-caked lips as she bit them. She was silent, however, and even her husband let out only a faint moan.

The priest stepped back and took a look at the stairs. Then he looked up at the building above, and Michal saw his hands tighten on the hammer and chisel.

"What is it?"

"See those cracks in the wall?"

Michal didn't, but he wasn't going to argue. "What of them?"

"The slab we have to move could be the only thing holding the wall up. If we move it off the woman, the wall may come down on whoever's moving it."

"Will one man be enough to move it if you work on it some more?" Michal hated to have to say this, but all the gods he'd ever seen worshipped anywhere couldn't have let him do otherwise.

"Not a man your size. Not even—no, wait." The priest stepped up to the stone, knelt, and ran his hands over it as if it were a fine horse. "If I crack off one more piece, two men should be able to roll it enough so that two more can pull the woman out. Then with God's help we can all be clear before the wall comes down or the fire gets closer."

The last seemed a greater danger than the stones. The flames were working their way toward the ground, and Michal felt his eyeballs ready to pop and melt in their sockets. The water poured on the woman earlier was rising in little whorls of steam. Michal hardly dared breathe for fear of crisping throat and lungs, but—

"With the help of the Father and the Warrior, I will do what I can for your kin if—they need help."

"I'll do the same for anyone you leave behind, Harzi."

Michal motioned the two nearest men to squat by the woman, low enough to grasp her arms but ready to leap up and backward. The woman's husband stared at them numbly; he was clearly past being of any use. Ulev motioned the rest of the people back and came up beside Michal; together they put their shoulders against the stone. It was already hot enough for them to feel the heat through their dampened wool tunics.

The priest squatted, felt the stone again, and tapped three or four times with the hammer while pressing his ear against the stone. Then he picked up the chisel, rested one end in a shallow groove in the stone, muttered what sounded less like a prayer than a curse on the stone if it didn't split correctly, and swung the hammer.

The slab of stone that fell this time was the size of a full-grown goat. Michal felt the stairs begin to rock back and forth, dug in his boots, and pushed hard as they rocked back. The woman screamed, her husband howled like a madman, gravel rattled as the woman was dragged across it, then everyone seemed to shout at once, "She's free!"

Michal felt the stairs rocking toward him, shouted, "Get out of here, you—!" to the priest, then felt the stairs start to slide in a way he knew no human power could hold back. He leaped away, gripping Ulev by one arm and the collar of his tunic. They went over backward into a tangle of arms and legs on the cobblestones for a moment, then sprang up in time to see the priest scramble out from under the slab of stairway just before it crashed down where the woman had been lying.

Michal looked up, saw cracks wide enough to hold a man's fist in the wall, and shouted a warning. The priest was just taking his first step backward when the wall collapsed, splitting halfway down. The lower part fell straight out in a single slab; the upper part came down in a rain of bricks, burning timbers, floorboards, and the hot coals that alone remained of the furniture on the upper floors.

Altogether, enough material to build a small cottage fell on the priest. By the time Michal could take his first step backward, the blood oozing from under the stones was already congealing in the fierce heat.

Michal didn't remember how or in what order he and his men retreated from the burning street, only that they all did it safely. He remembered or thought he remembered ordering someone to go on ahead and summon a Healer for the woman. Afterward Ulev said that he'd croaked something that might have been intended to be an order four or five times, but as it was no more sensible to human ears than the mating call of a bullfrog and they were all in some haste . . .

At last Michal was aware that there were other men and women and not just glare and heat and smoke all around him. Someone was pushing a leather bottle of water into his hands. As he drank, a voice from above said, "Well done, Captain."

Michal drank down the rest of the bottle except for what he splashed over his hands and face, then looked up. The First Magistrate was sitting on his big chestnut mare who was pecking and whinnying nervously at the fires in spite of the two Watchmen holding her head. Finally Joviz dismounted and came over to Michal.

Michal saluted. "I am to blame, my lord, if I disobeyed any orders of yours by taking my men toward the fires. But I had not been told to do otherwise at the time Master Coron's men relieved mine. It seemed best—"

A flickering change of Joviz's expression made Michal look to where the magistrate's eyes were aimed. Lord Volo was standing at the head of a half-score of his men, and more were riding up and dismounting, unhooking well-stuffed bread bags and dripping water bottles from their saddles. Michal nodded and continued as loudly as his parched throat could manage.

"—to fulfill our oaths as the First Magistrate's Harzis to go where lives were in the most danger."

"Certainly you did well," said Lord Volo. Another change of expression on Joviz's face. "You saved that woman at the risk of your life. Honor should be done you for that, great honor."

Michal saw the eyebrows of those of his men who still had any rise. He would have smiled, but even the most miserly movement made the skin of his face feel ready to crack and flake off in pieces.

There were half a score of witnesses to the woman's rescue, but Michal could not have claimed the honor of it had there been none at all. He'd sworn to make the life of the priest's kin easier, and he'd be foresworn at the outset if he robbed the dead man of honor. In the eyes of the Father and the Warrior, the priest was a man who'd fought under his command; breaking an oath to any such was an abomination.

Besides, a child could have seen that there wasn't the best

will between the First Magistrate, Michal's sworn lord, and Volo, a fine-honed schemer if there ever was one. When robbing a dead man of glory would also thrust Michal and his men straight into the middle of *that* quarrel—Michal hoped he'd be dead before he was ever so great a fool!

"Forgive those who have given me a name I don't deserve, my lords. I only led the man who really did the work to the place where he did it. He's—he was—a priest of God the Craftsman, and he's still there under half the house. Without him . . ."

"Do you know his name?" asked Joviz before Volo could even open his mouth.

Michal had his own mouth open before he realized that he'd never known the priest's name. Fortunately he was saved from having to admit this by someone shouting from the crowd.

"Valko Godinur. My sister married the journeyman who took over his shop after he acknowledged his Gift and went to the temple."

Joviz repeated the name, nodded, and looked at Michal. "The same," said Michal, as intelligently as he could. "I swore to aid his kin as much as I could, so if anyone knows where they are . . ."

"I'll find out," said Joviz briskly. "Meanwhile, Captain, you do have some reward coming, you and the men who followed you. I'll start by having you taken to the hospital at the First Temple of the Mother."

Michal had been thinking of asking for enough beer to properly wet his men's throats, but if his own was any guide there wasn't that much beer in all Koddardos. Besides, he'd hardly be worth his captain's shoulder cord if he assumed that none of them had hurts that needed tending, and the Healers of the First Temple of the Mother were the best in Koddardos likely to be available by now. The temples and shrines of the Healer would surely have been filled to overflowing long since.

"Thank you, my lord. I'll stay here until the whole squadron is relieved." He shifted his feet slightly apart and stared at Joviz, daring him to give any other order. "I'll start sending off the men, though." He rattled off the names of the men he'd seen with burns or minor wounds, hoping that if he forgot anyone he wouldn't be reminded too loudly. Mistakes made by a Magistrate's Harzi reflected ill on all other Harzis, and had a far bigger audience than those made guarding caravans. Far too many Sherrani always remembered a Harzi's mistakes far better than any good he did.

"As you wish, Captain," said Joviz. He seemed to be looking around for Volo, and as Michal looked also he saw why. Volo's men were keeping their distance from Joviz, like children of a stern father who still didn't dare defy him by actually running off. Lord Volo himself was sitting his saddle as if he had a sore in his crotch.

As Michal saw his men led off, he realized that he'd probably made an enemy of Lord Volo. Maybe he should have claimed at least a little of Valko Godinur's honor to protect himself?

Maybe, and if the Great Squid had only four arms it would be a dog. Neither the Father nor the Warrior protected liars, and a lie itself was seldom as much protection as a good mail shirt and steel kept sharp and close to hand.

XIX

"AND OF THY INFINITE GOODNESS, O GRACIOUS MOTHER, we ask Thee to comfort and succor all who suffered in last night's riot. We beseech Thee to move the hearts of all in Koddardos to feed the hungry, clothe the naked, shelter the homeless, assist the injured, and give strength to all of us to rebuild what has been destroyed."

A flute gave the note, and the crowd gathered for the morning prayers to God the Mother chanted, "Be it according to Thy will, Most Gracious Mother."

"We beseech Thee, in Thy infinite compassion, to comfort the bereaved, and grant to those who died the sight of Thy True Face."

"Be it according to Thy will, Most Gracious Mother."

167

To a flute accompaniment, the Reverend Lady Lilka spoke the Prayer for the Day.

"Most Holy Mother, Thou hast given us this day for our use. Grant to us the wisdom to do good work this day, neither wasting the time with trifles nor filling it with useless tasks. By Thy mercy may we refrain from doing evil to ourselves or harm to others, this day and always."

"Be it according to Thy will, Most Gracious Mother."

The flutes fell silent; the Reverend Lady turned and faced the hall, raising her arms and making the sign of blessing.

"Go with God's blessing and use well this day, God's gift."

The drums beat three times slowly, the flutes gave a final note and died away, then the drums beat the brisk rhythm that signaled the end of the service. Everyone began to rise from their knees, swiftly or otherwise according to their age and how much sleep they'd had the night before. Lilka was glad she'd been leading the prayers and able to stand; at her age she found it easier to stand than to kneel.

Lilka waited until the ordinary worshippers and unconsecrated workers not on duty had left, then walked to the door leading into the temple compound. She forced herself to walk as briskly as usual, since a few fools might take her dragging feet as an evil omen and many not so foolish might fear that the First Priestess was losing her strength. Then the curse of intrigue and conspiracy might descend on the temple of the Mother, and Lilka would stand until her heart burst to prevent that.

The past night's riot had at least one blessing: no one tried to speak on the way out of the hall. It was an unwritten rule that no one laid business or even pleasantries before the First Priestess until after she'd broken her fast, but there were always a few too new to the temple, too weak of memory, or too certain that rules meant for others didn't bind them.

Today, at least, everyone except the incorrigibly lazy had urgent work to do and knew it; the danger was not people stopping to ask foolish questions but a whole hallful of people trying to get out the same two doors at the same time. A few times Lilka wished she wore soldier's boots to apply to the shins or toes of people who crowded her too closely, but mostly the hall emptied itself in good order and almost in good time.

Lilka turned at once toward the hospital where the most urgent work was being done. Not as much as she feared, by God's mercy—fewer than a hundred people had walked or been carried in, and that included a score of the First Magistrate's Harzis. Nor had most of those hundred men been gravely hurt.

That was as well. The hospitals of Koddardos's three temples of God the Healer were intended either to train apprentice Healers or care for the desperately ill and injured. The Healer's shrines and those of the Mother took care of minor injuries and illnesses and gave preventive care, while the hospitals of the temples of the Mother took in those needing extended care. When really large numbers of people needed treatment all at once, they went to the hospitals of the Mother whose Healers decided whether they should remain, be sent to a temple of the Healer, be treated and sent home, or be given a draught to ease their dying.

Since the First Priestess of the Healer and the First Magistrate had not asked Lady Lilka to set that plan afoot, the temples and shrines of the Healer must have been equal to taking care of most of the injured. In that case, the riot had probably cost more in property and reputations than in shed blood and broken bones.

As Lilka reached the hospital entrance, she heard the familiar din of clattering vessels and Healers' chanted spells. She also heard the voice of Sirote Tashinura, the Chief Healer, rising above all the other noises if not quite drowning them out.

"—and you're going to sit there until I've finished oiling your burns and bandaging your shoulder. Otherwise I'll declare you needing a bed and have you clapped into it—"

"You and which regiment, wo— Reverend Mistress?" The voice was harsh, masculine, and unmistakably Harzi accented.

"The temple has enough able-bodied servants to—"

"Not enough to keep me or any of my men here if they want to leave, Reverend Mistress. And if you don't let me talk to them now I'll suggest that's exactly what they ought to do."

169

Lilka frowned. Sirote Tashinura was one of the finest Healers of people's bodies the First Priestess had ever known, but Sirote paid little heed to her patients' minds and none to their feelings. It was said that some of them got well because Death itself feared her tongue.

Lilka stepped through the hospital door into the outer chamber reserved for those not needing a bed. Stepping around two servants pushing a cart loaded with plates of soup and bread, she approached Mistress Sirote.

The Healer was sitting on the scarred black table she'd brought with her when she entered the temple, spreading oil on the bare chest of a Harzi who wore trousers and boots which smelled of smoke, and a venomous look. Lilka noted that he was taller than the average Harzi, if just as thickset, and that the tunic hung over a chair bore a captain's shoulder cord and also the badge of the First Magistrate. She raised a hand.

"Wait, Mistress Sirote. Is this Captain Michal shan-Ouvram who did such good work last night? No, I'm not trying to take honor away from Reverend Valko," she added, as the captain looked even less pleasant. "But you did much else, you and your men, and a good many other people in Koddardos owe you their lives."

"Lord Joviz thinks something of the kind," said Michal. "He had my hurt men sent here. I came to visit them as soon as my squadron went off duty. I never expected I'd have to run the gauntlet of this old—of this stubborn Healer. Damn it, I'm not hurt!"

"Maybe a Harzi would say he isn't hurt," said Sirote. "*I* say that he has a sprained shoulder and a good many small burns that will hurt less if they're oiled, not to mention a singed face and hands. I would be neglecting *my* duty if I sent one of Lord Joviz's best captains back to duty without using my skills on him. At the very least, he will sleep ill tonight if nothing is done."

Michal looked ready to boil over like a neglected stew pot. Lilka smiled. "Captain, you would do well to submit to Mistress Sirote's skills. Even I, the First Priestess, would submit to her in a matter of Healing.

"However, I understand your eagerness to return to duty. We shall not keep you, and if you do not make brawls before the sick and the hurt and the Face of the Mother you can take with you any of your men who say they are fit for duty." Sirote Tashinura looked stricken, but the expression on Lilka's face silenced her as thoroughly as it did the Harzi.

Finally Captain Michal nodded, although he still looked as pleasant as a wild white bull of the plains about to charge. "I will keep the peace and submit to Mistress Sirote's judgment of my hurts. Only don't take all day, Reverend Mistress. If my men perish of boredom here—"

Lilka turned away to hide a smile at both the Harzi's determination and Sirote Tashinura's glare. Her sympathies lay more with the Harzi, for all his harsh manners. Anyone who did not understand a Harzi's pride in enduring pain and being able to perform his sworn duty in spite of it had no business trying to heal even a single raw youth, let alone an experienced captain and a score of his men.

Yet she could not reproach Sirote for her sharp tongue, not in front of the Harzi. If she did this, Sirote would still give of her best as a Healer, but her position would be weakened in the hospital, where her sharp tongue had made enemies. Once more the curse of intrigue had to be kept from descending on the Mother's temple. . . .

And speaking of intrigue—Harzis were normally as quick to make much of their deeds as they were to make light of their hurts. What had caused Captain Michal to dismiss what was by all reports an excellent night's work by him and his men? Did the First Magistrate or Michal have enemies best not made jealous? If so, who were they? At least the ignorant fear of Harzis as child reavers was not a problem in Koddardos, God be thanked.

Lilka shook her head and turned for the door. If her thoughts were taking that course, perhaps the curse of intrigue had already descended and she had brought it. Yet how could she do her duty to the First Temple if she did not know of everything that might affect its safety—which surely included the rivalries of those lords who had brought young armies to

Koddardos? Where was the line that divided worthy innocence from foolish ignorance?

Did anyone know, save God?

If God made intriguers, God also made those who are generous in time of need. When Lilka returned to her chambers, she discovered that the Treasurer and her clerks had finished tallying the morning's offerings and sorting the letters accompanying them. The tallies filled two bronze bowls instead of the usual one, and the pile of letters was three fingers thick.

Atop the pile lay a wax tablet from the Treasurer with an offer to reply to most of the letters herself, leaving the Reverend Lady the lesser burden of answering only the most important ones. For in this time of trouble the First Priestess should spare herself—

Lilka did not spare a few pungently phrased thoughts about the Treasurer. She felt like throwing the tablet across the room. Then she stopped to think. The Treasurer's offer was certainly ill phrased, and if Lilka accepted it, most of the letters would just be added to the burden of the Treasurer's already over-worked clerks. Some officers of the temple tried to do every-thing themselves; the Treasurer not only didn't spare herself, she drove her clerks to the limit as well. By the mercy of God nothing had gone badly awry in the Treasury as yet.

Also, Lilka did not entirely trust the Treasurer's judgment as to who could safely be thanked by an officer of the temple and who would be insulted if the reply came from anyone but the First Priestess. The Treasurer was a most unworldly servant of the Mother to hold her post—or perhaps she saw the world only as a place from which gold and silver came and food, clothing, and baths went out. . . .

Still, if Sherran was entering a time of troubles, the temples of the Mother would need more offerings than ever to do their work. If the offerings came in, the First Priestess could find herself spending the greater part of her time writing politely phrased letters of thanks—a task any merchant's daughter who'd memorized a book of etiquette could do. If the offerings did not come in—but Lilka refused to indulge in nightmares while awake.

She prayed that God would spare Sherran a time of troubles in which such decisions would have to be made by anyone. Then she put the wax tablet to one side and pulled the two topmost letters from the pile toward her. They were from the palace and from the First Magistrate, and she would answer those herself if the First Temple were about to be swallowed up by the serpent of Belozal Wormsbane!

The letter from the First Magistrate was in the handwriting of his Secretary Lanach Tashinur. No surprise in that; the First Magistrate had been not only up but in the saddle all night. Nor was there any surprise in the contents—a simple accounting of the money sent to the First Temple: how much as a regular offering, how much as a special offering, how much for the Healing of the Harzis, and so on.

Trust Joviz and Lanach to keep such matters in order, though the world were falling about their ears. The only surprise would have been if they hadn't. She slit open the letter from the palace.

No surprises in most of this letter, either, apart from the size of the offering. Kantela must have either found the Privy Purse fatter than she'd expected or else decided that the need was too great for close reckoning. The conclusion made Lilka drop her knife and purse her lips.

"This offering is made jointly in the name of Kantela, Queen of Sherran, and Bakarydes Linzur dar no Benye, Captain-General of the North in the army of Sherran."

The lip-pursing turned into a soundless whistle. Nine veyselas out of ten in such an offering had to come from Kantela, if not nineteen out of twenty. Bakarydes couldn't have raised a quarter of such a sum without selling everything he owned except his horse and war gear.

Yet Kantela must have known that Bakarydes wanted to help the victims of a situation he'd had to stand by and watch, helpless to prevent, nearly helpless to remedy. So she'd made the offering in both their names, so that Bakarydes could at

173

least appear to have done something. He would receive honor he certainly deserved, even if not for his work last night.

But—Bakarydes was notorious for his pride in the fact that he'd fought his way to the captain-generalship without help from anyone except his family, and lately not even from them. He'd earned everything he'd won. And now this . . .

Lilka was as sure as if she'd actually seen them bedded together that Kantela and Bakarydes were lovers. Until now she'd listened to those rumors with half an ear, knowing that rumor could make lovers of two people who barely knew each other's names. Nor had it seemed very important. If they were not lovers, Bakarydes was still sufficiently welcome in the palace, whatever the reason, that Kantela was likely to be receiving the benefit of his sound and honest advice. If they were, he was even more likely to be remaining by her side and filling that empty place at her council table—something Kantela needed filled far worse than her bed.

Now Lilka had no more doubts. Kantela would not have made such an offering for someone bound to her by no more than ties of wise counsel. But Lilka would also have wagered the entire sum that Bakarydes's pride would not have let him accept it, unless—had Kantela been unwise enough to make the joint offering without telling Bakarydes? Lilka decided to send a discreet message to Kantela alone with her thanks and that very question more politely phrased. If Kantela had been unwise, thanking them together would whip up Bakarydes's pride until he might do or say something foolish.

She drew a clean wax tablet toward her and was reaching for a stylus when a cough reached her ears and the smell of hot food reached her nose. She turned. Bitrino Jankura stood beside the desk, one hand resting on the handle of a cart laden with covered dishes.

"Reverend Lady, have you eaten since last night?"

Lilka hesitated, and the hesitation let the cat out of the bag. The steward frowned and began pulling covers off plates and bowls. Steam and appetizing smells rose from sausages, fried vegetables, flatcakes, boiled eggs, and honey bread with nuts.

"Reverend Lady, God gave us food for the nourishment of

our bodies that they may be fit to perform those duties that are assigned to them."

It occurred to Lilka for at least the fiftieth time that this homily was the midden pit complaining of the musk goat's smell. The steward was an immensely tall woman, who might have been handsome in an austere fashion if she hadn't always looked as if she hadn't eaten for a week. Certainly she fed five hundred people a day—and fed them well, too—without ever allowing herself to sit down and eat a proper meal.

"This is true indeed," said Lilka. "Therefore I ask you to join me in the Blessing over the Food and in the meal itself. You've brought enough for six landsmen or even perhaps one sailor. Surely you aren't plotting to kill me with overeating?"

The steward frowned again, and Lilka realized that jests about plotting might not make very agreeable hearing, and that Bitrino Jankura had little sense of humor anyway. "Forgive me, but I doubt if you have any duties that won't allow you to join me in breaking our fast. If you do, tell me and I'll have someone else perform them."

"As you wish, Reverend Lady."

Lilka rose and bowed her head. "Most Gracious Mother, we thank Thee for Thy precious gift of food. Give us, we beseech Thee, the wisdom to use it, not abuse it, at this and every meal."

Silently she added a prayer of her own, "God, grant that Bakarydes is the man Kantela so greatly needs, the man she can laugh with."

XX

THE FIRST MAGISTRATE CONSIDERED REMAINING SEATED when Lord Volo entered, but quickly rejected the notion. The man was only under suspicion of criminal conduct, and petty slights accomplished nothing in great matters. Joviz would have been interested to hear the reasoning of anyone who thought last night's riot was no great matter.

He doubted that their arguments would have satisfied Izrunarko or even a petty lord's tax clerk.

The two doors of the chamber were already open; at Lanach Tashinur's announcement of his name Lord Volo strode through. Joviz rose; they bowed simultaneously and to the same angle. This was a discourtesy, since his office gave Joviz a higher rank in Koddardos than Volo, but so slight a one that Joviz saw no reason to regret rising.

It did not leave him in the most charitable mind toward the man, however, nor did Volo's next words improve matters.

"Your secretary seems determined to remain within hearing," said Volo. "I thought this meeting was to be private."

"Lanach Tashinur is under the Spell of Discretion and sits where he does by my order," replied the First Magistrate. "Nor will I order him to depart."

Volo managed to look around the room without moving more than his eyes, which were still red from smoke and lack of sleep. His silence and assured stance, along with his flawlessly cut tunic and trousers, compelled Joviz's grudging respect. No one could have told that Volo had done anything more improper last night than drink too much Figuri wine.

"Volo Deningkur, we must deal with the people responsible for last night's riot in such a way that nothing like that will happen again."

"That is in God's hands, is it not?" said Volo. "A city altogether without riots would be a city whose people had milk in their veins instead of blood, I should think."

"I do not speak of riots caused by ill-timed cold porridge or hot words, Volo Deningkur. I speak of riots caused by the men of great and small lords, brought to Koddardos—" he rejected the phrase, "for reasons doubtful in the eyes of God and man alike," in favor of "—and then left without proper occupation."

"My men do not break discipline no matter where they are!" said Volo. Obviously the pride of a man who still thought of himself as a soldier was touched.

Just as obviously, he was telling the truth about the discipline of his men. They'd come to his command like a

176

pack of good hunting dogs when the master whistles. They would have done good work in sorting out the riot area, too, if Captain Michal hadn't been thinking ahead of his orders—and God be thanked that he had!

It would be hard enough to deal with Volo now, when he was only under grave suspicion of giving unlawful orders; it was a near-certainty that his well-disciplined men wouldn't have fought Lord Bihor's without such orders. If the First Magistrate had also been under an obligation to Volo's men for restoring order in Koddardos, it would have been damned near impossible to deal with their lord.

"Your men did their work well, insofar as they were called on to work at all."

"They did. And in that work eight of them were killed, two by common thieves after being disarmed by your Harzis. Twenty-five more were hurt."

Joviz left unspoken the reply, "Thirty of Bihor's men are dead and more than a hundred hurt, some maimed for life." He shrugged slightly. "At the time the two were disarmed, my men did not think the riot would go on so long that all the scum of Koddardos would have a chance to rise to the surface and make a stench in the nostrils of honest men. I think some arrangements can be made for their kin, if there is no danger of their swearing false accusations against my Harzis."

If Volo didn't prevent a lawsuit (in which no magistrate would award more than Joviz was planning to give anyway), either he did not have the kind of authority he claimed or he was prepared to harry the First Magistrate himself.

"My men are lawful Sherranis, and so are their kin. It is their right to appeal to the magistrate if they have grievances—"

"Then I suggest that you settle those grievances before they reach the magistrates, by whatever other lawful means suggest themselves to you."

Volo didn't flinch, but Joviz pressed on. This point had to be driven home, both out of loyalty to his Harzis and out of hope that he could discourage Volo from any notion of making them the next victims of his intrigues. That would threaten still more disorder in Koddardos by forcing some of the magistrate's best men to guard their own backs instead of the peace of the city. It also threatened to rouse all the ancient prejudices against Harzis, which might mean trouble elsewhere. Volo had never seemed the sort of man to risk such disasters to others for his own petty gains, but perhaps he'd decided that this time the gains were not so petty. . . .

"My Harzis are not men with milk instead of blood in their veins. Yet I think they have committed no crime except stealing your men's chances of redeeming themselves for starting the riot. That is no crime in the eyes of the people of Koddardos or of the First Magistrate.

"You will prevent any lawsuits against my Harzis. You will prevent your men from brawling with them or worse. You will give up to the justice of the Throne and the First Magistrate any of your men who forget their orders on this matter.

"Oh, yes. You also will give no unlawful punishments to the village of Niza's Forge for taking lessons in self-defense from Captain Michal shan-Ouvram. As I am sure you know, he is their guest-friend and would feel sworn to avenge any wrongs done them."

Volo jumped to his feet and took a deep breath. If he'd been wearing a sword he would have drawn it, and Joviz almost signaled Lanach to summon the squad of Watchmen standing within call. He'd been of two minds about dragging them into this matter, but he'd decided that even though the Watchmen might be cautious about laying hands on a great lord, the consequences of having Volo manhandled by Harzis hardly bore thinking about.

"Do you think I'd stoop to persecuting a whole village because of what might be a grievance against one—Harzi—in your service?"

"You stooped to giving orders to your captains to start a fight with Lord Bihor's men while throwing the blame on them. Now, some of your captains may have exceeded their orders. Lord Bihor's men behaved like the rabble they are. And once the fighting had gone on long enough—well, we

178

both know that when the dogs are fighting, the rats feel safe in leaving their holes. Or at least I *thought* you knew that."

Volo let out another long breath. "If you have evidence of all this, why are you accusing me here and now, instead of before the Throne?"

Joviz felt an old cavalryman's joy at seeing the enemy's line begin to crumble under the impact of his charge. Time to press the charge home. "Because the danger of the peace of Koddardos and Sherran is the presence of your men in the city, not any ambitions you may have hoped to advance by bringing them here. You have served Sherran well in the past, and I don't see that you've lost your wits to the point of being unable to serve it again in the future. Not as king, I think—" and he smiled at Volo's shrug "—but however else God and the Throne see fit.

"As for me, God and the Throne have seen fit to charge me with the peace and good order of Koddardos, and I will maintain these as the laws and customs of Sherran and my own good sense dictate until God or the Throne relieves me of that burden. I have all the evidence I need against your men, and that may well be enough to have *you* place your hand in the Fire of Truth to bear witness about your own orders."

The last statement would not have stood the test of the Fire. The Fire demanded not only nothing but the truth but also the whole truth; the whole truth was that much of the evidence came from spies who would be compromised and Harzis whose bearing witness would generate more ill will toward them. Volo probably knew this; Joviz prayed that he had not become the sort of man who would willingly fall if he could bring his enemies down with him.

Volo shrugged again, more broadly. "My men and I would spend more time before the magistrates than your Harzis, if matters went that far. Well, I suppose it is in my hands to see that they do not. I also suppose that you have some specific proposals to make, rather than mere accusations against my own ethics and the discipline of my men?"

"I do. I think an edict from the Throne would be best, limiting both you and Lord Bihor to a hundred or perhaps two hundred men apiece within two days' ride of Koddardos. I am sure you have enough lawful business in the city to give occupation to that many. I think the hammering that they took last night will keep Bihor's men tame for a while."

Volo shook his head. "Your Excellency, that idea makes sense as far as it goes. Unfortunately, Lord Ikos has more than a thousand of his men ready to hand. If you ask Kantela to sign an edict that will leave Ikos the strongest lord in Koddardos, she'll tell you what to do with it in language borrowed from her new bedmate."

Joviz frowned, not understanding the last phrase at first. Then he raised his eyebrows. "You think Bakarydes is, ah, Her Grace's lover?"

"Of course. Don't you?"

Under other circumstances, Joviz reflected, it would have been interesting to observe how dispassionately Volo was seeking to regain dominance over the meeting—and how close he was coming to success. However, the present circumstances precluded such esthetic pleasures.

"Volo Deningkur, I think the question of—what mare the Captain-General rides at night is not the most important matter facing us. You say that Her Grace has some reason to fear or distrust Lord Ikos if he is left with more freedom of action than he has enjoyed with your men and Lord Bihor's in Koddardos. I know that he was guilty of improper conduct toward her on the night of Pijtos Sherran's death and that his ambitions are notorious. I also know that he is an exceptional soldier and that his men are by all reports a well-ordered, formidable band. Do you know anything else that might influence the Queen in this matter?"

"Not so much the Queen as Ikos himself. It's not something I would know myself if my elder son's wife wasn't of the House of Rishi, whose secret it really is."

Joviz quietly signaled to Lanach to have wine and cakes sent up. Even in the unlikely event that Volo decided to tell this story quickly, the negotiations for getting his men out of Koddardos promised to be a moderately lengthy business.

180

Now that he'd gained his point, Joviz had no intention of appearing to be hasty or lacking in hospitality.

Lanach had brought in the refreshments and Volo had eaten half the cakes before Joviz noticed that they'd come at all. This was a tribute of Volo's storytelling skills—and as he listened with a more alert and critical ear, Joviz realized that he was not listening to a story rehearsed as part of Volo's defense. The man occasionally fumbled for a name or went back to add a detail; he hadn't planned to be discussing this matter today.

The sum of the tale was simple enough. Three years ago Ikos had been about to contract a betrothal to a woman of the House of Rishi, in fact the last unmarried sister of the mother of the wife of Volo's elder son. It seemed that he had really loved her, insofar as it was in Ikos to love anything but himself and power.

However, rumor and perhaps more than rumor reached him from the palace, that Pijtos was about to name an heir to the throne in case he left none of his body. Ikos's name was well to the fore on the list of heirs—indeed, Joviz recalled, it had been so every time such a list was drawn up, whether in fact or rumor. As little as most might love Ikos's ambition, few denied his skill at leading men or managing his money and land.

In any case, Ikos believed that he should be free to contract a more advantageous marriage. It was for that reason that he'd delayed so long in seeking a wife; as long as he was unmarried hopes of a marriage alliance might earn him at least goodwill among his fellow nobles.

Now it seemed best that he be free again. The betrothal was broken off; Volo did not know in detail the reasons given for it, but apparently they had been insultingly insufficient.

"Ikos had always been one for letting his ambition run around naked," added Volo.

"God be thanked for that," replied Joviz. "Or his other gifts might have let him be taken for a wise man."

Ikos waited and hoped, but nothing happened. Pijtos did not name an heir, and suddenly the rumors that he was even planning to do so died away.

"I can't swear to the truth of all this," said Volo. "Some of what I heard may have only been fine tales to win my silver. Still, the tale goes that it was Kantela who persuaded Pijtos not to name an heir, that she'd even claimed to be with child to force him to abandon the matter entirely.

"By the time Ikos decided that the throne was out of his reach, so was Lady Tarina. Not wishing to take second place to Ikos's ambitions, she'd contracted a betrothal to Zunik Rivur dar no Saviz, and is now the mother of his heir.

"Ikos ended with neither throne nor lady and blamed it all on Kantela."

It was not a pretty tale, nor one in which Ikos came off smelling very sweet. He would have smelled still worse if Joviz hadn't known far too well what rumormongers could do when they put their tongues to it. If he were King of Sherran, Joviz had long since sworn, he would revive the ancient penalty of piercing the tongues of gossips and slanderers with red-hot needles.

Meanwhile, even if Kantela did not know of this particular reason for Ikos's hatred, she knew that she could not afford to run any risks with him—such as leaving his men the strongest fighting force in Koddardos. This was something to be considered in any scheme to relieve the city of its burden of riotous retainers, a problem still crying for a solution.

"Volo Deningkur, you certainly gave some thought to—whatever caused last night's disturbances. Have you given any thought to ways of preventing more, other than the one you have just said Her Grace would reject?"

"Yes. What about an edict from the Throne, expelling all lords whose seats aren't in Koddardos from the city? Also, when they come back they can bring only enough men to guard their quarters and baggage."

"About forty of those lords have town houses, including you, Bihor, Ikos, and Arkan. Enough men to guard one of those could still make a good deal of trouble."

"True. But five times that many lords have to hire lodgings for everybody and everything they bring. How much trouble could they cause with only enough men to guard their strongboxes and horses? How much would they be worth as allies? And if they could do nothing either on their own or as allies of the great ones, how many of those would find it worth the trouble to come at all?"

Joviz didn't know whether Volo was delivering a well-rehearsed defense or was merely such an accomplished intriguer that he was stocked beforehand with arguments for every occasion. From what he'd heard of the man, the latter seemed probable.

Still, while Volo's suggestion was worth discussing and even putting before the Queen, it would be foolish to appear too eager for agreement. Having been spared the need to be grateful to Volo by the mercy of God and the sharp wits of Captain Michal, Joviz was not about to tempt fate a second time.

So they argued over what should be done about the retainers of everybody else, from great merchants with caravans as large as a village to traveling craftsmen and even street entertainers with one boy to guard their baggage. They argued over whether some lords should leave first or all leave together, and Joviz warned Volo against any effort to be the last to leave. They argued over a joint contribution to the temples by all the lords whose men had been devouring the substance of Koddardos. They argued over so many matters great and small that by the time they finished, three plates of cakes were empty and enough jugs of wine for Joviz to be feeling the effects were empty. The shadows were a good deal longer, and a ring of crumbs lay around Volo's chair.

He stood up, brushed more crumbs into the ring from his trousers, and held up both his hands. "Your Excellency, I've had enough of haggling. Call in your secretary and have him write down what we've agreed to lay before Queen Kantela. The sooner she issues the edict, the sooner I can stop worrying about either staying here and guarding my back every moment or losing reputation by leaving someone else in possession of the field. I'll geld myself before I see Ikos playing cock in Koddardos, let me tell you!"

He poured the last of the wine into their cups and raised his. "There've been rumors since Bakarydes came to Koddardos that we can expect the Momaks over the border in more strength than usual this year. Have you heard anything about this—that you can tell me, that is?"

Joviz had heard those rumors too, but nothing of substance except Bakarydes's opinion—which was worth quite a bit, come to think of it, but was not something to tell Volo. Still, there'd been something almost wistful in Volo's tone when he spoke of the Momaks coming. He'd had to leave the army he loved when he became head of the House of Tivest. Had he come to Koddardos and staged the fight with Bihor's men just so he could feel like a soldier again?

Joviz felt a sudden sense of comradeship and couldn't hide a smile. "Nothing certain. I'll tell Her Grace that you're ready to offer men, if we need to raise strength beyond the regular army. If you restore your men's discipline and obey the edict, you won't be refused."

Volo grinned and raised his cup. "To good comrades and enough enemies to go around!"

They drank the old frontier army toast, clinking cups instead of actually linking arms, but that was enough. Joviz was sure that hope of being able to lead his men against the Momaks, even under Bakarydes's command, would make Volo not pliant—he didn't have that in him—but willing to intrigue peacefully for some time to come.

"Lanach!"

"My lord?"

"I'm ready to dictate. Use the form for a petition to the Throne."

"Yes, my lord."

Michal was examining his mount's left forehoof when he heard footsteps on the straw-covered stones of the stable floor behind him. He looked around. The patch of sunlight cast by one window had turned redder since he knelt to examine the horse's hooves. The other window was almost blocked by the head and shoulders of a woman.

"Niko!" Michal stood up and snatched a handful of hay from the manger to wipe the dung and dirt from his hands. His breeches, he feared, were past praying for; they would need boiling rather than washing.

"I went up to wake you for dinner, but Yiftat said you'd already gone down to the stables. By the way, I have a bone to pick with your friend. He let you take your nap by shouting 'Be quiet! The captain is sleeping!' so loud I'm surprised you did sleep."

"When I've had a long night, I could sleep through the end of the world."

"Well, not everyone else is such a sound sleeper or did so much last night, and some of them needed their sleep too and didn't get it because your friend was so determined you would get yours. Next time, do you suppose he could just stab noisemakers quietly and toss them in the kitchen midden?"

Michal grinned. "I'll see what I can do. But if you think you've met stubborn Harzis before, wait until you try arguing with Yiftat."

He finished wiping his hands and tossed the hay to the floor. "By the way, I've found the trouble with the Banner Troop's horses. I had to clean off the floor of two stalls to find it—"

"Oh, is that all? I thought you'd been rolling in the manure pile."

"Don't complain—you had the stalls cleaned free. You also have cracked stones in the floors in two or three places each. It was bits of stone working their way up into the hooves that lamed the two Banner mounts."

"Damn! That means relaying the floor. If I don't, more bits will lame more horses. Pretty soon it won't be easy to clean the floors, and then I'll be breeding hoof rot and God knows what else. . . ."

"Masons aren't cheap, but considering what you must be making off this inn—"

"Is much less than you think, my friend." To Michal's inquiring look she returned a smile. "Indeed it is, I swear by all the Faces of God. Would you ask me to say more, when you would hardly tell me the details of one of your contracts if *I* asked?"

Michal wondered if the Sherrani had been dealing with Harzis so long that by now they were all learning the art of bargaining themselves.

"Well, if you need a mason, there are always the kin and friends of Valko Godinur to—"

"Michal, they owe me no debt. I can't honorably take advantage of their good will toward you."

That was a sentiment fit for a Harzi woman, even if not expressed quite Harzi fashion. *Did* Niko have Harzi blood?

"I wasn't thinking of asking them for free work. The Guild of Masons would probably throw them off the guildhouse roof and you off your own. No, I only thought that for a friend of mine, any kin of Reverend Valko would do good work for the lawful price. You wouldn't have to worry about little tricks in the work or the price that any good craftsman knows and that his guild will never punish him for."

Niko rolled her eyes toward the ceiling. "God knows *that's* true. There's one vintner I'll never be able to charge with watering his wine unless a frog jumps out of the barrel in front of the First Priestess of the Mother."

She looked out the window at the sunset, then turned back to Michal. "Michal, the bathhouse should be empty now. I'm going to scrub the stable off you and then massage you until you can get a good night's sleep."

Michal looked at Niko's round cheeks and her arms solid with work-hardened muscle and didn't stop looking there. He rather liked what he suspected he was about to see.

Niko met his eyes with a smile that touched hers. "The bath has a good massage couch. I used to work in a bathhouse myself. It was a very respectable establishment, of course."

"Of course. And you—?"

"Was quite as respectable as the establishment." She put an arm around his waist, trying to avoid the patches of filth. "Although I confess I always preferred giving massages to the men, for some reason."

XXI

A NEW MAP HAD JOINED THE ONES OF SHERRAN AND Koddardos in the chamber where Joviz now sat facing both Kantela and Captain-General Bakarydes. It was a standard military map of the northern frontier lands of Sherran, thin-cut pine on a brass backing, folding into four leaves for easier travel in a saddlebag.

No, not quite. The map had been framed and the wood of the frame polished until it reflected the lamplight. Also, the pins marking the locations of Sherrani garrisons and camps had blue coral heads; the pins marking the last known (or guessed) location of Momak tribes and clans were red headed.

A nice combination of palace and saddle, thought Joviz. Rather like the man who sat on the Queen's side of the table, whose new wine-colored tunic and trousers could not make him look much less warlike and who might have discarded them if he'd thought they did.

It would take more to turn Bakarydes into a man who looked at home in palaces than it would to turn him into a Queen's lover, if in fact that first transformation had occurred.

Joviz realized that contemplating the map was giving him no answer to the Queen's last question. He forced his mind back to it and still found no answer. God, he was tired! But Kantela would show charity, and if Bakarydes in his young soldier's strength did not—

"Your Excellency, are you not well?" asked Bakarydes.

Joviz smiled. "Only tired, my lord Captain-General."

"Then perhaps we can bring this meeting to a swifter close than we had intended," said Bakarydes. His tone was deferential, with a question implied, but he was speaking without looking at Kantela, let alone asking her permission. "Will Lord Volo accept any changes in the terms of this edict?"

"I think that would depend on the change," said Joviz. "I don't think small changes will cause trouble. Volo does not wish to dictate to the Throne—"

"At least not yet," said Kantela, with a wry smile.

Joviz nodded. "As to greater changes—after what I have said to him, he is unlikely to oppose the edict by any open means, but we would not have his goodwill."

"Do you value his goodwill so much?" said Kantela.

"Enough. Volo will support you as ruler of Sherran, I think. I would not lightly throw that away."

"I do not think refusing to let an ambitious lord dictate to the Throne is a light reason for doing anything," said Kantela. There was no mistaking the edge in her voice.

There was also no mistaking Bakarydes's own irritation when he spoke, although he still managed a deferential tone. "I do not say that we have only the choice between lesser and greater evils. I do say that Volo is certainly a lesser evil than Ikos, who will be much freer to do mischief if we do not have Volo's goodwill."

"Yes. Also, Ikos will have fewer scruples than Volo about dredging up allies from anywhere and everywhere. Consider how much the scum of Koddardos did without a leader to provide them with weapons and silver."

Kantela looked from one man to the other, and Joviz saw a trapped look on her face. He also saw that her eyes were red and she looked five years older than when he'd last seen her. She had not been in the saddle all the night of the riot and visiting temples most of her waking hours since, but she'd borne an even greater burden—that of bearing ultimate responsibility for what happened but being forced to sit and wait while others took action and only reported on the results, if that much. Under those circumstances it was easy to believe that you could do without food or sleep; when the enemy was actually in sight you either quickly learned otherwise or died.

Joviz thanked God that he'd never had to command more than a regiment, and also that Bakarydes could advise Kantela far better than he could on the wisdom of saving her strength. The Queen was looking positively mutinous.

"Forgive me, Your Grace," said Bakarydes. "If there are circumstances concerning Lord Volo that are known to you but not to us, we beg your pardon for appearing to urge you to a course of action against the Throne's best interests. Those and only those do we seek to promote, on my honor."

The line of Kantela's mouth softened a trifle. "I don't think there is anything to forgive, my lords. I can think of very few changes I would make in the terms Joviz and Volo discussed, although I don't want to put anything on paper until we've all had some sleep. I merely wanted to settle the matter of the Throne's right to make them at all, without having to haggle over every word. Much of the good the Throne's subjects will gain from this edict depends on its being proclaimed quickly."

Bakarydes nodded. "There's no other lord with Ikos's combination of strengths, but the sooner we get them all out of Koddardos, the better for the city and their own lands. Not to mention that God only knows what sort of rumors must be flying north toward the Momak lands. If they reach some hundred-head chief as a tale of plague, fire, and civil war that makes Sherran easy prey—"

"I think we can trust the Army of the North and its Captain-General," said Kantela. Joviz bit his lip to stop a smile as he saw her hand creep toward Bakarydes's as if to clasp it, then halt abruptly a span away. If they were not lovers already, it would hardly be long before they were. But even so, the deference Bakarydes was showing—as gracefully as if he'd sucked in court etiquette with his mother's milk—was clearly given out of respect for the Throne, not to flatter the woman who sat on it.

Bakarydes shrugged. "I hope so, but more than I would like will be in God's hands if a hundred-head chief comes south. There are eight or nine of those who can muster up five thousand warriors apiece. That's twice as many as our largest garrison and more than enough to swamp most of the smaller ones. Oh, we'd pull the army together and put an end to them fairly soon, but not soon enough for too many good men."

The courtier had dropped away like a discarded breechguard, and a soldier sat at the table. On the other hand, Kantela was every finger of her a Queen when she spoke: "It is the decision of the Throne that the edict shall be proclaimed according to the terms presented by Joviz Orasur dar no Vlana, the First Magistrate of Koddardos, and the penalties for defiance of the edict shall be those for treason against the Throne. Will you bear witness that this is the Throne's decision and enforce it with all the power that you command?"

In chorus, Bakarydes and Joviz replied according to the ancient formula: "This is the true decision of the Throne and we will enforce it with all our power and our lives, if necessary. This we swear by the lawful Faces of God, the names of our mothers, and our own honor in the service of the Throne."

Kantela swallowed a yawn and almost but not quite rubbed her eyes. "I think this calls for one toast and then all of us should get a good night's sleep. No, my lords, let me," as Bakarydes and Joviz both rose to bring the wine from a side table.

It was a very acceptable Elazig, but Joviz hardly tasted it. He was more interested in counting the number of times the Queen's eyes met the Captain-General's over the rims of their goblets and noting how their chairs seemed at least a span closer together than they'd been at the beginning of the meeting.

Whatever might lie between the Queen and the Captain-General, however, could not alter the fact that this was the first test of Kantela's power as ruler of Sherran. If the lords did not obey the edict, the Queen would have no choice but to bring them to trial for treason or die in the attempt. In either case, Joviz could see a dark night of chaos engulfing Sherran with no dawn beyond it.

But if Kantela had done nothing, not only would the Throne have seemed impotent when faced by unruly lords, something not seen since Veysel Sherran first sat on it, but letting them linger in Koddardos would have given all the Throne's enemies, from the lords to the Momaks, more time to work mischief. Kantela had put her finger with admirable precision on their greatest need: *time*.

Indeed, Kantela's Ruling seemed more admirable with each passing day. She was definitely no worse than uninstructed, and no piece of instruction she received seemed to be going to waste. (And were some of those lessons being given at night, and was it any of the First Magistrate's business if they were?) She lacked subtlety, but that would, or at least could, come with time, and far more easily than knowledge to the ignorant—or worse, to those who thought they already knew everything.

"With Your Grace's permission, I will approach Master Coron and the Council for Public Order for their support of this edict. When I visited him this morning, he promised that the council would 'act in the best interests of peace and good order in Koddardos.'"

"Promises come cheap, Your Excellency," said Kantela. "With Master Coron, I've heard that anything else comes very dear."

"I wouldn't be surprised. But I think we should at least learn what he means by that phrase. If one meets his price, Coron does good work, and he can buy and sell Bihor and Volo put together. With his friends joining him, he can buy enough of anything needed to cleanse Koddardos, from fodder to hired soldiers. He's already given five hundred orbs for charitable work and pledged as much from his friends, so he's certainly willing to spend freely for this.

"May I also say that Your Grace and the lord Captain-General have my heartfelt thanks as First Magistrate of Koddardos for your generous offering to ease the suffering of the riot victims? Due to press of business, the Reverend Lady Lilka may not have sent her formal thanks for the Throne's offering to the First Temple, so I thought you would wish to know that it has been received and—"

Joviz broke off, the first time he'd done that on an occasion of state business in three years. Bakarydes was staring at Kantela.

"Our offering?" he said.

"The Throne's offering, my lord."

"Yes, but did you make it in both our names?" There was nothing remotely like deference in Bakarydes's voice now.

"Yes, I did."

Bakarydes was staring at Kantela as if she'd grown scales and fangs. "Neither you nor Lady Lilka nor anyone else has spoken of this to me before." His tone not only lacked deference, it made Joviz glad his back wasn't turned to the Captain-General—and neither was Kantela's.

Joviz abandoned hope of doing any more business tonight and started to rise. As he did, he said, "If something has been ill done that my office may aid—"

"Nothing has been ill done," said Kantela. Her voice was not a bad match for Bakarydes's. Fortunately, etiquette called for backing out of the royal presence—once one had been dismissed. Joviz managed to avoid praying for that dismissal.

Kantela took a deep breath. "It seems that the lord Captain-General and I have some private matters which call urgently for discussion. You have leave to go."

Joviz hoped he would be stopped on his way to the door to also be given leave to approach Master Coron, but Kantela seemed to have no attention to spare for anyone but Bakarydes. Disappointment and irritation warred with sheer relief at being outside the chamber and clear of the storm brewing there.

XXII

WHEN THE CHAMBER DOOR THUMPED CLOSED BEHIND JOVIZ, Kantela fought down a brief urge to summon him back. She fought down a somewhat less brief urge to run in the opposite direction into her bedchamber where Bakarydes would hardly dare follow without her permission.

Instead she sat down again, thrusting her hands into her lap under the edge of the table to hide the twining of her fingers. "Bak—my lord Captain-General. It appears that I have given offense in some way. Would you do me the courtesy of explaining, insofar as you can, what that offense is?"

She had expected any one of a number of responses, but not Bakarydes's mouth gaping open. After a moment he closed it enough to say, "You really have no idea?"

"I have a number of ideas, my lord. That is not the same as knowledge—" she broke off before adding, "as Izrunarko told us." Imitating Lady Lilka was not always useful.

Besides, she had the horrible feeling that she did know why Bakarydes seemed to be mortally insulted. But if she admitted this, how could she explain why she'd gone ahead and made the offering without looking like a woman turned foolish by love or at least by a man's caresses? But Bakarydes would have to relearn what he seemed to have forgotten: that she was his Queen as well as his lover and not answerable to him for everything she did.

"You don't know," he went on, "after what I told you about my family?"

"I am not a drunken lancer you are judging for brawling in a house of cheap women!" said Kantela. "Assume that I had my wits about me when I committed the offense and that I have them about me now, and talk as you would to a rational being! Either that or end this display of temper that is unseemly to your dignity and is forcing me to abandon mine."

Instead of turning red, Bakarydes turned pale. He looked down the table, then rose and turned as far as he could without actually turning his back on her. Kantela found herself wishing and even praying that he would finish the turn. She could endure a breach of etiquette ten times more readily than reproaches from the frozen mask that had slipped down over the face she'd admired and kissed—

"Oh, God." She couldn't quite strangle the words, but Bakarydes might have been deaf. Just when Kantela was ready to scream or throw something simply to break the silence, he turned back toward her.

"Did it occur to you that most of the army and the lords know how little silver I have? And that if they know this, they will know that I gave only a small part of that offering, if any part at all?"

"Does it matter, if the offering is made and those who suffered in the riot are helped?"

"It matters very much that you have made a large offering like this without speaking to me or apparently even thinking that I had a claim to be heard."

If there'd been the slightest trace of animation in Bakarydes's face or voice as he spoke the last words, Kantela would have been tempted to beg his pardon on her knees. As it was, the chill face and chillier voice seemed a ghost of Pijtos reproaching her on one of those rare occasions when he really gave enough attention to a mistake she'd made to pass a judgment on it.

Please God, anything but that. I could not endure it again.

"You may speak now, my lord. I assure you that you will be heard."

"I do not know if there will be any purpose in talking to someone who has no—who does not understand—who does not realize what touches my honor."

If it hadn't been for the hesitations, it might have been a waterclock speaking. "Now it is my turn not to understand, my lord. Do you babble the nonsense that women have no idea of honor?"

"It—Your Grace, it begins to seem to me that we bandy words to no purpose. Is that your wish?"

It was Kantela's wish to break the wine jug over Bakarydes's head for using what had been one of Pijtos's favorite phrases when he did not wish to take a matter seriously and for saying it in a tone that made her wonder if Pijtos's ghost *was* suddenly before her. By God's mercy, the wish was gone before her mind could command her arm and hand to the necessary movements.

"It is not my wish that we part without speaking clearly. I do not wish to command you from the Throne to do so, Bakarydes Linzur, but I will if there is no other way of extracting an answer."

The long silence made Kantela suspect that she'd finally broken through. Bakarydes turned completely away from her, and when he spoke his voice was still completely flat, but the words did come, though slowly.

"You have tried to buy me an honor I did not fairly win, the honor of helping the victims of the riot. Since I first knotted my sash, I have tried to take no honor that I have not earned. Until this—offering—of yours, I thought I had succeeded in the sight of both God and men.

"Now, if I remain here at your side, it will be said that I am willing to have honors bought for me. How can I do my duty as Captain-General in the face of that? How can I serve the Throne if I cannot do my duty as Captain-General? Ka—Your Grace, you've cut your own throat as well as mine on a whim!

"And they'll be talking about you as well as me. You've tried not to seem besotted with love so that no one will doubt your judgment and my enemies will not become yours—"

"I didn't know you had any enemies except Momaks and Treasury clerks, and I don't give a pot of the Great Stallion's piss for either!"

The stiff shoulders trembled for a moment. "I will have enemies, after today. Enemies jealous of the influence I must have over the Throne to receive gifts like this. Other enemies, too—officers who lost promotions and posts to me who haven't been jealous before because they knew I took nothing I hadn't earned."

Suddenly his voice was close to breaking. "I have an army to lead, or are you planning to take it away from me?"

To Kantela he sounded like her brother Erzuli, seven years old and asking if his dog would have to be put down for killing chickens.

"Bakarydes, I have no one to put in your place, and you yourself have taught me that one does not leave important posts vacant. Particularly not this one, with the Momaks likely to come against us. The Army of the North is yours, as long as you feel that you are fit to lead it. If—if anything I have done or left undone has made you think otherwise . . ."

An iron band seemed to tighten about her throat. She raised her hands to claw at it, but her hands wouldn't move. She closed her eyes, but she heard the sound of Bakarydes's footsteps approaching around the table, then felt his hands on her shoulders, turning her around so gently that it seemed he was afraid she would break.

She was about to rest her head on his shoulder, then heard him laughing softly. She stiffened and started to pull away. How dared he laugh when she wanted to cry—would have to cry, or scream, or go mad?

"I'm sorry, Kantela," said Bakarydes. "I was just thinking of a young captain who did good work in our first battle against the Momaks this year."

"Kalaj Lesnur?"

"Have I mentioned him?"

"Every time you told the story of the battle."

"Oh. Well, I don't think I've mentioned that I thought of bringing him to Koddardos with me. I decided against it because I was afraid he might get into trouble over wine and women and talk too freely. Considering where I've ended up, *my* protecting *his* virtue would have been the blind leading the one eyed!"

"Oh God." The iron band dissolved, and Kantela found herself laughing and crying at the same time into Bakarydes's shoulder while his arms went around her and held her comfortably tight.

When she could speak again, Kantela pulled herself clear of Bakarydes's arms, tottered to the nearest chair, and silently filled two cups from the jug Bakarydes pushed toward her. The wine warmed her so much that she realized she must have been close to taking a chill.

She also realized something else. "Bakarydes, it wasn't just your own reputation you didn't want talked of, was it? It was your family's. Everyone who talked about how the Queen had bought you—whatever you want to call it—would also have been talking about how poor your family is. I think some of them would have said that you'd finally sold yourself to the Throne *because* your family was poor."

Bakarydes turned his head away before speaking and when he did his voice was shaking again. "Kantela, are you using magic to read my mind?"

"If I were, would I have done what had us fighting like—like this?"

"No." Then, more briskly. "But if you know this, why did you make the offering?"

"I don't think I knew that I knew it until this moment. If that makes any sense to you," she added.

He turned and nodded slowly. "Yes. I understand. It's like the first time you command in battle—somehow you find yourself giving orders you didn't know you'd ever heard and remembering the lay of a stream you've only crossed twice. Except that commanding a regiment, you have to find new memories a lot faster than when you're on a throne. It's a matter of life and death."

"Do you think that nobody will die if I do something stupid as Queen of Sherran? Or that nothing bad would have happened if I hadn't known that I was wrong—soon enough to keep you from walking out the door and riding—" She couldn't finish, and by the time he held her again she was crying so hard that she couldn't be sure where the wetness on his cheeks came from.

Even when she—or they—stopped crying, she went on standing comfortably in the circle of his arms, content with being held and not for the moment wanting anything more. She wanted to think of some way to reward his family, but no ideas came, and by the time they walked to the bedchamber she realized that this was not the time for giving Bakarydes anything else. The wounds she'd already dealt him had to be given time to heal.

A rare summer mist hung over the Golden River and the Island of Koddardos as Bakarydes rode into Queen Kopana's Garden. The mist smelled and tasted faintly of smoke, although all the fires in the riot area were out.

Gravel crunched under the mare's hooves as Bakarydes rode onto the path at Elktree Point. More gravel crunched, and a horse blew softly as Lozo and three Banner troopers closed up behind him. Here by the river the mist was even thicker, swallowing anything more than fifty paces away. Lozo wasn't prepared to wager his Captain-General's life on all the trouble-makers of Koddardos being cowed, dead, fled, or locked up.

If there'd been any purpose to arguing with Lozo, Bakary-des would have been happier alone with his thoughts. Not that they were unpleasant company he didn't dare share with anyone else; quite the contrary. He and Kantela hadn't said much after they went to bed, and indeed hadn't done much more than fall asleep in each other's arms. When the water-clock chimed the end of the westwatch, he'd risen as content as if they'd spent all the time making love, kissed a sleeping Kantela good-bye, and left for a sound night's sleep in his own bed.

He was glad she'd been asleep, or she might have seen how uneasy he was at having to leave her at all. He still valued her reputation, but he also wanted to go on letting her take comfort from being held—and give the comfort of holding him, which wasn't something he'd ever had any reason to expect from even the most congenial bed partner.

There was more about Kantela that set her apart, other than her being on the throne of—

" 'Ware, my lord!"

Bakarydes heard the sound of hooves on gravel himself, hard after Lozo's shout. They'd reached the other side of the point, where the path ran off between a line of featherbranch trees on the right and the embankment of granite blocks at the western end of the Island. A cluster of mounted figures was trotting out of the trees onto the path, just this side of where it vanished into the mist. As Bakarydes touched his sword hilt, one figure detached itself from the cluster and rode forward, a rider on a dappled gray and wearing a well-cut blue riding coat and trousers and light veil.

Bakarydes waved Lozo and his guards back and opened his hand in salute. Thank God he hadn't drawn his sword before he recognized the rider; he'd have looked more than a little foolish greeting Queen Kantela with a naked blade!

"My duty to the Queen's Grace," he said.

198

"Well met, my lord Captain-General." Her eyes shifted toward the trees. Obviously she had things to say not meant for any ears but his.

Bakarydes shook his head. Lozo's sense of duty left his Captain-General two alternatives. If he wished to be private, he had to do so in such a way that he could be protected by men stationed far enough off not to eavesdrop. If the situation didn't permit this, he had to risk being overheard. While Lozo's writ did not extend to the palace, here Bakarydes knew he would only look silly if he tried to defy it.

Kantela looked past him, back down the path to the beach at the other side of the point. This time Bakarydes nodded.

"Lozo, Her Grace and I wish to ride on to the beach and speak privately."

"My lord!"

Bakarydes turned his mount and let her match the pace of Kantela's gray. He could trust Lozo to deal with Kantela's escort of six armed grooms, who appeared to be hanging back as if trying to dissociate themselves from their mistress's folly. If the escort had been Swords, he'd have had to take a hand himself; Lozo hadn't forgiven the Swords for wrapping themselves around Bakarydes the night of the riot, as if the Banner troopers couldn't be trusted to protect him.

Armed grooms still seemed a rather light escort for the Queen, then Bakarydes remembered that this end of the Island was mostly homes and workshops for those serving either the palace or the King's servants. One street led directly from the palace westward to the slope behind the trees.

It was amazing how much he now knew about Koddardos that he hadn't known ten days ago. By the time of the next riot, he'd know enough to be more than a well-guarded spectator.

At the near end of the beach, a moss-grown stone bench stood under an isolated featherleaf. Kantela dismounted, then led her horse around to the side of the tree toward the river. By the time Bakarydes followed, Kantela had looped the reins over a stub of branch. She twined the fingers of one hand into her horse's mane and looked out at the river. A couple of small boats were crawling past at the edge of the mist, but everything heavier was either out in deep water or else not moving at all until the mist lifted. Even from the small boats, no one would have been able to recognize the two figures on the shore as more than a man and a woman wealthy enough to have a mounted escort.

"Bakarydes."

"Your—Kantela."

"You have many things to forgive me for, from last night. And do not talk nonsense or dismiss me as a foolish woman by contradicting me. We'd only quarrel again."

"I wasn't thinking anything of the kind, Kantela. I was thinking of how much you have to forgive *me* for—"

She held up a hand. "Please. Let me speak first." She took a deep breath. "The joint offering was foolish, I see that now. Then I made matters worse by not reading my letters yesterday. If I had, I would have found Lady Lilka's warning me of just that, and last night—could have been avoided. As it was, I failed in my duty. Yes, I was tired, but not so tired that I couldn't have opened a letter!"

Bakarydes listened as Kantela went through a list of her errors and follies. Long before she'd finished even those things Bakarydes would have agreed she'd done, he desperately wanted to take her in his arms and stop her. He also knew that would make matters worse—and realized with a start that he wouldn't have known this before he came to Koddardos. Was Kantela teaching him about women—or at least about herself—while he taught her about war and Ruling?

"Apart from all these matters," Kantela finished, "it is very much on my mind that I forced you to talk about your honor. I was taught that one sign of an honorable man is that he is very reluctant to make a show of that honor.

"I have also learned that if you are not an honorable man, then God made no such thing." He could not see her face, but he heard her swallow several times. "I—you have the right to ask me to make amends somehow, both as woman and as Queen, since I gave offense as both."

She turned toward him, and he wasn't sure if she was going to cry or smile. He put his arms around her, and she smiled.

"Only—please tell me what you think is fair and honorable. I'm afraid my first attempt to reward you for your good advice wasn't quite the success I'd hoped for, so in this matter I will need still *more* advice."

She pressed against him, his arms tightened around her, and the desire he hadn't felt last night suddenly blazed up in him. She felt it too and perhaps shared it; her own arms tightened and her breath came quickly. Bakarydes laughed and gently pulled free; he was afraid of what kissing her or even continuing to hold her would do to his discretion.

When he was sure that his voice would be steady, Bakarydes said, "I think all the amends I need are for you to forgive me for most of what *I* said. I felt betrayed when I had no cause for it, and nearly betrayed you. Away from the frontier, there aren't many people I can trust besides my kin. I was a fool to betray either the woman or the queen, and I ask both to forgive me."

She kissed him, and since he doubted that she could command her voice, he decided to be content with that. Much to his relief, the kiss seemed to make his desire ebb.

"Since we are here—do you think your grooms will hold their tongues if we share the morning bread and wisdomfruit?"

"They'll be holding their tongues in their hands if they don't," said Kantela.

Bakarydes wasn't at all sure she was joking. He turned back to his mount and started opening his saddlebags.

"Oh, plague and—!"

"What does the Great Stallion have to do with—?"

"I'm ten kinds of witling. I forgot the wisdomfruit, on this morning of all mornings! God, where were my thoughts last night?" He slammed his fist against the tree in rage and frustration, hard enough to make him wince.

Kantela seemed to be choking on silent laughter. "Bakarydes, if you'll stop trying to cut down that tree with your bare hands . . . Thank you. I won't say that your thoughts being elsewhere was all my fault, although if we'd—well, under other circumstances it might have been a different matter.

201

"I brought some bread and wisdomfruit myself. If you—if you don't mind taking another gift from my hands . . ."

Bakarydes lifted both her hands to his lips. "Thank you, Kantela."

Her bread was a white loaf from the palace bakery and the wisdomfruit was dried and lightly glazed. Bakarydes was drawing his dagger when he saw that Kantela had drawn one of her own.

"That's a Momak knife."

"Yes. My grandfather took it from a Momak chief he gave the Mercy stroke. My eldest brother gave it to me as a wedding present."

Bakarydes's opinion of Kantela's kin rose. However—
"Among the Momaks, to cut your bread with an enemy's knife means that you've made your peace with him."

"I suppose we've made our peace with the chief. He's been dead more than forty years. But the rest of the Momaks—"

"Very well. What about your knife—not your dagger, that one in your boot?"

"That's a Harzi knife."

"So?"

"Among the Harzis, a man and a woman cut bread together with the man's knife as part of the betrothal oath."

The silence was so long and so intense that Bakarydes could have sworn he heard Kantela's heartbeat. He certainly heard his own. At last she smiled.

"We couldn't do that without Lady Lilka, and she isn't here. But is that all a bread-breaking can mean, among the Harzis?"

"No. It's part of an oath a woman takes with a man who's leaving Harz-i-Shai, to accept no other betrothal than his for three years. It's also part of the oaths of blood brotherhood and kinship."

"What kind of kinship?"

"Take your choice. Most Harzis recognize more kinds of kinship than the kinds of weapons they carry, and since the average Harzi can stock a small arsenal all by himself—"

"Bakarydes, be serious. Is there a kind of kinship that would let me make some sort of a gift to your family, as Kantela their kinswoman instead of Queen Kantela?"

Bakarydes needed no further commands to be serious. He did need one to, "pick your jaw up off the beach, Bakarydes, and give some thought to your answer. I will not give them a loaf or a bit or a mug of beer without your permission, but I would like to have the right to do so without having to ask *theirs* from the Throne. They have given both the woman and the queen something precious, and if it won't seem too much like rewarding the shepherd who raised the prize ram—"

"Oh, God!" He hugged her, laughing into her hair as he conjured up a picture of himself at a farmer's fair, with a wooden plaque around his neck giving his owner and pedigree.

"Seriously," he said when he'd caught his breath. "As I remember, the degree of kinship is stated in the oath. There's a Harzi word for every one of those degrees of kinship, but I don't know half of them and most of the others don't make sense in Sherran. Let's just describe my kin and you in proper Sherrani and call God to witness it and hope that's enough. It will be for me, at least."

"Thank you, Bakarydes." He knelt to draw his boot knife, and she knelt beside him.

XXIII

"LIE DOWN ON THE BENCH."

"Yes, Reverend Master." The man gave the military salute of putting his hand over his heart—his left hand since his right had only a thumb and forefinger—and bowing slightly. Then he limped over to the bench and lay down on it, sighing with relief as he took the weight off his right leg.

After a moment he sat up and took off his tunic, then lay down again. His feet were already bare. "Will you bind me to the bench this time?"

Charko noted with approval that the man's tone showed no fear, only the intelligent curiosity of a good soldier who wants to understand his orders as well as obey them. This was not surprising; First Lancer Tholo Bekur had been a very good soldier indeed before the Momaks crippled him.

Tonight and for many days in the past, this good soldier had obeyed Charko, a priest of the Giver of Knowledge. Charko allowed himself a moment of pride in the fact that it wasn't only a soldier like Ikos who could gain the loyalty of a good fighting man, then shook his head.

"You did so well the first time, I have no fear of involuntary movements." Not to mention that this powerful a form of the Spell of the Inner Eye rendered a man completely incapable of moving while he was subject to it. It had to; the strain on the heart was such that more additional exertion than blinking an eye or twitching a finger could bring instant death.

Tholo began to murmur softly to himself. After a moment Charko recognized the prayer to the Warrior used before battle. "Lord of Hosts and God of Battles, we beseech Thee to look with favor upon us. Grant to us, we pray, the patience to wait when waiting is needed, and the strength of arm and heart and sword to strike when striking is needed. Above all do we pray for Thy gifts of wisdom and courage, that of Thy mercy we may refrain from all folly and vainglory, and remain true to our vows to Thee and to Sherran.

"As we set forth to battle, we beg Thy forgiveness if we have offended Thee in any way. Grant to Sherran, we pray, the victory this day, and to those who die the sight of Thy True Face. For Thou art our Sword and our Shield, our Strength and our Refuge, and our Captain of Captains, now and always.

"Be it according to Thy will, Lord of Warriors."

When Tholo had finished the prayer, he continued to murmur. After a few breaths Charko recognized some highly picturesque curses in frontier slang. Not that Tholo didn't have every reason to curse Momaks, but—

"Cease cursing, please. Or if you must curse, do not curse Marsh Wolf. Your mind must bond to his for the spell to be successful, and cursing can make that bond impossible. We do

204

not know exactly why, although we may when God gives us more knowledge of these bonds. We do know that it does happen."

"Yes, Reverend Master." Tholo fell silent, and after a moment Charko saw his shoulders relax and his chest begin to rise and fall steadily as he forced himself to be calm and await the working of the spell that would bring him vengeance on Marsh Wolf and the Momaks.

Charko turned to the corner where he'd left his pack on the least filthy patch of floor in the cellar. He'd been telling Tholo the truth, though not all of it. He wanted silence while he unpacked his apparatus and composed his own mind in preparation. The pack held not a veysela less than two orbs' worth of vessels, instruments, incense, rare earths, jewels, and scrolls. Nor could he have spent any less and obtained vessels of the required workmanship and materials of the required degree of purity. If he hadn't made more promises than he hoped he'd ever have to keep, he could easily have spent five orbs instead of two.

He would have spent it, if necessary. He intended to link his mind to Marsh Wolf's through Tholo's mind, using the bond formed between the soldier and the chief when they wounded each other. That bond was an uncertain thing at best; it would have to be strengthened enormously before the priest could be certain of reaching Marsh Wolf's mind for the purpose of putting into it the vision of an easy conquest of northern Sherran. Momaks placed great faith in the dreams and visions of their chiefs and seers; if Marsh Wolf could recount a sufficiently vivid dream, all the riders sworn to him would be on the move within days. They would be across the border within a week, so fast that they would be certain to win at least one victory, so Marsh Wolf would seem to have had a true vision.

Then other tribes would follow where Marsh Wolf led, and Sherran would face a major Momak invasion—from which a suitably forewarned Lord Ikos could save it. It would be hard to deny an Ikos who'd saved Sherran anything he wanted, even the throne.

It would also be hard for an Ikos placed on the throne of Sherran to deny any reasonable request from the priest of the Giver of Knowledge who'd put him there.

Did Marsh Wolf yet live to lead the invasion? Charko's agents on the frontier reported that he had been alive three moons ago, and since the raiding season was just well begun, the chances were that he still was. If he was not, it might still be possible to bring the Momaks south by sending his tribe a vision of the dead chief's spirit leading them to Sherran. But in order to be sure that the tribe would actually come, Charko would have to drag Marsh Wolf's corpse out of its grave to lend strength to the vision. While the priest was prepared to do this if he had to, for the first time he found himself hoping that a Momak was alive instead of dead.

First, however, Charko himself had to live through the necessary magic, and pushing a spell that was none too safe or reliable even within its normal limits far beyond those limits was like juggling with poisonous serpents. One had to be very sure that no impurity in one's materials or flaws in one's instruments existed to make all one's own care and skill useless at best or to end one's sanity or existence at worst. Indeed, Charko did not fear the death of the body so much as he feared the death of the mind while the body yet lived, and the fate of Pijtos Sherran had done nothing to ease this fear.

He'd loaded the pack so that what he needed first went in last; the waterskin and towel were on top. He spoke the blessing over the water: "God the One, God the Holy, God the Almighty, may Thou bless this water, that it and all it touches may be free from every impurity, and serve Thy gift of knowledge this night."

He poured water into his right hand and touched that hand to his face. "Cleanse me within and without, Most High Fount of Knowledge, that no defilement, error, or malevolence may corrupt that which I would do this night." He poured more water over his hands, cast water in each of the four directions, first to the east, then south, then west, then north, and then dried his hands.

Next he drew his dagger, and facing east, drew a symbol in

the air. "Wind of the east, wind of new beginnings. Guard and protect all within this place this night, that this work may be well begun without faltering or error. In the name of the One, the Almighty God, be this so."

He faced south and drew another symbol. "Wind of the south, wind of greatest strivings. Aid and protect us this night, that our strivings may be sufficient for that which I would do this night. In the name of the One, the Almighty God, be this so."

West, and another symbol. "Wind of the west, wind of judicious resting. Comfort and protect us this night, that we strive not to excess, and bring all to destruction. In the name of the One, the Almighty God, be this so."

North, and the final symbol. "Wind of the north, wind of all endings. Watch and protect us this night, that in the end this work may be both well and fully done. In the name of the One, the Almighty God, be this so."

The shields were now in place. Next he took the silver phial of *gilgram* and its brazier, filled the brazier with the dark red powder—rather the color of a Momak's hair, in fact—placed it in the center of the room, then lit it. The red smoke began curling up almost at once; he hurried back to the pack to finish arraying the rest of his apparatus before the sense-enhancing power of the smoke led him into minor mistakes that could have major consequences.

Lighting the brazier before arraying the apparatus was running a risk, but Charko wanted to save time. He could not be sure how much of that precious commodity he had, not even here in the cellar of an abandoned building deep within the area scarred and scorched by the rioting.

The building also provided privacy, which he needed so much that he was prepared to run the risk of physical interference. At least showing no lights, speaking softly, and locking doors were measures that needed no magic to maintain; he had used all the power he could spare for defensive magic on the shields. Moreover, if anyone passing along the streets outside or through the rooms above had enough of a Gift to recognize the aura of the spell, that Gift was unlikely to be great enough to prevent their being thrown into a daze. If they recovered from that with mind and memory intact, Charko and the spell would still be long gone before they could summon help.

Charko had not even considered asking Lord Ikos for help in this matter, although Ikos owned a number of buildings in Koddardos. Charko wanted Ikos forewarned only of the Momak invasion, but not of the priest's own efforts to bring it about. If Ikos knew that, he might have enough scruples where Momaks were involved to inform the Throne or at least the army. If he did, he'd probably be forgiven for not revealing what he knew about the stolen pay chests. As for Charko, the position of the sorcerer in this game of Siege would be strange and not at all desirable, if the king refused to move or even changed sides!

On the other hand, Ikos was unlikely to have enough scruples to test the wind of a gift horse. If the Momaks were already on the march when Charko gave him the news, the priest could always remind the noble of his own words three days ago, when the edict from the Throne came down, ordering the nobles out of Koddardos.

"For the moment, there's nothing I can do but obey. I'll look like a dog running off with his tail between his legs if I do, but that's not as bad as if I try to fight."

"Indeed. Have you been exaggerating your strength?" Charko had asked.

"Not by more than a few men and orbs. The problem lies in the strength of my enemies—Volo to start with, and once he comes into the field, a lot of petty lords. Arkan's men are on their way back to his warehouses and caravan camps, but he'd send silver. I couldn't face that kind of odds without fighting a battle I'd lose, whatever happened in the streets. Even if I ended up ruling the streets, Kantela's still got Bakarydes in her pocket as well as in her——. She could bring regiments down from the north, and once she had them in strength she could bring up Harzis from Hierandos—"

Charko had held up his hands. "I understand. I am not calling you coward or any other evil name. I merely wish to be sure that we both know all the facts in this matter, as Izrunarko said friends or allies worthy of the name always must."

Ikos's lips had moved in what Charko suspected was an uncomplimentary reference to the Teacher, but aloud he'd said, "Granted. If there were no regiments free to move, it would be another matter. But that won't be the case until the Momaks are on the march in force, and God only knows when that will be."

"God has also given us the ability to watch, learn, and speak. May I do that, so that you will have knowledge of their coming before any in Sherran away from the frontier?"

"Yes. I'll be leaving men in Koddardos, so a message can reach me by relay even if I'm all the way back at Stony Island."

The message could have been sent still faster if Ikos had been willing to take with him a Gifted man from the temple, one Charko could have reached with a simple mind-link. However, Ikos would have known such a man to be Charko's spy, so his usefulness would have been limited. Charko did not wish to press the matter.

They'd left it there. Now Ikos would—God willing!—have his warning of the Momaks' coming and much more besides, although he would never know how much more unless Charko's estimates of both Ikos's character and his Gifts were badly in error.

And if that were the case, perhaps Charko had not been given as much knowledge as he thought and should consider making his peace with the Throne and with God.

Charko recognized that last unbidden thought as an early sign of the *gilgram* smoke beginning to affect his concentration. It was time to stop considering either past actions or future possibilities and examine his apparatus to be sure it was all properly arrayed.

He stepped back from the corner, not noticing until he'd take two steps that he was still holding the Amulet of Tamonal in his left hand. He looked at Tholo, who now seemed asleep, then slipped the amulet chain around the man's neck and laid the amulet itself over his heart.

The lapse of attention made Charko a trifle uneasy; should

he continue? He would lose time by having to come back another night, true, but Tholo was a rare and priceless discovery who should not be put in any avoidable danger.

Yet time was also priceless, and once lost could never be regained. Also, he'd chosen the apparatus and materials with vast care; it was *not* overconfidence to believe that nothing could happen that made going ahead more dangerous than starting over another night. Considering that as the days passed, those who'd fled the riot area were beginning to move back as the buildings were cleaned and repaired . . .

No. He would go ahead. Otherwise he would begin to doubt his own courage and his own Gift and his own knowledge, and if he doubted any of these things . . .

He knelt in front of the apparatus and materials and counted the five phials, two of incense and three of rare earths, the nut-shaped golden case holding four sapphires and two turquoises, the antique mortar and pestle said to have belonged to a pupil of the Teacher himself, and the actual Spell of the Inner Eye on a parchment scrolled around a whale-ivory rod with golden knobs at either end.

"Most High Fount of Knowledge, Creator, Preserver, and Ruler of All! I ask Thy blessing on these Thy creatures and tools, that they may serve my purpose this night, and that what I desire, may with Thy aid be accomplished."

Charko stood and looked at Tholo. He was deeply asleep, and to any whose senses hadn't been made more acute by *gilgram* smoke he might have looked dead. Charko could count the hairs in the nostrils of his broken nose and on his forearms, see the tiny motions of his chest and the flicker of his eyelids, and hear the faint rumble of a stomach beginning to clamor for food after the long fast needed to prepare for taking this part in any spell.

Charko turned his awareness to his own senses. The almost womanly musk of the smoke clogged nose and mouth, every piece of grit on the floor seemed a nail driven into his bare soles, and he could hear mice chittering in the walls and even a spider spinning her web in a corner of the next room. What effect did spells of this kind have on the lesser animals, he wondered idly, and was there any chance that men would ever know?

Perhaps he would seek the answer, if Ikos Sherran made him the First Priest of the Giver of Knowledge and placed all the temples' wealth at his disposal. . . . But he was letting his wits wander under the burden he'd placed on his senses; he had to bring them back to the task at hand.

He had memorized the Spell of the Inner Eye, so placing the scroll within reach had largely symbolic value, though it was also an aid in case of a sudden lapse. He began the invocations.

"O Source of all that is, it was Thou who created the earth and all it contains.

"There is nothing in this world that Thou dost not know; Thou knowest the powers of every thing Thou has created.

"As Thou hast given power to all creatures of the earth, and to men the knowledge to use that power, I claim the power of these creatures of earth to accomplish my purpose this night."

He mixed the earths together in the mortar, placed them in another brazier, and set them alight. As the smoke rose he traced a symbol in the air and spoke two words in a language older than Sherran.

Next he took the turquoises and laid one on each side of the brazier.

"God the Creator of all! As Thou has created men and women and given us power both within ourselves and over earth, plants, and beasts, so also hast Thou charged us with liability for the use of that power. I claim the power of a man, knowing that Thou will be my Judge if I use it unworthily."

Another symbol, another word, and a glow appeared over the turquoises, which he had removed from good-luck necklaces given to children when they were old enough to wear them without trying to eat them.

Finally he took the sapphires and placed one in each of the four directions around the brazier, then took the incense and threw it into the brazier.

"Most High, Most Holy Source of all knowledge! Knowledge and Strength are Thine alone, and all that I have of these things is but Thy most gracious gift. Grant to me, I pray, the knowledge and strength to accomplish my purpose this night.

"Most Holy Giver of Knowledge, I trust in Thee; let not my trust be forsaken."

Only one ancient word this time, but he could sense the changes in the smoke. From the sapphires, symbols of thought, came a light which crept from stone to stone until it formed a ring of faint blue around the base of the brazier. Charko placed the flat of both hands in the smoke and prayed for a moment.

He stepped over to Tholo and shifted the amulet slightly, until it rested exactly over the man's heart. Then he placed his right hand on the man's forehead and began the Spell of the Open Memory, a powerful but simple Healing spell used on madmen still able to consent to being Healed. It required both consent and prolonged physical contact between the patient and a Healer whose own mind was sound enough to endure a sudden doubling of his own memory. Otherwise, since it permitted the use of another's memories as if they were one's own, it would have been forbidden after the War of God the Destroyer.

Charko had no doubt of Tholo's consent or of his own mental soundness. Even if he had ever doubted, he would not have permitted himself to do so now. A fundamental principle of magic was the belief of the magic worker in the efficacy of the spell or spells being worked.

One could fear or lust in many spells. One could not doubt: not even in the smallest piece of Healing magic for a burned thumb.

Magic came from God. One did not doubt God and still work magic.

Charko was covered with sweat and aware of every drop of it by the time he entered Tholo's memory. He went deeper than usual even with the Open Memory. Charko did not need all of Tholo's memories, but he had to draw up those he did need almost between one breath and the next. That was a depth not usually given the Open Memory, and when it was, it usually took several castings spread over weeks or even moons. To do so much at one session was not without danger for both men.

The point of greatest danger passed; Tholo's mind and body did not go into desperate spasms at Charko's penetration. Charko swiftly strengthened the spell and simultaneously began focusing on the memories he wanted, particularly memories of battle and above all the fight with Marsh Wolf.

He'd told Tholo what he wanted and the man had promised to do his best to offer it, but the best of a man both ungifted and untrained might hardly deserve the name. Charko mentally squared his shoulders and prepared to repeat the experience of one of his first attempts at the Inner Eye some years ago: a wearying search through a muddle of memories of pets, parents, recruit training, inept or uninteresting sexual experiences, hangovers—the motley array of memories of a largely dull life.

Within moments he found himself blessing both Tholo and his own foresight in asking for the man's cooperation. Tholo had brought to the forefront of his mind many of the memories Charko sought, including the most important one. Did he have some slight Gift after all, or was it natural wit sharpened by his desire for vengeance on the Momaks?

Izrunarko had said that vengeance was seldom the wisest course of action or as simple a one as it seemed. However, the Teacher had never said that all vengeance was evil.

Charko slipped down through Tholo's memories layer by layer, as if he were descending stairs from roof to cellar in an ancient castle tower:

A summer day in the north, gray-green plains before him, hard blue sky overhead, the smell of horse sweat and the swaying under him telling Charko that Tholo was mounted.

The gray-green plains sprouting black dots, then clumps of dots, swarming toward him like ants as the Momaks rode into sight.

The clumps turning into Momak clans and families, scores and then hundreds of warriors, with a faint rippling in the air over the leading riders as they drew and shot.

The whistle of descending arrows, the screams of men and horses, the sound of trumpets and drums signaling the charge

213

to the Sherrani, and new cries and hoof thunder as the regiments obeyed.

The Momaks growing larger and larger, dark brown men with hooked noses on scrubby little horses of every imaginable color.

With the soldier's knowledge he suddenly had, Charko knew that Momaks didn't usually advance like this, steadily and in good order. A chief must be wielding unusual authority over them to make them challenge the regiments this way.

Then sudden total confusion in which all the knowledge of a good soldier did no more than tell him which Momak was most dangerous at the moment, out of the fifty or so in sight, and which Sherrani was best placed to help him, out of thirty. Charko had heard that battles were often this way, but he had never had such a certain knowledge until now.

A Momak suddenly drove at Tholo from the left with a war ax of ancient pattern, a green-dyed wolf's tail flying behind his open-faced helm. The man was short even for a Momak but broad as a tall Sherrani, yet none of that bulk seemed to be fat.

Tholo cut at Marsh Wolf, and the boiled-leather armor of the Momak's left forearm opened halfway to the elbow where his mail began; after a moment blood followed. Marsh Wolf's horse turned practically within its own length, as a Momak mount could under a good rider, and his ax came down before Tholo could cut again. Blood poured from Tholo's right knee and leg, then his sword and three fingers of his right hand went spinning down into the dust. Now Tholo's mount was rearing and screaming from an ax wound in its neck—

But Charko took the memory-conjuring no farther. He had the moment of bonding firmly before his own Inner Eye, and the spell to hurl it across the distance to Marsh Wolf if the Momak yet lived.

That was something he would have to determine before he released the full power of the spell. He began the familiar words that would build the power of the Inner Eye until—

The power flowed. Charko seemed to be racing across an endless plain of hammered bronze with streaks of gilded glass

214

or perhaps something molten meandering through it in unbelievably complex patterns. Charko somehow knew that those patterns held profound secrets, and if he could just spend enough time in the spell world he could interpret the patterns, unlock their secrets, and find knowledge that God had withheld from all other men.

He also knew that although he seemed to be moving faster than a galloping horse, he stood motionless and erect, with a wind that was neither hot nor cold lashing his face without moving a single strand of his hair.

The power flowed more strongly, but Charko still maintained control. Now he was moving faster, faster than anything of flesh or of the common world could move, so that the patterns blurred before his eyes. He knew that he was reaching out with the bond between Tholo and Marsh Wolf as a blind man reached out with a stick, but this stick had to be more than a thousand miles long—

He swept over the edge of the plain into a midnight blackness where the stars were under him and on all sides as well as above. Then he was tumbling through the blackness, shouting in triumph.

In this moment, the spell was complete and perfect and ready to do its work, all the way from Charko to a living Marsh Wolf. That moment presented itself to each spell worker in a different way; to Charko it was this glorious fall through his own private midnight.

It was a moment as unmistakable as the supreme moment of the sexual act; for Charko it so far surpassed sex that it seemed blasphemous to mention such a lesser gift of God in the same breath as the knowledge of magic.

It was also a moment in which Charko had no doubts of himself or anything else. God could have brought all of creation to an end around him, and he would not have doubted even in the last moment of his own dissolution.

He let the ecstasy flow through and out of him until he had command of his thoughts again, and began to show Marsh Wolf what he wanted the chief to see.

* * *

Marsh Wolf knew that he was not awake because he felt his sleep furs against his skin, but he had never seen anything so clearly in a dream and hardly ever when he was awake. This had to be a spirit-seeing.

He saw a great war band of the People riding across land that he recognized—Sherran, to the south of the Great Vulture Pass. He saw them as he would have done if he'd been riding at their head, and looking up he saw his wolf's head on its pole going before the riders.

Then he saw fighting that would have taken half a day in the waking world but which here among the spirits seemed to be over in the time a horse could swim a small river. Each time the Great King's horsemen foolishly challenged the People, and each time they were beaten, dying or fleeing.

Each time the defeated band of enemies was larger, and each time the People came away from the battlefield with more armor and weapons to strengthen themselves, leaving naked bodies scattered headless for the carrion birds or staked out on the spirit-freeing mounds.

They came to one of the Great King's war towns; its men were defeated and it fell. When the war band rode on, the war town was a burning pyre for the Great King's dead and the People drove captive women in slave-thongs along with them.

It also seemed that the war band was larger, so much larger that it was as if other hundred-head chiefs had joined Marsh Wolf. Enough of his mind remained apart from what he was seeing to wonder where their standards were, but who was he to doubt that the spirits would have shown him this if they had wished him to know it?

The war band came to a river, and a Sherrani town on its banks seemed to melt into planks that formed themselves into rafts on which the horses of the People crossed the river. Marsh Wolf knew that while this was happening before his eyes, another war band of the People was fording the river farther upstream. The Sherrani thought the other war band was all the People there were in the land; they would learn otherwise.

They learned in a great battle fought over land so far inside

Sherran that it was all farms and villages and orchards. None of the People had been so far south since the first days of their coming out of the Land of the Mounds.

Marsh Wolf had not been so filled with eager anticipation since the day he had known would hold both his first battle and, if he survived it, his first woman.

The Great King's horsemen did not flee this time; they died and their bodies lay so thick on the ground that a man's mount could not find bare ground between them to set its hooves. The carrion birds blotted out the sun as they came for their feast.

Then at last a great city on an island in a river with flames and smoke rising from it. Again the villages on the banks melted into rafts that carried the Momaks to their final victory—for this was the golden city of the Great Kings, Koddardos itself.

Marsh Wolf's war cry sounded faint and far off, as if he were hearing himself from the far side of a wide valley. He did not know or care if he was awake or asleep as he leaped to his feet, although it seemed that he looked down upon the sleep furs from more than his own height and reached for his weapons with arms longer than his own.

He sprang through the tent door, feeling the night air warmer than it should have been and smelling odors that came from no campfire or horse pen of the People. The spirits were with him still. They would be with all of his warriors and all the People if they followed his vision and rode south to topple the Great King's throne.

He did not recognize his own voice as he began to shout this, for he seemed to be talking like a seer rather than a war chief. This did not matter; for this one night the spirits had made him a seer.

Someone was in his path, raising arms to hold him back. Marsh Wolf did not recognize the face or the voice but he recognized an enemy of his visions and therefore of the spirits. His knife was in his hand in one moment, and deep in the man's chest in the next. He drew it out and waved it over his head, shouting that the spirits had shown him an enemy of all the People. The drops of blood that flew from the knife seemed to glow like drops of molten iron, and puffs of smoke rose from the dust where they fell to the ground.

Marsh Wolf ran on, passing through the smoke and out into the moonlit common space of the camp, stopping every now and then to shout his war cry or some new part of his vision, as the warriors came swarming out of their tents to stand and stare and finally listen and begin shouting along with him. . . .

The cellar took shape around Charko again; he found himself seated with his back against a wall that felt only normally rough, and his lungs filled with air in which he could no longer taste every separate dust particle. Even without the doubled senses induced by *gilgram* he could smell a few things he hadn't smelled before he bonded with Marsh Wolf—his own sweat and vomit, dried blood, and—although this might be only his imagination—dung-fire smoke.

When he knew that his legs would support him long enough, he stood and staggered over to the bench where Tholo lay. One look at the pale skin and the already-dried blood from nose and mouth pooled around the head made Charko suspect what he would find when he felt for a pulse.

When he knew that Tholo was dead, Charko sat down on the bench and put his head between his knees, then breathed steadily until head and chest as well as limbs seemed fit to finish the night's work. He was not actually grateful that Tholo had died, but he had to admit that disposing of his body was the least demanding of the three ways the night could have ended.

If Tholo had awakened with his mind intact, it would have been necessary to cleanse it of all of tonight's memories—for his own protection even more than Charko's. No man could live easily with the memory of such a bond intact. The cleansing of Tholo's memory would have required yet another long and demanding spell, one which could still destroy mind or body.

If Tholo had awakened sound of body but empty of mind, Charko would have had to return to the temple of the Giver of

Knowledge with a helpless man bearing a spell-aura about him that would have called for immediate investigation. To have simply killed or abandoned the soldier would have been to spit both on his magician's oath to never deliberately harm another and his personal honor, for Tholo had submitted to him willingly.

As it was, only God would ever know what had happened to Tholo's mind; the bursting of his heart under its increased burden had put the matter beyond human knowledge. All that remained was to give Tholo's body a proper pyre.

Charko stood upright, faced the east, spoke two words, and made the gesture that banished the shields. Then he knelt to gather up his apparatus and stow it in his pack, ready for the quick departure he would be making when he'd set Tholo's pyre alight. As he worked, he prayed that Tholo would have not only a sight of the True Face of God, but also the knowledge that his death had purchased his long-sought vengeance on the Momaks.

Unless by some ill chance the unknown man Marsh Wolf had seemed to kill in his frenzy had powerful kin who declared blood feud with the chief, the Momaks would come. However much damage they did in Sherran, very few of them would return home. Ikos was quite enough of a soldier to make sure of that, and even to have the army follow him if Bakarydes did not survive.

On the whole, Charko rather hoped Bakarydes would survive to be the strong right arm of Ikos Sherran. Whatever bonds the Captain-General's flesh had knit between him and Kantela could hardly hold against allegiance to the man who defeated the Momaks, if that man showed him any sort of good faith, and if King Ikos took proper counsel he certainly would. . . .

The Momaks would come, Tholo would have his vengeance, and over Momak bodies Ikos would mount the throne of Sherran.

This thought gave Charko new strength, although his muscles were hardly unequal to the task of carrying one man's body through two rooms and laying it down on the floor. In spite of what Ikos might think, the discipline undertaken by the Gifted did not weaken muscle or sinew. This was one of many things Ikos would have to be taught eventually, so that Sherran might have God's greatest blessing—a Gifted Ruler.

The room where Charko placed Tholo's body had a narrow stairway leading up to the street. Since the building above was abandoned, the work gangs cleaning the streets after the riot had found the room a convenient dumping place for all sorts of rubbish they didn't want to bother carrying to the barges waiting at the waterfront. The rubbish now nearly blocked the stairway, and much of it would burn. Trapped by the stone walls of the cellar, the heat would give Tholo as fit a pyre as any man could wish, if in fact it did not set fire to the building above and bring it down to bury his ashes as well.

Charko arranged Tholo's body in a seemly fashion and emptied a flask of oil on the rubbish. "I bless and consecrate thee, O fire," he said, making the sign of consecration and striking sparks with his flint and steel. They fell on to the oil-soaked rubbish; the blue flames gushed up and began to spread.

"The sacred fire, the fire that frees," he added, backing toward the door before the onrush of heat and smoke.

He stopped in the room where he'd cast the spell to carefully gather up his satchel. By the time he'd done that, the heat and smoke had caught up with him, and he could hear the low crackle of flames beginning to feed with a good appetite. He faced the fire as he pronounced the Kin's Blessing.

"O God, set now Thy servant Tholo free from all impurity, and grant him the sight of Thy True Face. Farewell, Tholo."

Then he turned and hurried toward the open air his lungs had begun to crave.

XXIV

THE REVEREND LADY LILKA DIPPED HER PEN IN THE
inkwell and began to write on the ancient and much-scraped
sheet of parchment: "Seventeenth day of the Moon of Etdanu,
in the First Year of the Rule of Queen Kantela."

Her fingers itched to write "First Year of the Reign of
Kantela Sherran," but the First Priestess of the Mother must
deal with what is, not what she wished, even in a private
journal that no eyes but hers and God's would see while she
lived. She prayed that she would be able to change the style
soon.

The last of the lords covered by the Edict of Households
have now been gone from Koddardos three full weeks, and
the city is at peace for the first time since before the death of
Pijtos Sherran. I was not surprised that the lords obeyed the
edict, for none wished to be singled out as a traitor, but I
was surprised at how quickly even such turbulent spirits as
Ikos Muzkur departed. The only ones left after two weeks
were those who had persuaded Lord Joviz that they had
lawful business in the city, and Joviz is a hard man to
convince in such matters.

Lilka wondered if most of the lords, except perhaps for Ikos
and a handful like him, had been less in search of a road to the
throne than to easy pickings by the way. Certainly the warlords
of Izrunarko's day would never have departed so tamely—but
then, the lords of today were not petty kings with their own
armies, untaught except for knowing that the man across the
river was an enemy you had to kill before he killed you.

The Council for Public Order is taking the lead in
restoring business in the city, or at least says it is. No doubt
its members are actually doing a good deal of work, for

221

which they will in time demand a price, even of the Throne and possibly of the temples. Nevertheless, the offerings have flowed in until no one is without food, clothing, or a place to sleep as a result of the riot.

That wouldn't console the bereaved, heal the burned and maimed, or find work for those whose shops and warehouses had gone up in flames, but it was at least a beginning. Meanwhile, the First Temple of the Mother was no longer spending all its time taking in offerings and giving out charity; Lilka could think about sitting down with the Treasurer and discussing how to improve the work of her office. Preferably without finding a new Treasurer, but there would be one if such was required to see God properly served.

That idea turned the First Priestess's thoughts to the even more heavily burdened woman in the palace.

Queen Kantela is spoken of with much respect for her edict and her concern for the victims of the riot. Even those who wonder whose advice she took in the matter of the edict are willing to credit her with the good sense to take it.

The Sherrani might be quicker than Harzis in taking to new ways, but that didn't mean the idea of a reigning queen could take deep root in little more than a moon.

Captain-General Bakarydes is much in the Queen's company, and the rumors that they are lovers continue. However, the amount of work Bakarydes has done in putting the House of War in order and trying to settle disputes among the Treasury, the Purveyor, and the army is sufficient that few think he needs any other justification for the amount of time he has spent in Koddardos.

No one except perhaps Bakarydes himself, Lilka added mentally. Joviz had described Bakarydes as a man who could slay ten thousand Momaks with two regiments and then start planning how to do it with only one regiment the next time.

222

Nor did he tolerate theft, graft, or excessive waste in his command. This being so, he had no patience with the Purveyor's Office or the lower ranks of the House of War when they questioned his requisitions; he asked for what he needed and expected to get it.

While it had become necessary for the Captain-General to come to Koddardos, he would not have been happy at having to stay to do work that should not have needed doing in the first place. While someone else might have taken twice the time and considered himself to be doing well, Bakarydes would only count every day in Koddardos a day lost from his proper work. Such were his standards, and indeed no one else would have dared to set for Sherran's greatest living soldier the standards he set for himself.

But how was the Captain-General reconciling his duty in the north with his desire for the Queen? Lilka decided that she would find a plausible occasion to visit the palace and see Bakarydes and Kantela together.

Meanwhile, she would continue to pray that Kantela found someone to share her burdens. No one should have to bear what she bore alone.

Lanach Tashinur bowed as he offered Joviz the tray of letters to sign. Joviz went through them mechanically; he'd read them all before and only one wasn't purely routine: an inquiry into certain rumors about mishandled funds of the Council for Public Order. Even that would hardly cause trouble; the mishandling was at a very low level if it existed at all, and Master Coron would be absolutely ruthless with any underling who threatened to tarnish his reputation.

As fast as Joviz handed him the letters, Lanach folded them and sealed them with wax and the First Magistrate's seal. When they were finished, a neat stack of paper and parchment bundles lay on the tray and the air in the room reeked of sealing wax and smoke.

Lanach opened the shutters wider to let in what little breeze this hot summer afternoon could produce, then rang for the messengers. Joviz rose.

"Lanach, take the rest of the day off. I don't think there's anything more that I can't do myself or put into the hands of a clerk."

"Thank you, my lord." Lanach smiled. "Did you know that my niece and her husband are in the city?"

"At the Red Pheasant."

"True. It will be good to see them again, my lord, since I could not go to Hierandos for my name day, nor did they wish to come to Koddardos while the lords' men overran it."

"A good evening to all of you. And to make your dinner a trifle more agreeable . . ." Joviz placed on the table between them a silver spice box, with gilded feet and an enameled lid with a crystal knob.

"It's less than you deserve, Lanach, but I hope it will give you pleasure."

"Thank you, my lord." For one of the few times in his life, Lanach seemed at a loss. Joviz saved him further embarrassment by raising his hand in the sign of dismissal. The secretary bowed and went out.

The air in the room still smelled too strongly of wax. Joviz went to the window and thrust his head out to take a deep breath of air and look out at a Koddardos more or less at peace under the summer sky. If it hadn't been peaceful, Tashino Rikura and her husband would still have been in Hierandos. Zuko Danur was a senior clerk in the Assayer's Office for the Treasury, which meant that he had to be utterly honest. He also seemed to be frightened of his own shadow.

No, that wasn't quite just. A man didn't have to be a coward to doubt the wisdom of taking himself and his wife into the middle of a city where the Throne's power was uncertain and lords' men roamed the streets like fleas roaming a stray dog. Even if the man were a coward, he was married to Lanach's only living kin, the only thing Lanach cared for outside his work. It was not for Joviz to judge the man. Far better to reward Lanach.

Izrunarko himself had said that one of the marks of a just Ruler was to take pleasure in rewarding good service. Flattering, but Joviz wasn't sure that the Teacher hadn't been a little too optimistic there. He remembered trying a petty lord who'd been proud of the good pay he gave his men—men in the business of kidnapping women for hire to sell in the cities along the Inner Sea or even to the Eastern Momaks. Joviz had sentenced that "Ruler" to the gallows and his well-paid men to the mines without a qualm.

He could discuss the question of Rulers rewarding service with Bakarydes—yes, and with Kantela—when he dined with them at the palace tonight for the first time since the riot. Then he mentally gave himself a good hard kick. Was the heat of the afternoon affecting his judgment that he would even think of mentioning such a subject in the presence of those two, after Kantela's impulsive "reward" to Bakarydes made the end of a previous meeting so memorable? Joviz was still castigating himself for not keeping his tongue behind his teeth.

Ah well. Best write off that whole affair as good intentions gone astray and leave the rest to God, as Bakarydes and Kantela doubtless had. Still, it would be very interesting to know how Kantela was wrestling with the problem of rewarding Bakarydes for all his services—unless, of course, he regarded the chance to render one of those services as a reward in itself, and knowing Bakarydes that seemed excessively unlikely. . . .

Ikos watched the lance point kick up dust and clods before its shaft snapped in the rider's hand. Ikos spat into the dust.

"You're supposed to be a soldier killing Momaks, not a farmer plowing furrows!" he roared as the rider cantered past the wooden stake driven into the ground as a mark. "Get my horse and lance!"

Ironhead had lost most of the unruly manners he'd taken on through lack of exercise while his master was in Koddardos. His gait was smooth and sure as Ikos rode him down toward the end of the field, meanwhile exercising with the lance. It was only a practice lance of normal weight and length, not one of his double-weight battle lances. Even if he could have wielded it in today's practice, he would not have wished to reveal his ability to do so—and that reminded him to have two or three more of his battle lances made up at once. His battle helm and breastplate had a few dents, but nothing that spoiled more than their looks, although he suspected this would be their last campaign.

How many sets of double-weight war gear had he gone through since he discovered that in battle he could will into himself the strength to use it? Certainly he'd known that he had that particular Gift by the time he was nineteen, so figuring no more than two years for each set it must be eight or nine.

No one suspected the Gift, either. The armorers who made the gear assumed that it was for practice, and Ikos armed himself for battle. Also, he could only use the Gift in battle, at which time everyone else was likely to be too busy to notice anything strange about the resistance of Ikos's armor or the destructive effects of his blows.

No one *had* suspected the Gift, at least. Now there was Charko, with his vast knowledge of magic and a professional habit of suspecting everybody else of having secrets. Until Ikos was on the throne, however, Charko would most likely keep his mouth shut, and after that, it might not be a bad idea to reveal the Gift. It would be a thoroughly fit and proper Gift for a warrior king of Sherran, even if Ikos had no intention of letting Charko muddle it about with austerity diets and mystical maunderings.

Meanwhile, here was the end of the field, and there two hundred paces away was the white stake. Ikos turned Ironhead, shifted his grip on the lance, and dug in his spurs.

With his rider unarmored and wielding only a lance, Ironhead was carrying far less than his battle load. He took off down the field more like a rabbit than a horse. Ikos let Ironhead steady at the gallop, then set the lance into striking position. Its balance let him move it like an extension of his arm.

The world shrank down to sunlight, dust rising under Ironhead's hooves, the smell of his own sweat and the horse's, the glare of sun on the lance head, and the growing white blob of the stake. Ikos held himself steady so that he and the horse were a single being propelling the head of the lance forward, down, down a trifle more—

The impact shooting up lance shaft to arm, shoulder, and chest told him of a clean hit before cheers of "Hoaaa! Well struck, my lord!" did the same. He reined in Ironhead and looked back. The stake was split from top down to the ground and one half was leaning drunkenly.

Ikos pulled off his hat and waved it to acknowledge the cheers until they died. Then he put Ironhead up to a canter and shouted, "I want everyone to practice until they can do the same to a Momak's head, if they come. Judzas Tarilur, put out a new stake and have someone bring me wine."

Ikos sat on a camp stool until a steward brought the wine. It was a pale Chobani vintage, delightfully cooled in a jug lowered into the farm's well. Ikos drank three cups in the time it took to drive in a new stake.

If the Momaks came. Charko seemed more disposed to say *when*, and he wasn't the only one. However, no one could tell from what Ikos had been doing this past moon that he was wagering anything on the Momaks leaving their tents all summer.

Although he was as close to the frontier as the boundaries of his lands permitted, he was still inside them. This made for easier relations with the farmers whose fields his cavalry trampled and whose flocks they ate, and also made it easier to keep unwanted eyes and ears at a distance. He had no more men with him than he'd had in Koddardos—in fact, he'd sent some of the less trustworthy or the less skilled back to sweeping stables or boiling leather for armor. He was doing nothing with his men that any lord would not have done if they'd missed their spring training to follow him to Koddardos.

Not entirely to his surprise, he was also raising their spirits as he sharpened their eyes and toughened their muscles. It seemed that he wasn't the only one who was glad to see the last of Koddardos, where the people had ended by calling a Watchman if a lord's badge came within fifty paces. Now they were home on their own land, doing a fighting man's work with the hope of more to come. Even Ikos's own Household no longer missed swaggering about in their silvered armor and devouring pickled oysters and raisin-stuffed capons in the choicest taverns of Koddardos. They now seemed to thrive on hard bread and salt pork and their battle garb of dark red tunics and dusty green trousers.

If the Momaks came, Ikos expected to have a thousand men fit to ride at once to any point in Sherran, carrying everything they would need on their mounts or on pack animals. That would be enough to destroy small bands of Momaks, fight off most large ones, and be a reinforcement to the army that Bakarydes couldn't ignore.

It would also be two or three times what Volo could send and arrive sooner—unless Volo had been able to conceal preparations of his own from Ikos's spies.

Those thousand were not all the men that Ikos could send to war; if he had time or needed to defend his own lands, he could command four times as many. But he could not count on time, even with Charko's promise of foreknowledge (probably obtained by means and from sources best not inquired into), and he prayed to God that he would never have to defend his own lands against Momaks. To mount the throne of Sherran after such an invasion would be to take the helm of a sinking ship.

The smell of roast mutton reached Ikos. A moment later so did four scullions carrying a fully-laid table. Ikos rose and drained his cup, then tossed it to one of the scullions.

"Run and fetch Captain Malij Barjachur. Bring him back in a spell and the cup's yours."

The man scurried off. Ikos shaded his eyes against the sun and counted the men lined up to ride against the new stake. Definitely a second stake would be needed. In fact, why not set up a course of six or seven targets for lance, sword, dart, and bow, and use a watchglass to see how fast a man could ride the whole course?

It might work. If it did and he could give the idea to the army, Bakarydes would not love him the less for it. Ikos absently chewed on a slice of mutton as a picture of the course began to form in his mind.

The royal party rode into the shade of the ancient stone wall, the only part of some petty warlord's stronghold that hadn't long since been quarried for its stones. Kantela took off her broad-brimmed hat with the veil and waved it to her grooms. They pulled up their horses and waited for Lozo to divide the sentry posts between the grooms and the Banner troopers. Two of the troopers were already scrambling up the wall to find places that gave them a good view of the countryside around the old stronghold.

"How can anyone fight in this kind of heat?" Kantela asked.

Bakarydes grinned. "Mostly we don't have to. The passes are high enough that it's seldom this hot there. We always try to catch the Momaks in the passes before they reach the lowlands. Usually we succeed."

The grin faded, and Kantela knew he was wondering how matters were going in the north, in spite of all the useful work he was doing in Koddardos. She remembered his description of Chief of Horse Berov Godinur, commanding on the frontier in his absence.

"He's thorough but not imaginative. He's also twelve years my elder and thinks he should have had the Captain-Generalship. He hasn't let jealousy eat him up, but I wouldn't wager against his doing something foolish in an effort to prove that he's as good as he thinks he is."

He hadn't said whether that included not reporting trouble with the Momaks so Bakarydes would stay in Koddardos and Berov's command would continue. He hadn't needed to. By now they could talk without words about things other than desire.

Kantela looked toward the Golden River. Halfway downhill the path turned into a road, and the road wound down to level ground and then off toward the river through stands of fig and blackwood trees and little villages of whitewashed houses with tile roofs. Once the villages had held farmers; now they held mostly craftsmen who worked in the shops clustered around the Thunder Hill barracks. The half-mile square of gray barracks itself was invisible beyond the brow of the hill.

More villages, vineyards, and then the Golden River itself, so bright in the sun that it looked like an enameled river on the cover of a brass box. Koddardos also looked like a picture of itself, and even the boats on the river moved so slowly in the still air that one had to look for a spell to see that they were moving at all.

"I'd like to inspect the Thunder Hill barracks some day," Kantela said.

"There wouldn't be much to inspect now," Bakarydes replied. "The last of the trained recruits are long gone to their regiments, and the new ones won't come in until after the harvest. There's nothing there except camp hands—horse trainers, craftsmen, caretakers, and so forth—and whatever veterans aren't out running errands for the House of War."

"I wasn't thinking about going now," Kantela said. "I'd have to be out of mourning before I did. I confess, though, that I want to keep a closer eye on Sherran's army. Besides, the troubles with the Purveyor and the Treasury may have taken their toll at Thunder Hill."

"Maybe, but I think the worst of those troubles have been settled as well as they can be without removing Ikarotikos. You'd most likely find nothing worse than the bad habits old soldiers set in their ways can get into, particularly without a Great Captain to keep an eye on them."

Unspoken, it hung in the hot air between them—that Bakarydes would have to be back in the north before autumn and long before Kantela was out of mourning. Even if the whole Momak people vanished like the smoke from their fires, he would still be needed, if only to oversee the discharge of most of his men!

Kantela licked her lips, dry from the heat and also from fear of the impulse that had just struck her. It was an impulse, she admitted, rather than an idea—but she and Bakarydes were alone, and this time she would talk it over with him before she acted.

"There could be a Great Captain again, you know. It would be easy."

Bakarydes managed to smile when he replied, "There could also be a great many enemies for that Great Captain, and for the Queen who appointed him. I can't afford that many enemies, and you can't afford to make all of those enemies yours."

Since that was one reason she'd rejected marrying any of the lesser lords, Kantela knew that Bakarydes was making sense, as much as she wanted to find some flaw in his logic. "Very well. But the Captain-General of the North usually becomes the Great Captain unless he's too old to do more than become Captain-General of the Swords or simply retire. You won't be too old." She would not speak words of ill omen by mentioning the other way he might avoid becoming Great Captain.

"If I stayed in the north as long as I wanted to, I would be too old," said Bakarydes, and Kantela felt a small cold snake curl its way through her bowels. "But I'd better plan on leaving the frontier before I come to think I own the place. That way lies making even more enemies, and thinking you lead by right and God's will instead of by what kind of soldier you are."

"I'd trust you never to think that."

"Then you'd be trusting me more than I do myself," he said slowly in a tone that denied the possibility of argument. More briskly, he added, "There's also the problem of who would fill my saddle. Berov Godinur simply isn't fit for the job, but he'd probably intrigue against anyone else senior enough and make his life impossible.

"I think we'd best let the matter lie for, oh, five years. In that time a good many possible enemies will retire. Also, the Momaks will certainly ask for and get the kind of hammering that keeps them quiet for a generation. After that, any commander could do my job.

"Also, a good many of the younger officers are going to prove what they're made of in such a war. I can bring them

231

along first as Captain-General, then as Great Captain, until we're surrounded by men who owe their promotions to me, instead of men who've seen me promoted past them."

The queen in Kantela saw the sense of this, and the woman had too much pride to show what she thought of spending five years as Bakarydes's unacknowledged lover until he could formally divorce his twelve-thousand-headed acknowledged wife in the north. Both queen and woman appreciated Bakarydes's tactful and informative reply.

"Let's hope the war with the Momaks leaves some of the good men alive to promote," she said. He squeezed her hand and she saw in his eyes his gratitude for her self-control. Then he looked at the sky.

"Plague! It's getting on for the half-watch, and it's a quarter-watch just to the river. We don't want to keep Joviz waiting."

Kantela smiled. "We could save time by bathing together . . . Oh. So that's one of your dreams too. Well, I won't ask the others. Or maybe I will, some other time and place."

Bakarydes had almost stopped blushing by the time they rode out into the sunlight again.

Hakfor was telling the tale of how he'd helped a smith in his former employer's stables recognize and rescue his long-lost sister, who'd never been acknowledged by her father and who'd been sold as a small child. Having been sold, of course she could not go home to Harz-i-Shai and a true marriage, but Hakfor and her brother had managed to find her a respectable Sherrani husband in Hierandos.

It was a good story, even if Michal suspected that half of it was a patchwork of old tales told around the fireside for two centuries. Hakfor told it wittily and well, as he did every story, and he'd collected a respectable audience from among those in the Blue Falcon's main dining room who hadn't heard it before.

Unfortunately Michal had, at least four times that he could remember, and also knew that the tale would outlast not only the roast goose Hakfor was carving, but all that goose's broodmates and a couple of the Blue Falcon's famous game pasties as well. He was looking around for a route that would allow a discreet withdrawal when he saw a Harzi in riding dress enter, his red eyes huge in a dust-caked face.

The nearest serving maid promptly found him a table and a beer, which he drained without taking the mug from his lips. But Michal had noticed how he walked to the table—like a man whose legs were still locked around an imaginary horse—and how his eyes wandered everywhere without seeing anything. That man needed a good deal more than a drink.

Michal rose and walked to the man's table as the maid brought a second beer. He waited until she was gone and the beer as well, then said, "Clansman, I think any man who can help you is bound to give it."

"You can't help me unless—" the man began, then seemed to force into his eyes the ability to see things close at hand. His mouth gaped. "By the Warrior! You are timely come, Captain!"

"If so, I can be of more help if I know why. While it goes much against my habit to take a man away from his beer, this is not the best place to talk of matters you don't want overheard."

The man looked at his third beer, emptied it, waited until the maid brought a fourth, then paid her and rose. He wasn't entirely steady on his feet as he led Michal outside, but he didn't need to lean against the wall of the Blue Falcon. Michal very nearly did, by the time Zimrat shan-Bariv Lamenu had finished his tale.

The Momaks were over the frontier, all the warriors sworn to the hundred-head chief Marsh Wolf and more. Probably many more, because they were so far inside Sherran that they had to have overrun the patrols at the major passes before they could give a warning. No single chief, not even a hundred-head, could command so many warriors, although it seemed that Marsh Wolf had had a vision of a great Momak victory over the Sherrani.

As far as Zimrat knew, the first men to discover the Momaks were a hunting party of Harzis from a caravan guard, returning with fresh meat. They had stumbled across the field of a battle between Momaks and a Sherrani patrol, and found a couple of Sherrani still alive. With the answers the dying men gave to their questions, the Harzis tracked a few Momaks, and their answers to questions rather less gently put gave the Harzis a picture of the invasion worth writing down and sending south.

The party of riders from the caravan guard was ambushed by bandits, but the message went through and on to a Harzi working as a horse trainer on a noble's estate. His son rode south, killing two horses before he reached another trustworthy Harzi. . . .

So the message came, until it reached Koddardos in the hands of Zimrat. He'd stopped only to sew it into the lining of his left boot, in case there was someone in Koddardos who did not wish it known that Momaks were in the land.

To Michal, this seemed less than impossible. However much of a lackwit the Chief of Horse commanding in Bakarydes's absence was, he would certainly have sent enough messengers for at least one to reach Koddardos, though all the Momaks of the plains stood between the frontier and the city. That nothing had come to disturb the sleep of the Captain-General suggested that more than Momaks had been scooping up the messengers.

More than bandits, too. Neither Momaks nor bandits were good enough to stop not only news but rumors. That suggested treason or magic or both.

It was not yet time to take pride in the fact that bandits, Momaks, and magic hadn't been able to stop Harzis. The message still had to be delivered.

"I'm in the service of First Magistrate Joviz—"

"I recognize the badge."

"Good. I can bring you to him before the beginning of the northwatch. Give him your message, and your job is done."

"That is well."

Michal decided it would only draw more short remarks if he said that he hoped to see Joviz at the palace itself where the First Magistrate was dining. Now if only the Swords didn't refuse to let him see Joviz unless he stated his business—!

"Do you want anything to eat?"

"I had a sausage on my last half-watch to the river."

"Then come with me, while I call for our horses and a couple of guards."

Ulev would make one; he'd shown he had a cool head the night of the riot. Yiftat would be the other; he would do even better work staying behind to keep any wagging tongues still, but the man had earned a chance at whatever reward the bringers of this news would earn.

At least Michal thought it would be a reward. As far as he knew, Izrunarko had cured the Sherrani of the ancient custom of killing the bearer of bad news.

XXV

QUEEN KANTELA'S GAZE SHIFTED FROM ZIMRAT'S FACE TO Michal's and back again. Her hand rose to her face, then fell back as if she'd wanted to cover her mouth or pat her hair but then thought of her dignity before Harzis.

Michal entertained no illusions that the news of the Momak invasion coming to Koddardos in the hands of Harzis would afford either Kantela or Bakarydes any pleasure. Still, he did not fear injustice from either or folly from Bakarydes, and at least Lord Joviz was at the far end of the table, saying nothing now but watching everything.

"Are the names of all the Harzis who helped carry this message written down here?" asked the Queen, indicating the paper on the table between her wine goblet and a silver sauce bowl. The gesture was much more assured than the last one, even graceful. Michal was conscious that Her Grace was a distinctly handsome woman, in the dark Sherrani style.

"All the ones who aren't oath-bound to keep their names hidden," replied Zimrat.

"Good. That is some nine or ten men of Harz-i-Shai to whom the Throne may owe a great debt. God willing, that debt shall be paid." Both Joviz and Bakarydes nodded in approval.

"Zimrat shan-Bariv, are you prepared to submit to a test of your truthfulness in this matter?"

"Your Grace," said Joviz. "I do not know what oaths this man has sworn, but I cannot imagine that he would be serving in Sherran if they did not prevent him from lying in such a matter."

"As you say, Your Excellency, you do not know what oaths this man has sworn," said Bakarydes. "On the other hand, Your Grace, even the Fire of Truth would only reveal whether he believed what had been told him. If there is a lie somewhere along the chain of Harzis from the north to Koddardos, shaming this man would probably do nothing to find it."

"Perhaps," said Kantela. Michal had hardly ever in his life seen a woman trying so hard to hide disappointment that a man—her man—hadn't come to her aid. Before she could reveal anything else, she seemed to remember that this discussion was not for Harzi ears.

"Zimrat shan-Bariv, Captain Michal, you also have the Throne's gratitude. The Swords will escort you and those who came with you to a private chamber where you will await the summons of the Throne."

Both Harzis bowed; Michal said, "Our duty to the Queen's Grace" for both of them. Then they backed out the door to join Ulev and Yiftat as half a dozen Swords moved to surround the four Harzis and herd them out of the royal chambers.

The private chamber was part of the suite of rooms assigned to the officers of the palace. The benches, chairs, and rugs gave an air of comfort, but this room was not meant to sleep in. Michal hoped this meant their stay here would be short.

For the first time, he saw that Zimrat was uneasy. Finally Zimrat turned to Michal and blurted out, "Captain, would they really make me endure the Fire—"

Michal made the universal Harzi gesture against eavesdroppers. Zimrat took a deep breath and whispered, "Could it be— the Fire?"

"It could be," said Michal, and saw Zimrat blanch. "It isn't likely, though," he added hastily. "Lord Joviz knows our customs and trusts our oaths, and would speak against it. The

Queen wouldn't go against him unless she had Bakarydes on her side, I think, and he's a man of some sense."

"Not enough to keep him from discussing Harzis as if they were goats without the power to understand human speech," said Ulev.

"That only makes him a Sherrani, not a fool," said Michal. "You've been in Koddardos longer than I have, Ulev. You should know the difference."

"Maybe," said Ulev. "Oh, well, it would be a Father-forsaken bit of unwisdom to quarrel now. I could do with a drink."

"You'll do without unless you have some money," said Michal. "I didn't hear the Swords ordered to provide more hospitality than this room."

Ulev felt his purse. "Not fat, but not lean either. How much hospitality would a veysela win from the Swords?"

"More than I think we'd better take," said Michal. Ulev's cool head grew considerably warmer after the third cup.

Ulev caught Michal's tone and nodded. "Beer then, and a meat pie?"

"Two meat pies."

"Done."

Michal rose and walked to the door. "Swordsman!"

"Yes, Captain?"

Flourished silver brought at least a cheerful promise of pies and ale. Michal walked back into the room without feeling an itch between his shoulder blades for the first time since he'd heard the news of the Momaks. His report of tonight's activities would make a message that Daivon could hardly fail to remember.

Then the itch was back, as Michal realized this priceless opportunity to send valuable information was one he would have to pass by. If anyone ever learned what had been sent to Daivon, they would also learn that it must have come from a witness to the meeting in the palace—and the number of those was not so great that it would take a long search to find Michal.

Then nothing short of Joviz's threatening to resign his office could save Michal. The First Magistrate would not do that for a captain who had held his oath, if not in contempt, at least rather too lightly.

Michal cursed under his breath. There was more than his own advantage to be gained by telling Daivon that the Queen seemed inclined to distrust Harzis, and that Bakarydes would argue against that distrust from common sense. This was knowledge that the Chief of Chiefs *needed*.

Unfortunately, the Chief of Chiefs would also find a live and free Michal shan-Ouvram useful, and there seemed no way to have both. Michal racked his brains to find one, but he hadn't succeeded before the pies and beer arrived, and he realized that he was too hungry and thirsty to think about the matter any further at the moment.

To Joviz, the silence that had hung over the table since the Harzis left seemed to have lasted half a watch. He was trying to find neutral words to break it when Kantela saved him the trouble.

"Your Excellency, your concern for the honor of Harzis does you honor as well. But you seem to know things about them that I do not. Could you explain?"

Joviz could have wished for a better opportunity to instruct the Queen in the customs of Harzis, but at least Kantela didn't seem to be angry.

"Your Grace, I spoke as I did because I did not know what form of truth-testing you proposed. The Fire of Truth is reserved for traitors and other great criminals."

"It would not take a very hostile judge to consider that spreading rumors of Momak invasions was treason," said Bakarydes.

"I would consider it so myself," said Joviz. "But a Harzi who must submit to the Fire of Truth is little better than an outlaw, even if he passes the ordeal of the Fire. He is known as a man whose oaths were called into question. He cannot return to Harz-i-Shai unless he is willing to accept the most degrading work and still live ready to fight anyone who calls him oath-breaker. I have known Harzis to kill themselves

238

rather than go home, even though the Fire proved them innocent."

"I had not known this," said Kantela.

"No shame to Your Grace," said Bakarydes. "I don't imagine most of us have so many Harzis in our service that we have to be able to think like one in order to do our job. For me, it's always been enough to be able to think like a Momak. Frankly, I don't think I'd have the wits to do His Excellency's job, even if I had the patience."

"The Captain-General is gracious," said Joviz. "If Your Grace wishes my advice in this matter . . . ?"

"Do I look like a fool?" snapped Kantela. "I would have to be, not to want your advice!"

"Your pardon, Your Grace. I would suggest that the messenger be placed under the Spell of Truth Binding. That compels him to answer truthfully any questions put to him. It doesn't reveal his thoughts on any other matter or call his honor into question."

"That would be my choice, too, Your Grace," said Bakarydes. "Truth Binding has the limitation that you need to ask the right questions, but since we know what the trouble is, that's no problem."

"Very well," said Kantela. "That will be the Throne's order. I don't doubt that Zimrat is telling the truth as far as he knows, but he may not know everything. He may be able to tell us who would know more.

"This news should not have had to come in the hands of Harzis, my lords. That it did smells very much of the same trouble we had over the stolen pay chests—" Kantela's hand flew to her mouth and she looked away.

Bakarydes frowned. "Forgive me, Your Grace. I completely forgot to tell Lord Joviz the full story of the pay chests, even after we had word that the replacements were safely in the north." Then he proceeded to tell Joviz that there was a strong suspicion of unlawful sorcery's being involved in the theft of a convoy of army pay chests and how that same sorcery might have helped bandits and Momaks intercept army messengers with the news of the invasion.

Joviz was quite sure that Bakarydes was telling the truth about the convoy. He was quite as sure that he was being lied to about Kantela's having ordered Bakarydes to tell him, and for a moment he had to swallow indignation that was near to anger.

A little reflection calmed him. Clearly, Bakarydes had taken a place ahead of both himself and Lady Lilka as Kantela's most trusted adviser. Just as clearly, no harm would come of that for now. The Momaks might not be as numerous or as far into Sherran as Zimrat had said, but Sherran was now a kingdom at war. Who then could better advise the Throne than Sherran's greatest living soldier?

Kantela, meanwhile, seemed to be trying to both glare at Bakarydes and hold back the tears at the same time. Finally she pressed the heels of both hands into her eyes, and when she took them away Joviz saw her cheeks glisten suspiciously.

"My lords, it seems that we have some uninvited guests. How many we do not know, but even one is too many. Let us see what we can do to make them know they're not welcome."

Most of that work would fall to Bakarydes. He had eleven thousand fit men in his twenty regiments and another four thousand already in the north who could take the field—"if we can find replacements for them in the camps."

"Do we need to hold the camps?" asked Kantela. "I thought war against the Momaks was all movement."

"One still needs rations, arrows, horseshoes, fodder for our chargers since they can't graze, remounts, and reinforcements. All these have to be put somewhere, such as a fortified camp. Otherwise we have to choose between assigning field regiments to guard supply trains or losing the supplies to the Momaks. One way we eat our own tail, the other way the Momaks eat it. The Momaks can't take a fortified camp that's well supplied and defended by men who know which end of a crossbow does the damage, but we can't strip the camps entirely."

"If the lords and cities sent men, would they be good enough?" said Kantela.

"Many of them might be, if they came in time and weren't

240

massacred on the march by Momack scouts. I suspect that Marsh Wolf has discovered a few civilized tactics without any help from the spirits, and I'll lay odds that one of those tactics is cutting off our reinforcements and supplies."

Bakarydes refilled his wine cup without offering any to the others. "Marsh Wolf worries me more than anything else about this whole invasion. The last time the Momaks threw up a chief like him was in the time of Your Grace's grandfather, when they rode all the way to the walls of Dazkados.

"What saves us from more trouble with the Momaks most of the time is that they're not under one leader. Every hundred-head chief tries to go his own way, and most of the lesser chiefs are busy trying to collect heads. So in large numbers they can charge and they can run away, and that's about all.

"When they scout or raid, it's a different matter. There a leader has only picked men under him, and if he's shrewd he can do anything with them that I can do with a regular squadron and a few things I can't. Fortunately, we've managed to make scouting and raiding dangerous business, so those shrewd leaders usually don't live to take their hundredth head.

"Marsh Wolf did. We nearly bagged him a few times, but nearly isn't quite. Every time he escaped he learned more and taught it to a few more of his warriors, and they've taught it to theirs. So we could wind up facing Marsh Wolf having the same kind of hold over fifteen or twenty thousand Momaks that he used to have over a couple of hundred.

"If we do, we're in trouble. None of us except maybe me is going to end up on a Momak head-pole—" Kantela closed her eyes for a moment "—but it won't be the most auspicious beginning to Your Grace's rule.

"On the other hand, if this invasion can be trounced soon and thoroughly enough, Marsh Wolf's reputation as well as his warriors will be hammered. His vision will be suspected as sent by evil spirits, and someone might even save us the trouble of killing him. That will sow blood feuds and succession fights through his whole tribe for years to come."

Even if Marsh Wolf could be quickly trounced, they'd probably end up having to use the lords' men for cleaning-up operations. What Sherran needed right now was men already organized into units and fit for the field. The cupboard wasn't altogether bare of these, but it wasn't lavishly stocked either.

Of the lords' men, perhaps one in five might be fit to ride with the regiments—call it two thousand men. Take a regiment from Mindranas (if the ships to carry it could be found in time), half a regiment each from Thunder Hill and Hierandos, and odd troops and squadrons from here and there—another two thousand. Assemble three—call them "regiments" for want of a better name—of reliable Harzis, one from Svarno, one from the best caravan guards, and one from the First Magistrate's Harzis and Lord Uzichko's Fleet Guards—fifteen hundred more at least.

There were also small garrisons scattered all over southern Sherran "—but if any of them have fought more than pickpockets in the last two generations I'll serve a year in the ranks of the worst one," said Bakarydes. "Sending them into the field without training and remounts would only be giving the Momaks trophies."

There were also four reasonably fit regiments in Dazkados, but Bakarydes couldn't see how more than one of them could be sent into the field. After a doubtful look Joviz was about to agree, then saw Kantela shaking her head.

"Yes, Your Grace?"

"I would argue for sending three regiments from Dazkados. That was the nearest city to my father's estates, so I grew up knowing it quite well. They are very proud of how they rebuilt their walls and held them the last time the Momaks came, and still prouder of how they sent mounted men into the field to aid my grandfather. They have kept up both the walls and the City Guard ever since, so that with the aid of a single army regiment I am sure they could hold the city."

Bakarydes looked from Kantela to Joviz. "Your Excellency . . . ?"

"Her Grace does well to remind us," said Joviz. "Most of the city guards, I regret to say, couldn't hurt a Momak unless he broke a leg tripping over their corpses, but the guard of Dazkados is certainly fit for defense, maybe even for the field.

Also, they could mount some of the men with locally raised horses, instead of drawing on our stock of remounts."

"Indeed," said Kantela. "Also, consider that many of the lords who will be sending men have their lands in this area. Lord Volo is only the most powerful. With three regular regiments to stiffen them—" she looked a question over the term at Bakarydes, and he nodded "—they would be able to march more safely to the frontier, for they would be strong enough to fight any band of Momaks likely to ride that far into Sherran. Also, the regiments could see to supplying the lords' men instead of their having to buy or steal supplies on the way."

Bakarydes was smiling at Kantela not only like a lover but also like a teacher with his most gifted pupil. Joviz could imagine Izrunarko smiling at one of his most promising scholars in exactly the same way.

Joviz nodded. "I was not much impressed with the care many of the lords took to make sure their men were fed and paid once they were outside their own lands, nor their concern for what their men might do if they were not. I will certainly do everything my office allows to strengthen the City Guard of Dazkados, although I warn you that the magistrate there is no friend of mine. He thinks he should have had this office."

"God be merciful!" Kantela burst out. Then she controlled herself with an obvious effort. "Perhaps I should pay a visit to Dazkados, invoke my grandfather's memory, and see if the citizens allow their magistrate to drag his feet after that."

"Your Grace," began Bakarydes, "is it wise to leave Koddardos while—?"

"It's a damned sight wiser to leave Koddardos about the business of the throne than to sit on the throne and worry if your head's already some Momak's trophy!" Kantela shouted.

For a moment, Joviz would have given anything short of a sight of the True Face of God to be instantly transported elsewhere. Then he stole a look at Bakarydes. He had never seen a man simultaneously trying not to choke on his own laughter and not to take a woman in his arms.

243

Joviz had thought that with the news of the Momaks, Bakarydes would be on the road north under the moonlight. Now he changed his mind. If the Captain-General left before the Queen had a chance to bid him a farewell that took little account of discretion, any Momak who took him prisoner would find one vital part of his anatomy already missing.

XXVI

THIS WAS HIS HOME COUNTRY, THOUGHT BAKARYDES. THE hard blue sky that was almost too bright to look at, the half-ripe wheat and rye in fields separated by rough stone walls or gravel roads like the one he was riding on, the rippling green-brown horizon line. Somehow the hills in the north always seemed to be well off toward the horizon from where you were. The only place one could see further, so he'd heard, was beyond the frontier hills on the plains themselves.

"My lord," came Lozo's voice from his left rear.

"Yes, Lozo?"

"If you want to stop and rest the horses, we can visit your family as well. That road we passed a spell ago is the one to your uncle's house."

It would be good to see the family again—Bakarydes tried not to think "for what might be the last time." Besides, he had every intention of seeing what the Benye lands could contribute to the Army of the North in the way of men and supplies.

Bakarydes reined in his mount. The gelding pecked and slithered on the gravel and Bakarydes cursed him softly. Thank God he was at most two days from having Lightning under him again. For all his strength and speed, the war-horse was as sure-footed as a Momak pony.

Off to his left a lone blackwood rose at the edge of a wheat field. Bakarydes recognized the branch shaped like a shepherd's crook. That was the tree he'd learned to climb on, and in a little hollow out of sight was the pond where he'd learned to swim. . . .

"You're quite right, as usual."

"Yes, my lord."

Something in Lozo's voice caught Bakarydes's attention. His face, too. Bakarydes decided he didn't want that oh-so-respectful face or voice at his back when the time came to sit down with his kin and ask for their aid to the army. They wouldn't notice anything odd about Lozo's behavior, but they would notice that something was troubling *him*, and then the fat would be in the fire just as surely if not as soon.

Bakarydes reined in and shouted to the rest of the Banner troop, "Back to the last road and wait there!"

Lozo shot Bakarydes a relieved look, then added, "You heard the Captain-General. Now move!"

When the troopers had moved out of hearing, Bakarydes nodded to the Bannerbearer. "All right, Lozo. Tell me man-to-man what's on your mind."

"It's not what's on my mind, my lord. It's the road you're on. You know it could lead to the pyre as well as to the throne."

"All roads lead to the pyre in the end, Lozo."

"There's a time and a place waiting for every man's pyre, or so I've heard. No need to pile the logs and pour the oil yourself." Lozo's eyes asked a question he didn't dare put into words.

Bakarydes shook his head. "No, I haven't been asked, and I wouldn't be interested if I was. I won't be asked, either. Not with Pijtos's pyre barely cold."

Lozo frowned. "Not the throne, then. But that's not all she could give you."

"No, it isn't, and she did ask me about being Great Captain. Not ask me *to be* Great Captain, just whether I would accept an offer if she made it."

"That's more sense than I thought she had," Lozo's respect for the throne didn't keep him from being blunt about any particular occupant of it.

"Kantela has more sense than most people thought she had, including both the late Pijtos Sherran and your Captain-General."

"I'm still surprised she did it that way, after what she did with the offering."

"You heard about that?"

"I don't remember that anyone was much for keeping it a secret, my lord. Although I admit I had more time to listen to things like that."

"No doubt." This time it was Bakarydes who didn't dare put a question into words.

"Nobody said anything I had to notice, my lord. Don't worry about that."

Bakarydes grunted with relief. Lozo's way of "noticing" people who made disrespectful remarks about the Captain-General had been known to put the people in the hands of a minor Healer for half a watch or so.

"I thought you must have settled it yourself," Lozo added, "or we'd have long since left Koddardos."

Bakarydes stifled a groan. Was it just his imagination, or was his skull suddenly as transparent as a thin silk bed robe, so that everyone could see his thoughts? Lozo had known him for twenty years, so perhaps the Bannerbearer's questions proved little. But Kantela had been damned near as keen sighted, after knowing him barely ten days.

If he'd been coming back to the frontier permanently, it wouldn't have mattered. The only people he had to fool about his plans were the Momaks. But if—call it circumstances— would be taking him to Koddardos every few moons . . .

Meanwhile, Lozo was on the scent, and there'd be no whipping him off, not after asking him to speak man-to-man. "We did have a few words—more than a few, actually, although most of them were mine—about the offering."

He gave a judiciously revised version of the quarrel and the talk the next morning, carefully putting himself in as unfavorable a light as he could manage without telling any too obvious lies. When he'd finished, he looked at Lozo's careful lack of expression and realized that his notion of "obvious" was hopelessly inadequate in the face of the Bannerbearer.

All Lozo said, however, was "Did you make that big a fool of yourself, my lord?"

246

All Bakarydes could answer was, "Not really, Lozo."

After a long silence, Lozo nodded. "I don't suppose you did." After a shorter silence, he added, "Chief Berov's Bannerbearer, Talzo Rikur, has a brother who's an armorer in Crowsford. I reckon he might be able to make a really good suit of armor if you could give him the dimensions."

"Why should—anyone we know—need armor?"

"I'm thinking that if she can't keep you down south, she may want to come north from time to time. You and she'll both sleep easier and argue less if she's got armor between her and Momak arrows."

"We might at that," said Bakarydes. He allowed the silence to go on until it was obvious that Lozo had no more questions, then dug in his spurs. Gravel rattled as the gelding pecked and slithered again before working up to a trot.

The brass railing of the balcony where Kantela sat finishing her breakfast gleamed with the night's dew and the spray from the mountain stream boiling past ten paces below. Fifty paces downhill, the stream flowed into a granite-walled canal and wound its way out of sight through Dazkados, to emerge on the other side and flow into the Tarnspill River, one of the tributaries of the Golden.

Dazkados owed its existence to being at the head of navigation on the Tarnspill and indeed on the whole system of the Golden River and all its tributaries. The magistrate's house where Kantela was lodged owed its existence to Veysel Sherran, who'd quartered his first garrison for the city in this spot, which had unlimited fresh water and a good view of the city.

Trees, houses, and gardens now covered a fair part of what had once been open ground between the house and the city walls, but it would still be hard for any evilly disposed person to come within bowshot of the balcony without being seen. This was not something Kantela would have noticed two moons ago, but she had profited from Bakarydes's instruction in this as in other matters. She had also taken great pleasure in

247

pointing out this fact to the magistrate, when he politely grumbled at her exposing herself on the balcony.

"The Swords and the City Guards can deal with any handful of enemies. If there is more than a handful of men in Dazkados who wish my life, especially now, then perhaps you have not been performing the duties of your office as the Throne has a right to expect."

In fact, though Magistrate Goros kept more state than Joviz and Bakarydes put together, he had not neglected the duties of his office. In three days in the city, Kantela had found little to complain of in the City Guard or anything else that affected Dazkados's ability to defend itself. Kantela suspected that the Chief of Horse commanding the four regiments of the garrison had a hand in this. The better the City Guard, the better his own chances of taking his men to the frontier instead of sitting on his hindquarters.

Whatever the reason, the work had been done. The three regiments told off for frontier duty would be able to leave as soon as the lords' men they were to escort and the supplies for the march were all assembled. That work did not need the Throne's hand, so Kantela had already made plans to return to Koddardos the day after tomorrow. This would preclude all but the briefest of visits to the Tinos lands and her brother Gaida, but all that she had to say to him could be said in such a visit. In the fifteen years since she left for Koddardos and her wedding, she and Gaida had grown to have little in common, and the rest of her surviving kin were scattered from Svarno to the Cities of the Plain; it would have taken a year to visit them all.

Meanwhile, she could do a fair amount of the Throne's business here, besides traveling about the city and its surrounding villages and invoking the memory of Kalaj Kopanur and the city's famous stand against the Momaks. That seemed to be a powerful memory, from the way they cheered every mention of her grandfather's name and the other heroes of the war.

"Your Grace, Master Captain Drako Trunjur craves audience."

It was the captain of the City Guard commanding the duty watch of sentries. The Guard and the Swords of her escort alternated watches; the Swords grumbled at this but their captain was prepared to admit that the City Guard deserved the honor and was fit for the work. She doubted that he would have admitted as much if he'd known that one reason she allowed the Guard this duty was that too many of the Swords reached Dazkados so exhausted from a ride that left her merely pleasantly tired that she doubted their fitness for more than palace duty. She would have gladly turned all the Swords over to Lozo Bojarkur or someone like him for two moons' vigorous training and then sent the survivors off to fight Momaks; giving some of their work to other men was the best she could do for now.

"Bid Master Drako enter," Kantela replied, patting her hair into order with one hand and signalling the servants with the other.

The Master Captain was about Bakarydes's height but twice as wide and so built that he did not look fat in spite of his bulk. His bow was workmanlike rather than graceful, and his "My duty to the Queen's Grace" seemed to rumble up from somewhere below the level of his brass-studded belt.

"You have honored the Throne and shown a great sense of duty by riding so far from the sea," said Kantela. "The least I can do is ask you to sit down and join me for breakfast. I've already eaten once, but I find this mountain air gives me an appetite I don't have in Koddardos. I've heard much the same is true of sea air. Indeed, it would have to be, if sailors are fed on moldy bread and salt meat as I've heard."

Drako Trunjur smiled and sat. "Thank you, Your Grace. You've heard right for the longer voyages, to the eastern end of the Inner Sea or out onto the Ocean. For shorter voyages, say to Mindranas, a good wind will take you there before the bread can spoil or the water turn green."

"Indeed. Did you have any such troubles on your voyage from Zaramy with the horses?"

"Fewer than I'd expected, but not so few that I don't think the men earned their pay." He went off into the tale of the horse convoy's voyage. Kantela suspected that he was telling it as concisely as he knew how, but it was still overfull of bilges and halyards and tillers and cookboxes and other words that might as well have been in Momak for all the sense they made to her.

Finally she held up a hand. "I am more than persuaded that the men earned their pay, as long as the horses are fit." One thing she did know was that horses, being sensible land-dwelling beasts, often finished a long sea voyage in poor health.

"The army farriers had passed nine out of ten when I left," said Drako. "They were even talking of forming up the first remount herd to ride north with the army squadrons from Hierandos."

"Excellent," said Kantela. "I am grateful for all the good work you and your crews have done. Now, if you will answer one further question: Is there time to make another voyage east for horses, or should the ships be turned to bringing men from Mindranas? Please try to answer as you would to a child. It is not something to be proud of, when so much of Sherran's wealth comes from Mindranas and our sea trade, but ships and the sea are as much a mystery to me as the rites of the Momaks."

She half-expected the Master Captain to protest that without using the precise words he would be talking nonsense. Instead he nodded and smiled. "Bless Your Grace for being a gentle teacher. It's not often enough that I have cause to remember how to talk to people who aren't sailors. I'll do my best."

His best was quite good enough, and when he did stray off into thickets of seafarers' words he was always ready to be brought back and to explain in plain Sherrani what he'd been trying to say. It seemed that the horse transports might not make another voyage in time for their second cargo of horses to be useful in anything but a long war, running at least into the autumn. On the other hand, they would need a thorough cleaning before they could safely carry men, and that also would take time.

"Far better to send us for horses again, because the army will need remounts even after the war," Drako concluded.

"For the men of Mindranas, the Throne had best think of chartering some more ships."

"It shall be done that way, then," said Kantela. "If you are not sailing again at once, I will ask you to take a commission from the Throne to find the—how many ships to carry a regiment?"

"Eight at least, and big ones if only that many."

"To find and charter enough ships to carry one regiment from the garrison of Mindranas. Choose a reliable deputy for the work, or have Lord Uzichko give you one, so that if you have to sail before the work is done he can finish it."

She could almost hear Bakarydes saying, "Always have somebody ready to step into the shoes of every man in an important job, even if the replacement's not as good. It's bad enough if something's done ill, but worse if it's not done at all because there's no one to do it."

"As Your Grace commands."

When Master Drako had left, Kantela realized that her second breakfast had grown cold without her touching it. She'd had no attention to spare for anything but the man before her.

At least it seemed to have brought results. He'd quickly learned how to explain things to her in ordinary Sherrani, and just as quickly agreed to take on a job that she suspected would involve much thankless and frustrating negotiations with merchant captains.

Nor was this the first time that she'd been able to win agreement, cooperation, enthusiasm, or even silver since coming to Dazkados. The magistrate, the Captain of Swords, several officers of the City Guard, merchants, local land-owners and village heads, even an old Healer who remembered tending the wounded of her grandfather's victory—they all seemed ready to follow where she would lead.

It seemed to her that she'd never known such willing reception of her orders. In the palace there'd always been someone to frown and say, "But, Your Grace—" Or had there been? Looking back, she saw that they'd only been able to prevail when she was uncertain. When she had made up her mind, no one except Pijtos had been able to oppose her.

Still, she'd been the queen. No one except Pijtos *could* refuse her if she gave a direct order. Besides, an enthusiastic reception didn't mean that the order would be carried out. Bakarydes had also told her, "Don't give an important assignment to anyone you know can't be trusted, but don't assume that just anyone will get the job done. You can't keep your rein on everyone, but examine the essential jobs every so often, to make sure that *they're* being done." In Dazkados, the essential jobs and a great many others gave every indication of being done.

She had been queen; she was now Ruler. Were her fellow Sherrani beginning to accept that? If so, God be thanked. Or could—could there be a Gift for ruling? The thought crossed her mind that Pijtos had never been received with such enthusiasm in Dazkados or even in Koddardos. He'd been the king, and no one had questioned his Ruling. Kantela was not the king, nor did she have Bakarydes's experience with gradually increasing amounts of responsibility all his life, yet she could already see many things that Pijtos had done that he should not have done, or left undone that he should have done. If she could see these things after only two moons, then maybe she did have a Gift.

But if so, where could she find anyone, from Svarno to the Inner Sea, to teach her to use it? Even Bakarydes, as much as he'd taught her, knew nothing of Gifts. And when could she find the time to even look for someone both wise enough to teach her and discreet enough to keep the Throne's secrets?

She had no answer to any of these questions but one, and the answer to that was thoroughly unsatisfactory.

She could see about her Gift only after the Momaks were back on their own side of the frontier.

"—and had to go to the Healer because the blisters on his hands from hauling those blackwood logs festered and he might have been sick for a long time or even lost his hands. By God's mercy and good Healing he came to no harm."

Bakarydes smiled. "You haven't changed at all, Uncle," he

said, which wasn't entirely intended as a compliment but was certainly God's own truth. Uros Tarinur dar no Benye spent the first few watches of any visit by his nephew talking of nothing but the family lands and what had happened on them since Bakarydes's last visit, as if he really couldn't imagine anything of more interest to the Captain-General. It was all part of a visit home, and Bakarydes would have missed it if Uros really had changed.

Usually, but not now. This wasn't a visit, anyway, just a stop to rest the horses and find out how many men the Benye lands could send to the frontier without being left completely defenseless.

Uros now started on what promised to be an equally long tale of a fire that had destroyed half the supply of thatch in the village of Bear Heights. Bakarydes managed to keep from fidgeting, but found his attention wandering around his uncle's study.

That hadn't changed much either. The tiles of the floor had been patched in a few places where they'd been cracked the last time. They were also cracked in as many or more new places. The two shutters were still in place, but they'd lost the last of their paint and were so badly warped that Bakarydes doubted they'd last the winter. The little table with the shelf of scrolls underneath it still glowed with the sheen of fine wood tenderly oiled and rubbed over many years, but it was one of the few really good pieces left in the house. However, there was a new tapestry on the wall, of a rather plain design but of good quality, instead of the badly flaked and faded painting of Izrunarko defying the warlord of Ravenscroft.

"How did you come by the tapestry, Uncle?" said Bakarydes, rising and walking over to it in order to stretch his legs. Between the long days in the saddle and the long ramblings of Uncle Uros, he seemed to be spending all his time these days sitting. At least he'd had a quick bath—in a bathhouse with one corner of its roof missing.

"When Rezi Kuzlur over at Stork's Rest died, I knew his sons would be selling up to meet his debts. I paid a visit before the traders got there. This was the only thing worth bidding on, really. They took my offer of sixteen veyselas."

"An honest trader would have given them twenty, and resold it in Koddardos for at least thirty-five. Besides, for sixteen veyselas you could have relaid the floor in here."

"The floor, yes, but to get at the leaks, it would have been necessary to tear out and rebuild half the walls and the windows. That kind of silver I didn't have."

Stumbling footsteps approached the door and a slurred voice called, "Hello, cousin. How was Koddardos?"

That was another thing that hadn't changed. His cousin Karos Bitrinur still spent most of his time on home leave drinking, sleeping, or recovering from a bout. He wasn't a slave to wine, but he definitely craved more entertainment than either a frontier regiment's camp or the Benye silver allowed him. At least he stayed sober most of the time on duty, and wine was a cheaper and less dangerous vice than gambling, women, horse racing, or brawling.

"Koddardos hasn't changed, thank you," said Bakarydes. "I found myself staying longer than I'd expected, because Her Grace wanted some advice on matters to do with the army."

"Advice?" said Karos, his face hovering on the edge of a leer.

"Advice," said Bakarydes levelly. "One thing I advised her to do was appoint a Great Captain. Most of what I ended up having to do could have been done long since if Pijtos had filled that office."

"Ah well, God made Pijtos a priest and men had to make him a king," said Uros. "No good can ever come of that."

"No good has come of it, at least as far as our facing the Momaks is concerned," said Bakarydes. Uros could maunder on about religion at greater length and to less purpose than he could about farming. Bakarydes wanted to head him off.

"Momaks? We've heard nothing of them," said Uros. Bakarydes doubted that he'd heard nothing, not even rumors, but was prepared to let the matter lie for now. Nothing except Karos's disgrace could come from discovering that he'd ignored a summons to return to his regiment because he'd been too drunk to understand it when it arrived.

"Well, you're about to hear of them now," said Bakarydes, and briefly told what he'd learned in Koddardos. "If you haven't heard anything here, it's possible there may be even more bandits than we feared." Or more potent magic at work, but he'd be impaled before he told any of his kin *that*!

"Bandits or Momaks," Bakarydes went on, "you'd best raise the men of our lands. If there aren't enough bandits to keep everyone busy, we can use every man and boy on the frontier."

"Well now, that's not something to be done overnight, what you're asking," said Uros dubiously. "We haven't horses to carry more than a hundred, and there's weapons, saddles, shoes . . .

"If matters are desperate enough, we could send six hundred. They'd hardly be less naked than when they were born, of course, so you'd have to be giving them most of what they needed."

Bakarydes frowned. The magazines and storehouses of the Army of the North would be barely equal to equipping the regiments already on duty. This wouldn't change until the Treasury opened its hands, although Kantela had sworn half a dozen times to do that or send Bakarydes Lord Ikarotikos's head.

In the meantime, a full-sized war against the Momaks was no place for ill-equipped or ill-mounted men. The frontier army needed reinforcements, not Momaks' prey, especially not men who'd been Bakarydes's playmates as a boy and whose widows would be girls he'd kissed as a youth.

"We won't be able to take anyone who doesn't have at least his own weapons, clothing, shoes, and a few days' food. Think of how many men you can give that and tell me when—"

A polite cough interrupted him. All three men turned to see the doorway occupied by the tall, stooped frame of Ketus Deningkur, the steward.

Bakarydes rose. Ketus had been the Captain-General's

friend when he was a boy, tolerating a reasonable number of practical jokes and filched snacks and applying a leather strap when they got out of hand. Bakarydes had always wondered whether he would have received toleration or the strap if Ketus had known that his daughter Deningka had been Bakarydes's first woman when she was seventeen and he was sixteen. It had been a rather muddled occasion, but Bakarydes had always thought of Deningka with affection, even now when she might well have a son old enough to be killed by the Momaks. . . .

He jerked his mind away from that line of thought and back to Ketus. "Yes, Ketus Deningkur?"

"There's a Captain Kalaj Lesnur, who's ridden in with a message for Master Bak—I mean, for the lord Captain-General." He lowered his voice. "The captain's got the look of a man with bad news."

Bakarydes stifled a groan. "Send him in."

Kalaj Lesnur was coated with dust and slimy with sweat, and under the sweat and dust his face seemed to have aged ten years in the last three moons. The bad news might have been his own death sentence—and come to think of it, for a captain like Kalaj, who would surely be in the forefront of any battle . . .

Bakarydes had been a soldier too long to find consolation in any poetic notion that the boy would at least die well. Not when he would die when he'd barely begun to live.

"Greetings, Captain Kalaj. You have news of the Momaks?"

Kalaj nodded jerkily and still more jerkily handed Bakarydes a sealed letter. With his dagger Bakarydes picked off the seal—Commander Chukan's, he noticed—tore open the letter, and fought to keep his face straight as he read it.

When he was finished, he had to resist the temptation to tear the letter to shreds. "That *umgrutzhag* Berov Godinur led the Third and the Seventh out of Camp Coldwater to meet what he thought was a couple of clans' worth of Momaks coming to join Marsh Wolf. I suppose he wanted a cheap victory to make himself look good.

"What he got was another whole tribe under Five Spears. Four thousand warriors at least. About a hundred of our men got back to the camp. Berov didn't, thank God. I've never wished a man on a Momak torture mound before, but if they did take that *chazrappig* to drink his spirit, he may do us one last favor if they drink his stupidity and vainglory! May *emptfandls* use his head for a football!! May dung-fed brood mares miscarry upon him!! May—" He couldn't think of anything vile enough in Sherrani, so he shifted to Momak and swore in that until a familiar whinny sounded outside.

Bakarydes broke off, stared at Kalaj, tried to speak, and discovered that he'd sworn himself into muteness.

"Here, Master Bakarydes." Ketus handed him a full cup of wine. It was thin and sour, but it restored Bakarydes's voice to something more than a hoarse croak.

"Kalaj, if I didn't know it was impossible I'd swear that was Lightning outside."

Kalaj nodded. "It is, my lord. We brought him along when we rode out to look for you. I thought you would want to have him as soon as possible. He must have heard your voice or—"

"Kalaj, either Lightning must have been bored out of his wits or else you have horse magic. It's a miracle that he didn't put you in the hands of the Healers."

"Well, my lord, your groom did give me a few hints about Lightning, and my father always said I had good hands with a horse."

Bakarydes decided not to ask if the groom had provided those hints free of charge.

"My thanks, Captain. It's just as well you did bring Lightning because I'm going to have to do some fast riding."

He waved the letter at his audience. "Berov's losing two regiments wasn't the end of it, either. The commander at Camp White Fox knew he couldn't hold against a whole tribe, so he loaded and mounted up everybody and put them on the road west. Five Spears's scouts caught them. The commander had time to make a circle of the wagons before he went down himself.

"The Momaks would still have finished everybody, except

that a message had reached Camp Cloudcroft. Commander Erzuli brought up the Fourteenth and beat off the Momaks. He lost half his men and took a belly wound himself doing it, though."

The silence in the room was something thick enough to reach out and gather up in handfuls, like lint on the floor of a weavers' hall. Bakarydes made an elaborate business of folding the letter neatly and stuffing it into his belt pouch. It gave him the time he needed to think, and when he raised his eyes he had at least the first few orders in mind.

"We obviously can't do things tidily any more," he began, "such as taking on new men only after we get fresh supplies from the south. We'll have to take men with whatever they can bring and do our best to make the one loaf we have feed all our guests. We may wind up stripping dead Momaks to equip our new levies, but that's better than losing any more camps or regiments."

Uros nodded. "I can have a hundred and fifty men on foot ready to march tomorrow night. I don't think they should move without a mounted escort, though. Fifty of our horse can be ready too, but we really don't have a fit captain for them—"

"You do now," said Bakarydes. "Captain Karos, you're on detached duty from the Fifteenth as of this moment and in command of the mounted levies from the Benye lands."

"With—I mean, yes, cou—my lord Captain-General!"

Bakarydes couldn't tell if Karos was that drunk or merely stunned by the news. If the former, he would sober up fast enough. Three regiments and a camp lost to the Momaks was news fit to sober up a Chimpantegli wine spirit.

"If Uncle Uros can really produce those levies, the hundred fifty on foot and the fifty mounted, you can lead the whole two hundred as far as Camp Thunderstone. I'll write out warrants for equipping them and also for sending gear for the other four hundred men back here. We'll send a squadron with the wagons, and it can be the mounted escort back to the camp. Kalaj, do you write a good hand? If you do—"

"Begging your pardon, my lord, but I brought Reverend Balar's clerk because I thought you might be needing to write a good many orders. With your permission, I'll go out and send him in, then find who has the freshest horses. They can take the messages to your family's people, and—"

"By the Great Stallion's dung! That's the first time I've heard of Balar being generous with anything except words. How did you persuade him to loan you the clerk?"

Kalaj's blush nearly turned him back into a boy again. "Well, my lord—I didn't exactly persuade him. I just asked the clerk and assumed that Balar would have given permission if I'd asked him."

Bakarydes grinned. The promise the boy had shown in his first battle wasn't a one-time affair. "With a habit of making assumptions like that, you will either lose your sash or rise to Chief of Horse before you're thirty. Probably both."

"Is Konja Valur going to be in trouble over this? If he is, I can say I ordered him—"

"He won't be in any trouble, but Reverend Balar will be if he so much as raises an eyebrow. Forget it, and send the man in."

"Yes, my lord." He saluted and went out.

"Does this mean you won't be dining with us, Bakarydes?" asked Uros.

"Quite the contrary," said Bakarydes, sitting down and pouring himself another cup of wine. "I'll probably be eating breakfast before I've done writing out orders and counting up your men."

"Good. Ketus, tonight we feast!"

"Yes, my lord."

He went out too, and Bakarydes sipped at his wine. He no longer cared that it was wretched stuff. Part of what was making him feel better was Kalaj's obvious competence. Part of it was being home with his kin, the best place for a man to hear even the worst news. Part was the prospect of being able to take Lightning for a gallop before dinner, instead of the day after tomorrow.

The greatest part of it, though, was simply being back on the frontier, with his army, doing the work to which he'd been putting his hand and heart and wits for twenty years. For today, at least, everything in the south might as well have been a dream—except for Kantela.

He raised his cup.

"To the Throne!"

XXVII

THE LAST SLIVER OF THE SUN WAS VANISHING BELOW THE horizon as Joviz's barge bumped against the palace quay. Joviz stood while the outboard oarsmen rammed their oars into the bottom to hold the barge against the quay. His information hadn't been faulty; a familiar four-man litter was approaching from the Palace Square, two guards walking behind it.

"Lady Lilka," Joviz called softly.

The guards turned; Joviz saw that one of them was a woman, taller and sturdier than her male companion. The First Priestess's gray head poked out through the curtains.

"Lord Joviz?"

"Yes. May I offer you my barge to take you back to the temple?"

"Gladly."

Accompanied by the male guard, Lilka walked briskly to the quay and climbed down into the barge without needing Joviz's offered hand. Only when the barge was heading out into the river again did she lean back against the cushions.

"How did you come to meet me, Joviz?"

"I had business on the south bank that I thought might keep me past the closing of Market Bridge, so I took my barge. As for the rest—I knew that you were visiting the palace tonight, about when it is your custom to leave, and what route you take back to your temple. If I can learn these things, then others can."

"Speak plainly, Joviz. You think I travel either too often or with too little guarding?"

"Yes."

"God's business will not wait, and every pair of hands put to guarding me is one less to do work more useful than protecting an old woman."

Since that was closing the door quietly but firmly on any further discussion of the matter, Joviz thought it best to retreat gracefully.

"When you are an old woman, men will have forgotten where my ashes lie."

"Are all magistrates so smooth-tongued?"

"On the contrary, Reverend Lady, we are sworn to tell only the truth."

Lilka laughed and patted Joviz's hand. "You must have been a dreadful menace to susceptible women when you were a young officer."

Joviz acknowledged the compliment with a smile. "How does Her Grace?"

"Well enough, for one who works from dawn to dark. She is not stinting herself on sleep or food, you understand, but she hardly leaves herself a single spell to sit down and take a deep breath."

"If the work is well done—"

"It is, as far as I know. It also keeps her too busy to worry about Bakarydes. This she told me herself."

Joviz wasn't surprised. The tales of the pace Kantela had set on her journey to Dazkados might have grown in the telling, but Joviz had seen some of the Swords who'd ridden with her. They had the look of men tried to the limits of their endurance. Kantela, on the other hand, had looked as if the whole journey had been no more than healthy exercise to give herself an appetite for dinner.

"As long as she does not put her hand in where it will make her enemies, no one will be the worse for it."

"One hopes so. She is certainly doing much of the work of the First Lord of the Treasury herself, and this will not make a friend of Ikarotikos."

"Only God could make Ikarotikos anyone's friend at this time. I do not think we can ask Kantela to let the affairs of the Treasury wait on a miracle."

"No, indeed. But—Joviz, have you some advice for her that she won't accept in plain Sherrani?"

It was well that he was not as easily read by anyone besides Lilka, Joviz realized. He could hardly perform the duties of his office otherwise. But the First Magistrate of Koddardos and the First Priestess of the Mother had seen a good deal of each other even before they had agreed to adopt Kantela as their daughter in spirit.

"Yes. If she must ignore Ikarotikos, she should be careful to defer to the Second Lord, Mugla Zenur."

"Isn't he cut from the same cloth as Ikarotikos?"

"Only outwardly," said Joviz. "He has little imagination and knows it, but also a great deal of good sense. He could never be bribed, but he could be flattered into cooperation, and Kantela seems to have a knack for such flattery."

"Then why not retire Ikarotikos at once?"

"Ikarotikos may not have friends, but a good many people in the Treasury owe him their careers. If they were to take offense, neither Kantela nor Mugla could overcome their opposition. Also, I do not think Mugla would accept the first lordship unless Ikarotikos were to die. His only ambition is to serve honestly for another few years, long enough to make a settlement on the last of his children. He has seven, by the way, yet has never taken a bribe. I do not think anything in the Throne's gift would make him take the first lordship."

"I will *not* start praying that anyone become less honest than they are, not at my age. Do you have any other ideas?"

"None at the moment." It occurred to Joviz that if the Third Lord's health were to worsen again, there would be a vacancy at the Treasury that might be filled by someone who could then be promoted to First Lord. Mugla Zenur would not resent that.

Unfortunately, Third Lord Firus Tarilur seemed to have taken a new grip on his office with the news of the Momak invasion and was showing great if probably misdirected energy in all his duties and as many more as he could grasp. Since Joviz had the same scruples about praying for a man's sickness as Lilka had about praying for his corruptibility, there seemed little more to be done in the Treasury.

The talk turned to the affairs of Koddardos itself. "Kantela said that you and she had agreed it was too soon to spend men and silver preparing the city for defense," said Lilka.

"Yes. Berov Godinur's defeat may mean a longer war then usual, but that doesn't mean we'll have the Momaks at our gates. We'd do better to prepare the city for receiving the levies and garrisons coming up from the south."

"Will it be the lords' men all over again, God forbid?"

"The Purveyor will feed and pay the army men, and also the levies once they're sworn in. The levies might be under poor discipline, though. Put extra guards on the temple's strongrooms and food stores, if you won't guard yourself."

"Can you lend me some Watchmen?"

"I can even lend you some Harzis. They won't be going north for another moon."

"That can't have pleased your Captain Michal."

"Quite the contrary. I told him that he would do more to bring victory over the Momaks by seeing that order was kept in Koddardos, but a Harzi who hears trumpets in the distance is sometimes deaf to reason. As long as he's not deaf to his oath, however, I won't worry."

The barge heeled slightly. Joviz looked ahead to see that the helmsman and rowers were taking it in toward the quay by the First Temple without waiting for orders.

Please, God, send our Kantela fifty men who know what to do and will do it without waiting to be told. That, Joviz knew too well, was asking for a great deal, but fifty such men would serve Kantela and Sherran far better than ten times the number of Ikarotikos and his ilk.

Michal took another swig of beer and stared moodily across the taproom of the Full Trough. He took still another swig and considered the merits of getting thoroughly drunk. It might wash from his mouth the bitter taste of being kept on a leash to guard Koddardos, when there were more Momaks than anyone less than sixty could remember swarming across the frontier.

He rose to refill his cup and look for some wine, when he heard footsteps behind him. He turned to see Hakfor shan-

Melech, a broad grin on his face and a wine bottle in his hand. At first glance Michal thought Hakfor was drunk, then realized that the bottle was still sealed and the grin was the drunkenness of delight, not wine.

"Ha, Michal. Let's drink to enough Momaks to go around. I'm leading Coron's guards north tomorrow."

Michal didn't know any words in any language including Momak really adequate to the occasion. He gripped the table until his fingernails bit into the wood and wearily put aside the idea of getting drunk. Hakfor would not think well of him for doing it, or well of himself for having made Michal do it with ill-timed news.

Besides, tomorrow would be as busy and as long as today, and so would the day after and the day after that. Perhaps with work to occupy his days and Niko to occupy his nights, he could live as a chained watchdog, at least once.

"I'd say that the Warrior blesses his faithful servants, except I remember the woman for hire you threatened to tell the man's wife about. What did you use on Coron?"

Hakfor looked pious. "Nothing of that sort. Master Coron's life is as chaste as a priest's—well, almost. Besides, the merchant with the woman was letting my men go short on pay and rations."

Michal had to laugh at the virtue written so blatantly on Hakfor's face. "I won't say I'm not jealous, because I am. Joviz is keeping his Harzis here in Koddardos to keep order as the levies come in from the south. That means I'll be one of the last into the fight."

Hakfor's face turned sober. "I'm sorry to hear that. Perhaps if Coron went to Joviz, he would give you a leave of absence—"

Michal shook his head. "He wouldn't, and I wouldn't ask. I'll fight at the head of my own men or not at all. The older ones think I know my business and the younger ones think I'm lucky, so we'll all be better off."

"You're no doubt right," said Hakfor. "Although I'd be doing myself a favor if you did go north with me. Coron is sending three squadrons and a couple of troops of baggage boys."

"By the Warrior! Has he been hiring Harzis by the clan since I left him?"

"No, he's just sending all he has. No caravans are traveling north of Koddardos now except on army business. The Cities of the Plains are mostly shutting their gates and closing their markets and wharves until they see which way the eastern Momaks will jump. Even the shipping is being hired up for carrying horses and the garrison from Mindranas. Coron's not going to lose any money by taking a season or two off from trading to become a purveyor of fighting men, so why shouldn't he?"

"No reason at all, except that—" Michal broke off as Niko's voice sounded from the hall.

"Welcome to the Full Trough, Captain Hakfor. Thank you for breaking the news. I was afraid I wouldn't have the courage."

Hakfor turned and glowered at Niko in mock anger. "Just how would you know what my news was?"

"One of your baggage boys is brother to a maid at the Full Trough."

"One of my baggage boys is going to be turned over my knee and spanked with a sword scabbard the next time he lets his tongue wag," said Hakfor, breaking into a grin. "Meanwhile, I've brought a bottle of Coron's best wine, maybe even good enough for this occasion."

After Niko went to see that Sapsko had finally gone to sleep, they retired to her private chambers for the wine. The talk turned to matters of war.

"Coron's giving us the best of everything and a cartload of weapons and armor so we can accept volunteers who ride in at the last minute. It's said that the other merchants on the Council for Public Order are doing the same." Hakfor looked from Michal to Niko and back to Michal, who nodded to indicate that Niko could be trusted.

"It's Arkan Batur dar no Chintek they're thinking of, almost as much as the Momaks," Hakfor went on. "He's supposed to be raising a whole regiment from his guards alone and another from his estates' watchmen and sending both north. The merchants fear that if he outdoes the Council for Disorderly Private Parts, the Throne will grant his petition to be made a member of it. So they're trying to raise two full regiments of their own.''

If the Throne did grant his petition, Arkan would have a foothold in Koddardos again. He was the least ambitious of the great lords, but that was only saying that lung fever was not as bad as lung rot. It was on the tip of Michal's tongue to say that the Queen didn't seem the sort to let gratitude overwhelm her judgment, when he realized that he'd only make Hakfor wonder how he knew. He remembered an old captain's warning to him some years ago: "It's not wanting to know everything that will put you on the pyre before your time. It's wanting everyone to know that you know everything.''

The captain's words no longer seemed so amusing.

By the time the wine was gone, Niko was yawning unashamedly. Hakfor rose. "I'd best not overstay my welcome, Mistress Niko. Feed Michal well, mind you, so that he'll have all his strength after a hard day of testing wine for water and telling farm boys to piss in the privies and not the streets.''

Niko gave him a sisterly kiss on the cheek. "God be with you, Hakfor, and give you plenty of fighting and some new stories to tell, so you won't always have to be scraping the mold off your old ones!''

In the bed, Niko proved much less tired than she'd seemed "—because you needed more than wine or Hakfor's secrets, Michal.''

"Am I that much an unrolled parchment to you, Niko?''

She laughed softly. "Men aren't nearly as good at keeping secrets from women as they think they are. Even Harzis.''

"Are you glad I'm staying in Koddardos, Niko?''

"That's a foolish question if ever I heard one. It's asking if seeing you unhappy makes *me* happy. What do you think I am?''

"I think you must have Harzi blood yourself, if you really want to know.''

266

She raised herself on one elbow and looked down at him. "My father was from Koddardos but my mother was from Svarno. What that says about my blood God only knows, because they were both dead before I was sixteen and without telling me or my sister who their fathers were."

Her smile told him that this was all the answer he was going to get. After a little while he decided that it was all the answer he really needed, and put an arm around Niko's shoulders to draw her down beside him again.

As Ikos reined in, a flock of carrion birds rose from the dead ox in the ravine before him. He looked down at the already half-stripped carcass with distaste but also with relief. Some farmer's strayed animal, falling into the ravine in the dark and breaking its neck. Not a sign of Momaks anywhere. Still, there was long grass just outside bowshot; best to be certain.

"Varjan Kuzlur!"

"My lord?" replied the chief of Ikos's scouts.

"Search that field as far as the tree line."

"Yes, my lord."

Five or six spells' worth of field searching turned up no sign of any human life except a camp fire that might have been burning half a moon ago. It had been at least that long since it rained around here; the dust that had given everyone an extra layer of armor in a single watch made that plain enough.

"Well done," Ikos told Varjan. "Now ride back and pass the word for a quarter-watch halt. Water the horses and feed the men. When you come back, bring the other half of my guards with you. They'll be under your orders until we camp on the Heights."

Varjan Kuzlur was too experienced a soldier to have much faith in Ikos's guards for scouting work, but too loyal a servant to say anything to Ikos. His face made an interesting sight until experience and loyalty reached an armed truce, and he rode off.

Ikos would never have sent the guards out ahead on their own; they could fight well enough against an opponent they could see but were hardly better than children against ambushes. He doubted there were any Momaks ahead, though. They didn't care much for fighting in rough or wooded country, and most of the Kyreian Heights was both.

However, to do what had to have been done in intercepting the army messengers so that Ikos could be forewarned, someone (let's call him Charko) must have become the paymaster for all the bandits and outlaws in the northern Sherrani countryside and some of the common thieves and cutpurses in the towns as well. That didn't mean they would follow orders once they'd finished with the messengers, not when Ikos's supply train would be a tempting target. Indeed, it was most unlikely that they *had* any orders that would permit them to identify Ikos as someone not to be robbed.

Not unless Charko is a witling, and I will believe many things before I believe that.

The Heights would be an equally good refuge for bandits or for Ikos. It was possible to hide twice his two thousand men on the wooded spurs jutting north and south from the Heights because only one road ran up on to them and along the bare grassland of the ridge, a road easily guarded at either end. On the other hand, that road was an ideal place to ambush a supply train, strung out as it would have to be on a road only just wide enough for a single cart.

Ikos looked ahead to where the pale green ridge line of the Heights bulged the horizon. His troubles wouldn't be over once his men got there.

There was water, firewood, and grazing in abundance, but everything else would have to be brought in, including fodder for the horses after more than a few days. Every journey off the Heights meant one more chance for a wine-loosened tongue to reveal his presence here, much farther from the frontier than a loyal Sherrani lord had any business being at this time.

Ikos dismounted and let his grooms deal with Ironhead while he strode up and down, washing the dust from his throat with watered wine and walking the stiffness out of his knees and the ache from his thighs. They'd been on the road since there was enough light to tell a white horse from a black one, over country that was no promenade.

Ikos's major concern at this point was that he'd had neither word nor sign of any Momaks in the area, and he should have had one or the other by now. Either they hadn't come at all, or they were still so far away as to turn his advantages of stealth and fresh fighters into very nearly their opposites. Without Momaks to fight and a reputation to gain from that fighting, all the silver Ikos had spent to raise and equip his men would be wasted. In addition, he'd taken many hands from the farms of his own lands. If the war went on until crops rotted in the fields for lack of hands to harvest them, he'd have to spend still more silver to buy food. At that rate, next winter he'd be doing well to be able to purchase half a measure of beer!

Ikos looked at the line of the Heights again. Perhaps he should seek out some bandits while camping on the Heights, waiting for news of the Momaks' whereabouts. That would keep his men exercised without exhausting them, and he could probably recoup some of what he'd spent from the bandits' hoards. Also, a few-score bandits' heads would buy a fair amount of friendship and closed mouths among the villagers and farmers the bandits had preyed on until Charko's silver made it worth their while to go after more dangerous game.

That seemed the best course. Every step ahead meant further danger: of being discovered, of bandits, of wearing out men and horses in search of Momaks to engage, of being found by more Momaks than he could fight. Until he knew more, to continue his march beyond the Heights would be carrying boldness to the point of foolhardiness, and that was no road to the throne.

Bakarydes's desk was mostly covered with papers being packed up for tomorrow's move to Camp Ruchan's Victory. In the middle of the largest open space was a sealed letter addressed to the Captain-General. Even from the door Bakarydes recognized Kalaj Lesnur's handwriting.

No doubt it was the captain's fifth petition to return to his regiment. Bakarydes sat down and started mentally composing his fifth refusal. Kalaj would have his chance to lead his squadron or at least *a* squadron, but right now his versatility made him far more valuable as a staff officer. He was tireless, tactful, ingenious sometimes beyond the bounds of common sense, able to get along with Lozo—

As if Bakarydes's thoughts had conjured him up, the Bannerbearer appeared in the doorway.

"Permission to enter, my lord?"

Bakarydes took a second look at Lozo's face. "Yes, and close the door before you give me the bad news."

"It's your cousin, Captain Karos," began Lozo, after he'd closed the door and seated himself. "He's billeted the last of the Benye levies in the tents on the north side of Barn Street."

"That's a good site," Bakarydes said. "I'm glad to know Karos is taking care of his men—or is there something else I should know?"

"Well, the Camp Commander assigned the site to the Ninth Regiment. They're coming in from Dazkados tomorrow. A messenger just brought word. I met him at the gate."

He'd have to pay Lozo the cost of whatever he'd used to bribe the messenger without asking the Bannerbearer how much it was; that was a familiar ritual between them and not urgent. His cousin's—call it excessive zeal—was.

"Has the Camp Commander ordered Karos to leave?"

"No, my lord. His secretary said that he assumed Karos had billeted his men with your permission."

Chalk up another bribe to pay back to Lozo, and another mark against the Camp Commander. Not that his failure to act and his lame excuse for that failure were any surprise. Vuko Abelur should have retired long since—would have retired this spring, probably, if Bakarydes hadn't quietly suspended the retirement of everyone who could still hold a weapon and see a Momak in front of him. Bakarydes now realized that he probably should have made Commander Vuko an exception, but that didn't solve the problem of cousin Karos.

It might look as if he were unwilling to have his kin dealt with in public, but he couldn't see any better way at the moment. "Lozo, take my ring to Captain Karos and order him to move his men at once to a billet assigned by the Camp Commander. Then go to Commander Vuko and tell him to have a billet assigned to Karos' squadron before you leave his headquarters."

"My lord."

After Lozo left, Bakarydes turned to the map. Like Kalaj, Karos might be chafing at the bit out of sheer boredom. Should he give each man a squadron and send them out on the flanks of the main column to deal with as many bandits as they could find?

Yes. Kalaj could handle an assignment like that on his head, and if Karos couldn't act on his own, better to find out now against bandits rather than later against Momaks. Picking men for him would be harder, but with more than five hundred men from the Benye lands now in camp and the remounts and supplies beginning to arrive, it shouldn't be impossible.

In fact, it might not be a bad idea to plan a whole secondary campaign against the bandits while keeping his main strength for the Momaks. If their numbers weren't pruned and some sense knocked into the survivors, the bandits would be a menace to the supply convoys and a danger to peaceful citizens of every sort until the Momaks were turned back. A few hundred bandits hanged or left headless in their lairs would hearten both the army and those civilians who hadn't fled.

Was the magic the bandits (or others) were using strong enough to be dangerous to men warned of what to expect? Bakarydes could do no more than guess, and his guess was no. Even if he were wrong, the only magic workers with the army were the Healers, and they were too busy with men, animals, tainted water, and the like to ride around with cavalry squadrons looking for magic they probably couldn't fight if they found it. He would have his bandit catchers note down everything that even smelled magical, and then send the whole pile of paper off to the College of Priests for them to deal with.

How long could he spare men for bandit catching before the Momaks were on the move again? The map gave him no ideas he hadn't been turning over in his mind for several days.

The Momaks were still flowing over Great Pass and

Sweetwater Pass into what had become a Momak enclave around Camp Coldwater. Few seemed to flow out of the enclave again, which suggested that they were massing under Marsh Wolf's command. That didn't mean they would all obey him indefinitely, of course, and even with mounts who could live by grazing, an army that might now be more than twenty thousand strong would have to search for new grass sooner rather than later. When they moved, Marsh Wolf's control over them would be weakened, and that would be the time for the Sherrani to strike. Bakarydes wouldn't pretend even to himself that he knew how and where.

"War isn't quite as terrifying if you remember just one thing. The other commander knows no more than you do and almost certainly has just as many problems."

"My lord?"

It was Lozo in the doorway again. Bakarydes realized that he'd been speaking out loud to a woman who, if seated at a desk at all, was in the palace of Koddardos a thousand miles away.

"Yes, Lozo?"

"I found Captain Karos in the Twining Vine. Drinking but not drunk."

"Yes?"

"He went right off to the squadron when I gave him your orders. When I got back from Commander Vuko with their new billet, they were already packing."

"Very good, Lozo."

XXVIII

THE TOWER WHERE DAIVON SHAN-YASI'S AUNT DAMIA lived on the uppermost floor had been built in the days before the chief of Clan Kadran was the Chief of Chiefs. The walls were as thick as three men and each timber of the floors had been cut from a single tree.

Now the chief of the Kadrans could call at need on the Oath-

Bound, two thousand sworn fighting men drawn from all nine clans. It had been an easy decision for Daivon to turn the tower over to Damia when he succeeded his uncle. She did not wish to interfere in the new household, knew that she would do so anyway if she remained in the Great House, and moved the day after the funeral feast for Araz. The days when the Kadrans might need to pack themselves into the tower and defend it with arrows and boiling water against battering rams and scaling ladders would not come again.

Daivon was as sure of this as he had ever been but also knew that other dangers had taken the place of hostile clans. It was to listen to his aunt on some of these other dangers that he'd ridden down from the Great House.

Damia's best table, its legs inlaid with walrus ivory, stood by a window chiseled out wider to give a view of the kitchen garden on the terraced hillside below. Daivon saw that the table was set with much more than the ritual oatcakes and ale: a bowl of mutton stew, a silver jug from Sherran holding wine, a plate of smoked fish, and another bowl holding dried apples.

"Greetings, son of my husband's brother," said Damia, gripping Daivon's hands with more than ceremonial courtesy.

"Greetings, widow of my father's brother," replied Daivon with equal dignity. Damia was more stooped than the last time he'd seen her, and most of the gray in her hair was now white. She hadn't lost any weight, though, and her cheeks were still round and bright. It had been the Father's will that Damia outlive not only a husband and two sons but also nearly all of her generation.

Might the Father be pleased to let her live a while longer, because Daivon knew he badly wanted her advice in what he'd begun to suspect would be trying times.

"You seem to be expecting either a long visit or other guests," he added.

"No other guests, Daivon. Even the servants have been sent below. As to the length of your visit—if it is to ask me to move back to the Great House, it will be as short as my answer. If you wish to discuss how matters go in Sherran, on the other hand . . ."

"The Great House is no longer so ill served that it needs your hand," said Daivon, smiling faintly.

"I have heard otherwise."

"It is served well enough for me," said Daivon. "Besides, if you moved back, I could no longer hold your doing so as a threat over the heads of those who neglect their duties."

Damia was silent. "Do not again ask me to consider marrying again," Daivon went on. "You know what my answer to that will be."

"There are as many reasons for it as ever, Daivon."

"There are also as many reasons against it. Each time we talk of this, Rakal is closer to being of age, and there is still no rival to the chieftainship who would not be fought by the Oath-Bound. Why should I breed up a litter of rivals to Rakal from my own loins?"

"I do not admit that your reasons are stronger than mine. I do admit that if we go over each one again, this meal will grow cold before either of us so much as mentions Sherran or the Momaks."

They sat down. Daivon accepted the ceremonial offering of oatcakes and ale, then poured them both some wine. He raised his cup.

"To the downfall of the Momaks."

Damia smiled. "What would Clan Manoded and Clan Lamenu do if there were no more Momaks to fight? They would feel as useless as teats on a bull. And are you sure that we can hope for the downfall of the Momaks rather than the downfall of Sherran?"

"It will take more than a surprise attack, even by a hundred-head chief, to bring down Sherran, especially since the thousand-head chief is back in the north. Indeed, were the affairs of Sherran in their usual good order, all we should have to do is reckon up the veyselas the clans could earn before the end of the fighting. Now, though, we must be on our guard against the 'more,' and look for it in Koddardos, not in the north."

"Will Bakarydes be able to wield his Army of the North as before, after dallying in Koddardos?"

"It is only rumor that he dallied. It is rather more than rumor that he swept through the Purveyor's Office like a winter wind, chilling a great many little schemes. That may have made him enemies in Koddardos, but none among his own men, who have been suffering from those schemes for two years or more. No, Bakarydes will be as great a hammer to the Momaks as ever."

"The Father and the Warrior be thanked for that."

Daivon's own thanks were silent but even more heartfelt. An old nightmare of the Harzis was an enemy invading Sherran in such force that it could not be stopped, then turning north. That had been done once, after all.

No doubt any Momaks who might do that would destroy so much in Sherran that they would gain little to help them invade the Land of the Clans; and certainly one man of Harz-i-Shai was the equal of five Momaks. Still, it would be a war to the death of one people or the other.

"What concerns me more is the delay in the news of the invasion reaching Koddardos," said Daivon. "There is an ugly smell of magic to that. Old magic, forbidden magic, and used by someone of high rank or one of his allies."

"Why of high rank?"

"Who else would gain anything worth the cost of using Momaks as a weapon?"

"It could be an army rival of Bakarydes."

"Impossible, Damia. Such an army rival would have to be willing to slaughter his comrades *and* assume that the Momaks would kill Bakarydes without putting him in danger. He'd still have to fight, though, or he'd be a marked man. Momak arrows are no respecters of intriguers' schemes. Oh, I will grant you that such a man might exist, but you must grant me that he'd be the next thing to a madman."

"True enough, and we know of none such high enough in the army to be a rival of Bakarydes. Nor will I propose that we go looking for one, either."

Whether they agreed or not, Damia always forced him to array his arguments like the oath-bound arrayed for battle, until flaws in those arguments showed up like rusty spots on armor. That was the greatest blessing of talking with her.

"It doesn't greatly matter who's begun using the magic," Damia went on. "Where one leads, rivals will follow in fear or hope of gain. Do you fear the War of God the Destroyer again?"

Daivon was glad to be able to say no. That was an even worse nightmare than a Momak conquest of Sherran. The Sherrani would not die without taking a great many of the horsemen with them, but if they ruined themselves by another war of spells and mutual slaughter, leaving the land devastated and plague ridden, and throwing trade into confusion from the Outer Ocean to the eastern end of the Inner Sea . . . Daivon could think of nothing worse.

"Any Sherrani sorcerer who can cast a spell stronger than one of our forge spells is known to the College of Priests and works under its eye."

"At least one has escaped that eye."

"One sorcerer or even a few can't bring back the War. If more than a few start hiring themselves out to intriguers, the college will surely notice and put a stop to it, unless the Throne opposes them."

"It might, Pijtos Sherran favored the temple of the Divine Essence beyond the bounds of custom. Suppose the sorcerers at work are of that temple?"

"I find that hard to believe, Damia. The priests of the Divine Essence are the most unworldly set of scholars and meditators you'd never want to put to practical work. Also, they've renounced personal wealth and kin ties, so what would they gain?"

"Knowledge is a form of wealth that even an unworldly scholar can covet, Daivon."

"Then perhaps we should look for our sorcerer in the temple of the Giver of Knowledge?"

"Perhaps. Certainly that temple all but has the College of Priests in its pocket. If one of the Giver of Knowledge's priests were the intriguer, he'd be even safer than a priest of the Divine Essence with the Throne on his side."

Daivon notched up another point brought to his awareness by talking with his aunt. "I just realized that we have no idea whether Kantela favors the Divine Essence as much as her husband did."

"We probably won't have any chance of finding out until she has done with mourning. After that—would our clansman in the First Magistrate's service have a chance of learning?"

"Better than anyone else, I should think."

Certainly it would be a better chance than any Harzi would have of learning the workings of the College of Priests, or of any temple except perhaps that of God the Craftsman. Daivon hardly resented the Sherrani showing enough respect for their gods not to let those who didn't worship those gods serve the priests, but it made knowing much about the Sherrani priesthoods a chancy business. Now, when what happened in those priesthoods might mean life or death for a good many Harzis—well, one had to pray to the Father for patience and the Warrior for the cunning to find a way where there'd been none before.

Daivon refilled the wine cups and served them both with stew and fish. "One thing we can do that will show the world we don't sit on our fleeces while the Momaks make trouble—I'll lead some of the Oath-Bound down to join the Manoded and the Lemenu."

"Their scouts haven't reported any Momaks."

"The scouts may not have gone far enough. With five or six hundred of the Oath-Bound to strengthen them, they can go farther and fight anything they are likely to find. A thousand or so Momaks dead without any Sherrani having to set foot into stirrup will be no bad thing. Besides, the younger men among the Oath-Bound need a little battle experience."

Daivon knew that those words were a mistake the moment Damia's eyebrows went up. "Indeed. Then are you planning to take Rakal?"

"I hadn't thought of it, but—"

"Your son and heir also needs seasoning, and if he can prove himself as a warrior in the eyes of the Oath-Bound . . ."

Daivon cursed his own tongue. Damia had the right of it, but if he took Rakal to war this summer the battle over his remarrying would have to be fought all over again. She would point out with perfect justice that if he and Rakal both fell, Edruz would be five years short of lawful age. He would need allies to hold even the Oath-Bound, allies such as the kin of a stepmother with no sons of her own.

"A wife's kin would have to be prepared to swear the Oath of Iron and Fire to support Edruz," said Daivon slowly. "Otherwise I'll hire out as a fighting man before I marry again!"

"There might be such women, if Rakal and Edruz swore that their stepbrothers would inherit if both of them died without sons of their own. That is a heavy oath to lay on the lads, I know, but Rakal at least is of an age where he must start learning what it is to be Chief of Chiefs. And you are laying no light oath on the woman and her kin to protect your sons."

"Do you think I'm so lack-witted that I'd marry a woman who wouldn't see her duty or with kin who wouldn't see theirs?" Damia was silent. Daivon swore mentally. What she thought was perfectly true; left to himself he would take no second wife. Yet if she thought the risk of rivals to his sons by Yanima was worth facing—well, Damia had seldom been wrong, and a man was wise to keep peace with his kin even when they were.

"You would know better than I where such a woman might be found," said Daivon, rising. "I give you leave to search for her, *quietly* if you please. I do not want half the heads of families in the land camping outside the Great House, trying to sell me a wife."

"Of course, Daivon." Damia almost kept the triumph out of her voice.

XXIX

Camp Ruchan's Victory straddled a ridge with the barracks on one side, the stables and workshops on the other, and the officers' quarters on the ridge line. Since the ridge line was the highest part of the camp, the officers shared it with the two watchtowers.

Bakarydes strode back and forth across the twelve paces of the platform on top of the south tower, trying to squint against the sun and the dust and thinking how much better it would be if he could stop breathing. On a scorching hot day like this, the smell of the stables on one side of the ridge and of privies on the other seemed to meet and linger over the watchtowers. Probably it wasn't as bad when the camp had only its normal two regiments and camp hands, but when a fair-sized army was packed into and around it, there was no escaping the smell.

Actually, Bakarydes was happy to pay this small a price for having a force with real striking power under his hand where it could move to engage the Momaks in any direction with only a quarter-watch's writing of orders: nine regiments, plus one more expected any watch and another marching east with a supply convoy to Camp Cloudcroft; two thousand camp hands mounted and ready for the field; four hundred assorted Harzis under Acting Commander Hakfor shan-Melech; seven hundred miscellaneous men of varying quality, including the rearguard of the Benye levies.

Under Karos's command, most of his family's men were on their way to Camp Cloudcroft with the supplies. Those without horses would be used for camp defense; at the very least they could stand on top of walls and hit Momaks over the head as they climbed scaling ladders. The mounted men could be used for sorties. They would stay under Karos's command; his cousin had earned a good name while bandit-hunting, although ugly rumors floated around that not all the loot he recovered from the bandits' strongholds had been turned over to the army as the law required.

The situation with regard to the bandits' magical helpers was less satisfactory. Plenty of bandits were prepared to bear witness that magic had been used without knowing what kind or by whom. One man rumored to have behaved like a sorcerer—or what ignorant bandits thought a sorcerer—had died by his own hand before he could be questioned. Another man of whom the same was said vanished so thoroughly that he might indeed have used magic to do so; the soldiers had found neither his body nor any traces of his going or any scrap of his possessions. What had been a mystery in the spring was still a mystery in the summer on the eve of battle with the Momaks.

Still, Karos and Kalaj between them had left the flanks of the march clear of bandits, bringing in more than a hundred living or dead and driving several times that many into the wilderness. The Momaks would doubtless take their toll of these, and so would the Harzis if any fled over the Harzi border to get away from the Momaks. By the time the survivors trickled back, the army should be free to give them its undivided attention and a very short shrift. From the attack on the pay convoy through the last ambushed messenger, the bandits had killed more than two hundred soldiers, and the men of the frontier army had as long a memory for blood debts as any Harzi.

At least the army would be free if the Momaks could be brought to battle in the next moon or so. Bakarydes didn't expect to have the strength to meet the united Momak horde in the open field, but neither did he expect that Marsh Wolf's dream could hold together so many different tribes, clans, and chiefs of all ranks much longer. Even if the worst happened— the united horde moving south toward the heartland of Sherran—Bakarydes was prepared to cut in behind it and block the passes that led to the plains, then harry its rear until he had gathered the strength to crush it.

The cloud of dust rising in the south now had a moving dark line at its base. Bakarydes squinted again and said, "That looks like the Thirty-First from Dazkados. They're a day late."

Commander Chukan frowned. "Unless the Momaks have sent a column around to the south. Then we could be having visitors."

"We'd have had warning of the Momaks, I think."

"Unless they came in such force that they swamped our scouts."

Bakarydes made a mental gesture of despair. Chukan was the best staff officer and the worst pessimist he'd ever known. Perhaps the two went together, since Chukan not only saw everything that could go wrong but made plans to prevent it.

A moment later Chukan nodded. "You were right, my lord. I can see the sun on armor." He looked again. "Although it looks like more than one regiment."

"Well, however many they are they deserve a proper greeting. Will you ride with me, Commander?"

Half a watch later, Bakarydes and Chukan waited with the Banner Troop on the exercise ground beyond Little Cascade Creek as the Thirty-First filed past the mounted sentries. The squadron that had been exercising was drawn up to either side of Bakarydes—Chukan's pessimism at work, he was sure, since the nearest cover that could have concealed an archer was three times long bowshot from the edge of the grounds.

The Thirty-First *had* grown, Bakarydes realized, or else someone had joined them on the march. The line of dust-covered horsemen and pack animals didn't seem to end. At last a small cluster of horsemen broke out of the column and rode toward Bakarydes, and the mystery was solved.

"Volo Deningkur," said Bakarydes, returning the noble-man's crisp military salute with a smile. "You are very well met indeed. I hadn't expected any of the lords' levies for at least another week."

"You'll be seeing some of Arkan's Harzi guards before long, if rumor speaks true," said Volo. "Ikos is also said to be raising men."

Not wanting to be drawn into a discussion of intrigues by an intriguer, Bakarydes pretended to be inspecting the men riding by. Then he was no longer pretending. Finally he smiled again.

"You've taken care with their arming and mounting, I see. How many did you bring?"

"No more than three hundred, but as you said, I took some care with them. Most of them have at least fought bandits if not Momaks, and all the officers are army veterans except my son." He motioned one of his escort forward. "My lord Captain-General, may I present my elder son, Rajos Marinkur?"

"I am honored to be serving under the lord Captain-General of the North," said the young man, giving the mounted salute awkwardly but enthusiastically.

Bakarydes hoped Volo had arranged to have his veterans keep an eye on his son; youth and inexperience pitted against Momaks meant almost certain death. He was searching for some reply that wouldn't raise the young man's hopes too much when he saw a mounted messenger with two escorts trying to cut through the tail end of Volo's men. The messenger's horse was stumbling and lathered, and he himself was swaying in the saddle.

"Lozo! Help that man!"

The man's horse carried him to Bakarydes, but the man himself stumbled as he dismounted and would have fallen without the help of his escorts. Bakarydes saw that he had a bloodstained bandage around one bare arm and another bloodstain on his left thigh. His tongue was too swollen for speech, but he pointed at his belt pouch, and Bakarydes pulled out the letter in it while Lozo brought his water bottle and sent one of the escorts for a Healer.

By the time Bakarydes finished the letter, he knew that everyone around him must have read bad news from his face. All the looks were sober; some were grim.

The looks changed to stunned bemusement as Bakarydes laughed. "The Momaks are on the move again. Ten thousand are besieging Camp Cloudcroft."

"Ten thousand?" exclaimed Chukan. His eyebrows seemed to be trying to crawl up his high forehead into his hair. "Then either we've been completely wrong in our estimate of their strength or—?" He looked expectantly at his Captain-General, who nodded.

"Or they've split their forces and sent one we can handle to where we can strike it. We'll find out soon enough."

"My lord, your cousin and his men—?"

"Reached the camp in time, along with the convoy. So Erzuli Kalinur has plenty of men and supplies to hold off the Momaks until we get there. He sent the Eighteenth back too, so they wouldn't be shut up where their horses would be useless."

Commander Erzuli's survival was a gift of God to both him and the army. The Momak arrow that had hit him in the stomach drove through the abdominal wall, but carried with it the silk shirt he was wearing next to his skin. The shirt kept the arrowhead from penetrating any internal organs, leaving only a flesh wound, painful but well within reach of the Gift of any Healer worthy of the name.

Chukan looked down at the now-unconscious messenger. "I suppose he outrode the regiment and ran into either bandits or a small band of Momaks. I'll send out a couple of squadron-strength patrols to make sure which and guide the Eighteenth in. With your permission, my lord," he added.

"You have it. When you've done that, send messages for all the commanders to meet in my quarters for dinner. We're going to need a little council of war before we march, I'm thinking."

"My lord!"

Chukan turned his horse and put the spurs to it. Volo's sober look had turned to one of delighted surprise. Suddenly he looked hardly older than his son.

"Lord Volo, your men will have to camp with Coron's Harzis by Little Cascade Creek. I'll have one of my troopers show you the way and where to post your sentries."

Too late, Bakarydes remembered Volo's humiliation at the hands of the First Magistrate's Harzis. Any impulse to change his orders vanished when he saw that Volo's grin hadn't even flickered. The Captain-General suspected that Volo would have bedded down with billy goats, let alone Harzis, if it meant a chance to lead his men in a full-scale battle against the Momaks.

Kantela moved a piece of paper from the pile on her left to the pile on her right, meanwhile pulling a wax tablet toward her. Joviz noticed that the hand holding the paper was thinner than it had been a moon ago, and that the full sleeve of the Queen's robe trailed dangerously close to the flame of the oil lamp on the table.

"Will the barracks at Thunder Hill be adequate for the new levies?"

"For now, yes."

"How long is 'now'?"

"If the work on the roof of the Blue Fortress is done by next week—a moon, at least."

"Do you think we should start renting quarters outside the gates? The Treasury will not stand against it."

The Treasury, Joviz suspected, would hardly dare stand against Kantela if she wanted to melt down all the coined silver in Koddardos and cast it into a statue of Veysel Sherran. Lord Ikarotikos knew that his continued tenure depended largely on convincing the Queen that it was less trouble to keep him on than to get rid of him and do the work herself—which she was very nearly doing anyway.

"Not yet, and then only in places where the men's comings and goings can be watched. The Camp Commander at Thunder Hill found it very useful to confine the Hierandos City Guard to barracks last week after they sacked that bakery."

"A wise man. What is his name?"

"Malko Vanur."

Kantela wrote it on the wax tablet. "Is he fit for service in the field, commanding a regiment or even more?"

"Your Grace—"

"Joviz, do you wish to be Great Captain?"

Joviz refrained from gaping. "No. My soldiering is long done. I might know the work or most of it, but the House of War would never believe it."

"Then if you will not relieve me of the necessity of being my own Great Captain, at least give me as much help as you have given me in being First Lord of the Treasury."

"Yes, Your Grace." It would be of little use to say that if she continued to try to do too much she would end up doing too little. If she left matters to others even less would be done. For the first time Joviz felt ready to curse the memory of Pijtos Sherran. He had served his God and his God only, even when on the throne, and now both his people and his widow seemed likely to pay a most ungodly price for it.

"Commander Malko is past sixty and suffers from several old wounds. Also, he came up from the ranks, and I cannot imagine a man who better knows what mischief young soldiers or those in unfamiliar surroundings may get into."

In fact, Joviz had had First Lancer Malko Vanur in his own squadron thirty years before. He'd been one of the officers who decided to see if promoting the man and giving him responsibility would give him something more than practical jokes on which to exercise his considerable ingenuity. It had; Troopmaster Malko's men became the pride of the squadron, the jokes ceased, and Malko was destined for further promotion. He'd ended up a highly honored commander, and if some sneered at his origins by calling him a *fening-ferg* behind his back, none did so to his face.

"Very well. Then he stays where he is." She made another note on the wax, almost gouging out pieces of it with her stylus.

"Have your Harzis marched yet?" she asked when she'd finished.

She was smiling; Joviz accepted the peace offering and smiled back. "Yesterday at dawn. Captain Michal showed exceptional restraint in waiting until the day after we decided to quarter the new levies at Thunder Hill before asking me for leave to go north. He showed even more by waiting two more days until there were enough Harzis to make up a second squadron. Once they'd sworn to follow him, though—well, a man with his trousers on fire is a model of calm by comparison. I think he would have sacrificed to the Bee Father of Pythrad for a magical journey to the frontier."

285

"I hope he won't rush into a Momak ambush. Two squadrons is too few to fight a battle, but more men than Bak—than Sherran can afford to lose."

Kantela, Joviz decided, could not forever be forgiven her ignorance of Harzis, but he would do so this time. "Michal is not so eager when the lives of men sworn to him are at stake. If he threw them away, he'd have to kill himself before their kin found him."

"Even if he chose exile?"

Michal would not choose exile, Joviz knew, but knowledge like that was not something to be passed about in casual conversation. Instead he said, "In the matter of such a blood debt, any member of the same clan as one of the dead would count himself kin. Every city in Sherran and most of the Cities of the Plains and on the Inner Sea hold Harzis of every clan. All would have long memories."

"Then God give Michal a swift safe journey and all the Momaks he wants in reach of his sword," said Kantela. She blinked. "Lord Joviz, the watch is half-passed and I am growing unfit for business. Is there anything else you wished to discuss?"

"No, Your Grace," said Joviz, accepting his dismissal with some feeling of relief. He did not really expect an invitation to join Kantela for her evening devotions, nor, indeed, did he want one. Whether Kantela prayed as woman or Ruler or both was God's business and no one else's. After the First Magistrate had given the Queen all the help his office and strength allowed, he could only join his prayers to Lady Lilka's and, he hoped, those of all other Sherranis, that God would provide the rest of what Kantela and Sherran would need.

Bakarydes rose and looked down at the letter on his camp table. It was short, and he was leaving it with Commander (Acting Chief of Horse) Chukan Vodarkur, to be sent to Queen Kantela only in the event of Bakarydes's death.

It should be longer; it held only a request to confirm Chukan in his Acting rank and an acceptance of all responsibility for the disaster which the Sherrani might have suffered at the hands of the Momaks. But what could he add?

An account of the Council of War? No, because a short one would convey little and a long one would be as dull as the council itself. A Council of War could not be very interesting if everyone present agreed with the Captain-General.

Not that there was that much room for disagreement. All the Sherrani forces were quite fit to make the march to Camp Cloudcroft that Bakarydes' strategy demanded, including a final thirty miles by night in the hope of achieving surprise. Their scouts were good enough to detect any Momak reinforcements, ambushes, or retreats. Once the Momaks were brought to battle, armored horsemen always had the edge over unarmored ones if they could avoid being drawn into futile charges until they'd exhausted their horses.

Bakarydes rose and started walking up and down the chamber between the table and the bed, eight paces in each direction. He'd never anticipated having to write a love letter, and his mind was as bare as the Menolean Wastes of ideas on how to do it.

He considered the notion that Kantela could not bear a declaration of love from beyond the pyre and immediately rejected it. That was not only nonsense, it was an insult to Kantela.

What *was* a man to do, when he'd found what he never knew he was missing, and found it moreover in the palace of Sherran? Anyone who'd predicted such a turn of events three moons ago, Bakarydes would have given over to a Healer trained in disorders of the mind.

What this man was to do, he decided, was to follow the maxim of one of his old tutors in tactics: "Better what's good enough on time than what's perfect two days late." He sat down, picked up his pen again, and wrote:

I have no regrets about even one moment of the time we spent together. I only regret that time could not be longer. You have shown me—

He hesitated, considering *what it is not to be alone*, then rejecting that as an insult to both Lozo, for so many years watchdog and conscience, and his kin. Finally he added:

—that there is more to life than I'd dreamed for many years. God give you a prosperous reign and all the happiness you deserve as both woman and queen.

He'd just finished sealing the letter when Lozo entered. "Here. This is to go to Chief Chukan. The instructions are on the outside."

Lozo read them and nodded. "Chukan's wild as a stallion in greenfly season over being left behind."

"Doesn't he know it's a compliment that I'm trusting him to be able to hold the frontier if we lose in front of Camp Cloudcroft?"

"I think so, my lord, but I'm not sure he appreciates it."

Bakarydes threw up his hands. "Oh, well, only God could please everybody at once and God has the sense not to try." He sat down on the bed and began pulling off his boots. "Lozo, did Berov Godinur's Bannerbearer leave any children?"

"Two and a widow. They'll be going to his brother's house, is my thought."

"Then we can make it easier for the brother to aid them, by the price of at least one suit of armor."

"For the—person we were talking about?"

"Yes."

"Can you give me the measurements—oh, I beg your pardon, my lord!"

"Never mind," said Bakarydes, trying to stifle laughter. Lozo was actually blushing, as he realized how his Captain-General must have obtained the Queen's measurements. "I think it's time we were both in bed. I'll have the measurements for you in the morning."

"Yes, my lord."

Lozo helped Bakarydes off with his boots, then poured him a cup of tea before stuffing the letter into his belt pouch and going out.

XXX

"THREE VEYSELAS WOULD BUY A FULL-GROWN OX, MY friend," said Michal genially. "If that calf's been two moons weaned, I'll eat the head without salt."

"Two veyselas six, then, although I really should charge you more for doubting my word."

"Two veyselas and not a brass more."

"That's a calf from my best heifer, Captain. It would insult the Face of the Mother to sell him for less."

"I don't want to breed him, my friend. I want to roast him for my squadron."

"No doubt, but your men being hungry doesn't mean you can steal my calf. Two veyselas four, or see if you can find anyone willing to sell for less before the sun goes down."

Michal looked toward the west. The shadows were beginning to lengthen, and they'd be doing well to make another fifteen miles tonight even if they bought the calf here. If they had to spend any more time hunting up meat for dinner, they'd lose a quarter of today's march, and Michal grudged every unnecessary spell not spent shrinking the distance between his men and the Momaks.

He decided that the reputation of the Harzis for close bargaining had been sufficiently upheld for today on this north country farm. The farmer also deserved something for not sending his children into hiding at the sight of two hundred armed and mounted Harzis. The First Magistrate's badge was not so well known here, ten long days' ride north of Koddardos.

"Two veyselas four, then. It's only petty theft."

"I'm surprised you didn't ask me to roast it for you." The farmer took Michal's money, counted it, bit a couple of sample coins, and slipped them into his purse. "I'll have my cowherd halter the—"

"Captain! Look over there!"

Michal turned, realized that Ulev was pointing at something that could only be seen from horseback, and swung back up onto his mount. Now he could see it clearly—a dozen or more horsemen cantering along the fieldstone wall that marked the bank of a small stream as well as the boundary of the farm.

"Bandits!" Michal said. His orders were to join the Army of the North as quickly as possible, but not to neglect any opportunities to fight bandits that allowed him to carry out his first orders. A dozen bandits barely outside bowshot was certainly such an opportunity.

Michal used hand signals to get the thirty men with him mounted and on the move, since the wind was blowing toward the bandits. It was a wasted precaution; the bandits must have seen the Harzis moments after Ulev saw them, judging from the way they pulled their horses around and dug in their spurs. The speed of their departure at least removed any lingering doubts about their identity.

Michal dug in his own spurs and drew his sword. "Archers to the front. Try for the horses!" A horse was an easier target at extreme range than a man and less likely to be wearing armor. The archers dropped their reins, controlling their horses with their knees, as Michal and the other riders of the vanguard swerved to give them clear shots.

Two horses went down before the other riders started to scatter in all directions. Michal thought he saw only one rider catch a comrade's saddle and be carried off to safety. Then he was too busy shouting orders; before he'd finished he'd ridden past the fallen horse and into an open field. On the far side of the field the ground began to rise toward the impressive ridge shown on his map as the Kyreian Heights.

Michal reined in briefly to study the Heights. They would make a fine stronghold for bandits; half a dozen bands could find room up there. The thirty men with Michal were too few to fight anywhere near that many, or even search the Heights for them. Calling up all his men would mean delaying the march toward the frontier, which settled the matter for Michal. He would beat the bushes for the bandits who'd scattered, make his camp near here tonight to keep them from coming back, and call it making the best of a bad job.

Not much to Michal's surprise, the bandits turned out to know their ground. Neither the men he took with him nor those he sent back to guard the farm saw any trace of them. It took Michal no more than a quarter of a watch to decide that he'd delayed his march by enough for one day and turn back toward the farm.

As he rode past the spot where the bandits had scattered, he saw the two horses lying where they'd fallen, flies already gathering over noses and eyes. There was no sign of the fallen bandit; the men returning to the farm must have taken his body with them.

Michal reined in to see if the horses's harnesses and saddles had been salvaged, saw that they had, and also saw that the horses were well-shod and sleek-flanked, grain-fed rather than grazed. One had had its tail docked, like the mount of someone who wanted to make a show.

Either the men who'd scattered hadn't been bandits, or else bandits in this part of the country lived like lords and kept their mounts in appropriate style. Since the country hadn't been eaten bare, Michal inclined toward the former theory. He was inclined to dig in his spurs and return to the farm at a gallop.

"Where's the dead bandit?" he shouted to the first of the farm guards to greet him.

"What dead bandit?" the man said.

Michal glared. "The bandit who didn't get away when we killed his horse."

"There wasn't any body. At least there wasn't any by the time we stripped the horses," he added hastily.

"How long was that after the bandits scattered?"

"Only a spell at most," said Ulev, coming out of the barn door. "So he couldn't have crawled away, or been carried far enough that we wouldn't have seen the people carrying him when we rode back."

That was true. There were no dense stands of brush or trees or long grass anywhere on the farm. Carrying anyone through the wheat fields would have left a visible trail, and the Harzis had ridden behind every wall, fence, building, and tree close enough to serve as a refuge in time.

"Ulev, post two men by each building and have them stop anyone who looks as if he doesn't belong to the farm. Politely, mind you, but stop them. Keep six men with you to help any of the guards who may need it. I'll take the rest back to the horses."

That would give Michal eight men, enough to handle any natural opposition he expected. As for other kinds—he'd worry about that when he knew he was facing it.

As Michal had suspected, there was no hope of finding a trail leading away from the dead horses. Too many Harzis had ridden or walked back and forth, trampling whatever traces might have survived on the hard ground. Was he imagining things, being put falsely on the alert by horses whose condition could be explained by their being recently stolen? Had both bandits managed to remount, or had the one who hadn't still been able to run for cover and find it within a few breaths?

Michal looked around him. The grass at the foot of the wall was too short to hide anything larger than a snake, and on the far side lay the steep bank of the stream—

"The stream! Did anyone search along its banks for caves?"

Blank faces gave Michal his answer. He wanted to curse and laugh at the same time. "No, I haven't had a vision from the Warrior. I just had a little hideaway under the bank of a stream when I was a boy. Very snug and almost impossible to find unless you were looking for it."

He pointed downstream. "Yiftat, you go two hundred paces that way while I go two hundred paces the other way. We'll work toward each other. Examine both sides of the stream, keep your swords ready, and don't worry about getting wet."

The first knowledge Michal had that he'd guessed right was a shout from Yiftat, "Don't kill him, you idiot!" followed by shouting, breaking branches, splashes, and high-pitched cursing. Michal turned to look downstream, slipped on a stone, and went into a neck-deep hole. He arose spluttering and adding a few of his own curses to the din.

By the time Michal joined Yiftat, two Harzis had forced to his knees a wiry, nut-brown man with close-cropped gray hair. The rest were staring down at a hole gaping in the bank where a number of tree roots had been pulled aside. When the roots had been in place, the bank would have looked as if the roots of a large blackwood a few paces away had broken through. Nothing to arouse suspicion, if one wasn't looking for trouble.

"We still might have gone right past it," conceded Yiftat. "Our friend here was trying to cast a spell, though. He was talking soft, but the stream wasn't making enough noise to cover it. He—"

"A spell?"

"Damned if I know what else it could be," said Yiftat. "Our missing bandit's down there, dead or senseless, and our friend was doing something around his head with powders and an amulet."

Michal's right hand came up as if it had a life of its own and made a gesture of aversion, but with his left he pointed at a man. "You. Ride back to the farm and bring Ulev."

Ulev had learned to read while serving as a guard on the estate of a family who was sending its second son to the temple of the Giver of Knowledge. Both the son and the scholar-apprentice who'd been tutoring him had let Ulev read many of their books, including those dealing with Sherrani magic. Like most Harzis other than smiths, Ulev had no Gift himself, but he had more knowledge of what Sherrani magic looked like than anyone else under Michal's command.

Ulev must have ridden as if his sister's virtue were at stake; he seemed to gallop up on a lathered horse almost before the messenger was out of sight. He flung himself out of the saddle, ran to the bank, and swung himself down to the hidden hole.

He was climbing back up again in less than a spell, covered with mud and bits of bark and muttering an interesting selection of curses not quite under his breath. "It's the Spell of the Second Face," he said briskly, and started scraping the mud off his boots with the back of his knife.

No good ever came of interrupting Ulev when he was

293

working on his boots, so Michal simply crossed his arms on his chest and ignored the stares of everyone around him, including the prisoner. Finally Ulev straightened up and sheathed his knife.

"It's an old spell from before the War of God the Destroyer. It gives a dead man's face a different appearance until the body starts decaying. That breaks the link of the spell with the last of the—oh, call it the life force—and the face goes back to normal. It began as a spell to give a good appearance to embalmed bodies that had to be on public display before being burned, back when that was still the custom.

"It didn't stop there, though. Someone discovered how to use it on a living man, as long as he was asleep or senseless. That was harder. In fact, it was downright dangerous. If anything went wrong or the man woke up, he'd be blinded or mutilated. After that, it was an easy step to using it as a weapon. It was one of the popular feud spells in the War of the Destroyer and outlawed afterward."

"Is it still outlawed?" asked Michal.

"As far as I learned twenty years ago, yes. Maybe some master in the College of Priests could get permission to work it, but I don't think our friend here is one of those."

"Somehow I don't think so either," said Michal. He looked at the small man, who was now sweating a bit more than before but otherwise might have been listening to a discussion of fletching arrows.

A nice dilemma. Illegal magic was definitely something to bring before Joviz, who'd probably turn the man over to the College of Priests for a thorough investigation. If the man was found guilty, the least he could expect was a heavy fine and a term of forced labor. If he'd used the magic to commit any crimes, he might find himself in the mines of Mindranas or even on the gallows.

On the other hand, he'd have to be sent back to Koddardos with an escort strong enough to defeat any rescue attempt by the "bandits" whose friend he seemed to be. That meant at least twenty men under a good leader, enough to considerably weaken Michal's squadrons for fighting Momaks.

Besides, while illegal magic was no light matter, right now it had to take a place behind the mysterious "bandits." Who were they? What were they doing here? If the spell caster knew, how to make him tell?

Michal decided to sacrifice the lesser prize for a chance at the greater. The only other way of getting a quick answer from the man would be torture, which Joviz forbade anyone under his command to use except as the very last resort. Besides, the torture of a free Sherrani by Harzis, no matter whom they served, always meant trouble for the Harzis, even when they had justice on their side.

"My friend, the Spell of the Second Face is illegal, and I believe you know that. So we have the right to bring you before the magistrate, who will probably send you to the College of Priests. Not just you, but everybody who might have knowledge of your spell working. Your wife, your children, any servants—"

"I've always practiced alone," the man blurted out. "Nobody else knows." The beads of sweat formed into drops and began to trickle down his face.

"That's not a matter I can take your word for," said Michal. "However, if you're concerned for your family and friends, there's a better way to protect them than lying to me." He prolonged his silence while staring at the man until the prisoner was biting his lip.

"What is it?" the man finally asked.

"Who was the man down there, the one whose face you were changing?" The man swallowed and shook his head. Michal shrugged. "If you told me, I might see about ignoring the illegal sorcery. You probably haven't done any real harm. I'd rather not treat a mistake or idle curiosity as a crime, but if you leave me no choice—"

"The man is—was—one of the lord's captains. I was changing his face so that none of you men from Koddardos could recognize him. He said he'd served there this spring."

"What lord?"

"I—we don't know. He's just—the lord—and he has his

men up there—" with a gesture in the general direction of the Kyreian Heights. "He's waiting for news of the Momaks and meanwhile he's killing bandits. He's done a lot for the villages around here, so we don't ask who he is or why he's waiting."

That wasn't much information. Captains in the service of half the lords of Sherran had been in Koddardos this spring. Michal decided to count it as enough.

"If you've told the truth, you have nothing to fear," said Michal, dismissing the man and his guards. With another gesture he gathered Yiftat and Ulev to him.

"We camp here tonight with the guards set as if Momaks were about," he said. "This—lord—might have enough men to think he can snatch a prisoner out of our hands with surprise on his side." Both men grinned and Michal added, "Let's not be too ready for a fight. We may have stumbled on to something that isn't really unlawful."

"Or that we'd never be able to prove was unlawful," Ulev added.

"As long as we're in Joviz's service, the two are the same," said Yiftat.

Michal nodded. "Now, what I need is a dozen or so good climbers. Clan Avanat men first, but you can take anybody you know has a sure foot and a good head. I'm thinking that the Heights must have a few approaches our mysterious lord hasn't picketed because he thinks nobody can climb them undetected."

"He's about to find out otherwise," said Ulev, with a grin.

"He's not going to find out anything unless he's guilty of a crime. Even then he'll find out only after we've joined Bakarydes. What odds would you give on our being able to beat him with two hundred men, or going unpunished if we did and he was innocent? Joviz would have our heads for destroying his Harzis, and he'd only be the first in line!"

Ulev looked sufficiently crestfallen for Michal to drop the matter. Ulev was like so many of his men, eager for a fight, afraid they'd be too late for the Momaks, and beginning to look around for some other opponent.

"What about our spell-working friend?" said Yiftat.

"He stays with us until we're a day's march beyond the Heights," said Michal. "If the lord of the Heights turns out to be doing anything suspicious, our hedge sorcerer stays with us longer than that. I promised to pardon illegal sorcery. I didn't promise to pardon aid to traitors or rebels."

XXXI

THE FALSE DAWN HAD LONG VANISHED BY THE TIME THE Sherrani scouts reached the bank of Hilyar's Run, but the darkness didn't cause the Sherrani veterans much trouble. Lozo dismounted to spare his horse, then watched in silence as the leading scouts waded the run and took positions on the far bank, holding up white flags to mark the ford.

Lozo thought yearningly of a long drink of water, then decided to wait until true dawn. A thirty-mile night march at the end of five days on the move had left him thirsty, but it had also brought him within striking distance of the Momaks besieging Camp Cloudcroft. The battle might be today, and certainly there'd be plenty of fighting to drive in the Momak scouts and pass the supply and reinforcement convoy into the camp. That prospect made Lozo feel better than he had since the night the pay convoy was robbed, more than good enough to ignore thirst.

An occasional rattle and thump marked the passage of the scouts across the run. The banks were strewn with rocks, some of them large enough to be called boulders, scarred and chipped by flash floods. There weren't many unavoidable noises; not only were the scouts all veterans but the two column leaders had both served years at Camp Cloudcroft. They knew every trick of all the valleys and hillsides for miles around. Neither of them was senior to several under their command, but rank meant very little on the frontier when there was scouting to be done, at least to men who wanted to come home alive. The first thing Lozo did after Bakarydes gave him charge of a reinforced troop of scouts was to send back to their regiments a couple of overaged and underbrained boys who seemed to have forgotten this rule.

Being so close to the Momaks even made Lozo willing to stop worrying about being so far from Bakarydes. The Captain-General *was* able to take care of himself, and Lozo was beginning to suspect that Captain Kalaj Lesnur would be more help than hindrance. Besides, if all went at all the way they'd planned, Bakarydes would be coming up to wherever Lozo was before more than a single watch of serious fighting had passed.

The plan was simple, a virtue Bakarydes always tried to give to his battle plans. "Things you can't control always make a shambles of your plan when the fighting starts," he'd once said to Berov Godinur. "Make sure that things you can control don't do the job before you even see the enemy."

Well, Berov Godinur had proved himself a wretched pupil, and if there was any justice at all that would cost him his sight of the True Face.

The last hand of scouts was on the bank. Lozo mounted to join them, and as he did he saw a faint tinge of gray in the eastern sky. True dawn was at hand. He decided to halt the patrol for breakfast just below the crest of the next hill.

On the far bank the senior column commander, First Lancer Ludo Zelenur, was waiting. "Orders, Bannerbearer?"

Lozo upended his sword scabbard to make sure no water had leaked in. "Spread the men out in a single line abreast. Ten-pace intervals. Everybody keep their eyes open."

Ludo nodded. They both knew this kind of hillside, with enough natural cover to hide men in bowshot of a stream, was a Momak favorite for ambush.

The scouts were already spreading out as Lozo mounted again. By the time he'd taken his place at the center of the line the right end was already halfway up the hill. The more rugged ground on the left seemed to be holding the men there back; in the slowly growing light Lozo saw that a couple of the left flankers had dismounted and were leading their horses.

Lozo was about to order the right flank to halt until the left caught up, when Momak war cries rose shrill and harsh from

298

the crest of the hill. A moment later the crest was swarming with dark figures.

"Archers, shoot!" Lozo yelled. "Left flankers, draw in on me. Right flank, back to the ford." The men on the right had gone farther up the hill, but their retreat lay across smoother ground.

From ahead came Sherrani war cries answering the Momaks and the *snik* of crossbows. The bolts drew a good deal of screaming on the crest from both men and horses, as well as an answering shower of arrows. A quick look showed Lozo visible gaps in the Momak ranks and none in the Sherrani.

It looked as if the Momaks had sprung their ambush just a spell or so too soon. They were silhouetted against the dawn while the Sherrani were still in shadow, and they'd started shooting at long range for good practice against dimly seen targets. Lozo decided to ignore the odds; he would take a hand or so up to the crest of the hill and see what lay beyond it. These Momaks might be a band that had gone off to play with their horses by themselves, but with Marsh Wolf leading the enemy they could also be a regular picket guarding an approach to the main Momak army.

"Ludo! Tell off two hands and follow me up to the crest."

Ludo didn't waste time answering; he just nodded and started pointing at men. Like Lozo, he must have seen that there were well over a hundred Momaks, and that they were beginning to mount up.

Lozo led his eleven riders to the right, slanting up toward the crest as sharply as he dared to reduce the time they'd be exposing their flank to the Momaks. The going was good, and only the steepness of the slope kept them from galloping. Bending low in their saddles, they were barely a hundred paces from the crest before they lost their first man.

"Keep moving, you——!" shouted Lozo at the two riders who'd dropped back to help the fallen man. This was one of those times when the frontier way of the helping hand had to be changed. They had to reach the crest, see what lay beyond it, live to tell what they'd seen, and then pick up fallen comrades on the way out of here.

Fifty paces to the crest, and the mounted Momaks were beginning to move out. Some were on the way downhill, and some of those were already dropping as Sherrani archers let fly from behind boulders. The rest were riding at Lozo, helterskelter into the line of fire of their own dismounted archers. Either the chief of this band had been put down already, or else he didn't know his arse from a quiver sling! Lozo saw two Momaks shot out of their saddles by "friendly" arrows, and signaled his men to let fly themselves. Another three or four Momaks went down, then the Sherrani reached the crest of the hill and the surviving Momaks reached them at the same time.

Lozo saw three Momaks riding straight at him, but what he saw beyond them nearly made him forget to draw his sword or unbucket his lance. A lower hill stood in the shadow of this one, and from the base of the second hill a Momak camp stretched for miles. Tents, common grounds, horse corrals, fire pits beginning to haze the morning air with dung-reeking smoke—Lozo had never seen and barely imagined such a gathering of Momaks in one place.

He managed to control his awe enough to keep from being killed in the next breath. He spitted one Momak's horse with his lance; it took the lance out of his hand but also trapped its rider screaming under it. The screaming stopped as one of the man's comrades rode straight over him to reach Lozo. The Bannerbearer pulled his horse around so that the two remaining Momaks weren't coming at him from opposite directions. One reined in to nock an arrow to his bow; Lozo rode at him, forcing the other Momak to turn also. Lozo closed with the archer before he could shoot or abandon his bow in favor of steel and took him out of the saddle with a dart.

This gave the third Momak time to catch up with Lozo and get inside his guard, but Harzi-forged mail held the soft-steel blade away from Lozo's flesh. His own sword slashed down; the Momak rolled out of the saddle, clutching the ruined left side of his face.

With no opponents close enough to need all his attention, Lozo backed his horse and looked down the slope toward

Hilyar's Run. The mounted Momaks who'd ridden down there were quite a lot fewer than they had been, but the ones left were threatening Lozo's line of retreat and his wounded. He had with him only eight of the eleven men he'd started with, and all of them were riding tired horses.

It was time to think about bringing news of the living Momaks in the camp, rather than killing any more on this hilltop.

Lozo jerked a hand toward Hilyar's Run. "Ready your bows."

Bolts *sniked* into place.

"Shoot!"

Three mounted Momaks became dismounted ones and one dismounted Momak became a corpse. The reply sent one Sherrani down with an arrow in his neck and left several more with blood seeping out around arrows driven through their armor.

"For Sherran! Charge!"

Eight riders launched themselves downhill, a compact fist of steel and flesh.

The first thing Bakarydes did when he received the messenger with Lozo's report of the Momak camp was to ask if the Bannerbearer were still alive. When he'd been told yes, he ordered the column to halt and summoned Captain Kalaj to draft orders for the two scout leaders. They were to withdraw all their men not engaged with the enemy to within sight of their banners and not send out any more detachments without orders from Bakarydes.

Kalaj wrote this down with a questioning look. Bakarydes decided that a small lesson in tactics would not take too long. Unlike Berov Godinur, Kalaj knew that he could profitably receive instruction in war from a qualified teacher.

"We know where the Momaks are now, and they'll soon know we're close. That means we don't need to cast a wide net with the scouts. We need them concentrated enough to fight Momaks in force and close enough to the main column to both warn it and then fall back on it."

"What about finding Lord Volo's men?"

Dawn had revealed that Volo's men, placed on the right flank of the army when the march began at sundown, were nowhere to be seen. A few cautiously scattered patrols hadn't even found a trail. Bakarydes refused to believe that Volo's three hundred men, plus fifty Harzis and two troops of army scouts, had been spelled away or overwhelmed by Momaks without leaving any trace. He could believe that an overbold leader whose men had become separated from the main army during the night might have decided to press on and hope he would rejoin the army before he met any Momaks. In that case, Volo and his men might have seen their last sunset.

"If they haven't been found or found us, they've either ridden very far afield or else the Momaks have done for them. We'd have to send a couple of regiments to search for them now. I can't imagine that Volo himself would want that."

"Very good, my lord. But suppose we ordered the advanced body to follow a line of march that lets them search ground we haven't searched already? The advanced body is supposed to be three regiments and the rest of the Harzis, so—"

"We certainly can. Thank you, Captain Kalaj." Bakarydes was grateful, embarrassed at his own lapse, and thoroughly impressed in about equal measure. He looked at Kalaj with new respect. Profitably receive instruction, indeed! If he received enough instruction, Kalaj might be sitting in the Captain-General's saddle himself before he was forty.

One battle at a time, though. Bakarydes drew his field map from Lightning's saddlebags and spread it on the ground. The Momaks weren't exactly where he'd expected them. They were a good ten miles further south of Camp Cloudcroft than would have been logical. Did Marsh Wolf's knowledge of civilized tactics not extend as far as the Sherrani had thought, or was it his authority that had failed? Or did he have some unintelligible reason that still seemed perfectly sound to him?

Without either a traitor in Marsh Wolf's camp or spells outlawed since the War of God the Destroyer, there was no discovering the enemy commander's thoughts. But by reading the map, Bakarydes decided that the advanced body, intended to draw the Momaks out and force them to battle on ground of Sherrani choosing, could indeed add a search for Volo to its mission. It could swing south through virgin territory, then turn north again as soon as the Momaks came on in strength. That would encourage the Momaks to believe that the Sherrani were coming from the south.

It would have been agreeable to be able to cut in behind the Momaks and take Hungry Fox Hill overlooking the Red Ford over the Jaropik River. That would cut the main Momak army off from the one ford within a day's march that a large army could cross quickly without degenerating into a rabble. It would also cut them off from any reinforcements that might still be on the far side of the Jaropik.

It would have been agreeable, but it wasn't going to be possible. On the way to the hill the country was rugged and short of water; the advance would be slow and vulnerable to ambush. Also, if the advanced body alone took that route the main body could not join it fast enough if the Momaks took the bait. If the whole army took that route, it would be too far from both water and Camp Cloudcroft. The Momaks would be free to move at will in any direction except due south. A movement that at first glance offered tempting prospects of victory would in fact be dangerous and probably futile.

Bakarydes would also have to keep the supplies and reinforcements for Camp Cloudcroft with the main body until after the battle or else release them right now. If he took them south and then released them before battle was joined, they'd have a long trek north to the camp with only a couple of squadrons for protection against God-only-knew how many Momaks.

He'd send the extra crossbows and bolts; the bags could be slung on the saddles of regular cavalrymen and the camp would need them if the Momaks made a desperate attempt to storm it. He'd also send orders against sorties from the camp. The rest of the supplies and reinforcements could enjoy the hospitality of the main body for the rest of the day—or longer, if the Momaks weren't brought to battle at once.

Bakarydes was fairly sure the Momaks would fight at once. Even if they found the main body as well as the advanced body, they would still have a three-to-two edge in numbers as well as the confidence that their victory over Berov Godinur had given them. They would fight, and they would be smashed. Berov's folly would help his comrades avenge, not him, for he deserved no vengeance, but the good men he'd led to their doom.

Bakarydes stood up, brushed gravel off the map, and was folding it up as the first messenger rode off with the orders to the scout commanders.

XXXII

LOZO LET FLY AT A MOMAK AT EXTREME RANGE. THE BOLT bounced off a rock and nicked the man's horse in the withers. As the Momak drew completely out of range, he was fighting with more desperation than dignity not to be dumped to the stony ground.

Lozo glanced at the bolts laid out on the ground beside the rock that hid him. Only three left. He cautiously looked around the line of rocks held by the twenty-eight survivors of his scouting troop. Most of the other men seemed to be doing the same thing.

"How many bolts?" he shouted.

A gabble of answers came back. Nobody seemed to have more than five left; some had shot themselves dry. There wouldn't be any more in the saddlebags, either. They'd emptied those before they left the horses in the hands of the holders and moved up to the rocks.

"All the men who are dry, take a couple from a friend," Lozo shouted. It wasn't a life or death situation yet. The whole troop was tied in with the right flank of the Fifteenth, and their commander wasn't a man to forget even orphan detachments when it came to supplying water, fodder, rations, bolts, and Healers.

Lozo raised his head again and looked down the hill. Maybe there wouldn't be any danger for a while. The third Momak charge seemed to have been pretty well broken, although not smashed the way Lozo liked to see: scattered across the hills with every band for itself.

These Momaks might have the heart to come again, and they'd probably left archers or knifemen close to the Fifteenth's positions. There'd been a good deal of cover in the form of boulders, gullies, and stands of dwarf blackwood. Now there was even more in the form of dead men and horses. Mostly Momaks, but farther out Lozo could see mail-clad bodies from the Fifteenth and its flanker the Eighth, proof that the Momaks had taken the bait Bakarydes offered them.

Lozo rolled over on his back, picked up a pebble, and stuck it in his mouth to suck while he looked up at the sky. It was gray and lifeless, but it hardly made the day cooler. It was more like a wool blanket tied over a bed, and the rocks didn't help. They seemed to be throwing back half a moon of soaked-up heat.

If the clouds had held promise of rain, Lozo would have been happier. The Momaks didn't much care for fighting in a storm. They thought evil spirits rode the lightning. They were also on lower ground, so it would be their camps that got washed away in any flash floods.

But those weren't rain clouds, unless God had changed the rules for weather. At least nobody would be fighting with sun in his eyes, and sunlight on armor wouldn't reveal a column miles off.

"Bannerbearer Lozo Bojarkur!"

Lozo turned toward the voice. A train of seven mules was making its way down the slope behind his troop, and the soldier walking beside the lead mule was hailing him. Behind the train came a score or so of men whom Lozo recognized as camp hands. They wore no armor except helmets and boiled-leather corselets and carried only swords and crossbows.

"What is it?"

"Message from Commander Belas Rivur. You and your scouts are to report to him at once. These men and your horse holders will defend this position until the reserve squadron comes up."

Lozo looked from the messenger to the camp hands, then back down the slope toward the Momaks. Maybe they wouldn't attack, and maybe if they did the camp hands could hold them, and it certainly wasn't worth losing his sash for disobeying a direct order.

"Scouts! Mount up! Commander Belas's invited us to lunch."

The scouts reached Commander Belas's post on foot, leading their horses over the last quarter mile. Commander Belas met them with waterskins and a preoccupied look. He was a big man, running to fat but known for swordsmanship and shrewdness as well as looking after his men.

"Are your men fit for another scouting mission?"

Experience had taught Lozo that most of the time, senior officers didn't want completely truthful answers to questions like that. Fortunately he could both tell the truth and also please the commander.

"We need more bolts and a meal, but after that we'll be ready to ride. Where are we going?"

"You won't be going anywhere until you've changed your clothes. We want you to put Momak dress over your armor and ride to the Jaropik River, then along it to Hungry Fox Hill. We just had a message from the Eighth. One of their squadrons drove the Momaks back far enough in their last attack to have a glimpse of the hill. There was fighting going on, Momaks attacking uphill against someone holding the spurs."

"Volo?"

"Maybe. He might have ridden off east, then turned north. Hungry Fox Hill would be the first place he found where he could stand off the Momaks."

With no more than four hundred men, Volo wasn't going to do that much standing off, and none at all after the water or the bolts ran out. Lozo said as much, and added, "Since time's important, I'm thinking that maybe we should forget about the Momak clothing and—"

"Thinking is what you're not doing. That hill means a good ten miles' ride inside Momak-held territory. Without Momak clothing and a few Momak speakers, your last man might get halfway. I want you to reach the hill and send word, or if you can't send word, reach the hill and join up with whoever's there until we come up. If I let you and your men just hare off among the Momaks and never come back, the Captain-General will break me to recruit latrine digger, if he doesn't hang me with my own sash!"

"All right, Commander. Oh—could you ask for volunteers from Momak speakers among your men? I'd like to have at least forty or fifty men if we're to send messengers. We lost a few more of my people on the way back from Hilyar's Run." *Not to mention that all our walking wounded really aren't fit for a ride like this, whatever stories they may try to tell me!*

"Certainly. I'll have them sent up while you and your horses are being fed. I'll also send a message to Chief Valos."

The look that passed between the two men said all that was necessary. Chief of Horse Valos Remur dar Galej wouldn't oppose the mission if he were told about it before Lozo left, but he undoubtedly had some young officer he wanted to advance and thought better qualified for Lozo's job. If they lost the time needed for Valos's man to come forward and pick his own men (Lozo's would hardly follow him), the mission would be pointless.

"Bear right here!" shouted the lead rider in Momak. Lozo waved acknowledgment as he saw the ground beginning to open into ravines running down to the bank of the Jaropik. A hundred paces farther on, cliffs twenty paces high in most places dropped to the shingle beach along the river.

Should he take the scouts down and use the concealment of the cliffs? Better not. He didn't remember if there was a way up onto Hungry Fox Hill from the riverbank until you got all the way to the Red Ford. Also, there might be Momaks watering their horses down below. It wouldn't take many Momaks to hold the beach or the head of one of the ravines against fifty Sherrani long enough for reinforcements to come up.

No, the scouts would stay on open ground and rely on Momak clothes, speed, good lookouts, dust, and the blessing of God the Warrior to get them to Hungry Fox Hill. So far these had taken them through the Momak lines and halfway to their goal.

Lozo turned his horse on the heels of the lead rider's and looked back to make sure that everyone was following in the loose formation of Momaks, not in the orderly ranks of Sherrani. That could betray them from farther off than their clothing would. By the time they were a mile into Momak territory, the dust had coated them so thickly that from more than a hundred paces it would be hard to tell if they were wearing clothes at all.

Another two miles passed in silence and without incident. Twice Lozo saw respectable bands of Momaks, one riding down a ravine to the river, the other halted to tend their horses and wounded. Among the second band Lozo saw a handful of Sherrani prisoners.

He cursed under his breath. Other scouts who saw the prisoners cursed out loud, but had the wits to do it in Momak. There was nothing to be done for the prisoners, except pray that Bakarydes came up soon enough to rescue them or at least force the Momaks to kill them quickly.

Another half mile and Lozo stopped the band while he rode forward to study Hungry Fox Hill. Its lower slopes began to rise less than three miles away, but he couldn't see the spurs that ran off from the crest to the south. He could see a dust cloud rising from beyond the crest and another from the western end, which probably meant fighting but could also simply mean Momaks on the move.

The slope was too rugged for mounted men to climb rapidly. That might protect Volo's rear if he still had one, but it would also slow down the scouts' reaching Volo or whatever else lay beyond the crest.

Unfortunately there wasn't any other way onto the hill that didn't lie along the river or through the Momaks at the western—

"Bannerbearer. Look."

Ludo Zelenur was pointing west. About three hundred Momaks had ridden into view from a fold of the ground and were slanting toward the riverbank at a point about half a mile ahead.

"Hold up here," called Lozo in Momak. Those who understood held back those who wanted to spur their horses in the hope of passing ahead of the Momaks. Lozo could see no chance of their doing that, not without coming so close that their disguises might not hold up. Even breaking into a gallop might destroy the disguises—and a fight against six-to-one odds with the Momaks able to choose their ground and range could end only one way.

Lozo looked for a place where his men could make a dismounted stand. That wouldn't change the outcome of the fight, but would make it more expensive for the Momaks. A frontier motto for two centuries had been, "Don't make it easy for the Momaks. The one you take with you today might have killed your best friend tomorrow."

The suitable places turned out to number exactly two. One was the slopes of Hungry Fox Hill itself, still three miles away. The Momaks were closer to it than the scouts, and these Momaks seemed to be expecting trouble if not suspecting Sherrani. Their lances were dipping and many of them had unslung bows.

The other place to stand was a brush-grown hillock less than half a mile away on the edge of the cliffs. Not bad, except that one of the ravines down to the river lay directly beyond it. More Momaks could easily come up the ravine into the Sherrani rear.

It was still better than nothing, Lozo decided. He rose in his stirrups and was about to call, "Follow me," when the ravine erupted Momaks.

Lozo invoked every Face of God and most of the Great Stallion's anatomy and bodily functions in a long, fluent, disgusted bout of cursing. There must be at least a couple of hundred Momaks in the newly arrived band. Added to the first band, that meant ten to one against the Sherrani. With those odds they couldn't even hope to die usefully.

The first band of Momaks raised their lances, slung their bows, and broke toward the new arrivals helter-skelter, until they were spread across half a mile of ground. Only a handful on the flank toward the Sherrani kept any sort of formation. Lozo decided that he would charge those men and see if a few of his scouts could break past them to the hillside. It was a slim chance, but better than no—

Movement and light rippled along the new arrivals, the familiar pattern of crossbows being raised. Then a wind seemed to sweep through the Momaks coming to greet their friends, a wind strong enough to knock horses off their feet and riders out of their saddles.

"Sherran!"

Lozo shouted the war cry knowing that the new arrivals were Sherrani, without worrying about what they were doing here. The Sherrani were closing on the surviving Momaks at a gallop after their one volley, but the Momak flankers facing Lozo were digging in their spurs for flight. If enough of them got away soon enough to carry a warning—

This time Lozo did shout "Follow me!" and dug in his own spurs. He was out in the lead before anyone could respond to his order, but the war cries and hoof thunder behind him told their own tale. He'd taken his men through the Momak lines at a horse-saving trot, and the scouts' mounts could respond when called on. Sherrani horses were faster than Momak ones to begin with, but only a fool galloped without need in a battle.

Some of the Momaks with their main body saw Lozo's charge and wheeled their mounts. This left their backs to the Sherrani from the ravine. Crossbows went to work again and more saddles suddenly lacked riders. The rest of the Momaks joined their comrades facing Lozo, riding among and through them, seeking the place of honor as Momaks often did when there was no chief to give orders. For half a spell or so the Momaks facing Lozo could neither shoot nor charge nor run away.

At the end of that spell Lozo's charge struck them.

The world around Lozo disintegrated into a chaos of

shouting men, screaming horses, swords striking sparks from armor or other blades, a few Sherrani using lances or darts and a few Momaks using bows but everybody else just hewing and slashing and hacking as if they were all drunk or mad. . . .

Lozo wouldn't have used his lance even if he'd had one. He didn't want to give even one Momak the few extra breaths' life that setting a lance would take. Reason told him that a Momak might use those breaths to get away. Instinct told him that he would simply feel better if he killed with the sword.

Lozo fought for what he learned was nearly a spell in a red rage that clouded his vision so that he sometimes killed with no awareness of the act except feeling his sword bite into something solid. His vision cleared as he was thrusting his sword down into the throat of his last victim, to show him ground littered with dead and wounded, mostly Momaks. Beyond the litter of bodies the improbable but well-timed Sherrani were milling around, except for a few who were chasing even fewer Momaks toward Hungry Fox Hill.

A tall Sherrani in a poor imitation of Momak clothing rode toward Lozo, undoing the headcloth that had concealed his helmet. Lozo's mouth opened in a soundless gape.

"Captain Karos! What in the name of the Great Stallion's spavined sire are you doing here?"

"The same as you, Bannerbearer. Killing Momaks." He finished undoing the headcloth and reined in. "As to how we came to be doing it here rather than someplace else—perhaps I'd better tell that story when we're on the move again. Some of those Momaks are bound to reach their friends with word of what's being done."

Karos was right, Lozo admitted. However, there was such a thing as being right in a way that annoyed people as much or more than being wrong did. Karos seemed to have the habit of that sort of rightness.

Sherrani casualties had been so few that it was possible to not only pick up the wounded but the dead as well, instead of stripping them of weapons and leaving them until the battle was over. Lozo counted Karos's force as two slim army squadrons and about two hundred irregular cavalry, the Benye mounted levies. He noted that the army men went about the job of gathering up the dead and wounded as efficiently as usual, but that the levies seemed as concerned with stripping the bodies of dead Momaks. He also noted that only a hand or two of the levies joined the troops thrown out on a picket line, while ten times as many dismounted to collect loot.

Lozo kept his own men at their work and his own mouth shut.

The united four hundred Sherrani were on the march again just before Lozo reached the point of throwing good sense to the winds and goading Karos. Once the march order was set, Karos dropped back to ride beside Lozo and tell him how the Benye levies and two army squadrons came to be so far behind the Momaks.

"The Momaks around Camp Cloudcroft had been reinforced by the time the two squadrons rode up with the extra crossbow bolts. I saw they weren't going to be able to break through to the camp without help, so I led the mounted Benye levies out. We broke through the Momaks, but they charged us again and cut us off from the camp."

"How many Momaks were there around the camp?"

"At least two thousand."

"Marsh Wolf must not be getting his orders obeyed, if that many bands have moved against the camp. Two thousand men will make a big difference in the main battle. If they win that, the camp's theirs for the looting."

"I don't know if Marsh Wolf is even on this side of the Jaropik. We took a few prisoners and none of them mentioned him. They did mention someone called Five Spears in a fight down south on Hungry Fox Hill against a Sherrani 'hundred-head chief.' They described Volo's banner, too."

"Very good. Excuse me a moment, Captain."

"Why?"

"I want to send off a few of my men to try getting word to Commander Belas. He sent us out here on a report that Volo was on the hill."

"Wait until we reach the hill."

"But Captain, the Momaks will—"

"Bannerbearer, my orders are that no men will be sent back until we reach Hungry Fox Hill."

"Yes, Captain." Lozo put his best tone of respectful reproach into his reply, but it seemed to go over Karos's head. It was possible that Karos was concerned for the men, but it was absolutely certain that the Momaks would be too thick on the ground for anyone to get through them by the time the Sherrani reached the hill. If Karos had any hope of grabbing the glory of finding Volo by being the one to send the message, he was going to be disappointed. Lozo only hoped that nobody was going to get killed on the way to disappointing him.

Since the Momaks had managed to get not only between Karos and Camp Cloudcroft but also between him and any route back to the main army, Karos had decided to head south along the Jaropik and look for stragglers. (Lozo didn't suspect deliberate defiance of orders, but he couldn't help wondering if Karos had made as thorough a search for a way to join the main army as he would have done if he hadn't seen a chance of winning glory by finding and possibly rescuing orphan detachments.) They'd managed to get far enough downriver to meet Lozo thanks to their rough disguises as Momaks, keeping their distance from real Momaks, surprise, and the fact that the Momaks to the rear of the main battle area seemed to be widely scattered.

"We'd seen you about two spells before we came up, thanks to a couple of hunters with eyes like eagles. It's a good thing we came up when we did, isn't it?"

"It is, Captain."

Lozo wasn't going to pretend to be ungrateful for his life and the lives of his men, even if Karos did seem inclined to preen himself over his ride along the river. Indeed, it was something any captain might be proud of, and if Volo was holding Hungry Fox Hill, doubling his strength might save him. Karos had been overbold, but overboldness in a man his age was something a few harsh lessons could cure.

So Lozo rode in silence, not mentioning to Karos that he should be back at the head of his men and sending out scouts to see if the lower slopes of Hungry Fox Hill were already held by Momaks. If Karos delayed too long in sending out the scouts, Lozo would volunteer his own, using one of the polite formulas he'd polished up long ago for dealing with senior officers when their pride won out over their judgment.

XXXIII

BY THE FIRST QUARTER OF THE SOUTHWATCH, THE SHERRANI advanced body had drawn most of the Momaks in its area against it and killed many of those. Bakarydes reformed the army into a northern column under Valos Remur and a southern under himself, then gave the orders for a general advance.

Valos would have four army regiments (one transferred from the southern column to replace casualties), a regiment of camp hands, and all the Harzis—about three thousand five hundred men. Bakarydes would be leading five army regiments and a second regiment of camp hands, slightly less than four thousand men. Moving about two miles apart, the columns would be within supporting distance of each other and able to turn the area between them into a killing pen for overbold Momaks.

Bakarydes formed up his army for its advance in a somewhat irritable frame of mind. Lozo Bojarkur had ridden off on a dangerous scouting mission in search of a man who for all his courage was probably dead and certainly didn't belong on a battlefield like this. Lozo had ridden off on orders from Commander Belas Rivur of the Fifteenth, orders given without consulting with Chief Valos. Valos was angry enough to take Belas's sash if Bakarydes gave him the least encouragement, which Bakarydes did not intend to do.

Farther north, the mounted Benye levies had ridden out of Camp Cloudcroft, joined the squadrons bringing bolts to the camp, and charged off God knew where in search of God knew what. Karos had left the camp against orders—although to do him justice, they were orders he had not received at the time he left the camp and might not have been able to obey after he joined the army squadrons. He still seemed likely to have his name written down on the same bloody ledger as Berov Godinur's, which vexed Bakarydes both as Karos's kin and as his Captain-General.

Most frustrating of all, it was beginning to seem that Marsh Wolf was nowhere on the battlefield, that in fact the Sherrani were not fighting men under his orders. That considerably increased their chances of crushing *this* Momak army; it also considerably increased their chances of having to do the whole job over again—and again and again until Marsh Wolf was dead. Rumor said that the Momaks had already lost three to four thousand; it might even be true. Bakarydes would have gladly seen all of them brought back to life in return for Marsh Wolf's head in a Sherrani saddlebag.

All of which was to say that this battle was going no worse than most and better than many. The Sherrani could hardly do worse than a draw, although that would still leave too many Momaks alive who would have to be fought again, and had a fair chance to win a crushing victory.

As for Lozo and Karos—God did not promise that men would survive in battle merely because they were your comrades or your kin. Still, he took a breath to pray: *Let them live, O God, please!*

Bakarydes's column had just overrun a small band of Momaks and stopped to let their horses breathe when he saw Belas Rivur riding back from the head of the column at a canter. Bakarydes prepared for important news and hoped it would be good news as well. Belas would not be cantering in this heat on a horse he might not be able to water short of the Jaropik without good reason.

"My lord," Belas called. "My scouts have returned. They saw that Hungry Fox Hill is completely surrounded by Momaks. Fighting is going on along both the northern and southern slopes. They have also seen a banner on the crest that could be Volo's."

Bakarydes must not have reacted as calmly as he thought,

because Lightning began to prance. He gentled the horse and asked, "Where is the main Momak strength?"

"To the north and west of the hill."

"Then the Red Ford is only lightly defended?"

"That seems to be so, at least on this side of the Jaropik. The scouts couldn't get close enough to the river to see what the Momaks had on the far side."

What the Momaks had on the far side of the Jaropik might as well have been in the Cities of the Plains if the Sherrani could hold the near side of the Red Ford in strength. The Jaropik was much wider than bowshot, and no one could charge across the Red Ford.

Bakarydes looked up at the sky, which now showed only a few scattered patches of cloud. The rest of the battle would be fought under a scorching sun. He consulted his mental map of the area around Hungry Fox Hill.

"Commander Belas, send the scouts with the strongest horses to Chief Valos. They are to tell him what they've seen and order him to lead his men against the Momaks to the west of Hungry Fox Hill. We'll ride for the south side of the hill. As soon as we know the enemy's strength, we'll either move together against the south side or divide. If we divide I'll take three regiments and the camp hands against the hill. Belas, you'll advance to the Red Ford and hold it as long as you can without losing contact with me or risking being cut off yourself."

"My lord!"

That was giving Belas the kind of independent command he loved and also trusting two regiments to the judgment he'd shown earlier. It was only common sense to remove Belas and his regiment from under Valos, who now disliked him too intensely to make the best use of him. It had also given Bakarydes a valuable subordinate who just might find himself a Chief of Horse by the end of the day. However many Momaks died today, it looked as if Sherran was in for another long war against the horsemen. This meant a larger army that would need more good senior officers.

316

Bakarydes looked up at the sky again. His army would have plenty of time both to reach the battlefield and force a decision before dark. The Momaks would also have plenty of time to detect his advance and retreat or even lay traps.

Still, if Valos attacked west of the hill and Bakarydes to the south of it, they shouldn't be out of touch for too long. The Momaks to the north of the hill would be cut off from the ford whatever Belas did. If all else failed Bakarydes and Valos could send messengers over the hill itself! Was wagering that much on Volo's ability to hold out for at least another half-watch in the face of God only knew how many Momaks gambling for higher stakes than Sherran could afford? If the Army of the North was crippled today, the Momaks would not over-run the land, but the throne on which Kantela was so precariously seated would be severely shaken. Even if Bakarydes could reconcile it with his honor to survive the defeat of his army, he would have lost much of the reputation that made his advice such a useful prop to Kantela. . . .

Bakarydes decided that he was not gambling too much, considering what might be won, as well as what might be lost. He made a mental note to try to analyze how and why he knew this, so that he could explain it to Kantela the next time they met. Then he laughed.

"Does anyone have any questions, comments, advice, protests, or insults to my ancestors and habits?" Belas laughed, but without mirth. Kalaj smiled.

"Then let's be off!"

Kalaj waved the Captain-General's banner at the signalers, and their horns blared in reply. Bakarydes urged Lightning forward. *Captain of Captains, send us strength and wisdom this day, and victory to Sherran—and the Throne.*

"Here come the dung-spawn again!" someone shouted. Lozo didn't need the warning. He could see the Momaks swarming up the draw, both on foot and on horseback.

"Aim at the horses!" Lozo shouted. The moment the words were out of his dust-coated throat he knew that the order was unnecessary. He hoped it didn't sound as if he was losing his head from the heat, the dust, and what seemed to be the endless numbers and determination of the Momaks around Hungry Fox Hill.

The handful of Harzis mixed in among the squadron of Sherrani defending the spring under Lozo's command were already shooting, lofting their arrows to hit the mounted Momaks in the rear of the attack. Some of the Sherrani crossbowmen were shifting position to any boulder or hump in the ground that would give them higher command. Lozo was proud to see that none of them were retreating up the draw toward the crest of the hill. If the Momaks overran this spring, there would be only one source of water left inside the Sherrani position, and that one at the far western end of the hill's crest.

Enough arrows and bolts seemed to be hitting the mounted Momaks to thin their ranks and slow their charge. Even a Momak pony wouldn't step on a writhing corpse, let alone climb a steep, rocky slope with its tongue hanging out from thirst and perhaps an arrow sunk a span into its flank.

The Momaks on foot were still coming on, though. Lozo decided to find smoother ground for himself. If he had the edge in speed as well as in reach and striking power over his opponents, he'd have a much better chance of coming off this hill alive.

He'd covered five paces when he saw that the Momaks were closing too fast to let him move any farther. At least the remaining mounted archers had ceased shooting, some perhaps for fear of hitting their own comrades, others (Lozo prayed) because they were out of arrows.

Lozo stepped in front of a Sherrani limping with an arrow in his thigh and trying to tug another out of his shoulder, drew his sword, and shouted the rally. Then the first Momak was in reach, and Lozo's sword leaped out to carve a bloody path across his boiled-leather jerkin and the rib cage inside it.

The Sherrani weren't as well equipped for fighting on foot as the Harzis, who had shields and shorter, handier swords. The Sherrani sword was intended to be used mostly from horseback, and needed two hands to wield it effectively for long on foot.

Still, a strong and skilled man like Lozo could use the Sherrani blade with devastating effect against the lightly protected Momaks. Lozo killed three Momaks before one of them even touched his armor. As fast as the three went down, the wounded Sherrani knelt beside them and cut their throats with a dagger held in his left hand.

Here on Hungry Fox Hill Volo's men faced many times their strength, and there was no way to guard prisoners and nothing to be learned from them anyway. Besides, not even a Momak deserved to be made to die a finger at a time under this broiling sun. God heard the curses of men who died like that on those who didn't give them cleaner deaths.

It took Lozo a while longer to kill his fourth opponent, but after that he found the ground in front of him momentarily clear. Looking to either side along the Sherrani line, he saw that it was just barely holding. In a couple of places Momaks had actually reached the spring and were hurling rocks into it. A small band of Harzis was moving in a tight circle around the spring, efficiently dispatching the Momaks and trying to pull the rocks out; but there were always more Momaks, and one by one the Harzis were going down. The Harzi archers had mostly stopped shooting, but Lozo saw some of them slipping out of the fight—not to the rear, no Harzi would do that—but forward to replace their arrows from the quivers of dead Momaks.

By the Face of the Warrior, let no one ever tell me again that Harzis aren't almost as good as they say they are!

Then fresh Momaks were coming up the draw, this time mounted men each with an archer or swordsman clinging to his stirrups. A cold hand seemed to grip Lozo's bowels as he saw the stirrup hangers dropping off and running up the slope on either side of the draw, around the ends of the Sherrani line and toward the cover of the scrub growth on the crests of the flanking spurs. Then Lozo's world shrank down to a score of horsemen cantering at him, through and over the survivors of the previous charge, then shrank down further to a single rider and stirrup hanger coming straight at him.

319

Lozo cut the rider out of his saddle but the stirrup hanger jumped clear. Lozo slashed at him, giving another rider time to close and thrust with his lance. The rider came on so fast he knocked the stirrup hanger to one side and nearly trampled him, but the lance tip caught in the crest of Lozo's helmet and jerked him backward off his feet.

He landed with a bone-jarring thud, not sure his neck wasn't broken and his skull cracked but thrusting upward with his sword anyway. The steel drove into the Momak's mount, and it reared with a scream, spilling its rider instead of coming down with both hooves crushing Lozo's chest. Lozo rolled to one side and found himself rolling straight onto the fallen Momak. The man cursed and clawed at Lozo's face, gashed his skin with filthy fingernails, and tried to sink his teeth into Lozo's throat. Lozo threw both arms around the Momak in a wrestler's grip and twisted until the Momak was underneath, then slammed the Momak's head against the stony ground several times until he felt the man relax, then several more times until he felt the impact become squashy.

Sherrani horns and war cries, the thud and rattle of trotting horses, and the sound of swords sinking into flesh jerked Lozo to his feet. Twoscore Sherrani horsemen were picking their way down the slope to the left of the draw, not a real charge but definitely more than the Momaks there were willing to face. Some of them stood and died, others ran and died at the hands of either the horsemen or the survivors of Lozo's men. By the time the handful of living Momaks reached the bottom of the draw, the litter of dead ones on the ground was a good deal thicker and the survivors seemed to have no heart for another charge.

Lozo now had time to note that the horsemen wore Volo's badge and were led by Volo himself in his unmistakable blued armor. Lozo wasn't surprised to see either the charge or Volo leading it. Volo was taking great care to keep the remaining horses fit by forbidding any man to ride in more than two consecutive charges, except for Captain Karos and himself.

Karos, Lozo suspected, was either seeking more glory or else didn't trust the discipline of the Benye levies unless they were under his eye. Every man on the hill knew why Volo rode in every charge. His son Rajos had died of wounds at the end of the first eastwatch, and since then Volo had fought as if killing enough Momaks could bring the young man back to life.

Lozo was about to call to Volo to send down more bolts and men to hold the spring, when he saw that Volo had turned in his saddle and was cursing with frontier fluency. Lozo felt like doing the same when he also turned his gaze toward the spring.

It was completely blocked with a pile of dead horses, horse dung, dead Momaks, rocks, and some other things Lozo didn't really want to identify. The Harzis who'd been defending it lay dead to the last man on the lower slopes of the spur to the right. The upper slopes of the spur and the scrub along its crest were alive with Momaks, a couple of hundred at least. They weren't in easy bowshot of Lozo or Volo or the others in the draw, but they could rain arrows on anyone trying to reach the spring to clear it.

There was nothing to do here except retreat up the draw before the Momaks gathered for another charge, and save the men to defend the last remaining spring. Every man Lozo could save would be none too many because the Momaks on top of the spur were also well placed to charge right onto the crest of Hungry Fox Hill. If they did that, they would cut the men on the eastern end of the crest off from the last source of water closer than the Jaropik.

Then if nightfall did not bring Bakarydes, dawn would see Hungry Fox Hill peopled only by corpses and carrion birds. Most of the corpses would be Momaks because the Sherrani and Harzis weren't short of either weapons or determination. Still, of the eight hundred men who'd reached the hill today, a hundred were dead, two hundred wounded, and half of those unfit to be moved.

Could they still break out if they abandoned the wounded while the horses could still move? Perhaps, but no one who'd fought on the frontier would do that. Volo wasn't like Bakarydes, a man to follow anywhere, or he wouldn't have been on this hill today, but Lozo saw no shame in dying under Volo's banner.

As Lozo's men retreated up out of the draw after Volo's horsemen, Lozo learned something from the lord's cursing. It seemed that Captain Karos was supposed to have charged the other spur when Volo charged this one, but for some reason hadn't done so.

If it was Karos's failure to charge that had let the Momaks seize the spur, ruin the spring, and take a long step forward toward victory today, the captain was going to need a very good reason indeed for not charging, and Lozo didn't care *whose* kin he was!

Michal looked down at the sluggish brown waters of the Jaropik and began counting the bodies floating in the channel or stranded on the near bank. When his count reached a hundred he spat into the brush in front of his horse and turned in disgust. "Well, they've started the party without us."

Ulev nodded. Yiftat didn't even do that much; he just grunted like a sleepy bear.

Most of the bodies were Momaks, which suggested that the battle was going well for the Sherrani. On the other hand, Sherrani bodies seldom floated until the gases of corruption overcame the weight of their armor and brought them to the surface again. Only the Father could say what might lie beneath those brown waters.

It would be no insult to Bakarydes and the Army of the North to swing away from the Jaropik and not ride straight into a battle where the advantage might be changing every half watch. It would only be hoping for the best but guarding against the worst, an ancient law of war.

Michal still felt like cursing his luck as he gave the orders that would probably keep his men out of the battle even longer. He would have cursed Joviz's taking so long to permit his Harzis to go north, except that only a madman cursed his sworn lord on the eve of what might be a battle. The Warrior remembered such curses.

Michal did curse Lord Ikos, the "lord" of the Kyreian Heights. The climbers sent up the cliffs that night had discovered Ikos's identity with even less trouble than they'd expected. They'd eavesdropped on a few indiscreet sentries, then waylaid one of them and completely stripped him as bandits would have done. Even a man as shrewd and suspicious as Ikos was said to be was unlikely to suspect anyone else of being responsible for the naked sentry with the sore head found the next morning.

If Ikos hadn't been lurking on the Kyreian Heights for what was probably no good purpose, and forced Michal to lose a day's march in his attempt to find out what it was, the First Magistrate's Harzis could have reached Bakarydes yesterday, in good time for the battle.

Michal only hoped that Ikos hadn't killed enough bandits *or* Momaks to prevent the Throne's asking pointed questions about his conduct. Making trouble for His Craftiness Ikos Muzkur was about the best recompense Michal could now expect for missing the battle.

"Captain!"

One of the sentries was signaling the approach of a friendly mounted force. Michal rode over to the sentry post in time to see the scouts of Lord Arkan's regiment of Harzis ride up. He greeted them politely but absently, while doing sums in his head. Arkan had sent three hundred Harzis but no captain who outranked Michal. Five hundred Harzis could safely go where two hundred would be foolhardy.

Michal grinned. "If your captains will agree to follow me along the bank of the Jaropik, I think we can join the party before all the drink is gone." The answering grins told him that he wasn't the only man who found the lees of a battle a very bitter cup.

Bakarydes struck the Momak line at a canter, not looking back to see how closely the Thirty-First and the Tenth were following him. He'd be killed faster by taking his eyes off the Momaks around him than by being isolated in the middle of them. There were so many Momaks that Bakarydes sometimes wondered if they *were* coming back to life to be killed over and over, but they seemed far more scattered and less organized than he'd expected. Was Marsh Wolf dead?

Never mind wild hopes; here was a Momak ideally placed for a lance thrust. Bakarydes delivered the thrust, the Momak's pony galloped off with an empty saddle, and Captain Kalaj rode up to his left with the Captain-General's banner in its bucket on his saddle. Bakarydes had time to note that Kalaj had found time to wipe the blood from the staff, then the dusty chaos of a cavalry action swallowed them again.

The Momak force now in front of him was hardly more than a thousand strong, and some of the Momaks Bakarydes saw already bore wounds. It was barely a worthy opponent for two Sherrani regiments, but Bakarydes wasn't interested in fair fighting; he was interested in seeing that a few Momaks as possible left this battle alive. Perhaps he couldn't kill Marsh Wolf, but leaving the war chief without any warriors alive to follow him would not be a bad second-best. . . .

A Momak lance broke into Bakaryddes's thoughts by whispering through Lightning's mane, a finger from his neck. The near wound to his mount put Bakarydes into a greater rage than a similarly narrow escape for himself. His sword lopped off the head of the lance in one stroke, the Momak's arm in another, and his head in a third. Bakarydes gave a wordless cry of sheer rage and blood lust, then looked around, half ashamed and more than half hoping that no one had seen or heard him.

If anyone had they gave no sign of it, and the odds were good that no one had noticed. The surviving Momaks were giving way, and the Sherrani regiments were breaking into squadrons to follow them. Bakarydes reined in Lightning and watched to make sure that none of the squadrons were breaking into troops. A troop was too easy prey for even scattered and disorganized Momaks, while a squadron could at least fight its way out of any trouble it couldn't defeat.

With a chance to look around him for the first time in several spells, Bakarydes realized that the last charge had taken the left flank of his column a long way closer to the base of Hungry Fox Hill itself. About half a mile of broken ground concealed the actual bases of the three spurs running off from the crest to the south. It was difficult to tell what was happening, because of the distance and the dust rising from several places on the spurs. Bakarydes thought he saw a banner on the crest and knew he saw the glint of sunlight on armor.

That meant Sherrani were still holding on the hill itself. More dust, practically a miniature storm, was rising from the western end of the hill. That would be Valos and his column coming into action, as the last messenger from the chief had promised.

Bakarydes faced a delicate decision. Should he split his own column as he'd considered, sending Commander Belas toward the Red Ford with two regiments and taking the rest of the column straight to the hill? If he did, he'd catch the Momaks there between two solid forces of Sherrani.

He'd also have both forces in a position to cut off the Momaks' retreat to the Red Ford, whatever Belas did. Could he afford to spend two regiments protecting his rear against Momak reinforcements that might or might not be on the other side of the Jaropik? The Momaks didn't seem to be under the kind of leadership that would immediately send such reinforcements, and the two regiments would add a useful amount of weight to the main battle around Hungry Fox. . . .

"My lord Captain-General!"

"Yes, Captain Kalaj."

"Messenger from Commander Belas. A scouting party he sent south has found five hundred Harzis moving up the river. The First Magistrate's men and Lord Arkan's, mostly. Belas thinks that with the extra men he's justified in moving to the Red Ford."

He probably was. In fact, five hundred Harzis might be able to do most of the work themselves. All the arguments in favor of bringing Belas onto the hill still applied, though.

But so did the argument that if Bakarydes waited for Belas to come up he would delay the attack on the hill. If he didn't wait he would lose the advantage of having Belas with him. If he called Belas back at all, he would look like a Captain-

General who had turned, if not precisely timid, then at least away from his usual decisiveness.

He'd also crush Belas's belief that the Captain-General really trusted him with an independent command, a blow that could cripple him as an effective senior officer.

No, Belas could ride for the Red Ford with Bakarydes's blessing. If he survived the day, he'd be an Acting Chief of Horse, and also have a place in Bakarydes's next discussion with Kantela about the wisest way of handling subordinates.

Kalaj saw Belas's orders written on Bakarydes's face, and again in the way that face turned toward Hungry Fox Hill. He grinned and made a tiny adjustment to the angle of the banner pole.

"Kalaj, send a messenger to the Fourteenth and the camp hands. We'll advance toward the central spur as soon as they come up. All regiments will guide on the Captain-General's banner!"

Kalaj looked as if he wanted to cheer, instead of only nodding and saying, "At once, my lord!"

Lozo straightened up from examining Ludo Zelenur's wound and grinned at the First Lancer's rebellious look.

"Nobody's going to be saying the Kin's Blessing over you for a while, if you have the sense to take yourself to the Healers and then do what they tell you."

"That's the midden pit saying that the musk goat stinks," replied Ludo. "What about those?" He pointed to assorted bloodstains and bandages on Lozo.

"Oh, they'll do until the fighting's over."

"I could say the same about mine."

"You could. I could also say that I'm a Bannerbearer and you're a First Lancer."

"Yes, lord." Ludo saluted mockingly and let four of the walking wounded Lozo had assigned as litter bearers carry him off.

Lozo looked westward toward the fighting at that end of the hill. The amount of dust and the number of armored horsemen he could see told him that the Sherrani had arrived there in some force. So far they hadn't driven the Momaks there either north or eastward onto the hill, which was just as well. Sooner or later the Momaks to the south would nerve themselves for another charge, and they still had the strength to sweep the crest of Hungry Fox Hill clear of living Sherrani. Clouds of dust behind them and toward the Red Ford might be Sherrani, but they might also be Momak reinforcements. The dust that had been a blessing when Lozo and his scouts plunged into Momak territory was now becoming a curse, making it next to impossible to tell who was doing what to whom where.

A messenger trotted past on a foam-flecked horse and dismounted beside Lord Volo, who was squatting in the shade of his own mount. Lozo was close enough to hear the messenger's report without having to listen too obviously.

"The Momaks to the west are beginning to retreat. There's four or five army regiments against them from the banners we counted."

"Four or five? Bakarydes wouldn't have sent a force that size by themselves. He has to be somewhere around here with the rest of his men."

Lozo couldn't quarrel with Volo's logic, but that didn't answer the question of where Bakarydes was. He looked south again, screwing up his eyes as if that would let them penetrate the dust clouds and the broken ground. He thought he saw armor flashing in the dust toward the Red Ford, but knew that might also be reflections of sun on the river.

Then half a dozen voices were shouting, "Here they come!" Lozo saw Momaks on foot running up the spur above the spring, some of them stopping to shoot but most just running with swords, spears, and knives in their hands. Although he heard no death song, this could be only one thing—a final charge by Momaks sworn to take the crest or die.

Somehow Lozo doubted that any of them would be foresworn. *Captain of Captains, look upon us with favor, that we may have the strength to do our duty and meet our fate.*

Volo's men were mounting up while the archers took their

positions, the few surviving Harzis standing in the open and the Sherrani behind what little cover the crest provided. Lozo had assigned other lightly wounded Sherrani to reload the crossbows of the best archers, so bolts quickly started tearing into the advancing Momaks.

Volo's men were mounted now. From the far side of the crest Lozo heard the horns of Karos's squadrons. Maybe Captain Karos would be in the right place at the right time for once. That wasn't really just, though; at the time Karos had been supposed to be attacking down the spur above the spring he'd been fighting off a mounted Momak attack on the north side of the hill. Maybe the men there could have done the job without him, probably he'd charged a little too far, and certainly no one believed his tale of having killed a major chief, but only God could say for sure whether he'd neglected his duty and disobeyed his orders.

The Momaks coming up the spur were now scrambling over the writhing bodies of their comrades but they were still coming. Lozo drew his own sword and waved it to signal the litter bearers to move in and help any wounded Sherrani. In two places Sherrani had thrown down empty quivers and useless bows and were defending themselves desperately against odds of four or five to one.

Lozo had just decided that his place now was down there with his men as just one more sword, when everything seemed to happen at once. Mounted Momaks and archers seemed to rise from the ground or materialize out of the air, surging up the spur toward the crest like an incoming tide. Sherrani war horns blared from inside the dust behind the oncoming Momaks, and Lozo heard cries of "Sherran!" and "Bakary-des!" Volo drew his sword, tossed it over his head, caught it by the hilt, and waved it in the direction of the Momaks. His fifty-odd horsemen didn't need a second signal; they plunged toward the Momaks.

Lozo wanted to fling himself bodily in front of Volo's mount and stop this unnecessary and futile charge. The Momaks weren't trying to sweep the crest; they were trying to get away from Bakarydes tearing into their rear. He did shout, "Stop, lord! Stop!" but he might as well have tried to outshout a thunderstorm. Karos's men were coming up over the crest at a trot, in good order, adding their own war cries and hoofbeats to the uproar and their own dust to the cloud that was swallowing the crest.

As the dust swallowed Volo and his men, it opened a little further down the spur, and Lozo shouted again, this time in triumph. The Captain-General's banner that he'd carried in a dozen battles was climbing steadily up the spur, with a familiar figure on a huge gray horse riding close beside it. Every horseman whose mount could find room on the spur was following close behind the banner, and in the draw what looked like at least another regiment was coming up more slowly, scouring the ground like a gardener's rake.

If he hadn't been tired, hot, thirsty, and sore, Lozo would have done a sword dance for sheer joy.

In a couple of spells there were no live, free, fighting Momaks anywhere in sight. Lozo was counting off the Sherrani wounded who could walk to the Healers and those who would need to be carried and had just decided he'd better recruit a few more litter bearers when he heard someone shouting: "A Healer! A Healer! In the name of God, a Healer!"

The voice was cracking with fear or pain. Lozo's head snapped up and around. A cluster of mounted Sherrani were riding toward him, two of them on either side of a third who seemed ready to tumble out of his saddle. Lozo saw three arrows sticking into the man's mail—then cursed under his breath as he saw the mail was blued.

He ran forward as a Healer ran up from the other side and Lord Volo's comrades helped him out of the saddle. He could not stand, so they laid him in the shadow of a large boulder and started making a tent for him with saddlecloths and lances. Others took off his helmet and were about to start removing his armor when the Healer stopped them.

"Wait! If he has broken bones or inward hurts, the less he is moved the better."

Healers didn't care for audiences when they were working, so Lozo played sheepdog, herding all the would-be gawkers to a safe distance. Some took the hint more gracefully than others and went off to join the litter bearers.

About three spells passed while the Healer examined Volo. Except toward the west the battle sounds were dying away. Bakarydes's banner was out of sight again, but from the orderly way the Sherrani in sight were moving about, Lozo knew that the Captain-General was on hand, doing his usual thorough job of finishing off an opponent.

At last the Healer straightened up, his face trying so hard not to reveal his verdict that everyone who saw him knew it at once. Volo managed a parody of a smile.

"What's the matter, Reverend Minjo? Afraid you won't be paid? You'll have your fee, and it even looks as if you'll live long enough to spend it."

"My lord, there is a chance for you, if you don't exert—"

"There may be, but it's a damned slim one, isn't it?" The Healer couldn't even shake his head. "Well, then, I'm not going to behave like a corpse until I am one. Bannerbearer!"

"My lord?"

"Prop me up some place where I can see what's going on. I might survive the wounds, but I doubt if I'll survive boredom."

"My lord!" Lozo motioned to four of his litter bearers. They started pulling down Volo's tent and transforming it into a litter as the Bannerbearer knelt beside the nobleman.

"If I don't last until Bakarydes comes, swear to tell him what I think of Karos."

Lozo blinked. He owed Karos his life and the lives of his men, but a dying man's last message was a sacred trust. Complicating this dilemma was the fact that criticism of Bakarydes's kin was very low on the list of things Lozo really cared to put before the Captain-General.

His face must have been a trifle too revealing, because Volo managed a faint laugh. "Not—that bad. Just that Karos is—as greedy as he is brave. Maybe—they'll balance each other. But have Bak—treat the boy—treat him like Joviz treated me. Keep him busy. Keep him busy."

Volo couldn't or wouldn't say any more, so Lozo stood up and looked around again. Toward the west the Sherrani—no doubt under Valos—were steadily driving the Momaks before them, out onto the open ground north of the hill. To the south the dust still shrouded most of what was going on, but at the Red Ford Lozo could now make out what must be at least two regiments of Sherrani. A third regiment that looked like Harzis was close by.

The Captain of Captains had sent Sherran the victory this day, and anything that deserved the name of battle was over. What was left would be no more than a killing match, and with armored horsemen against unarmored Momaks, many no longer mounted, there could be no doubt about who would do most of the killing.

"My lord," said one of the litter bearers, "we're ready to move you if you'll tell us—" He broke off and signaled urgently to Lozo. Lozo bent over the nobleman. It didn't really matter where they put Volo now. His eyes were open, but they would never see anything again.

Lozo wiped the trickle of blood from the corner of Volo's mouth and signaled to the litter bearers to cover him. Then he stood up and silently said the Prayer for the Newly-Departed. It would not take away the ache of knowing that Volo had died leading an unnecessary charge against Momaks already routed and fleeing, but nothing would do that. Nothing, that is, except the knowledge that came to any soldier with Lozo's experience, that such things happened in battle and to let them ache too much or too long was to court madness and question the judgment of God.

His years as a soldier would not help him, however, to decide whether to tell Bakarydes of Volo's last words about Captain Karos—and if so, how much and when.

"So there the levies were, wallowing in that pile of Momak loot like pigs in a puddle. We weren't in the best of tempers ourselves, but all would have been well if somebody hadn't

331

sung out, 'Hoy, Harzi. Want something to take back to your girl? We're selling cheap!'"

Hakfor nodded sympathetically. "What did you say to that?"

Michal shrugged. "*I* didn't say anything. Ulev shouted, 'We bring our women what we've bought with our blood, not with silver from thieves!' Our friend in the levies said that no sister-futtering child-reaving Harzi called him a thief, and they'd both drawn steel before I or the levies' captain could reach them. We stopped matters before any blood was shed, but since the captain didn't seem disposed to apologize for either the blood insult or the pile of loot, I decided we'd best push on."

"Describe that captain," said Hakfor. He wrapped a piece of middle-aged cheese in a slab of fried flatbread and munched on it as Michal described the man.

"You did the best thing," Hakfor said, when Michal had finished. "That was the Captain-General's cousin Karos Bitrinur. He killed Chief Five Spears—"

"Really? I heard his men boasting about it, but I thought—"

"No, he really did put a lance through the man. Five Spears led the biggest war band this side of the river, so killing him made the rest of our work a good bit easier. He also saved the life of your friend Lozo Bojarkur and did quite a bit else worth boasting about. It's not only Bakarydes who'll think that Karos is at least as much use as you are."

"Lozo's a friend and I won't pretend not to be grateful for his life," said Michal. "And I won't quarrel too much with any man who kills Momaks. But he'd better keep quiet about Ulev, though. . . ." The two Harzis exchanged speaking looks.

They changed the subject to the fighting at Red Ford. The Momaks on the far side of the Jaropik had made only one effort to get across and help their comrades, but that had been enough to make the ford live up to its name. On the near side, there'd been enough retreating Momaks so that most of Michal's men ended the day with bloody steel, and Belas

332

Rivur seemed good at leading Harzis. If there was in fact going to be a moon of campaigning to clear the Momaks back across the frontier and Hakfor was able to procure him Acting Commander's rank, Michal would have to admit that the Warrior had not been altogether heartless.

"Just as long as we don't have to serve under Lord Ikos," Michal concluded.

"Ikos? He's not with us. Anyway, I thought it was Volo you had the quarrel with."

"It wasn't exactly a quarrel, or at least it wasn't after Joviz gave Volo the choice between making his peace with Harzis or facing the Fire of Truth. Besides, Volo's gone where nobody has a quarrel with him anymore."

"True. But he's left the House of Tivest to a son ten years old and a grandson still at the breast. I don't think Volo was the only one of that House who didn't think well of Harzis, but he was the only one brought to heel. Some of the others may have lived through today, and now there's no one to rein them in. But you were asking about Ikos, I believe?"

"I'd heard he was raising men, and we passed through a couple of villages where his levies had been chasing bandits. From the tales we heard, you'd not want them at your back with Momaks to your front. Ikos himself is no bad soldier, or so I've heard, but he seems to be short of officers worth their sashes."

"That doesn't surprise me," said Hakfor, and took the hint in Michal's voice by changing the subject to praise how well Lord Volo had fought after putting himself in a situation he shouldn't have been in at all.

Michal listened with just enough attention for good manners. It seemed that Ikos hadn't joined Bakarydes after all, yet the sentries Michal's climbers had overheard said that the nobleman's two thousand soldiers had been on the Kyreian Heights for some days. Ikos could have joined Bakarydes easily if he'd wanted to.

Therefore, he hadn't wanted to. Why? It did not seem to Michal that he was being paid enough to speculate on Ikos's motives. It was his duty to lay the matter of where Ikos had been when he should and could have been elsewhere before Lord Joviz, then let the magistrate speculate. It also might be best to lay the matter of Karos Bitrinur before Joviz, if only because the magistrate insisted on knowing of anyone who might interfere with his Harzis doing their duty. That was one of the unbreakable rules of his service. Since that would also leave in Joviz's hands the decision of what to lay before the Throne or the Captain-General (and if the two were close to the same, as rumor ran . . . ?), Michal was quite happy to follow the rules.

His only remaining decision was how much to tell Daivon, and he could put that off until he returned to Koddardos after a moon or so of chasing Momaks. Both prospects delighted him so much that he only regretted there was no wine at hand for celebrating.

XXXIV

CHARKO CLOSED THE DOOR AGAINST THE SOUNDS OF rejoicing in the hall outside his chambers and knelt.

"My God, my God, how have I offended Thee? Why is Thy Face turned from me?"

He went through the Litany in Time of Doubt with covered face and closed eyes, as he had done every day since the news of Bakarydes's victory reached Koddardos. Then, still kneeling, he entered upon his meditations.

The Momaks had not done as he expected them to do, indeed as they must have done for his plans for Ikos to succeed. Ikos had warned him of this— "Momaks aren't pieces to be moved about on a Siege board" —and so it had proved. Clearly Ikos's knowledge had proven greater than that of a High Master in the service of the Giver of Knowledge.

God could give knowledge to anyone. Had he, Charko, been given the knowledge he needed to bring his plans for Ikos to fruition? That was the question he had asked every day, but so far he had not found an answer he could be sure was true knowledge from God and not the counsel of his own desires and fears.

Faint sounds of rejoicing reached him from the hall, in spite of the closed door. Not that he felt the rejoicing to be unseemly, even here in the temple of the Giver of Knowledge. God had given Sherran a great victory over its enemies; rejoicing was fit and proper.

Nor would he deny the claims of those who had suffered to bring about the victory. Three of his scholar-apprentices had been given leave to return home to assist in the mourning for dead kin. He himself was paying for a Healer from the First Temple of the Healer to go to the Rishi estates to tend two of his kin who would be returning home with wounds that needed expert Healing if they were not to be permanently crippling.

He would also pay one blood debt. His principal man among the bandits in the north had fled to save his own skin when Bakarydes sent the army against the bandits. A scholar-apprentice had remained behind, done what he could to keep the soldiers from learning anything, found that was not enough, and defended Charko's secrets and God's with his life.

Charko did not now have the time to ferret out whether the coward still lived, and if so where. But a time would come when that coward would learn that there was no hiding place from Charko's vengeance. He owed his apprentice that.

At the head of his men, Ikos rode south along the dusty back road. Varjan Kuzler, his chief of scouts, rode beside him. Ikos did not expect trouble, not after the defeat of the Momaks and with his own men a good hundred miles on their homeward ride already. He rode with Varjan because the man was normally so taciturn that it wouldn't even occur to him to try lifting the mood of his lord with unwarrantably cheerful remarks.

Ikos needed not only time to be alone with his bleak mood, he also needed time to think. The plain fact was that he and Charko had been defeated, though not (God be thanked!) routed. Since he was a soldier and the defeat was due to poor tactics and not faulty information, it was more his fault than Charko's.

Who would have thought that the Momaks would begin their campaign like civilized people, massing their men to achieve superior numbers? If they'd come on helter-skelter in their usual fashion, Ikos could easily have made a name for himself smashing small or even fairly large bands. He also would have been the only lord with men ready to reinforce the Army of the North and play a decisive part in its victory, or had it been necessary, in covering its retreat.

As it was, Marsh Wolf kept his warriors in hand until there was time for a warning to reach Koddardos, Charko's magic and bandit allies notwithstanding, *and* for that *parodi's* daughter and her bedmate to act on that warning. When Five Spears finally slipped his harness and led fourteen thousand men off to fight Bakarydes, he met a Bakarydes reinforced and ready for him. He also met death for himself and for ten thousand of those who followed him. Bakarydes lost at most fifteen hundred, and by the time Marsh Wolf had to decide what to do next, Bakarydes had received four thousand additional reinforcements. His army was stronger than the one that had already defeated a larger force than Marsh Wolf had left.

What Marsh Wolf decided to do was lead his eight thousand surviving men homeward. Since it was the men who'd ignored his spirit-vision who had died and those who stayed with him who returned home, he would have more authority and more allies among the seers than before. Marsh Wolf *had* seen a truth—and the next time he came, he would not only come with more warriors but with warriors who would follow his orders and nobody else's.

When the chief came again, Ikos might have another chance to win a reputation. Meanwhile, his own best course seemed to be the same as his foe's—accept defeat, gather his men, ride home, and start planning his next move.

He'd not been so philosophical at first; indeed he'd been angrier than ever before in his life. Two things kept him from giving vent to all that anger. One was the knowledge that if he did, even his sworn men would think he'd gone mad, not to mention learning that they'd been committing treason. The other was that the person he was angriest at, next to Kantela, was himself. He'd been so determined to put himself in a place where he could win a victory of his own over the Momaks that he'd missed a chance to join Bakarydes in ample time to take part in the Captain-General's victory.

Shared glory might not put a man on the throne, but it was better than no glory at all, and riding home without having struck a blow.

He would have to ride home quickly, too, in order not to lose a good part of his harvest. If he did, there would go more of his silver to feed his people this winter.

He'd not ask Charko for any of that silver, either. If he couldn't act independently of that schemer, however gifted he might be, they would inevitably reach a point where it was just a question of who told the Throne about whom first. After that, it would be an equally simple question of whether they were impaled side by side or separately—unless that *parodi's* daughter borrowed a lance from her bedmate and did a personal job on him. . . .

Ahead, the road climbed toward the crest of a hill, and the sky was vanishing behind rolling thunderclouds. Ikos saw the lightning flicker and pulled his hat more tightly down on his head. At least he could thank God for one favor: Volo hadn't survived the battle. If the man who had tied down four thousand Momaks and brought about Five Spears's death had survived to be rewarded by the Throne for his valor—Ikos didn't care to think about what Volo's reward might have cost *him*.

Kantela slipped on her sandals. Summer was giving way to autumn; it was too cool this late in the day to sit outside barefoot. Then she slipped her arm through Bakarydes's again.

"If I can get the household officers to agree, I will proclaim the end of formal mourning at the middle of next moon. That can also be the occasion when Lajos Zenskur is promoted to Third Lord of the Treasury."

"Won't that seem like a slap in the face to Ikarotikos?"

"That *umgrutzhag* deserves more than a slap, and not in the face either."

"I wouldn't use that word for Ikarotikos. He's not a weakling. If he were, he'd have done less damage."

"What does *umgrutzhag* mean, then?"

"It means a wretch who will let himself be buggered by the stallion who was driven out of every herd and so has no mares."

"I see. That wouldn't be Ikarotikos. It might be Ikos—but he's not a weakling either, even though he may be a traitor."

"I thought you were sure."

"What I thought and what I've learned since summer are two different things. The only evidence against Ikos suggests that he knows something about how magic has been aiding the bandits this summer. That may mean he knows what stopped the Army's messengers, but even the evidence we have is only what one Harzi says a sentry told him.

"The Throne has requested the cooperation of the local magistrate in gathering more evidence, but I'm not hoping for much. Ikos is a great lord and apparently did a lot of bandit catching. The local farmers are likely to be grateful and closemouthed, and so may the magistrate, for that matter.

"If I were to have Ikos subjected to the Fire of Truth on the evidence we have now, it would be said that Queen Kantela has irregular notions of justice. People will forgive me irregular bedmates much more readily, as indeed they should."

Bakarydes muttered something untranslatable in Momak, and Kantela rested her cheek against his shoulder for a moment. "I know. It galls me too that we can't simply send Ikos to Mindranas or at least impose a fine that would take half his lands. I'm sure as I can be of anything that he has the blood of your messengers on his hands. But I think we'd better continue as we've begun, having the College of Priests study the illegal magic until they can point a finger at someone. That someone will be under suspicion of treason, and when *he* comes to the Fire we will learn how much Ikos knew."

She sat up. "Let's leave it to God to punish the evil and think about rewarding the good, which is somewhat more in our power right now. You wouldn't object to receiving a small amount of silver, would you?"

Her heart lifted to see him smile. "If it was *very* small, no. Perhaps two veyselas—" and he ducked as she made a playful slash with an imaginary sword.

"Draw up a reckoning of your extraordinary expenses and present it to the Treasury," she went on. "I'll see that it's dealt with properly. Now, about your cousin Karos—he's going to be promoted to commander, isn't he?"

"He could be, but I think it would be better if the promotion waited until there's a vacant regiment. Otherwise he'll be at loose ends, and then he drinks. He'll drink if you give him a palace appointment, too."

"I wasn't thinking of a palace post. I was thinking of a standing force of men sworn directly to the Throne, not part of the army." Bakarydes looked interested but unconvinced, so she rushed on. "It strikes me that leaving so much of the work of patrolling the roads and chasing bandits to the lords is what has given them the excuse to keep private armies. If we don't take that excuse away from them, they will still be able to make trouble, even if the Edict of Households keeps them out of Koddardos for now.

"Look at Bihor, for example. He can't pay his men properly no matter where they are. What happens if some of them decide to join the bandits instead of catching them?

"If we had a Queen's Levy, much of the work now done by the lords' men would be done directly under the authority of the Throne. It couldn't take over all the work at once, of course, because it wouldn't have anywhere near enough men, but over five or ten years—"

"Wouldn't it be simpler just to add the appropriate number of regiments to the army?"

"It might be, but it would also be much more expensive. I've discovered that the lords have fallen into the habit of withholding some of their taxes on the excuse of paying their men, so the Treasury is going short. If we deprived the lords of that excuse, we could tighten the reins on their tax payments and have the money for both the Queen's Levy and more regiments. We'll need both, unless you think we can manage bandit catching *and* Momak fighting with the men you have left after this year's casualties."

Bakarydes laughed. "God spare me from even having to try. Forgive me, I just wanted to see if you'd thought the matter out clearly. I see that you have."

Kantela assumed a pose of mock indignation. "I might condescend to forgive you for testing me in this matter, if you'll let me appoint your cousin Karos as Commander of the Queen's Levy."

"I won't stand in his way or yours. But—Kantela, it's a big jump for him. He's never commanded more than four hundred men, and you'd need at least a thousand in the Queen's Levy for it to do any good."

"I was thinking of giving him a good—staff officer, is that the term? Someone who can take the paperwork off his shoulders."

"He'd need one, and—Kantela, I feel rather silly proposing this, but if you really want to reward the House of Benye—"

"I'll be wanting to break your head if you don't stop apologizing for thinking that they deserve something."

"All right. What about appointing my uncle Uros to the staff of the Queen's Levy? Karos is—let's say, not experienced in handling money. Uros has always been able to make one veysela do the work of three. It's thanks to him that the House of Benye has any silver at all.

"Besides, if Karos ever needs to interrogate some captured bandits, all he need to do is lock them up with my uncle and have him talk farming or religion at them. Inside of a watch they'll be begging for the chance to tell all they know."

"Then by all means let's make the Queen's Levy a family affair, at least for now."

Bakarydes gave her a brotherly kiss on the cheek and they sat in companionable silence until the sun went down. Then they rose and went inside. Duty would claim them tomorrow, but tonight was theirs.

ANDRÉ NORTON

GORDON R. DICKSON

☐	53068-3	Hoka! (with Poul Anderson)	$2.95
	53069-1		Canada $3.50
☐	53556-1	Sleepwalkers' World	$2.95
	53557-X		Canada $3.50
☐	53564-2	The Outposter	$2.95
	53565-0		Canada $3.50
☐	48525-5	Planet Run *with Keith Laumer*	$2.75
☐	48556-5	The Pritcher Mass	$2.75
☐	48576-X	The Man From Earth	$2.95
☐	53562-6	The Last Master	$2.95
	53563-4		Canada $3.50
☐	53550-2	BEYOND THE DAR AL-HARB	$2.95
	53551-0		Canada $3.50
☐	53558-8	SPACE WINNERS	$2.95
	53559-6		Canada $3.50
☐	53552-9	STEEL BROTHER	$2.95
	53553-7		Canada $3.50

Buy them at your local bookstore or use this handy coupon:
Clip and mail this page with your order

TOR BOOKS—Reader Service Dept.
49 W. 24 Street, 9th Floor, New York, NY 10010

Please send me the book(s) I have checked above. I am enclosing
$_____ (please add $1.00 to cover postage and handling).
Send check or money order only—no cash or C.O.D.'s.

Mr./Mrs./Miss _____

Address _____

City _____ State/Zip _____

Please allow six weeks for delivery. Prices subject to change without notice.

CONAN

☐ 54238-X CONAN THE DESTROYER $2.95
  54239-8   Canada $3.50

☐ 54228-2 CONAN THE DEFENDER $2.95
  54229-0   Canada $3.50

☐ 54225-8 CONAN THE INVINCIBLE $2.95
  54226-6   Canada $3.50

☐ 54236-3 CONAN THE MAGNIFICENT $2.95
  54237-1   Canada $3.50

☐ 54231-2 CONAN THE UNCONQUERED $2.95
  54232-0   Canada $3.50

☐ 54246-0 CONAN THE VICTORIOUS $2.95
  54247-9   Canada $3.50

☐ 54248-7 CONAN THE FEARLESS (trade) $6.95
  54249-5   Canada $7.95

☐ 54242-8 CONAN THE TRIUMPHANT $2.95
  54243-6   Canada $3.50

☐ 54244-4 CONAN THE VALOROUS (trade) $6.95
  54245-2   Canada $7.95

Buy them at your local bookstore or use this handy coupon:
Clip and mail this page with your order

TOR BOOKS—Reader Service Dept.
49 W. 24 Street, 9th Floor, New York, NY 10010

Please send me the book(s) I have checked above. I am enclosing
$_____ (please add $1.00 to cover postage and handling).
Send check or money order only—no cash or C.O.D.'s.

Mr./Mrs./Miss _____
Address _____
City _____ State/Zip _____
Please allow six weeks for delivery. Prices subject to change without
notice.